Nicholas Barrett was born in rural Lincolnshire. He grew up in a house which was shared by a ghost known as "Mr Goodman" who was polite and very tidy. Educated in Grantham, and then at Lincoln College of Art, Nick went on to do a variety of jobs including session musician, rock drummer, stand-up comedian, roadie and manager in a large company.

He now lives in rural Essex. Having always had the urge to write, he did just that. Embarrassingly, most of the incidents which happen in his book did occur! He has drawn on many of his varied life experiences for the book – but has used washable crayon, so it will probably wipe off...

He misses his drum kit – but the laptop takes less time to set up!

He guarantees that reading this book will be the best fun that you have had whilst fully dressed…

To Bob and Rosemarie:

MICHAELMAS TERM
(OR – WHY IS THAT BOY NAKED?)

With my
Very Best Wishes
Enjoy!

Nick Ball

Nicholas Barrett

MICHAELMAS TERM
(OR – WHY IS THAT BOY NAKED?)

Vanguard Press

VANGUARD PAPERBACK

© Copyright 2016
Nicholas Barrett

The right of Nicholas Barrett to be identified as author of
this work has been asserted by him in accordance with the
Copyright, Designs and Patents Act 1988.

A CIP catalogue record for this title is
available from the British Library.

ISBN 978 178 465 164 0

Vanguard Press is an imprint of
Pegasus Elliot MacKenzie Publishers Ltd.
www.pegasuspublishers.com

First Published in 2016

Vanguard Press
Sheraton House Castle Park
Cambridge England

Printed & Bound in Great Britain

To Dolores – for everything, now and always.

And in loving memory of Mollie O'Farrell, an Irish Rose who made me smile every day… and always will.

Acknowledgements

How do you possibly begin to thank those wonderful individuals who have given you such love and constant support throughout the process of writing? Like this, I hope...

To Mum and Auntie – thank you for love, light and laughter.
To Mike, Jacquie and Patrick – for being there.
To the greatest of true friends and a constant source of inspiration – Mr Steve 'Loopy' Newhouse; thanks for all of the "Dink" moments! I could never have done it without you, Mate. Sincere thanks for giving me your unending support – I shall wear it every Christmas.
To my dear friend and fellow conspirator Mr Neal Price – Rocker, Historian, Scientist, Pilot, Mean BJ Player, and constant inspiration. My trousers are almost dry...
To Freddie Mercury, Roger Taylor, John Deacon and Dr Brian May – For providing the sound track to my life. I humbly salute the majesty that is the band Queen...
To all of my ex-colleagues – Bob S, Bob T, Eddie, Dennis, Malcolm, Mark G, Jan, Tony, Peter Reid, Terry, Martin M, and everyone who I bored silly with plot details. If I haven't included you – then my apologies!
My humble and sincere thanks to Jasmine Molton, Suzanne Mulvey, Andrew Smith – and all at Pegasus Elliot Mackenzie.
To the pupils and staff of St Onan's Academy.
And let us please be upstanding and raise our glasses to:

The truly wonderful and much missed genius... Sir Terry Pratchett.

Chapter One

Squatting as a medieval toad of learning, under the rock of ignorance and social depravity in the World outside its boundaries, stand the grey bastions of education which have become famed as the hallowed towers of Saint Onan's Academy.

Betwixt the angry sky and the slumbering town, the walls of St Onan's stand as a secure defence against the influences of the Modern Age – in which it is determined to play no active part, thank you very much. Time passes slowly within these walls, because it is told to do so – and it never ever runs with scissors.

These venerated walls hold back a torrent of young men, whose educational lunchbox has been filled to capacity with the junk food of literacy – leaving the student to belch ineffectually, but with the confidence of a job well done, and style.

With the shock of an open fly at a prize-giving ceremony, St Onan's prepared itself for the fresh intake of impressionable young minds...

Now tuck your shirt in, sit up straight, and read on...

Well, if it was to happen at all, it would have to happen today. This was the kind of day that snaps off keys in the lock for no other reason than pure malicious entertainment, when a finger will be slashed whilst opening a new box of sticking plasters, and when the surreptitious breaking of wind occurs with alarming solidity. Oh yes, today was the day by crikey...

The letterbox vomited a clutch of lonely envelopes onto the front door mat. Mother absent-mindedly scooped up the heap of paper, expecting to see the usual postal detritus destined for instant recycling. She then spotted the buff envelope which completely failed to comply with the "Send back your enclosed lucky prize draw numbers urgently – and you will be included in our prize draw to win a free Bluetooth-enabled hip replacement" script. This envelope was longer, slimmer and altogether more formal, and contrived to look more threatening and aloof, amongst its more mundane travelling companions.

Transfixed in a state of apprehension, Mother walked to the kitchen table, carrying the envelope as if it were an incontinent wasp. What was this communication which seemed to radiate unspoken menace? She hoped against hope that it was not in any way connected to the recent incident where her ten year old grandson had been apprehended whilst playing "Doctors and Nurses" with his eleven year old cousin.

Performing the appendectomy in the garden shed had perhaps been ill advised, but surely no-one could complain about the neatness of the stitching?

Could it be (horror of horrors) some further legal repercussions from the hotel catering manager who had witnessed just how one-armed Uncle Frank had made the holes in his doughnuts? Had some outraged member of the public taken issue with Uncle Stanley dropping his trousers in the middle of a busy Granchester high street, in order to liberate a trapped bee? It was merely bad luck that the whole incident had been conducted in front of a coach load of nuns.

Mother firmed up her resolve with a large glass of "Toledo" cooking sherry. This refreshing drink was known to remove the finish from tungsten steel, but was adequate as a mouthwash for hard-working Adalucian mules, and flavouring the Sunday trifle with all of the European luxury that the Co-Op was able to provide. Mother squared up to the envelope with the butter knife...

Out of the envelope fell a heavily embossed vellum sheet bearing the commanding crest of St Onan's Academy. Mother skittered to the back door, and called out to her youngest son, Nicholas, who was currently upside down at the top of the plum tree.

'Come in quickly,' she stammered, 'this letter says you're going to be an Onanist...'

The fall from the tree had somewhat stunned the boy, who had fallen at the base of the trunk like unwashed laundry.

'What's up Mum?' he enquired.

'You've passed!' said Mother, her face now glowing with pride.

'No I haven't,' he replied, 'it's only a plum juice stain – it will wash out.'

'I think that you had better read this letter,' said Mother.

Whilst he read, and tried to fully absorb the contents of the letter, Mother sprinted to the telephone to share the good news with her neighbour and arch-rival Mrs Hislop.

Mrs Hislop was the stalwart and unofficial generalissimo of the village Chapter of the Women's Institute. The focus of her life were her two daughters, Jocylena (God help anyone who shortened her name to "Jossie" – you were risking the hardened stem of a pre-church display dried flower in the eye.) and Isabella. Jocylena had proved to be the whizz kid at the village primary school, and sailed effortlessly into the local private girls' school known as Saint Gertrude's Academy for Young Ladies. Mrs Hislop was only too willing to extol the virtues of her offspring's educational prowess at length to any ear passing on a casual basis.

Indeed, if you had informed Mrs Hislop that your family had just returned from a holiday in Tenerife, she would have informed you that she and her brood were booked up to holiday in Elevenerife...

'Oh hello, Gwen,' said Mother, 'I just thought that I would let you know that Nicholas is going to St Onan's.'

'Oh how nice,' came the terse reply – 'I didn't know that they were advertising for cleaners…'

The force with which Mother slammed down the receiver tore the telephone shelf out of the wall.

So the camera pans back to the top of the plum tree. Hanging inverted and contemplating the swollen fruit which swung like gravity-defying sweet bruises, the boy realised that his world too had now been turned upside down. Just how would he, a happy little minnow from a small village pond, cope with the sharks in a bigger and altogether more terrifying sea?

He was well familiar with the sight of the boys of St Onan's as they paraded through the town in their quirky, yet regal uniform. These were boys who seemed to regard all other kids as one might regard someone who had just stepped into fresh dog poo. Not only did they act as if they were the owner of said hound, but that you should consider yourself highly honoured to have soiled your shoe – since the dog has longer and nobler pedigree than you are ever likely to achieve. Still contemplating the gravity of the situation, Nicky was brought down to earth when gravity decided to contemplate him –

The branch broke...

With the long days of the summer holidays stretching before him to the horizon, and the urgent need to fill in the void with stolen fruit, tree houses to be built in the vertiginous branches of tall trees, and go-carts to be constructed, raced, and crashed in Action-Hero style, the village kids would group together at the earliest possibility in order to plan their latest assault upon the unsuspecting residents of the sleepy hamlet.

Such a gathering was now taking place in the depths of a crater which had been left in the "big field" by a German bomb during the Second World War. Nature had long since reclaimed the crater, which now formed a natural amphitheatre, and which lent itself to all kinds of conspiratorial meetings (and more importantly, was well hidden on all sides from prying adult eyes).

Its varied and sunken terrain became the arena for the myriad games that young minds could conjure up – and thus became "Planet Quareeg", Darkest Borneo jungle, Burleigh Horse Trial grounds, "Dead Man's Neck" in the Wild West, Agincourt (until Stewart snapped his bow), and for some unknown reason, Budleigh Salterton.

During a break from raising the Titanic again, the group were discussing their proposed secondary schools – and who would be despatched to which school.

'Did you get your letter yet, Squid?' asked Mike.

'Yep – I'm going to Central, same as our Jack,' replied Steve "squiddy" Squire.

'I've got St Wilfred's,' said Richard. 'Got yours then, Mikey?'

'Yes, I've got Westborne Secondary – I can't wait,' answered Mike as he casually reloaded his catapult. 'I must have done very well in the Church Scholarship exam, 'coz Dad says that when I get to Westbourne, I'll get what I deserve…'

'Come on then – what did you get, Nicky?' asked Peter, as the group scattered to avoid crisp crumbs sprayed out like potato shrapnel. Nicky hesitated, knowing that when he replied, it could well in all probability result in a rift between himself and the rest of the village gang.

He drew in a hesitant breath, and muttered, 'I'm going to St Onan's…'

'Oh my God… Toff Central!' cried Mike, aghast.

There was a leaden silence, as glances shot between the members of the gang. Nicky did not know which was worse, the silence of his friends, or the explosion of laughter which followed.

'What's wrong with Westborne or Central then?' demanded Mike.

Then, the inquisition began from all sides.

'How come you got into there?'

'I thought we were all going to go to Big School together?'

'What makes you so special then?'

'But the place is full of complete Arses!'

'Are you too good to mix with us now then?'

'They are a bunch of Posh Tossbags.'

'Yeah, they are so posh that they think Lego is spelt with a silent T as in Merlot.'

'Merlot – was that King Arthur's wizard?'

'Why can't you go to a proper school like us?'

Safety catch suddenly disengaged from his tongue, Nicky took the bait and let fly…

'Well, maybe I don't want to go to Westborne, where the school uniform includes a stab vest, or crummy Central where you can learn how to hot-wire a getaway car, and Wilfred's have after school classes in shoplifting… at least at St Onans I will get a proper education.'

As the sound of the full stop faded, Nicky knew that he had gone too far, and had just successfully ignited several bridges.

Another shorter silence was broken by Mike – who growled 'Well you can have a proper think about not coming to my birthday party on Saturday for a start – we don't want any snobs there expecting us to serve ice cream with cravat.'

'Caviar,' corrected Pete.

'I don't care – you can stay away. Get off to your snooty St Onan's, and from now on you can play with yourself… '

The rest of the gang turned and headed out of the crater, making tracks toward the top end of the village.

Nicky had been comprehensively banished.

The hot summer days slouched on, and Nicky amused himself in reflective solitude. He did not seek out the companionship of his gang, nor did they seem in any hurry to readmit him into their circle of fun and general mischief. Daunting as the concept was, for him, the start of the new term could not come soon enough. He passed a lot of his time browsing the aged books in the local town library. As a gesture of intransigence, he found time to place his used chewing gum firmly up the left nostril of the bronze bust of Sir Winston Churchill, which scowled from the first floor landing of the library.

Normally, he would have caught the local bus from the town back up into the village, but today he decided that he would walk the two miles up the long hill and use the time to plan his next move. He would normally have sat down and discussed the whole thing with Mother, but she was burstingly proud of his achievement of being selected for St Onan's, and was in all probability already selecting her finest needles for sewing name tags into what would be his new school uniform. What he needed was a totally objective opinion, and unbiased guidance given by someone with a vast and varied worldly experience.

He would consult his Oracle.

Mr Prentiss was an elderly gentleman who had lived in the village for his entire life (apart from World War II; he was in Belgium when the first shot of the war had been fired – and was under his bed back home in the village when the second one was fired).

Every one of the children who lived in the village had been given their first bicycle which had been made by Mr Prentiss. More than one child had ridden to school on a penny farthing made by Mr P – whose bicycle manufacturing career had been ruined by decimalization. He was universally known to all and sundry as "Uncle Joe", and was loved and respected by everyone. He was a war hero, ex-racing driver, Grand National jockey, photographer, surgeon, journalist, expert horseman, and compulsive liar.

He claimed to have worked at one stage for MI5, but now hated them, as they did not deliver the wardrobes which he had ordered on time.

His sometimes outrageous memoirs included assisting in the abdication of the king, who he helped to hide at local Belton House with Homer Simpson.

Uncle Joe had a healthy disregard for all forms of authority, and would ensure that fools suffer. He could always be relied upon to give brutally honest advice, and was just the person to calm the nerves of youth in a situation such as this. If anyone could help him feel better about the future, it would be Uncle Joe.

As he walked up the long garden path to Joe's house, Nicky could firstly hear, and then see Mr P marching up the path from the back garden, with a spade in the "slope arms" position. He sang a verse of a marching song as he went:

'I don't know, but I've been told, a polar bear's arse is mighty cold…

'Oh hello, Boy, I've just finished burying the last of the stolen gold bullion from the Brinks Mat job; come into me office, let's have a mug of tea and a wad.'

Uncle Joe's shed followed the style of grandfathers' sheds everywhere. It contained treasures beyond belief to a young boy, with old tobacco and Oxo tins full of every conceivable nut, screw, washer and bolt. Joe was the village wizard who had a part with which to repair any broken toy, and had stopped many a tear from a child with the right nut, washer, and a humbug. His shed had shelves which were bowed under the weight of weird and wonderful objects. A huge, sad stag's head hung on one wall, sporting a black eyepatch and a red clown's nose. A stuffed owl stared down at the lathe, and a skull (hopefully not real) sat on the shelf next to a glass-fronted box containing a pike with an expression of haughty disinterest.

Joe himself had a face that radiated joy and mischief, and to Nicky always reminded him of a walnut starring in a haemorrhoid ointment commercial.

Whatever hideous act you may have perpetrated, Joe had the solution.

Man and boy sat in threadbare armchairs opposite one another, whilst Mr P poured two mugs of steaming tea, out of a teapot last cleaned during the Blitz.

'What's troubling you then, laddie?' said Joe, 'You look like you have been caught playing marbles with Granny's glass eye.'

Nicky explained that he had taken the Church Scholarship examination, and had been selected to go to St Onan's Academy. He told Joe that now he had told his friends where he was going to be attending school, they had turned their back on him. He hadn't meant to cause any offence to anyone, but now it seemed that everyone was against him just because he had passed a stupid exam to get to a stupid school. He spluttered out his fears that the boys at St Onan's would hate him for being a poor kid from the village – so he would have no friends at all.

Joe smiled a crafty smile, and took a sip of tea. He got up slowly and headed for one of the shelves opposite. Moving aside an old gas mask and a cricket ball, he reached to the back of the shelf and pulled out a long, thin mahogany-framed photograph. Joe blew the heavy patina of dust from the photograph, which caused an epic coughing fit and sneezing of a violent nature. 'Got yer, you little bugger,' grinned Joe.

Joe turned the photograph around, and Nicky noted four rows of schoolboys, one row above the other in long lines.

'Right, lad, what do you see front row, second from the right?' asked Joe.

'Looks like a dead moth,' said Nicky.

'Not that, you daft little sod – I mean, do you recognize the boy with the sticking-up hair?'

Nicky peered through the grime of the photograph, and scanned the boys grinning at the camera. Suddenly, a shock of realisation hit him as he recognised one particular youth in the position which Uncle Joe had indicated.

'Uncle – that's you isn't it?' said Nicky.

'My word, yes lad, year one, form 1B.'

'Now look at the school crest at the front of the bottom row,' said Joe.

'Uncle – I never knew that you went to St Onan's!' exclaimed Nicky.

'There's plenty that no-one knows about me, lad, nor needs to know,' Joe said, with a wry grin. 'And I'll be thanking you not to tell a living soul that I have that Enigma machine in my shed.'

It may have been a 1933 Remington typewriter heavily encrusted with grime and dust – but with Uncle Joe, you could never be really certain.

Joe swilled his tannic potion around his mug, and smiled hugely. 'Look, lad, you've done well to get to where you are going. You have made your mum and auntie very proud, and being given the chance of a great education is nothing to be ashamed of. How you do is up to you, but school is what you make of it, and it's up to you to make sure you come out at the other end with a head crammed with everything you will need for a good life. You will get benefits there that others at different schools might not get – so be grateful for it, you whining little sod… ' Joe went on, 'Your mates will soon get used to it, and they'll come around in their own time, and if they don't – then you haven't lost bugger all, have ye? Just don't become an internationally hunted spy like me, having to watch me back night and day… '

Here ended the sermon, and Mr P saw that his congregation was well pleased. Nicky felt more hopeful and positive than he had in days.

'To think, Uncle – you at St Onan's… !' laughed Nicky.

'Weren't for long, lad' said Joe. 'I were expelled.'

'What for, Uncle Joe?' Nicky asked tentatively.

'Diamond smuggling,' Uncle replied.

Chapter Two

It appeared that July had reluctantly changed its name by deed poll, and thus August slouched onward in the heat haze of high summer. Occasional surly teenage thunderstorms sulked across the evening horizon, slamming around leaden skies – having been told to tidy its bedroom. Random paparazzi flashes of white and green illuminated the little village, which flinched in thatched apprehension as the storm concussed the air.

Nicky watched the storm as it loitered over his village, and considered just what form his own gathering storm would take. Was he in any way ready to accept the challenge of the impending cataclysm of St Onan's? He hoped that he would not be swallowed Jonah-like by this impending monster. Before he fell asleep, he spent a long time contemplating his football team wallpaper (having spent several hours adding red stripes to the white shirted players in order to resemble his favourite team), and began to wonder exactly which side he would find himself on. He had a strong suspicion that he would end up on the bench with the wheezy kids who had brought a note from mum. Mainstream education seemed a very frightening thing at this point in his life, and he could only hope that it would not include a ducking stool.

He awoke draped across his bed like a nonchalant cat. Out of his bedroom window, he could now see the curls of wraith-like mist which wove their spectral fingers across the field. The sun was an orange badge of morning promise, and life looked distinctly more hopeful than it had done last night. The overnight storm had blessed the peony roses with a heavy bounty of rain, out of which tiny rabbits were drinking. All was perfectly lovely with the world – until he heard the letter box rattle.

He spotted the dreaded envelope straight away. It bore the sententious crest of St Onan's, and radiated yet more menace behind its gummed facade. Nicky made the decision not to hide it under the doormat, or set it alight, hoping that he could explain away its charred condition as the result of friction. He took the post to his mother, who received it with the glee reserved for Premium Bond winners.

She spent several minutes perusing the contents of the letter, which amounted to six written pages and two quite comprehensive lists. 'Well, young man,' she said, after taking a sip of now cold tea. 'It looks like we are going to be rather busy tomorrow.' The first page of the letter was a summons to attend the school outfitters, to be sized, measured, and (as far as Nicky saw it) imprisoned in the finery demanded by St Onan's. He tentatively picked up one of the pages detailing the items required in the way of uniform. There seemed to be an endless inventory of apparel without which (it seemed to him) it would be impossible to look like a complete prat. He was sure that the list of items recovered from the tomb of Tutankhamun had not been as long as this.

He began to feel a rising panic when he read, "Waistcoats, maroon (light, summer) Old Gold (Ceremonial); as well as, "Full cricket whites, boots and gentleman's protector" and he hoped that he could get to and from school without being seen in the "Straw boater with colour band". If the "gentleman's protector" was in fact a bodyguard, it may well be the only useful thing on the entire list. All that seemed to be missing was a full suit of armour, and he had a horrible feeling that this may well be lurking on page two.

Oh well, cometh the hour, cometh the bus to town. Mother was dressed in her finest coat and best scarf with a small cameo brooch which showed a miniature portrait of a galleon in full sail at sea, and this was her outfit that really meant business. Nicky was just as immensely proud of her as she was of him, as they sat together on the antiquated bus which rattled its way to and from the town. They set off down the green tree-lined hill on their mission. Halfway down the hill, the bus slowed to allow a milk float to pass, and Nicky was sure that he saw Mikey and Squid untying Richie from a tree (although tying him to the tree was the more likely scenario). They looked happy and full of fun, and Nicky began to feel even more despondent.

Simper and Crouch were the clothing firm known to provide "Everything for the Modern Gentleman" (so the legend in golden italics above the front door proclaimed, and this may have been so, if the gentleman in question was Charles Dickens). The shop stood as a living time capsule on the Granchester high street, and was reputed to be so high class that pigeons were only allowed to leave their droppings upon its roof by strict appointment.

The Art Deco shop door opened to the jangling of a discreet bell, and an assistant appeared, gliding swiftly from a side room.

'Good day, madam, sir. I am Gripp. How may I assist you today?' said the small man immaculate in pinstripe trousers and waistcoat. He gave the impression that he would not own a single item of clothing which would carry a crease, and would pass on any stained garment to an expensive solicitor.

'We are here to be fitted out for St Onan's,' Mother declared, in hushed tones which the store seemed to demand.

'Excellent, madam, and may I add my personal congratulations to sir. Could I perchance humbly solicit your vertical advancement to the upper storey?' purred Mr Gripp.

'Could you repeat that please?' said Mother, taken aback,

'My apologies, madam, would you care to traverse the perpendicular footway to the second most echelon?'

Mum and Nicky looked at each other, and both gave a shrug.

'I am sorry, what exactly are you asking?' Mum said, after a pause.

'Upstairs and first on the right please,' Gripp replied, with just a hint of disappointment in his voice. He had now put back the cut-glass accent into its silk-lined box, for use later when the next bulging bank account came in through the door.

Gripp called to a young assistant, 'Thomas – Onan's, full Monty please.'

He then produced an ancient tape measure from about his person, and proceeded to make mystic Tai-Chi movements around the startled boy, whilst all the time calling out sizes and imperial measurements to the out-of-sight assistant. Nicky was startled as a tape measure was thrust Ninja-style into his groinal area and down to his ankle. 'Which way does sir prefer to dress?' asked Gripp.

'Away from the window, and quickly if it's frosty,' answered the boy.

Ignoring this reply, Gripp turned to Mum and asked, 'Will sir be requiring the latest hardwearing worsted fabric trouser just in? They really are the pinnacle of taste for this season, and an absolute bargain at twenty guineas per pair?'

'We will, I think, prefer something off the peg,' Mother hastily retorted.

The demeanour of Mr Gripp instantly changed, and he adopted a sad, hurt face – as if someone had just thrown confetti at a funeral.

Somehow the laws of physics were transcended, and in seconds the assistant began to zip backwards and forwards bearing garments, packets and bundles which soon formed a small mountain on the chaise longue behind Mum and Nicky. Packets of white shirts were produced, which appeared so crisp that Nicky was certain that they would include a small blue packet of salt inside. Socks and ties materialised in bundles marked with the venerable crest of the school. Mother had already taken stock of the price labels of shoes and overcoats, and had already planned to equip her son with items that did not require the selling of a kidney or all of the household furniture, from another local shop. Nicky noticed that Mr Gripp and his Mother did lock eyes after he proffered a pair of black brogues for inspection, but the poor man wisely decided to back down before he became a casualty.

'Well, madam, it would appear that sir is now fully catered for… ' stated Gripp. 'May I request that madam and sir accompany myself to the lower floor and agree remuneration?'

Mother, Nicky, Gripp and Thomas descended the narrow staircase laden with the items like safari bearers. Mr Gripp glided over to the highly-polished counter, and took up station behind the ornate and ancient cash register. Nicky just managed to restrain himself from asking 'Do you play requests?'

'May I presume to ask how we will be making payment?' oiled Gripp.

'We have the Church Scholarship Bursary,' said Mother.

'Then perhaps madam and sir would accompany me to the ante-room,' said Gripp, without feeling.

Nicky felt himself beginning to go red – not with embarrassment, but with anger. This slimy little creep was sending us out of sight of the rest of the customers, as if getting a grant was something to be ashamed of. Hang on a moment – We came to this bloody shop because we were bloody told to, not because we wanted to bloody well see how bloody posh people buy their pants. Were Bursary grants not good enough to put into their rusty till? Was the front of the shop and counter reserved for those rich bastards who were so rich that they paid for everything "on account" (eventually, when prompted by a solicitor's letter)? Never had he been made so acutely aware of the social division which he now saw. He made a mental note that come what may, retribution would be exacted upon the house of Simper and Crouch. Keep smarming Gripp, he thought – 'cos yours is on its way.

The rest of the transaction was completed in silence, with just the rustle of brown paper and large carrier bags to provide a soundtrack to humiliation. They gathered up the purchases, and left unescorted through the narrow front door. Nicky then tore off a piece of brown paper from a bundle, bent down, and said, 'Hang on Mum, I forgot something.'

He went back into the shop, re-emerging a few moments later with a stern look on his face.

'What did you go back for?' asked Mum, 'Did we forget something?'

'No Mum, we didn't forget anything, but Mr Smartarse will have a surprise when he finds what I have just put in the pocket of "This seasons must-have camel hair coat".

Mother regarded her son thoughtfully for a moment, and then said 'Let's have dinner out as a treat… '

"Initiates' Day" was the day on which the Academy doors were thrown open for the new students to acclimatise themselves with the layout of the school and its environs. It was assumed that entrants would thus feel less intimidated by the historic buildings. The specific and descriptive (if, in many cases biologically impossible) graffiti applied to the outer walls of St Onan's would seem to suggest that pupils from the other town schools were not in the least bit intimidated. Adorned with slogans applied in florid colours, a passing observer would perhaps liken the Academy to a "Hip-Hop Gormenghast". There would be no trace of this left by the time visiting day arrived.

Name tags had been meticulously sewn into all items of uniform, and even Auntie (Ninja seamstress and extreme ironer) had lent her support to the task. Since passing the entrance exam, various gifts of congratulation had come into Nicky's possession. So far, he had amassed seven pen sets, four geometry boxes containing a variety of plastic mysteries guaranteed shatter-proof, and a bizarre and lethal looking compass set from Uncle Joe – which he swore had helped him save the life of a British pilot, and aided him when he tunnelled out of a prisoner of war camp. Nicky was impressed how Uncle had kept them in such pristine condition. The tale of how come the slide rule had no slide was altogether too graphic to repeat, but all that Joe would say was that he hoped that the German general did in fact eventually "work it out".

Okay – so the day had arrived, elbowing its way through the queue of lazy late summer days too idle to move. Nicky had not slept well last night; he had a rather terrifying dream that he was being chased down cold stone corridors by huge black bats, which were all wearing mortar boards upon their carnivorous heads. He had awoken very early in the pre-dawn light, covered in sweat (at least he hoped that it was sweat).

He got dressed early, and went downstairs, where Mum was already pouring out the first and best cup of tea of the day.

'We will have to do something with your hair before we go to your new school,' said Mum.

'I suppose a Mohican is out of the question?' replied Nicky, hopefully.

'No, you want to create the right impression, even if it is only a look around,' said Mum.

Nicky would happily follow Mum's advice today, as he could see just how proud she was of her son, and his achievement of climbing the educational ladder. There would be no splinters – touch wood. He was the youngest of four, and Mum had always hoped that he would do well and go on to do great things. Moreover, she had always said that she didn't care what he did as long as he was happy. This was the mother who listened to him, and in whom he could confide implicitly. Moreover – she adored Rock Music, and loved all of the bands that he played endlessly at intimidating volume on the stereo system which his brother Steve had constructed for him. He had none of the pre-pubescent arguments which his friends spoke of with their own parents, and considered his life with Mum and Auntie to be darned near perfect.

Mum was generally fussing around him, tying his tie and straightening the new uniform which fitted him wherever in came into contact with his slight frame. As the deadline approached, Mum disappeared upstairs, and re-appeared looking as if she were attending a Hollywood premier night.

Uncle Joe had kindly volunteered to give them a lift into town in his vintage Ford Zodiac, which was always a treat, as this immaculately-kept vehicle only came out on high days and holidays – and was the envy of many who attempted to evade Joe's somewhat relaxed driving style.

Uncle knocked at the door at ten o'clock precisely, and they set off to meet their date with destiny. Nicky savoured the ride into town, sliding over the huge leather bench seat in the rear of the car with every corner which Uncle Joe took at speed.

Pulling up on Brook Street outside the school, Joe made his apologies, stating, 'I can't be long, I have a bloke from the SAS calling me, and I want to get the car well hidden before the Russians spot it on Google Earth. I will call back for you at half past twelve – don't be late.'

Mother exited the car in her usual regal fashion. Nicky got out and straightened his tie. Well, this was it then… As Uncle Joe purred the car into life and set off Nicky was made aware that all was not as it should be, as he had inadvertently trapped the hem of his blazer in the car door.

They were met at the school gates by a group of haughty prefects, who wore the maroon blazer which signified their elevated status in school. Parents and boys were shepherded through the imposing stone archway which framed the main gate. Nicky felt as if he had been swallowed whole by some stone colossus, and physically shrank in terror. They were then greeted by one of the masters, who introduced himself as "Captain Brayfield", and escorted them across the bottom right hand corner of the quadrangle to the assembly hall entrance.

Upstairs in the assembly hall was organised chaos, with parents and boys milling around like floating voters at a by-election. Trestle tables with wine and snacks had been set up around the perimeter of the hall. Various mothers and fathers were busy tidying up their dishevelled offspring, and a gentle murmur of anticipation pervaded the air. Soon, a kindly bespectacled gentleman navigated his way through the throng, and made his way to the front of the expectant crowd.

'Good day and welcome one and all,' he intoned, I am Mr Goodwill, headmaster of this noble academy, and it is my humble pleasure to welcome you all to our school today. I thank you all for attending, and hope that you will enjoy the brief presentation which we have prepared for you. Shortly, the young gentlemen will leave us for a short tour of the school and its environs, and we will see a presentation of the Academy and its achievements. Please do feel free to avail yourselves of the light buffet and refreshments provided.'

At this point, the prefects reappeared via the side doors, and lined up like the bad guys at the shootout in a cheap western. Nicky mentally noted that it was certainly number four that "done it" (he looked like a wrong 'un and no mistake).

'Gentlemen, would you care to convene your charges,' said Mr Goodwill – and the nightmare beginneth...

Nicky waved to Mum, and followed the band of boys who began to form a line behind the prefect. They led off down the stairs, and over the quadrangle to the "old block" where a master was holding open the double doors for them. 'Hello, chaps,' he said. 'Welcome to the Old School.' They found themselves in a wide, stone-flagged corridor smelling strongly of polish and disinfectant. The master led them along the corridor, pausing in front of the windowed wall which held plaques and varnished tributes to all those former boys from the Academy who had lost their lives in armed conflicts across the centuries.

'Dear fellows,' he intoned with a Shakespearean actor's timbre, 'we can trace our school heritage with pride and honour back to the time of the Crusades.' He appeared misty-eyed at this moment, but carried on. 'Were you most fortunate boys able to travel back in time and walk amongst the campfires of the troops of King Richard the Lionheart, as they prepared for their next engagement with the foreign foe, you would, I am certain, witness some Onanist enthusiastically buffing his helmet.'

The master gazed reverentially again at the Honour Boards, then smiled a kindly smile, looking directly at Nicky as one might regard a favoured nephew. He leaned down and ruffled the boy's hair, then declared, 'Very well, chaps – onward and upwards, my seekers of knowledge.' Nicky noticed that the man smelled distinctly of peppermints, old newspapers, and moreover of sixteen year old distilled Scotch whisky. As he led the troop of boys off up the corridor, Nicky heard a voice beside him say, 'That's why they call their hats mortar boards, you know.'

Nicky turned and asked, 'Sorry, that's what?'

'Their hats,' said the boy. 'They call their hats mortar boards, because everything underneath is plastered.'

The voice belonged to a friendly-looking boy with a genuine smile. He sported a mop of unruly brown hair, and had his hands dug deeply into his pockets with an air of someone determined not to be intimidated by the historic surroundings in which he now found himself.

'I'm Calderman,' he said. 'Call me Johnny.'

'Pleased to meet you, Johnny, I'm Shepherd – call me Nick,' he answered.

Calderman had not bothered to don his new school uniform for the visit, but instead had chosen jeans, trainers and a battered tweed jacket for the occasion. What impressed Nicky the most was the Queen tee shirt that the boy wore, and he knew that he had formed an instant bond with this fellow inmate.

Just then, the two were joined by a slightly smaller boy who introduced himself in hushed tones, 'Hello, I'm Merry.'

'Quite pleased myself, now you mention it,' responded Calderman.

'No, er, sorry, my surname is Merry,' said the boy.

'Could your parents afford a Christian name?' asked Johnny.

'Ah, sorry, yes – it's Gerald,' he replied, looking down at his feet.

'Gerry Merry?' asked Nicky, trying not to laugh.

Calderman gave the boy an appraising look, and declared, 'Welcome to the gang, Gerry Merry.'

The tour led on up the worn stone stairs, which echoed to the nervous feet of the boys, and the steel-tipped click of the master at the front of the company. They were halted in front of sombre looking double doors leading into a darker, narrower corridor.

'This, gentlemen, is the edifice in which the mysteries of Chemistry will be revealed,' intoned the master. The boys were herded into a wide room with high wooden benches, each with an ancient stained sink and double gas taps set into it. The laboratory smelled horribly of sulphurous and acidic residues, and Calderman whispered, 'I wonder where the bodies are hidden.'

Merry said quietly, 'If the assistant is called Igor, I'm legging it.'

Nicky stared up at the huge chart of the Periodic Table which hung above the raised dais at the front of the class, and wondered what horrors might have to be endured at the hands of a mad scientist within this room. He would hazard a guess that it would not resemble anything similar to the High Street chemist which had been his only contact with the world of alchemy to date. He noted the white laboratory coat hung on the back of the door, and hoped that weird and mystical punishments were not meted out to any boy failing to complete their homework.

The master led the boys out of the laboratory, and back along the parquet-floored corridor, pausing to indicate what subjects were taught behind the doors of each room in turn. Down another flight of prehistoric stairs the group went, until they emerged into the daylight of the quadrangle and crossed to the newer buildings which rose on the north side of the school.

Nicky noticed the similar fearful expression on the faces of some of the boys in another group of "tourists" as they passed on the quad, and took some comfort that he was not alone in feeling overwhelmed in the grasp of the Academy surroundings.

'This is the New Block, chaps,' said the master. 'It houses the biology laboratory, into which I am afraid, it is not possible to enter today. One may only postulate that some unspeakable barbaric and unnatural practice has yet again rendered the room temporarily out of bounds.'

'Upstairs are the language rooms, and top floor areas given over to art,' he went on. Nicky noted that the master placed the same distasteful emphasis on the word "art" as one might place on the term "haemorrhoids". This was obviously not a man who would hang a Turner in his living room, but Nicky was sure that he would certainly like to have had Turner hung.

'Boys, we will now traverse the quadrangle again, and visit the most historic and important building within the environs of this noble academy,' said the master, pausing for dramatic effect. He grouped together his charges and led them out of the New Block and up a walled path at the side of the headmaster's house and school offices. The path opened up onto a wide and well-manicured lawn on the left, framed by cherry trees in full blossom. In front of them rose the walls of a significantly older building, its ancient walls leaning and bowed like the last drunk on the late night bus. Moss clung to its venerable stone in comfortable patches, and two ravens atop the gutters regarded the boys with an intelligent, and unsettlingly evil eye. The master paused in front of the six stone steps which led up to the time-worn door which was crossed by studded ironwork. The door handle was a thick ring, which had been worn smooth by the turning of many hands across the centuries.

The tall man turned the handle with great solemnity, and held open the door as the boys filed into the long room with its high-vaulted ceiling, criss-crossed by huge oaken beams of obviously great age. The huge space instantly reminded Nicky of an inverted galleon of Tudor times (not that he was personally familiar with such a vessel – but you can learn a lot from comics, if so minded). The arched windows were high, and all other wall space was taken up by row upon row of books, which sat on the dark wood shelves with an air of haughty defiance.

'This, gentlemen, is the Academy Library,' spoke the Master. 'This is the fount of all knowledge, and you would all do well to visit often, and drink deeply.'

At this point, you could have heard a pin drop, as the boys took in their surroundings. No one, however, had brought a pin with them.

'In this very building, boys, the greatest Englishman, Sir Isaac Newton, received his education. As you are well aware, he went on to produce one of the most significant scientific tomes in history – namely, the *Principia Mathematica*. One may hope that you too may be inspired to follow his example and work diligently to produce great works of your own.'

Nicky whispered to Johnny that according to his Uncle Joe, Newton was the man who had strangled two hundred woodpeckers, before he realised that cider was in fact made from apples. He was unaware of the gravity of the situation until considerably later in his career. Luckily, this comment was out of earshot of the master, who Nicky was sure would not appreciate Joe's version of the Great Man.

With the master holding open the great door once again, the cluster of boys were taken down the path in the wake of the teacher who flapped onward like a black umbrella in a stiff breeze, only pausing when one of the vengeful ravens vacated onto his mortar board. They soon arrived at a large new-brick construction, and were ushered inside.

Two more sets of double doors opened up into the echoing void of gymnasiums everywhere. This was a world away from School Sports Day at Nicky's primary school, and he regarded the array of physical education equipment (mostly folded against the far wall) with some trepidation. The gym was the standard "rectangular box" design, fitted with the regulation loud squeaking floor. All over the floor were the myriad lines which marked out courts and boundaries for all manner of sport. This gave the overall impression of the Nazca Lines of Peru, but in vivid multicoloured hues. There seemed to be an overall smell of rubber matting and ritualistic humiliation.

'I could swing on those ropes like Tarzan,' thought Johnny,

'I could be killed if I fall from the wall bars,' thought Gerry,

'Is this where the Spanish Inquisition practise?' thought Nicky.

Their private musings were interrupted as the master spoke up:

'I shall now return you fellows to the bosom of your parentals, and the Head wishes to address you all in the main assembly hall,' he said.

The boys murmured their way back to the hall, where parents were awaiting the return of their much-travelled offspring. The cheese and wine provided seemed to have had an invigorating effect upon some of the parents, several of whom were so invigorated that they were swaying. The headmaster climbed the steps to the main stage, and addressed the gathering.

'Well, dear boys, I hope that you have found your little tour of our academy to be informative and uplifting,' he began. 'We Onanists are proud of our long, er, traditions, and I welcome you one and all to our venerated Seat of Learning. We do however; insist on decorum and punctuality as cornerstones of school life. Good manners are priceless, and should be displayed at all times. Take pride in the school gentlemen; make your parents proud of you, and stand proud on all occasions. Welcome to St Onan's. If there are no more questions, I will merely say adieu for now, and I look forward to seeing each and every one of you at the start of term.'

This well-delivered speech would have been uplifting, inspirational and motivating, and doubtlessly should have been so, had it not been delivered with an unfortunate and highly visible open fly.

Before the parents had reclaimed most, if not all of their offspring, Nicky sought out Johnny and Gerry. 'Well, what did you think to that?' asked Nicky.

Johnny answered with the collective decision which they had all subconsciously reached – 'I think that if we three stick together, then there is a chance that we may survive this ordeal,' he stated.

All three nodded in agreement.

'Where are you both from?' asked Nicky.

Johnny told him that he lived in the fairly local village of Lower Nethering, and Gerry was a native hailing from the one-horse settlement of Woldsham. There was no longer a horse, it had long since taken a course in Sociology at evening class, and moved to the Chinatown area of Bottesford. The boys exchanged telephone numbers, and calculated if a visit to each other's villages was within the scope of human endurance if attempted by bicycle. Mum must have noted Johnny's Queen shirt – as she invited him to come over and stay before the start of term. The new friends parted company, and said their "see you soons".

Nicky was still trying to absorb all he had heard and seen today, and was so deep in contemplation that he paid no attention to Mikey, Squid and the Village Gang hurling several eggs at the bus as it crawled laboriously up the hill from town on its homeward run.

Back at the family home, Mother insisted that he change out of his uniform and back into "civvies".

'Well,' she said, 'I thought that was very nice. It's a really lovely school, and the staff seem really friendly – I'm sure you will have a great time once you get settled in.'

Nicky thought of the long, dark corridors, the brooding stone buildings, and the opportunities to be ridiculed as a village peasant by the prefects which he had seen eyeing the new boys like sharks in possession of a pocketful of luncheon vouchers.

'Yes Mum,' he replied. 'I'm sure it will be okay.'

There was a coded knock on the back door. The source of the secret knock proved to be Uncle Joe.

'Now then, laddo – how did you get on down at the fun factory?' he enquired.

'Really good, thanks, Joe,' Mum answered. 'He'll have a great time, and he has already met two new friends.'

'Glad to hear it,' said Joe, casually glancing out of the kitchen window to check for any possible snipers. 'You can come over on Saturday and tell me all about it.'

'Yes, he will,' said Mum. 'Best make the most of it though, because soon he will be going to school on Saturday mornings.'

SCHOOL ON SATURDAY MORNINGS... Horror of Horrors; Nicky had forgotten all about that. Saturday mornings were for getting up early and plundering the dewy fields for delicious mushrooms with Auntie. Saturday mornings always consisted of sitting on the back door step, savouring the smells of cooking bacon which drifted down the row of houses, reading comics until your own breakfast was ready. Then it was time to test-fly the latest model aeroplane out in the Big Field, or take a trip into town with Auntie – at weekends you had earned the right to completely forget everything that you had learned under torture during the week. This was simply an outrage.

Uncle sensed his unease, and made his apologies stating, 'I can't stay and chat, I have promised my old friend Fingal that I will install a Sky television dish in a cave which he has bought.'

With that, the running man runneth out of small talk, and scarpereth…

Chapter Three

For the remainder of what was left of the school holidays, Nicky decided to cram in as much fun as he could. Ponds were waded, ancient trees climbed, and ancient village residents were mildly terrorized in a "not so terrorizing" way. He had even been surprisingly reunited with his former partners in crime, during an unplanned visit to "the bomb crater" one afternoon.

'Oh Hello and What Ho, it's Toff Boy,' said Mikey.

'How was it then – do they make you write with your little finger sticking out?' joked Squid.

'I dunno really,' replied Nicky. 'It's a massive old place and I didn't really get to see all of it, but I guess I am stuck with it.'

'Well if the Toffs get on your nerves, you can always ask for our help to sort them out good and proper.' Squid laughed.

Mikey seemed to have forgiven Nicky too – as he responded, 'You know what I say, if you can't join 'em – beat 'em.'

Nicky knew that deep down; he was worried that even if he could manage to beat them, someone was bound to see the join. He hoped that his somewhat rural upbringing would not be the focus of derision at the Academy, and that he would not become lost in the labyrinthine corridors of the school – to be found years later as a well-educated skeleton in extremely short trousers.

Then there was the satchel…

Auntie had gone into the town and spent what was obviously a significant amount of money on a high-class satchel for him. It was a superb piece of leather crafted luxury, with various compartments and a shoulder strap capable of tethering a wild rhino. It sat on the kitchen table and gave off the aroma of stables and a farrier's gift shop. The front buckle had come straight off the boot of Long John Silver, and the leather would in all probability stop a bullet at close range. When opened (using considerable effort), the leather creaked and groaned like a new saddle. It gleamed like a new conker, and would obviously spit out anything placed inside which it considered to be unworthy or vulgar.

'Now you really will look the part when you get to school,' beamed Mother.

If that unforgiving buckle and leather got the better of him, Nicky knew exactly which part he would look like. He wondered if he would live long enough to be able to beat it into submission.

'It's really lovely, auntie,' he said. 'You should not have spent all of that money on me.' Nicky was sure that it was sneering at him. He would tame the beast later, by writing his name inside the front flap – or perhaps use a branding iron on it, if it resisted.

Now it was Sunday, and Mother was busy pressing, smoothing and preparing his new uniform so that there would be "No rush at the last minute". He wasn't due at the Academy until Tuesday morning, but Mother practised the precise advanced planning of a rocket scientist. New shoes were polished by Nicky using the method that his brother, Mike, had shown him, with a hot spoon on the toecaps, and circles of spit and polish - until they yielded to a mirror finish.

Nicky had two older brothers. Mike was the "Action Man" of the family. He had joined the Paratroops. He often reappeared at home driving a huge Army lorry, or a smaller jeep – which Nicky couldn't wait to get to ride in. He was Nicky's very own hero, who rode great old British motorbikes, and better still, hurled himself out of aircraft for fun.

Steve was Nicky's other brother. Younger than Mike, he too had joined the Army briefly, but soon left as he considered it "too cissy"for his liking. He worked as a demolition expert using a variety of high explosives. In Nicky's opinion, he did have a tendency to wear a kilt more often than was strictly necessary, and he hurled other people out of aircraft for fun.

The other sibling was his sister, Janey. She had also passed the Scholarship exam, and went to St Gertrude's College (for young Ladies), and after leaving school (as a young Lady) had met and married a Wing Commander in the Royal Air Force. This connection with the RAF and fast planes gave them both godlike status in the eyes of a young boy. They now lived abroad after postings around the world, but Mum would regularly speak to her daughter on the telephone, so that she could complain about the size of the bill.

Sunday afternoon was proving to be strange. All of the lawns around the house had been preened to perfection by Auntie, and there were no more chores that required his immediate, if sometimes unenthusiastic input. Now, the fear and apprehension was really beginning to make itself felt. He was beginning to feel as nervous as the time during last winter, when he had decided to make use of the heavy snow which lay over the whole village like a chilled duvet – and try his hand at the world of sculpture. Mother had taken him to task over the construction in the front garden of what she had termed "Snowmen which are far too anatomically correct". He shuddered as he reminded himself of the neighbour's smirks, as he was forced to knock off the "extra snow" with the small coal shovel.

Apart from a few minutes spent gently ridiculing the born-again Christians who sang with such exaggerated facial movement on the evening broadcast of *Songs of Praise* (he marvelled that they sprang into life as soon as they realised that the camera was on them), there was little else to take his mind off the approaching cultural tsunami. He did find the time however, to ask himself what exactly was the mathematical probability that so many people in jaunty hand-knitted sweaters would need to go to the toilet at the same time. Also, surely, any of the "Born Agains" would logically have two belly buttons. He made a mental note to pose this theological question to a suitably learned teacher, as soon as he got to the Academy.

He was unusually withdrawn during Sunday tea, and could not wait for darkness to fall, and provide him with the raw material for one of his most treasured pastimes. Mum and Auntie had bought him a superb refractor telescope for Christmas, and he spent as many evenings outside gazing up in wonder at the heavens as the weather would allow. Uncle Joe seemed obsessed with planetary observation, and continually asked him, 'Have you managed to see Uranus yet?' Nicky got the impression that his enquiry may not have been entirely scientifically based.

When the ink-black yet bejewelled curtain of night had fallen, Nicky hurriedly set up his telescope on the side lawn. He began to sweep the constellations for a glimpse of his favourite star clusters, and home in on the fainter deep-sky objects which were at the limits of his observing capabilities. His mind began to wander again, and he pondered the question of life in other galaxies. He would bet a year's pocket money that at this very moment, some poor pre-pubescent creature was being forced to parade in front of its parent species wearing tri-leg coverings which concertinaed at the bottoms, and was being told, 'You soon will grow into them, young N'Karak, and those land-limb pods will fit you a treat in a couple of graddz.'

These thoughts put him completely off his stride, and he decided to cut his losses and pack up for tonight. It was at times such as these that Nicky wondered what his father might have made of all the carry-on. His father had been absent since he was born. The story was told that he had just nipped out for a packet of cigarettes and some custard powder; but that was in 1960, the shop was round the corner, and it was (allowing for gossip from the shopkeeper to be passed and received) unlikely that the queue would have been this long. Rumours abounded that he had run off to join the crew of a Nottingham herring trawler, or that he had been kidnapped by contract plumbers who held him for ransom in Bottesford's Latin Quarter. Should Nicky ever encounter a fisherman who spoke fluent Latin – he may well ask some searching questions...

So, the condemned boy ate a hearty breakfast. (Well, Weetabix – if you must know, but trust me, he ate it with all of the heart which he could muster.) Today was Monday, and was his last day of freedom. He resolved to go out in the beauteous early sunshine, and have a good old slouch around the village. The other kids would have started at their respective secondary schools today, so there would be less possibility of taunts or sarcastic questioning.

He began his meanderings with a slow walk up the leafy Church Lane. He paused at the top of the lane by the huge old farm gate, and turned to admire the church. He missed the camaraderie that he enjoyed whilst being a part of the church choir, and wondered what the Africans did with all of the tins of out-of-date peaches collected for them at Harvest Festival.

Pondering on, he passed Mr Thompson the farmer.

'Morning, Mr T, how's it going?' Nicky called out.

'Too fine to tell, lad – ta for askin',' replied the sunburned man.

'Can I ask you something?'

'Fire away, son'

'Have you lived in that little falling-down farmhouse all of your life?'

'No – not yet'.

As replies go, this seemed to end with a very large full stop, so Nicky waved to the smiling man and walked on. He ambled up to the very top of the lane, and sat in the long grass admiring the view out across the Rutland plain to Belvoir Castle. Down to his left was the worn track that led down to a group of stalwart elm trees. Up aloft in their muscular branches sat the tree house which he and his friends had constructed at risk of life and limb several summers ago. Rather than risk attack from the family of homicidal owls which were reputed to now own the airborne shack, he cut along the rear of the new estate, up to Green Street and the Old Chapel.

Walking up the long street would take him past the house where he lived until he was six years old. He always had a real affection for this house, the barns in the yard, and its capacious gardens which were a safe playground for a young boy. The village had seemed like a huge patchwork of fields to him then, but he was already noticing that it was beginning to shrink in his eyes. Now thirsty, he decided to head back home and pass some time back in the Big Field and "The Bomb Crater".

He felt safe and content in this dimple in the landscape. It held so many happy memories, and was the scene of some epic events in the lives of the village gang. Was this not the place where Mikey hung trouserless for over forty-five minutes until he could be released from the big oak tree by his dad? Was this not the very arena where Squid had risen to the challenge of a dare, and had run three times around the trees with his underpants filled with stinging nettles? Would anyone ever forget the day Nicky accidentally peed on the electric cattle wire? He deeply loved his tiny little village, its winding alleys and its friendly, familiar inhabitants. He did not want to be separated from this bond, or to be seen as wanting to be kept apart. He may be a "son of the soil", but he had grown accustomed to the odd patch of mud on the carpet.

Nicky still had the feeling at the back of his mind that he would eventually be exposed as an impostor, with no real right to be at St Onans. He visioned the dark day when the classroom door would burst open, and large men in black suits with sunglasses and radio earpieces would muscle into the room and manhandle him out of class and into a waiting limousine. There would be no conversation in the back of the car. He would be dragged hooded into a small room with a single unshaded light bulb. The biggest of the men would then pull a cosh out of his inside jacket pocket, lean toward him menacingly, and ask in a low and intimidating rasp, 'How come you can't tie a proper Windsor knot?'

He didn't want to go to a school where spelling a word incorrectly would earn you a session in the stocks – and the signs no doubt all said "Keep off the Foie Gras".

Chapter Four

Indiana Jones slowly opened his eyes. The light was pouring in through the small window in the square room. He did not remember falling asleep, but was now awake with the alertness of a hunting tiger. He could hear human sounds some distance from his cell, and began to plan his escape. He dressed silently, carrying jacket and shoes carefully as he slunk down the steep stairs. A creak on the edge of hearing him made him crouch and check behind him, but there was no huge rolling ball thundering down the stairs. Absent too, were concealed holes in either wall, out of which poison darts should by now have been propelled to halt his progress. At the bottom of the stairs, the floor looked completely solid and devoid of snake pits or covered traps. Scarcely daring to breathe, he eased his careful way forward. Flexing his fingers, he gripped the handle of the door in front of him with surgical care, as his heart hammered in his chest. Opening the door carefully and silently (in case a rusty hinge betrayed his presence) he entered a larger room with trepidation.

'I've done you egg, bacon, mushroom, tomato and fried bread,' called Indiana's mum, as she placed his breakfast on the kitchen table.

'Don't get ketchup on your new shirt or trousers,' she warned.

His Action Hero alter-ego now evaporated, Nicky again began to contemplate his own "Temple of Gloom".

Mother and boy sat at the table together and ate their breakfast, whilst Mum hummed the melody over the words of the weather forecast on the radio.

'Any mention of road closures cutting off the town?' he asked.

'No – now eat up.'

'Earthquakes?'

'I think we might just have noticed.'

'Escaped tigers, lions or ravenous carnivores necessitating the public to remain calm, but stay indoors with all doors and windows locked?'

'There has been no mention so far... '

'Are the local Buddhists holding their bi-annual Save the Earth sit-in clad only in saffron body paint, making it essential to shut off all major transport routes?'

'I didn't see it advertised in the local paper.'

'Has an eight-foot tall man blocked the road in protest at climate change, and are police waiting for a trained negotiator to talk him down?'

'Not that I am aware of... '

'Has, by any chance a mystery figure closed off the town by threatening residents with radioactive cheese?'

'No, Nicky, your Uncle Joe is away today visiting his sister.'

'Any curious bands of juggling goats, holding up traffic?'

'Look dear, you will enjoy it when you get there, now finish your breakfast and get ready – you don't want to miss the bus, do you?'

'I take it that is a trick question, isn't it, Mum?'

(Mum 1: Nicky 0. Mum will now take on Juventus in the Quarter Final...)

On went the tie, jacket and shoes. The mocking satchel was fed with the various items of technical equipment, creaking threateningly all the time. Nicky kissed his mother, and opened the front door with all of the trepidation of a smaller version of Neil Armstrong.

'Have a nice first day, dear...' beamed Mum. 'Don't forget – you are every bit as good as they are, so keep your head held high.'

Yes, high on a pole, he thought.

Nicky began the walk up the long front path, looking as if he were trudging to the gallows. He joined the four other passengers awaiting the arrival of the asthmatic bus run by the village company. It didn't so much run, as sidle for money. Just as the bus pulled into the stop, he deftly whipped off the hated straw boater and rammed it into his satchel. He paid his fare, and then found an empty seat, waving to Mum as the vehicle set off in random gear. It would not be long before some of friends would join the bus, and he was mentally bracing himself for a ribbing.

Mikey, Squid, Richard and Pete got onto the bus two stops down the hill, spotted Nicky sitting anxiously, and gave him their greetings as they passed him on their way to the back of the bus:

'Mornin', ToffBoy – What Ho!' (He had fully expected.)

'Good Day, milord.' (He had sort of anticipated.)

'Woah! It's Dickie the deckchair!' (He could probably live with.)

'Why – it's Little Lord Fartleroy!' (He was not pleased with at all.)

Luckily, the lads passed him and formed a huddle at the rear of the coach. He considered that he had got off lightly, but would no doubt have to run the gauntlet of further barracking when he got off. Traffic was light, and the bus soon pulled up at his stop. He hurriedly stood up and headed for the front door of the bus. It was at this moment that the satchel decided to display its homicidal tendencies toward Mankind, and swung out viciously on its strap, catching an unsuspecting passenger a telling blow about the head. Nicky apologised profusely, but could hear the gales of laughter from his friends on the back seats as he escaped from the bus.

He rearranged the leather assassin, and set off on the walk to St Onan's.

He was joined on the march by several other pupils, whom he noted looked just as apprehensive as he. Wordlessly, they all settled into the lazy pace of schoolchildren everywhere, who never seem to be in any hurry to get to school. They crossed the busy road, and walked the few short paces up to the imposing front arched gates of the Academy. Outside, eyeing the entrants suspiciously (and no doubt looking for any small sign of weakness which would be noted, and exploited later) was a gang of prefects. A short, rotund master was directing boys to the notice board on the left of the quad.

'Your form and room is displayed on the board, gentlemen,' wheezed the master, 'And your form masters will be pinned up on the boards adjacent.'

'Seems a bit harsh, for a first offence?' said a familiar voice behind Nicky.

It was Calderman, who was now fully decked out now in the school finery, and with a grin that spread from ear to ear.

'Good to see you, mate!' he said. 'Don't bother with all that tosh, Shep – we are in Form 1A, room 9 on the Old Block first floor. Merry is over there somewhere, fighting with his trousers.'

Around the three boys thronged the crowd which comprised the conglomeration of established scholars, and the new intake. The "New Bugs" were easily distinguished: as they were milling around in the Brownian motion of first-day pupils everywhere. Most had the look of bewildered penguins, which were flapping around whilst attempting to camouflage themselves as deck chairs on a busy Brighton beach. Trousers were being worn "generous" for this season. Last year's intake were already talking and laughing in small groups, or hurrying off on the well-rehearsed daily routines not yet implanted into the new boys.

'What do we do now?' asked Nicky.

'We'll drop our stuff in the form room, and wait for assembly,' his well-organised friend answered.

The boys hurried up the worn stone stairway to room 9, where they deposited their satchels and sundries on top of the row of low cupboards which ran the full length of the corridor under the windows. Just then, a tall, thin prefect appeared as if from nowhere. 'What the hell are you chaps doing?' he shouted, 'No boy is to be in the rooms or corridors before assembly.'

'I have come already fully assembled,' answered Calderman.

'Oh, Mr Clever are we?' fumed the prefect. He strode right up to Calderman and hissed into his ear. 'I am Piper, and I will be watching you three – one step out of line, and you will be accompanying me to the head's study for a thrashing.'

'It's very nice of you to offer to join us, but only come if you really feel that you want a thrashing too,' Nicky heard himself say.

'You, especially, I shall watch,' the prefect said to Nicky with menace.

Piper stormed off up the corridor, and when he had gone, Calderman turned to Nicky and Gerry. 'See, I told you,' he said. 'If arseholes could fly, my friends, then this place would be an airport… '

The Academy bell sang out its call for all to assemble in the huge main hall. A pressing throng of boys funnelled through the double doors and began to fill the wide space in front of the stage. First Year students were ushered to the front, and the older sixth-form boys sat on chairs placed on a small raised dais at the back of the hall.

A pleasant yet nervous master then entered, and took his seat in front of the organ.

There was then a general murmur from the crowd as the staff filed onto the stage through the rear doors, and muffled tittering as two of the masters collided mid-stage, each trying to beat the other to a preferred seat. The masters settled, and suddenly there was a muted rumble, as the entire crowd of boys stood up as the headmaster made his grand entrance. He strode regally through the boys, ascended the steps up to the stage, and took centre position in front of the lectern. There was an expectant hush as he attempted to straighten up the lectern, which was slightly off-centre to the audience. Despite using first some, and then considerably more force, the wooden structure remained glued to its peculiar spot. (This was indeed the case.)

'Good morning and greetings to you all, gentlemen,' announced Mr Goodwill. 'May I welcome you to Saint Onan's Academy, where we believe in the world of hard work, and hard play.'

'And hard luck,' ad-libbed an unnamed voice.

Ignoring this unscripted intrusion, Mr Goodwill rallied:

'You boys are setting off on a great adventure, an academic odyssey which will take you to places which you have never imagined. It is my duty, and, may I add, absolute pleasure to unfold the map and polish the compass for you on your travels, and to ensure that in any company, and in any situation – a boy of St Onan's will always hold his own.'

'We will now follow the tradition which reaches back through the centuries, and raise our voices in the singing of the School Song, which was by all account written by Sir John Fettles, a fellow of this Academy, at around 1749.'

'And finished at five past six,' Merry whispered.

He gave a respectful nod to the back of the hall, and the organ, with pilot Mr Newhouse at the controls, taxied out ready for take-off. The powerful instrument bellowed out the opening chords to the waiting masses, who sang the anthem with gusto, or disgusto, depending on how hard you were listening.

"Stride proudly all ye fellows-
Through tempest, storm or strife.
We Brotherhood of Onan
Shall grasp the Staff of Life

Within these walls of sanctity
Is seed of knowledge sown.
Amongst the rude society
We Onans hold our own

'Gainst injustice and adversity
Our members proud shall stand.
Rise up! Rise up! Saint Onan's'
And take yourself in hand…"

The mighty organ crashed out the last crescendo, and the head stood proudly to attention. Nicky felt that he should at least, salute…

'I can see us getting nil points from Belgium again for that,' Calderman said, out of the corner of his mouth.

Mr Goodwill then turned, gave a curt nod to the staff, and majestically swept down the steps and out of the hall, pausing to give a final narrow-eyed look of contempt at the lectern. The centre stage was then taken by the deputy head, who introduced himself as Doctor Chambers.

Here was a man so stiff and brittle that any glancing blow might well cause him to shatter. From the assembled mass of boys, there was now not just a complete silence, but a negative value for the phrase "sound".

Dr Chambers slowly and carefully produced papers from inside his jacket, straightened them, and turned a steely eye upon the assembled ranks of boys.

'Gentlemen, I shall briefly outline some of the Academy rules, for the benefit of the uninitiated,' he began.

'These rules are sacrosanct, and will be transgressed at the peril of the individual. Firstly, the use in school of any or all forms of mobile telephonic communication is expressly forbidden. At this academy we speak, communicate verbally, engage and cogitate. Thus, we enrich our minds and thus we develop and enrich our social skills. Tinny disembodied voices chattering aimlessly across the ether have no place or purpose within these walls. Neither will any boy use these devices to peruse what I believe is termed the "Interweb". The text you will read will be the venerable printed text which holds the accumulated wisdom of the authors, and which is available without subscription from our historic library. From the Latin "Liber" – book, and any boy who transgresses this rule will be swiftly brought to book; and looking around today, I can see one or two boys who may well subscribe to this.'

Scanning the pupils with death-ray eye, he continued:

'Hair length will be measured weekly; and any pupil whose hair is deemed to be of length which exceeds the standard will be suspended. Ties will be measured daily

– and we at this academy will not permit the sloppy and careless styles which I have seen adopted by pupils at some of the other local so-called educational establishments to be copied here. Transgressors will be suspended.'

Calderman whispered 'Any boy found attempting to hang himself will be suspended... '

Nicky and Gerry dared not laugh, but both began to turn a strange shade of purple.

It suddenly dawned on Nicky that the deputy head bore an uncanny resemblance to his late grandfather. He had (as long as Nicky could remember) always been a dour, severe character, who would have benefitted from a smile transplant. Grandfather had an inherent dislike of children it seemed, and would highlight the smallest misdemeanour committed by Nicky, and take great delight in punishing him severely for it. It was as if he lay in wait to witness the naughty deeds which were bound by the laws of childhood to be enacted.

He had passed away four years ago, and Nicky could still recall his grandfather's funeral with absolute clarity. It had rained heavily all day, and that seemed to perfectly mirror the general mood of the departed man during his life.

When the small crowd of sad, respectful mourners had slowly walked from the grave side, Nicky felt the urge to turn and go back to grandfather's final resting place. He approached the grave in a reflective mood, and hunched down at the side of the many floral tributes laid there. Although never really "close" to his grandfather, he thought that he should at least now say something appropriate.

He bent low and whispered, 'Now who's grounded... ?'

Suddenly yanked back into the real world, Nicky once again focussed on the imposing figure on the stage. Dr Chambers then hurried through a list of events forthcoming for the Upper School, and added, 'There are no names on the Walking List as yet – let us hope that it remains so.'

So, one general announcement and the Lord's Prayer later, the boys were filing out of the hall and out toward their respective form rooms. They lined up in the corridor outside room 9 in the Old Block, and were ushered into the classroom by an elderly master who from appearances may have been a schoolboy during the English Civil War. Under his dusty and battered black gown, he wore a tweed suit which had certainly come from a rummage sale held in the church at Naseby.

The man resembled a badly-laundered Winston Churchill. There were no words of welcome this time, just a barked instruction to each boy in turn to answer his name, and sit at the desk to which he was directed. Each boy was behaving identically, insomuch that they were scanning their fellow pupils – for any clue which may indicate if they were likely to become friend or foe. The classroom smelled of polish and chalk. Nicky could almost sense the history that radiated off the flaking walls and showered down over the assembled class. A significant amount of history seemed to radiate from the master, who now sat hunched over the large darkly-varnished desk on the dais at the front of the room.

'Settle please, gentlemen… I am Doctor Matthews,' began the master, reviewing the boys over steepled fingers. 'I will be your form master and history tutor for this first term. I am considered somewhat of an authority on the subject of the Palaeolithic or Old Stone Age. This is not, before some wag amongst you asks, because I was actually present during the period.' There was subdued laughter from the class.

'I shall firstly register the call, Ah… Call the Register, and hand out your form books – into which you will write your weekly timetable. I take it that all of you boys are armed with a pen? Good, then we will proceed.'

Dr Matthews rose awkwardly from his chair, and walked over to the stationary cupboard. He fumbled to free his gown from his jacket pocket, and began to search his pocket for the key. There was a curious clinking sound which accompanied the jangle of keys. He managed to get the key into the lock after four attempts, two drops, and a muted 'Damn and Bugger it'. There was a muted thump from the cupboard and the sound of an empty glass receptacle rolling to freedom, after which Dr Matthews reappeared laden with exercise books. He paused, pivoted slightly, and attempted to close the cupboard door with his foot. He missed the door completely, spun like a ballet dancer, and fell forward just enough to deposit most of the books into the waste paper bin at the side of his desk.

Regaining his composure, the master snapped 'A little help here, fellows, if you would be so kind… ' Gerry leapt out of his seat and retrieved the errant books from the bin.

'Should I hand them out, sir?' he enquired.

'Capital plan, that man – good show,' replied the master, grateful of the chance to retreat to his chair.

'I shall write your blacktable on the timeboard, and you will copy it into page one of your form books,' declared Dr Matthews, and for a second, confusion reigned supreme.

'Ought we not to call the register first?' asked a smug individual at the back.

'Yes indeed. Register, damn good point too,' answered the master.

So from Allenby, Ashworth, Barnet, and Baslow, all the way down to Yeardley and Zemburg, the new Form 1A was named and as yet, unshamed. There was a pause when Dr Matthews said, 'Oh my… there appear to be two Richard Wilsons, is this correct?'

The boys confirmed that this was indeed the case.

'Well… I don't believe it,' said Matthews.

He then excused himself and returned to the stationary cupboard, leaving the boys bemused at their desks. There was another clinking sound from within the cupboard, and it was followed by the attempt to suppress a forceful belch. He reappeared laden with another double-armful of exercise books, leaning like a tourist guide to the Italian city of Pisa.

'Right then, lads… ' he proclaimed. 'One each and pass them on please…'

Gerry and Nicky chimed up at this point. 'Thank you, sir, but we already have the books.'

'Really? Well, damn fine show, good planning those boys… '

As the master turned to take back the unwanted items, the front row were alerted to the cause of his confusion. There was a strong waft of Scotland's Finest, which reeled its way up the aisles to even the boys at the back. He steered himself somewhat unsteadily back to his chair, and reclined. The class sat in anticipation as he closed his eyes, awaiting their next instructions. There was an uncomfortably long pause, which was interrupted by the chainsaw snoring of Dr Matthews.

'The doctor will not be seeing any more patients today,' said Calderman.

The boys were confused as to what the next course of action should be, so they came to the consensus that they should copy out the timetable, leave a suitably polite note for the sleeping master, and go to their first lesson.

Now that they had "let sleeping docs lie", the lesson was Latin.

The troop of scholars marched to the doors of room 7, and each noted the impressive heraldic shield which was above the door. It bore the golden motto HABITUS OMNIA EST in gothic script. This was a room which a boy would certainly not barge into. One of the more adventurous souls knocked tentatively on the door, and the knock was answered by a cultured voice which instructed "Come".

They entered. The scene which greeted them was certainly not at all what they had expected. If any of the class had known what a bordello was (Nicky thought it may have been an exotic ice-cream flavour), then this is how they would have envisioned it. The windows had rich burgundy curtains with golden rope ties. Instead of the normal hanging globe lights, there were two majestic chandeliers which cast their elegant sparkle into every corner of the room. At either side of the master's desk stood luxuriant potted palms in ornate Greek urns. On the antique front desk was placed an onyx ashtray – in which was casually burning a black Russian Sobranie cigarette.

'Greetings, fellows and alumni,' intoned a voice with clipped, polished, and expensively manicured vowels.

' My name is Gideon Rundell, and it is my task to turn each of you into a lover and astute purveyor of the Latin tongue. Please do be seated; and do try not to scratch the desk tops – they are an absolute beast to polish.'

This was a voice that would obviously think that a "crèche" was a collision involving two Bentleys. The Master continued...

'You may call me sir, GR, or Imperator, but please, nothing distasteful or vulgar. We shall set off on a foray through the world of the Classical Civilisations, who have shaped our languages and given us form and purpose to our society.'

There was a murmur from the back row of the class. The Master paused in his speech to seek out the source of the interruption.

'Ah... Mister, let me see (he consulted the form list). Yes, Pratt: pray do enlighten the rest of the class with your comments... '

Pratt reddened, and answered in a timid voice, 'I was just saying. sir, that I don't see why we need to learn Latin, sir, seeing as how they are all dead, sir.'

The master smiled, as would a tiger in the long grass viewing an antelope picnic, and stubbing out his Russian cigarette, answered slowly and precisely.

'We learn the Roman tongue, Mr Pratt, in order that we enrich our knowledge and vocabulary. Latin gives us an insight into the major European languages of today, and will help you determine that *Pro Bono* is so much more than the lead singer of the band U2. Its use is prevalent in the legal profession, with whose documentation I am sure that you will become familiar in later life. In short, gentlemen – it is important that we learn that *In Loco Parentis* does not indicate that your Father is an engine driver.'

He then handed out volumes to each boy entitled *Latin for the Modern Scholar.*

'We will begin by looking at the verb Amare – to love.'

Thus began the explanation of how to decline the verb, and its various forms in Nominative, Vocative, Accusative, Genitive, Dative and Ablative. Most boys made an attempt to appear interested, some boys were making notes, and David DeVere was already secretly making plans to escape...

At the end of the lesson, Mr Rundell gave them their instruction to learn thirty words from the vocabulary book, in preparation for the next session. When the bell signalled the end of their tutorial, the boys gathered up their books, and filed out of the classroom door which the master held open for them. Nicky's last view of him before the door closed was as he calmly eased himself into the large desk chair, and lit another expensive cigarette.

Bundling on to their next study period, the boys were chatting.

'I really like Latin,' said a rather self-important classmate called Lordsley, in a haughty voice. 'It reminds me of when Papa took us to Rome. It was marvellous; I remember that there were tables and chairs out on the street.'

'We had exactly the same in my village,' said Nicky – 'but we called it eviction.'

Morning break time was now upon the boys, allowing them to mix and discuss the morning so far – and to dissect the various opinions on the masters which they had encountered.

'Do you think old Matthews is on some kind of medication?' asked Gerry.

'Indeed, and it's on special offer in our local off licence at £12 a bottle,' Calderman replied, laughing.

'Rundell seems quite nice though… ' said James Jackson, a tall, friendly open-faced boy from the village of South Wickham.

'Yeah, but he seems the type that would drive an ego-friendly car,' said Nicky.

The group of boys was now growing larger as new friendships were made. (The group was growing – the boys managed to stay the same size.) Calderman produced a packet of biscuits which he distributed unselfishly to all. Nicky was busy marshalling his thoughts as he turned around to take in the panorama of the Academy buildings from their position in the quad. He noticed that DeVere was over by the Physics block wall, seemingly pacing out distances, and taking a great interest in gratings and drain covers. He was busily writing notes into a small black notebook, which he swiftly put back into his jacket pocket when he noticed that he was being observed.

A familiar figure approached, and loomed over the group.

'I am putting you all on report for littering the quad,' said Piper the prefect in a smug tone.

'We haven't dropped any litter,' said Gerry.

'What do you call that then?' he sneered, pointing to the empty biscuit packet which Calderman was holding.

'I shall put it in my satchel, if it worries you so much,' Nicky told him.

'We recycle at this school, you loathsome little object,' Piper replied.

'I wish his father had', said Calderman, as the pefect stalked off to torment another gathering of boys.

Next lesson was History, back up in their form room 9.

The boys were all seemingly looking forward to the subject (and secretly wanted to see how Dr Matthews would further entertain them). They all sat in anticipation, books at the ready, when the door burst open, and a young master swept into the room.

'Sorry, chaps' he announced. 'Dr Matthews has had to nip out to collect a prescription, so I will take today's lesson. I am Mr Baker.'

'Is Dr Matthews all right, sir?' asked Peter Ashman.

'I am sure he will be; at ope – when he has collected his medication.'

' Anyway, chaps,' said Mr Baker, rubbing his hands, 'I thought it might be fun to have a General Knowledge History quiz – let's see what you brain-boxes really know eh?'

This was met with general approval. Foolscap sheets were handed out, and Mr Baker proceeded to ask historical questions dating from Biblical times to present day.

Thirty minutes later (and with many a well-chewed pen), the boys were told 'Righto, boys… now we will see who can do my job if I win the Lottery!' (There was a riotous laugh, and the Master had to call for quiet.)

'Please pass me the completed answer sheets up to the front desk.'

He made some hurried notes, and then walked between the aisles, returning the answer papers to their hopeful authors.

'I will read out your scores, and then correct one or two minor inaccuracies.

The following boys all scored twenty-two out of twenty-five:

Bellby, Morris, Wilson (1), DeVere, Jackson, Jenkins, Faroukh, Hennings, Money, Allman, Shepherd and Ritchey. Well Done!

Two boys scored twenty-three out of twenty-five:

Calderman and Merry. Congratulations gentlemen!

One boy scored twenty-four out of twenty-five:

Very well done to Lordsley !'

The master forced a short round of applause, which Lordsley took with all of the smug grace which befits a poor winner.

'The rest of you chaps did very well too, but I will just correct a few small points:

Question Four – Louie Armstrong was not the first man to set foot on the Moon.

Question Six – In religious history, an icon is not an optical illusion.

Question Nine – The PG Tips Company did not build the Great Pyramid.

Question Twelve – Magna Carta was not a famous Michael Caine film

Question Fourteen – The famed "Gordian Knot" was not a bunch of Greeks who recreated famous battles on their days off.

Question Sixteen – "El Dorado" is not a famous song by The Eagles.

Question Nineteen – The first dog in space was not called Pluto.

Question Twenty One – The "Terracotta Warriors" are not an American Football team.

'Apart from these points, I think that you all did well. Dr Matthews has left instruction that for your prep' work tonight, you should research "stone flaking in the Palaeolithic", so please be prepared for your next session.'

The whole class were beginning to wonder if "stoned and flaked out" might not be more apt.

They left the lesson feeling quite pleased with themselves, although one or two of them were harbouring feelings of retribution toward Lordsley.

Chapter Five

Meanwhile, something sinister was happening in the Kitchens...

DA, DA, DAAAAAH! (Sorry...)

Betty Bradley was the Head Cook of the school, or as she liked to upgrade her job description "Chief Executive in Charge of Provisions and Comestible Distribution". She had given long and committed service to the Academy since 1950, and was approaching retirement. This solid lady ruled her culinary kingdom with a rod of iron, or rather, a ladle of stainless steel.

She had twenty Staff under her.

She wore an immaculately starched apron.

She had respect.

She had a good pension to look forward to.

She also had 200 freshly-baked bread rolls, 15 roasted chickens, and 7 jam roly-poly puddings missing.

Again.

She was now extremely worried that her Empire was slipping out of her control. This was not the first time that food had mysteriously gone missing, but since it had not happened for a long while, she hoped that the problem might just have gone away. Things had returned to normal in the kitchens, and so she was taken aback by this latest disappearance of foodstuff into the Bermuda Triangle of Bakery.

The kitchens seemed to have a history of weird incidents, when utensils were moved, used, or taken. Staff would often complain of "shadows" seen fleeing into corners, and now the kitchen workers were nervous once again. Indeed, young Alice had one of her "little episodes" when she had discovered cupboard doors inexplicably opened, and small hand prints in the flour. Jewellery was of course banned in the kitchen under Betty's strict hygiene rules, but there were now one or two crucifixes being worn surreptitiously beneath aprons or tabards. Some member of her staff had taken it upon themselves to call in a local priest, but what Betty did to the unfortunate cleric with a spatula would take years of confession to be forgiven.

Betty knew that once again, something was afoot. (Ha! – we don't do metric, so see you in court EU bum faces.) There was little time to stand and dwell on the mystery, as there were two sittings of lunch to be prepared for the young gentlemen.

The younger girls were already laying out the long tables which provided the complete Dickensian Dining experience. There was always a vase of fresh seasonal flowers on the top table, to provide an ambience. No vases were allotted to the lower tables, to prevent having to call an ambulance. At each table were long bench seats which had been worn mirror-smooth by years of posterior friction.

Betty gave the room a thorough scan, and deciding all was as it should be, returned to her kitchen office to read up on Poltergeist and Demonic activity. She left her office door ajar, and went to flop into her comfy, cushioned chair.

Which was missing…

The bell had already sung out the call for the first dinner sitting. Boys were lining up outside the dining hall in two rows. Two masters stood at either side of the entrance door holding a long spike with a wooden end. At the instruction 'Boys may enter…' the queue began to file past the masters, who collected "dinner checks" from each pupil. These were plastic discs with a hole in the centre, which were placed onto the spike by the master as they were surrendered by the boys. The rule was: Grey for first sitting, yellow for second. Astute would-be diners had seen to it that there were many forgeries in circulation, which could be purchased by boys for a fraction of the normal cost of a meal. This was known as the "Brown Market", presumably taking its title from the colour of the gravy. It could of course, have been some acerbic comment on the quality of the meals provided.

It was the accepted convention that two boys from each table would perform "Porterage". This involved presenting themselves at the serving hatches, and collecting the large trays of food to be then taken back to the tables. The food would be served out onto a plate by one of the two masters who sat at each table, and the plates passed around to each pupil. This was somewhat time-consuming, and a diner could only look forward to warming up his dinner when the jug containing hot gravy found its way to him.

The saying of grace was another solemn ritual. The actual wording of the pre-meal thanks varied greatly depending on which master was saying it. There were various options, and boys soon got to know which master would deliver the most popular "speech".

'For what we are about to receive' was an old favourite, but the younger masters tended to lighten the mood with such witty renditions as, 'Oh let us be grateful, for this dirty great plateful', 'Dear Jesus, thanks for three courses and cheeses' and 'Great Creator, bless our meat, veg' and potater'…

At the end of a course, plates were collected in a high stack (beware the gravy that runneth over) and taken back to the serving hatch by the Porters. I tell you that verily didst oft the boy slip on an unseen gravy spill (I did warn you…). Any trip or fall by an unfortunate collector would be greeted immediately by a mighty roar, and banging on the table tops. Unpopular pupils or those likely to react by going completely over the top, were often subject to the cruel sport of "Servetipping". Victims were seen to arc through the air, and land in a hail of shattered crockery – after which points were awarded for style, reaction, and artistic merit. When these poor servers "went down", it was more vicious than the most annoying computer glitch.

Needless to say, some of these unfortunate mortals went on to suffer psychological damage in later life – and an unnatural phobia of custard.

Nicky, Calderman, and Merry were sitting together at one of the gargantuan benches. They had now begun a lively discussion with several other new pupils. It would seem that their parents had either a relaxed or vindictive attitude toward naming offspring. Among the new members of the group were Andy Mann, Cliff Topps, John Thomas and Philip Ardley. As Philip was the shorter of the two Ardley brothers at the school, and slightly older than his brother, Kevin, "Ardley Senior" seemed to be an appropriate title. The boy with perhaps the strangest Christian name was Mr and Mrs Money's son. Thanks to a cataclysmic error of judgement by his parents, they had chosen to ensure that the poor lad would go through life as Owen Money. There was a chap whose surname was Royd on the next table, and Calderman was hoping against hope that he had a sister – named Emma.

The instructions given during mealtime by the masters were identical to those usually given at home, i.e.:

'Do slow down, Merry, it's not a race.'

'Feel free to comment on the food, Thomas – but we do not wish to see it as you do so.'

'Baker, please cease your attempts to disprove evolution – use the cutlery, boy…
'

'Yes, Peters, the scar is impressive, but no-one wishes to see it during lunch.'

'Mann, if you are not intending to eat that tie, then remove it from your gravy.'

'Ardley, for goodness sake – you have the table manners of an inebriated yak.'

With this side order of enforced etiquette: shepherd's pie, chips and vegetables that died in mysterious circumstances were consumed.

Empty plates were stacked and returned to the hatches without incident, and "pudding" was collected on large metal trays. This proved, after forensic examination by a qualified scientist, to be the Cook's take on the theme of Chocolate Sponge. These rock-hard squares clung with adhesive defiance to the platter, and had to be loosened by brute force and gravity. Each boy was dealt a lump of the bizarre sponge, which hit the plate with a brick-like crunch.

It is, I feel, worthy of note to the reader that leftover sponge is never ever wasted by any educational establishment in the country. Surplus blocks of this unyielding inedible substance are donated to major aid organisations, who package them on pallets and fly them out of Brize Norton Royal Air Force Base where they can then be used overseas to rebuild hurricane-devastated communities.

They provide light, cheap and quick construction materials in disaster areas, with the added advantage that any family trapped in their storm shelter after reconstruction, can vary their diet during their period of confinement, by nibbling their foundation walls. (This is why so many people interviewed on American television news channels after yet another terrible storm has ravaged their town, have a house that is miraculously still standing, but really awful teeth.)

Thomas studied the leaden lump and declared, 'Sorry, sir, but I'm allergic… '

'Allergic? Allergic to what, boy?' asked the master.

'Death, sir,' answered Thomas, with considerable feeling.

Application of custard (watery and vaguely yellow, or thick-skinned and immobile –a sort of "unlucky dip") from the large, white enamel jug did little to soften the surfaces of the impenetrable dessert.

The unwanted pudding was fielded swiftly by Mark Davis, a young gentleman who may best be described as resembling two young gentlemen. He was a funny, pleasant and amiable boy, who it would be impossible not to like. He had already made dozens of new friends in just one morning. Rumour had it that he had a photographic memory. Rumour had it that most of the photographs were of cakes...

Lunch was now finished, and thus the lucky survivors filed out of the dining hall in orderly lines with Masonic precision. The pupils again began to congregate in the quad, whilst the next band of victims queued up for the second sitting. One or two older boys were handing out lapel badges to any First Years which they could find. Merry took a badge, and regarded it thoughtfully. It bore three letters in gothic script. Gerry asked the giver of the badge to explain the significance of the legend.

'It stands for Onans Is Knowledge,' answered the smirking boy. 'But we just used the initials to save space. We thought it might be a nice first-day gift for you New Bugs.'

Calderman scrutinised the badge, then exchanged a knowing glance with Nicky.

Merry thanked the older pupil, and looked genuinely pleased with his gift, until Calderman asked him, 'Gerry, have you recently had a blow to the head?'

'What do you mean?'

'The badge – did you look at it?'

'Of course I did, what's wrong with it?'

Nicky explained slowly and as kindly as he could:

'It really is a thoughtful gesture to be given a small gift on your first day at your new school. I expect that you feel a warm glow of acceptance, and that it helps you feel a true part of the bigger school community. You now feel a bond between all of the students in the Brotherhood of St Onan's, in which you are proud and privileged to play your part. You might just spare a moment to consider that you will be walking around in full view of masters and pupils, proudly announcing to the world in general that you are an OIK.'

'The Bastard... ' declared Merry, with narrowed, vengeful eyes.

He suddenly had a horrible flashback to when his Uncle Derek had taken an advertising job for a new company. They had assumed that their public profile could be enhanced by instructing employees to wear sweatshirts with the initials of the firm proudly printed on the front in jaunty script. And so it came to pass that dear Uncle Derek and his team went out amongst the people, to spread the goodwill of the Thames Water Advisory Trust – wearing a shirt proudly bearing the logo "TWAT".

His mother had made a hurried telephone call to his sister who was away at college. Knowing the mental torment and ridicule that Uncle Derek had endured, she demanded that her daughter refrain from purchasing any item of clothing which bore initials. She was well aware that the modern fashions had spawned shirts bearing logos such as UCLA and DKNY, not to mention the oh-so-naughty FCUK. This would normally have been harmless, but she knew her daughter was a member of the Cambridge University Netball Team, and was not prepared to take any chances.

With a few minutes to kill before the end of the lunch break, the boys had formed up teams for a game in the quad. Ball games were strictly forbidden, but some inventive soul had come up with the idea of "bottle-top football". Team games could still be enjoyed, and the evidence swiftly hidden if any of the masters should take exception to the sport. Nicky wondered how long it might be before Dr Matthews picked up the sound of a loose bottle top on his radar, and hurried to investigate.

Just as the captain of the victorious side was swooping around the quad in his lap of honour (having comprehensively trounced the opposition 33 – 7), the bell rang to signal the commencement of afternoon education.

The next class was English, which Nicky was really looking forward to. It was taught by a young master by the name of Mr Hyde-Jones. He was really popular with the boys throughout the Academy, and turned up in style each day in a red E – Type Jaguar sports car. This was the source of intense jealousy within the staffroom, and even worse, Mr Hyde-Jones had even been known to turn up at school on a Saturday morning wearing (cover your children's eyes, Mother)... jeans

He taught English with passion and humanity, and managed to fire up the imagination of any pupil lucky enough to be in his classes.

The form made their way across the quad and up the stairs of the New Block up to the classroom. The master held open the door for the boys, and instructed them 'Hi, chaps – go in and grab a seat.' He let the class settle, and then sat casually on the corner of his desk smiling at the room full of hopeful faces.

'So, how are we doing, guys?' he began. 'I hope that you will bear with me whilst I get to know who you all are.

This term we will be studying the works of Geoffrey Chaucer, the great Irish writer Sean O'Casey, the poetry of the First World War, and of course Mr William Shakespeare, a writer from Stratford upon Avon who you may have heard of. Trust me, lads, you will grow to love and respect these writers as I do – and if we have time, I promise that I will try and squeeze in a little education...'

A hand was already raised skywards at the back of the room. The owner of the hand was one William Trevill, who hailed originally from a small village in Dorset. His father had placed him halfway up the length of the country, in an Academy highly recommended by a man he met trapped underground for three hours down a pothole.

Trevill enquired in rich Dorset tones, ''Ere Surr, Ow come we 'as to lurn about thaat there Shakespeare bloke, cuz Oi can't understand Ee.'

The master smiled and replied, 'Mr Trevill, firstly, do not ever lose those glorious West Country vowels – be proud of your accent and heritage. Secondly, we learn about Shakespeare because he was quite simply the greatest English poetic dramatist. He employed language in the same way that the Welsh genius Dylan Thomas performed his own linguistic sorcery.'

'But woi carn't we learn about other famous wroiters – like wot they'm tellin' I at my other school?' asked Trevill.

'Like whom, in particular?' queried Hyde-Jones.

'Master John Diggle, the famous poet of Coltsford in the Wold, who was a well-known thatcher and wren-impersonator, who would 'ave no doubt gone on to wroite a-many great works, 'ad 'is memory not let 'im down...'

'How did his memory let him down?'

'He was a-wroitin' one of his great works whilst thatchin' the roof on a cottage.'

'And how should this affect his memory?'

'Well, see, He 'ad forgotten that the cottage was on fire at the toime...'

'Fascinating, Mr Trevill...' said Hyde-Jones, 'I will endeavour to include his work in our study as a mark of respect.'

(It would later transpire that there was more to our man Trevill than meets the eye. His elder brother had been the leader of a three-man gang who robbed banks and building societies in the Devon area. As a cunning disguise, the gang borrowed items of ladies' clothing from the girlfriend of one of the gang – who worked Saturdays in an "Ann Summers" shop. They conducted their raids decked out in various styles of rather racy women's lingerie – and so earned themselves the nickname from the local police and newspapers of "The Basque Terrorists".)

And so the lesson began in earnest (no, not Hemmingway – Hyde-Jones thought that his work most mostly a load of bull...).

The eager young minds were introduced to the world of Chaucer, which began with "The Knights' Tale". Strangely, Trevill proved to be somewhat of an expert at reading aloud the archaic verse. Calderman however, was in no doubt whatsoever as to exactly what hideous acts he would perpetrate upon "Chauntecleer" the damn cockerel, who he would like to introduce to Colonel Sanders at the earliest opportunity.

The reading of the text was shared around the room by the master, who helped the boys deal with some of the more complex translations required.

'You will see, boys, that this is the form from which our modern language has evolved,' said Hyde-Jones, 'and it is still evolving today. I will point out one very vital fact, chaps, which I want you all to remember and act upon. The word "nothing" does not contain any "fs", and never, EVER ends with a "k". Please remember this at all costs.'

Mr Hyde-Jones then brought the lesson to a close announcing, 'Okay, boys, we will read the next two chapters for prep tonight, and continue down the road to Canterbury in the next lesson.' The class then began packing yet more books into their bags and satchels, which were already beginning to strain under the load. As they left the classroom, Nicky fished out his timetable and saw the dreaded word… Maths.

The mathematics class was held on the very top floor of the New Block, at the rear of the building. There was a pleasant view out of the large, high windows over the Academy Library and the adjacent St Wilfred's church. The boys sat at the newer two-man tables in silence, awaiting the entrance of the master. DeVere was looking out of the window, whilst using a protractor to seemingly calculate the angle between the building and the nearby church spire – and noting down his findings in his little black book.

The door opened abruptly, and the boys all stood to attention as the master entered. Without addressing the class, the teacher walked sedately to the blackboard and began to write. A moment or two later, the board bore the legend "Mr Miles Bannister – Mathematics". The man now turned to face the class, and every boy shared a moment of terror which spread from pupil to pupil by telepathy.

The Master looked identical to the Great Horror Actor, Vincent Price…

'Good day, gentlemen,' he boomed. 'Be quiet now for goodness' sake – I'm talking to the class… ' None of the assembled pupils had said a word.

'We will begin by examining the importance of integers, prime numbers, and factors. All of life, science, and our understanding of our universe requires that we equip ourselves with mathematical skills,' said Mr Bannister, adding, 'Well look for it where you last had it, and stop asking me…' Again, the bemused class shot glances at each other.

He paced up and down the rows of tables, placing a thick volume in front of each boy.

'Please take these books home, boys, and cover them in suitable paper, if you would be so kind. NO, THEY MAY NOT USE THE PIGFARMERS WEEKLY,' he suddenly blurted out, causing each boy to flinch.

It would appear that Mr Bannister was engaged in a conversation with some other person who was invisible to the rest of the class. This was already becoming very disconcerting for the boys who were, after all, still getting used to their first day at the Academy.

'Well if you couldn't be bothered to lock it, then you deserve to have it stolen...' continued the master.

'Now, Boys, if you open our textbooks at page five, we will begin with the mathematical matrix and how it can assist us.'

Whilst they read the short introduction into matrices and their applications, Nicky began to panic. He felt like an early ape-man in the shadow of the huge black monolith of mathematics which towered over him. Even if it fell down on top of him, he doubted very much if any of its wisdom would rub off. It wasn't that he was stupid, but there had always been some unnamed factor concerning maths that he just didn't "get". He had been passable at the good old addition, subtraction and such – and could even manage long division given a suitable run-up. Numbers just did not hold any attraction for him, other than being nailed on the door of his closed mind.

Numbers were too clinical, too precise and literal for his comfort. You couldn't describe a perfect sunset with numbers (all right clever dicks everywhere – painting by numbers doesn't count), and a right or wrong answer had no shade or texture, just hard and sharp fact. So he did what he was aware of some other boys doing; in other words he frowned in what he hoped was an intelligent-looking manner at the book, in case the secret should leap from the page in a moment of divine inspiration.

It was at this point that a boy at the back of the class knocked his school geometry set off the table, and as convention dictates, the contents spread themselves over the widest possible floor area with a loud clatter.

'What on earth is going on there at the back...?' shouted Mr Bannister, in the sergeant-major tones of maths teachers everywhere.

Suddenly, without warning, the class quite clearly heard an elderly female voice snap back, 'Oh for heaven's sake, Miles, calm down – you are frightening the poor boy, and do think of your blood pressure...'

None of the pupils were sure exactly what was going on, and why the severe master was suddenly choosing to demonstrate his skill at ventriloquism. The female voice continued, 'You pay no attention, love, this is why he doesn't have many friends... '

'ENOUGH WOMAN, I SHALL SPEAK TO YOU PRIVATELY... ' Bannister growled in his normal voice. He gathered his composure, and instructed the boys to continue with the problems written on the blackboard. This they did, but all eyes were now furtively scanning Bannister for any further entertaining episodes.

Nicky was now suffering the mind-numbing panic of kids everywhere that had a similar terror of numbers, and unlike his primary school, there was no kindly hand to guide him safely through the snaking columns of impenetrable figures.

Andy Mann leaned across and whispered to Nicky and Calderman, 'My mum knows Bannister, he lives not far from us.'

'Did she say that he is a bit odd?' Nicky asked.

'No, but I know that his wife calls him "Four Minute Miles" for some strange reason.'

Time seemed to drag like a contestant in a three-legged race with one leg.

However hard he stared at that clock, Nicky could not turn the hands forward by effort of will. To the disappointment of all, the strange interruptions seem to have abated.

With more luck than judgement, he managed to more or less fully complete the questions which the Master had written on the blackboard. Mr Bannister now had a handful of printed sheets, which he handed out to the class, declaring, 'For prep tonight, boys, you will answer questions one to ten on the sheets using the Mean, Mode and Median averages... IT'S EGGS BENEDICT – NOT "BENEFIT"... My apologies, gentlemen, do collect your books, and I shall see you tomorrow and explain the operation of the slide rule.'

The end-of-school bell signalled their release. The boys left the class slightly confused as to what they thought they had just witnessed, and burdened with yet more books which could not be coaxed into their packed bags. They joined the urgent cascade of boys surging down the stairs toward the quad, and freedom.

Once out of the double doors into the fresh air, Nicky was trying to make sense of the day. History and Latin lessons had proved to be a bit weird (to say the least), and he was not at all sure as to what exactly he had witnessed during the last class.

The English lesson, however, had been a revelation. Words could drift in on the rolling breakers – leaving pools of wonder suspended upon the shores of his young mind. Ebb and neap tides left phrase and fable clinging as stranded starfish upon his consciousness.

Unfortunately – he was shite at maths...

Boys began to pour out of the great front doors of the Academy, happy to be released from the bondage of education. Prefects were again lurking to ensure that all pupils were wearing full uniform, and had not discarded ties or the hated straw boaters. Now, the urgency was to devise a route to the bus stop which would not bring them into contact with pupils from any of the other town schools. It was a known fact that the antique headgear of St Onans was a prized spoil of war - to be captured by any means, and no doubt flaunted as "booty" by other kids.

Luckily, there were no "raiding parties" in evidence as they left school today. The small group including Nicky made their way to the bus stop and awaited their repatriation to village life. Scanning the street for covert prefects, hats were speedily removed and hidden beneath blazers.

The bus eventually crept around the corner and into view. Nicky queued patiently and paid his fare to the driver, checking the already seated passengers for any potential mockery. He edged his way up the aisle (restraining the satchel to prevent any acts of aggression being enacted upon the public) and sat down. He found himself sitting next to Mrs Adcock, a neighbour from two doors up the row.

'Hello, dear,' she smiled. 'How was your first day at your new school?'

'It was good – thank you,' he lied.

The bus carried on its halting progress to the foot of the hill, then slowed to a stop. There had been some sort of incident involving a lorry carrying chickens, and there were broken crates in the road, and confused birds noisily celebrating their freedom in the roadway and along the grassed verges. Two drivers were nose to nose, engaged in a loud discussion in order to establish liability, although the language that was being used was far from what one might expect in legal terminology.

It was apparent that the bus would not be moving again for some time, and so Nicky decided to get off and walk the last half mile or so up the hill to his village. Dropping his various textbooks several times, he set off for home leaving bus, drivers, chickens, and amused bystanders to sort themselves out. He had walked only a short distance when there was a screeching of car brakes behind him.

'Hurry up, son… jump in and I'll give ye a lift,' called a voice.

Turning around, Nicky was happy to see the familiar face of Uncle Joe leaning out of the window of his gleaming Zodiac, and beckoning him toward the car urgently. He ran over and opened the car door, hurling his books and satchel onto the vast rear seat.

'Thanks, Uncle,' he began. 'I didn't expect to see you – I thought you were visiting your sister today?'

'Yeah, I was, but there was a bit of an incident, so I had to cut the visit short.'

'Can I ask what happened, Uncle?'

'Can't tell you a lot, son, obviously due to legal reasons, but let's just say that chutney, a fresh haddock, and a taser may have been involved…'

The international man of mystery known as Uncle Joe pulled up the car opposite Nicky's house, waited whilst the boy gathered all of his school paraphernalia from the back seat, and then sped off homeward – pausing to give the time-honoured two fingered salute to another road user who took exception to his scant regard of the Highway Code.

Walking up the familiar front garden path to his front door, a sense of calm and release began to settle once again on his shoulders, which were aching with the scholastic load bearing him to the ground. Nicky opened the door and squeezed through into the living room, dipping one shoulder to rid himself of his burden of books in the homicidal satchel. He whipped off his tie, carefully removed and folded his new blazer, and hurled it with feeling onto the back of the sofa.

Mum was in the kitchen, and greeted her offspring with an expectant smile...

She placed a cup of steaming tea and a plate of biscuits on the kitchen table.

'Well, come on then, tell us how you got on at school,' she gushed, sitting opposite Nicky in full "Mum paying attention and requiring full detail" mode. Auntie appeared from the garden, where she had been harassing a mole, and sat beside his mother.

'So... what is it like?' she prompted

'It's a bit big and old,' he answered.

'So is Cousin Sheila,' Mum said. 'But we want to hear all about your big first day.'

'It's a bit bizarre,' Nicky answered, feeling as if he were on a television quiz show – and hoping that he would do better in the General Knowledge round.

'What do you mean by "Bizarre?"'

'You know, peculiar, odd, funny, curious, eccentric, unorthodox, wacky, oddball... '

'I know what the word means; I want you to tell us what you did, who you made friends with, and what the lessons were like,' explained Mum.

'Mum, the place is huge and old and creepy (like Cousin Sheila presumably), and the prefects are evil, the masters we have seen so far are as mad as a hat full of spoons – one was drunk, one thinks he is Noel Coward, and one talks to himself and shouts a lot, and as far as I can see there is only the English master who can work out which is the correct way to put on his trousers... '

'Can you speak Latin yet?' Mum asked.

Nicky was silent...

'Why are you not answering?' she enquired.

'I was speaking Latin, Mum; there was no sound because all of the Romans are dead.'

Auntie paused mid-guffaw, as a digestive biscuit committed suicide by hurling itself into her tea cup. 'Imbecillitas Est...' said Auntie.

Mum and Nicky stared at her open-mouthed.

Auntie had always been, and still was, something of an enigma (although she herself would no doubt insist that an enigma is something given to relieve constipation). Since Father had gone out on his quick shopping errand all those years ago, Mum had insisted that Auntie should come and live with her and her son. She had worked in the munitions factory during the Second World War, and had some dangerous, and hilarious escapades at that time. She had recently retired from her job as a Technical Inspector at a ball-bearing factory, where she seemed to have acquired some surprising skills and some eccentric social contacts. Blessed with "green fingers" that could persuade a used lollipop stick to grow, her new kingdom was the garden which stretched down from the back door of the house, to the rustic fence which bordered the undulating field beyond.

She seemed to have some secret and inexplicable communion with all forms of wildlife, and was often seen chatting to a favourite robin which would perch without fear on her outstretched finger. Auntie also radiated a huge sense of fun, and when deciding which attitude to adopt in life, would usually decide to take the piss (anyone whom she considered to be "too far up their own jacksie" was walking a dangerous tightrope).

After a short while in her company, many had concluded that you did not need a telescope to see that there was more to Auntie than met the eye…

'Did you meet Ian at school?' Mum enquired.

'Yes, Mum, I sort of made a few new friends – but I know I'm going to hate it.'

'Look, dear, it's only your first day, and it is bound take a while to settle in.'

'Like dry rot,' Auntie chipped in helpfully.

'I don't think that was terribly helpful,' replied Mum. 'Anyway, you can tell us more detail after we have had tea – we're having fish, and Auntie has made a special trifle to celebrate your first day.'

Auntie grinned a knowing grin at Nicky. Her desserts were a legend in the village, and would contain varying amounts of alcohol guaranteed to make any function go with a swing (usually from the chandelier, if there was one available). They had floored many an unsuspecting guest, and temporarily incapacitated the vicar one Christmas. There is an old proverb which states that "The proof of the pudding is in the eating". The proof of the pudding in this case was approximately 94%.

Having finished their meal, they cleared the kitchen table so that Nicky could commandeer it for doing his homework. He read the Latin and tried to commit it to memory as directed; he made as much sense as he could of "stone flaking" for history, pondered through the sometimes undecipherable Chaucer for English, and bluffed his way through the maths, hoping there were no witnesses. This done, he thanked Auntie (who had volunteered to cover his new textbooks for him – wrapping expert as she is) and hurriedly changed into his jeans and tee shirt. He urgently needed to re-connect with his favourite spot in the big field, preferably perched aloft in one of the tall elms. There was still a lot of evening left, and he didn't want it to go to waste.

A gentle breeze fanned the field, but did not blow away the clouds of doubt about the future, which hung around like the kid with no pocket money at the ice-cream van. There was no football game with his village friends tonight, just a perturbed boy high up in a tree amidst the Constable landscape. He wondered if he would ever again feel the connection, the contentment, and the comfort of things returning to how they had been before he had walked through the doors of St Onan's. He closed his eyes and wished for things to return to normal.

His prayers were answered – the branch broke…

Chapter Six

Nicky awoke and shot a glance over to his Mickey Mouse alarm clock. He rolled out of his bed and discovered that he was still attached to the sheet by the sticking plaster which Mum had put over the graze he had sustained during his exit from the tree last evening. It was early, but the aromas of a "full English" were luring him powerfully downstairs.

'Morning Dear...' said Mum in her advert mum voice. 'Have your shower, and breakfast will be ready'. He was in and out of the shower speedily, having washed all of the bits which he could remember. They sat and ate together, when suddenly, there came a call outside the kitchen window 'Hellooo... Anyone there?'

'Oh, good grief, what does she want now?' exclaimed Mother.

The drive-by shouting was being perpetrated by their neighbour, Mrs Adcock, who was the search engine driving all gossip, long before social media took over. Her "window calls" had built up to several every day recently, and Nicky saw that this morning, Mum was not in the mood for Mrs A.

Mum got up and crossed to the kitchen window. She gripped the handle whilst leaning behind the curtain, and then swung it open suddenly. There was a bump, a sound of floral apron hitting the path, and a word that one would never hear on Radio 4.

'Sorry, Lily, I didn't see you there...' lied Mum.

The neighbour was scrabbling on the path for a second, then picked up some fallen object and lisped a response.

'I jusht wanted to shee how Nicky had got on at schcool yesterday,' she said.

'Oh fine, fine... ' Mum replied, 'I'm sure he will come up and tell you all about it later, won't you, Nicky?'

Covering her mouth, the embarrassed Mrs A retreated up the row to her own back door. Mum glanced out of the window, and said to her son 'Do go and tell her about the school – or we'll never get an end to these visits, and when you go, please return her bottom set of teeth because they make the lawn look untidy.'

Mother looked pleased to have "repelled boredom", and then said to her son, 'You can sort out Dave later, when you come home from school.'

'Mum – who is Dave?' Nicky ventured

'Look under the table, but don't disturb him – he looks so comfortable,' said Mum.

Nicky carefully lifted the table cloth to reveal a shoebox lined with straw on the kitchen floor. In the box was quite the most contented chicken that he had ever seen, who regarded him with a happy look (well it is hard to tell with chickens – but you get the point).

'He must have followed you home yesterday,' said Mum.

'Why "Dave" Mum?' Nicky asked.

'Well he just looks rather "Davey" don't you think?' she answered.

'I think that Dave may well turn out to be "Davina', don't you Mum?" said Nicky.

'In which case we must be thankful that we live in enlightened times,' stated Mum.

The happy fowl did indeed seem to possess a certain Davicity, so no more was said.

So, once again loaded down with the tomes of learning, Nicky plodded up the path to the bus stop like the heavy horses that ploughed the soil at village competitions. The satchel was stowed out of the way of the unsuspecting public, and so could not claim any early morning victims. Although his village friends joined the bus at their usual stop, they chose today to ignore Nicky completely, he sat in splendid isolation all the way into the town, until the bus coughed itself to a standstill at his stop.

He joined the throng of boys on the walk to the Academy, who were now becoming familiar faces. Today he did not feel the apprehension as he passed through the gates, and he thought that today might just be okay after all. His progress was halted by Piper, the prefect, who grabbed him by the lapel and hauled him to one side.

'Incorrectly dressed in public are we, Shepherd?' sneered the prefect.

Nicky suddenly realised that his hated boater was still in his satchel. Piper had a self-satisfied smile on his face, and Nicky wondered just how long he had waited there in order to catch him.

'You are on Report, boy… ' snapped Piper. 'See me at Morning Break.'

'But… ' began Nicky – but his words were stifled.

'You are in trouble, so I don't want to hear it,' said the prefect.

Nicky studied his tormentor; if he was in trouble already, then it was only a question of proportion. He thought to himself, 'What would Auntie do?' okay – here goes…

'Can I ask a question?' Nicky said

'Make it a good one' answered the prefect.

'Is being a complete pillock one of your A-Level choices, or just a hobby?'

The Prefect opened and closed his mouth like a goldfish from the fair. Finally he responded. 'Eleven o'clock outside the HM's study,' and strode off.

Calderman had appeared at his side, and Gerry stood grinning behind him.

'One nil to us, mate – Well done, now let's go and be assembled.'

The Faithful marched into the hall, and stood ready to receive the word of the great god known to his loyal followers as Goodwill.

The head tentatively checked the lectern before commencing his speech, but found that no tampering had seemingly occurred. He led the singing of the Academy anthem, and as the final organ chords ran for cover, produced sheets of paper from his pocket.

'It is with great sadness, gentlemen, that I have to inform you of the cessation of one of our Academy's most proud traditions. I am deeply sorry to have to be the bearer of such melancholy, but I felt that I should speak to you all personally, and not let rumour run its villainous course...'

All of the boys looked at each other, trying to see if anyone had any idea as to what dreadful incident had occurred. The head looked genuinely moved by whatever horrible news he had chosen to deliver, and all expected to hear of a tragedy.

'From this day...' said Goodwill, his voice faltering slightly, 'there will no longer be the requirement to wear the famous head apparel so long proudly donned by generations of Onanists. I know that you will share my feelings of loss for one of our most historic traditions. We shall all no doubt, mourn its passing...'

With that, the master seemed overcome, and swept out of the hall through the back doors, leaving the rest of the assembled staff somewhat bemused.

'What was all that about?' whispered Nicky to Calderman.

'I am happy to report that our Boaters have just been torpedoed,' he replied.

Dr Chambers hurriedly assumed centre stage, and blustered through the short list of announcements. He finished his short presentation with the notice that 'Auditions for parts in the Academy Drama Society's production of *Oliver* will be held in this hall at four o'clock prompt.' Dismissed without further ado, the boys filed out of the hall and prepared for their first lesson of the day.

Today, it was French class. The class sat in anticipation awaiting the arrival of the master. The door opened to reveal not the casually dressed, Gauloise-smoking teacher that they had half expected, but a short woman in a tweedy two-piece suit and gown with a look that would terrify a rampaging bull elephant.

'Bonjour, class,' she announced.

There were only three or four responses in the required tongue (although Nicky was certain that he heard one voice say 'Bondage, madam'). The teacher strode to the blackboard and wrote her name and subject in florid letters with screeching chalk.

'I am Mrs Penelope Dreadfall, and I shall teach you the beautiful mother tongue of France that you may travel widely across Europe and be welcomed everywhere,' she announced.

(There was little or no chance that she would escape being known informally as "Penny Dreadful" by all and sundry, but then c'est la vie, Sister...)

Nicky noticed that there was a new face in the class today, an intelligent looking lad with a mop of wild hair. He spotted Nicky's casual glance, and gave him a relaxed nod. He looked completely at ease with his surroundings, and not at all overawed by the Academy in general. He was also noticeable due to the fact that he was wearing a classic French beret set at a jaunty angle.

The teacher lasered in on the boy immediately, and demanded his name.

'I am Richard Wetherill, madame,' came his reply.

'Well, Mr Wetherill, much as I appreciate your display of enthusiasm for the subject – you will remove the headgear immediately.'

The trainee Frenchman complied with her instruction, the hat disappearing somewhere about his person.

The lesson progressed with explanations of French vowel sounds, and the naming of familiar household objects and the like. Mrs Dreadfall asked the class if anyone already spoke any French. Weatherill was first to raise his hand...

'My dad speaks fluid French, madame.'

'You mean "fluent?'

'No – he tries to speak French when he's pissed.'

This exchange brought the house down, and Merry had to be hit on the back to stop him from choking. Madame was definitely not amused.

She then made the class stand and introduce themselves in French. This went well, and there was a stream of passable attempts by the students – in the 'Bonjour, je m'apelle Ian/David/William' style. Things went slightly awry however, as Lordsley went to make his introduction. Just after he announced 'Bonjour, je m'appelle...' some unseen wit loudly inserted the name "Knobhead". Merry had to helped from the room.

'Mon dieu! I will have no further vulgarity, boys.' she demanded, her mouth now in the standard cats' bottom shape of disapproving ladies everywhere. 'French is not a vulgar language, it is a language of Art and Poetry – let us aspire to this.'

With much suppressed laughter and smirks aplenty, the lesson progressed through "numbers", "days of the week" and common French phrases (Madame would prefer the term "regularly used" in place of "common").

The boys left the lesson with the beginnings of a foreign language, and some knowledge of how to annoy this particular teacher – both invaluable skills to them.

Now it was time for the Himalayan trek up the endless flights of stairs for maths with Mr Bannister. On the way to class, Nicky and his friends introduced themselves to Dick Weatherill. It transpired that he lived in one of the small villages out towards Lincoln, his father ran the local pub, he had two sisters, and a mother who was either in therapy or grinning happily out of their conservatory window at sheep – assisted by her friend Valium. (Merry asked if her friend was Romanian, just to be clear.)

Dick was fascinated by the description of Mr Bannister's progress so far, and was looking forward to seeing the performance "live".

As the boys entered the classroom, the master was already seated bent over searching for something in his desk drawers. He was having an urgent conversation with his invisible confidante.

'Well I would, if you would ever give me a moment's peace...'

'I certainly will not be able to find it, if you persist with your constant interruptions, madam...'

'I certainly AM aware of what's going on... '

'What do you mean, "Look up now" then?'

This one-sided conversation had been witnessed by the class, who had been sitting in nervous silence. A somewhat flustered Bannister regained his composure and straightened his tie. 'Sorry about that, gentlemen, just dealing with something,' he announced. 'Whilst I collect in your prep work and check it, you will complete the question sheets which I shall hand out – on the subject of Elementary Geometry.'

Books were passed forward, and the master stalked between the tables placing the geometry question sheets in front of every boy.

'You may now begin,' he said.

'Good Morning, boys,' wouldn't have hurt you, would it?' – The female voice intoned.

'Madam, as you can see, I am somewhat busy,' said Bannister.

'Obviously too busy for manners...' came the terse reply.

Heads down in mock concentration, the class were fascinated by this latest exchange, especially as only one participant was visible. Weatherill sported a grin from ear to ear, and he could not believe his luck to witness at first hand, the events which his new friends had described. Bannister began to quickly mark the work in the books which he had collected, when suddenly the female voice came again in an urgent tone...

'Sorry, deary, must go – I think she's left the gas on again.'

The master looked up from the marking with a startled expression. 'Please do excuse me, you chaps – I must just attend to something,' he said, and walked quickly out of the classroom door.

'Told you,' said Calderman. 'Absolutely stark raving Banjo.'

'Hang on, let's be logical about this,' Nicky said. 'It may well be that Sir Strange is not strictly adhering to the rule about no mobile phones – he may have a concealed earpiece like the CIA.'

Wetherill chimed in. 'Yes, but would the CIA call their gran during a lesson?'

'Could be the earpiece picking up stray signals?' asked Gerry.

'Will you chaps pipe down – I'm trying to work,' snapped Lordsley.

'Shut it, "Le Knob", or you will pick up my stray boot,' growled Calderman.

Bannister returned, looking calmer. He smiled and told the boys 'Since this is a single period, we will break early today. Please read up on Pythagoras' Theorem if you have time – and thank you all for attending...'

As they left the maths lesson bound for chemistry, the small group of would-be detectives vowed to get to the bottom of the "Mystery of the phantom voices" - without enlisting the aid of some really annoying cartoon Great Dane.

The boys (except Weatherill) had already seen the inside of the chemistry lab. As they entered, they were each handed white lab coats by a sixth-form lab assistant (for safety), and a set of wrap-around clear goggles (for safety). They filed in and sat in rows, apart from Lordsley, who sat on his own at the back (for safety).

It was Captain Brayfield who entered the laboratory in military fashion. He was the Master that Nicky remembered as having shown his group around on "Initiates Day".

He was tall, very smart, and utterly terrifying. He stood in front of the wide front raised bench, and leaned over the front table with the air of ultimate authority.

'Gentlemen, I welcome you to the World of Chemistry. The very reason we exist is entirely due to chemical processes. Through years of painstaking experimentation, and sometimes a little luck, great minds have defined the science and made huge leaps to the benefit of Mankind. There is one abiding rule which is to be followed without question each and every time you set foot within these laboratory walls – and that is the rule of Safety. To ensure the safety of you and I, the rules of conduct which you see on the wall there (he indicated a large chart on the door side of the wall) will be followed at all times, and without question. Do I make myself abundantly clear, gentlemen?'

The awed class answered a respectful, 'Yes, sir...' Brayfield continued –

'There will be no, I repeat NO HORSEPLAY in this laboratory. Due to the nature of some of the materials with which we come into contact, any tomfoolery may be the first and possibly the last mistake which you will make. Chemistry can be dangerous, boys, and if I detect any stupid behaviour – so can I. It is my duty to ensure that you return to the bosom of your family with limbs and eyebrows intact. I will now run through a few important extra rules:

Do not touch or open the Fume Cupboard unless instructed to do so.

Turn off all gas taps securely.

If you do not know what a substance is – do not touch it.

If during an experiment you see me turn pale and run out of the door whilst something is smoking on the bench – please follow me quickly!'

At this unexpected humour, the class relaxed a bit. The master went on to explain the use of the Bunsen burners, test tube stands, clamps, and the other sundry equipment with which they would ply their trade. He explained the Periodic Table to them, and handed out copies for them to memorise.

As a bit of a first-time treat for the would-be scientists, he then placed several dishes on the front bench. The boys were told to gather round at a respectful distance, and they were shown how Lithium and Sodium behave when exposed to water – and the actinic flare of Magnesium when ignited.

This was more like it – now we were unfolding the mysteries of the Universe (well, in a small dish, but you get my point I hope). The Captain explained all about gasses, liquids and solids, and Nicky was disappointed when the bell sounded the end of the lesson. Forming an orderly line, the boys handed in their lab coats and goggles, collected their books, and filed out of the lab chattering excitedly.

It would be dinner break soon, and...

Just as Nicky was about to talk to Wetherill, a hand reached into the group of boys and pulled him out. It was Piper – who was furious.

'Where were you at eleven o'clock, you insolent peasant?' demanded the prefect.

Nicky had completely forgotten his summons to the prefects' study after their clash at the start of the morning.

'Right you, get to the head's study NOW,' shouted Piper.

Pupil and prefect marched across the quad, with the younger boy in front. A mocking cheer arose from onlookers, who enjoyed the fact that the person enduring ritual humiliation was not them. Nicky felt his face redden as they walked up the long path toward the headmasters rooms.

Outside the oaken door, the Prefect smirked as he knocked.

'Enter... ' said a voice, and the two boys went in.

'This is Shepherd, sir. I apprehended him this morning not wearing his correct Academy uniform, sir, in contravention of Rule 16a, sir' said Piper.

Mr Goodwill looked up from his newspaper, over the top of gold half-rimmed glasses.

'How was the boy improperly attired?' asked Goodwill.

'No boater being worn, sir,' snapped Piper, standing further to attention.

'I see... ' said Mr Goodwill, carefully folding his newspaper as the adjoining door to his study eased open, and the secretary, Miss Piggott, entered with a tray on which were a china cup of tea and biscuits.

'We have standards to keep up, sir, and we can't have boys letting the side down, sir... I mean it lets us all down, sir... ' babbled Piper.

'I take it that you are a new boy, Mr Shepherd?' asked Goodwill.

'Yes, sir, I am, but I didn't... '

Before Nicky could answer, Piper butted in, 'And when I challenged him, sir, he became rude and offensive, sir.'

Mr Goodwill considered this for a moment over steepled fingers. He asked the prefect – 'You are aware that the boater has of today been deleted from the list of required Academy uniform?' The prefect looked disappointed.

'Nevertheless, we do insist on certain standards of behaviour from our students, and we really cannot have rudeness or insubordination from our boys – or we open the door to anarchy.'

Nicky tried to explain, 'Yes, sir, but I was only… '

A wave of the headmaster's hand signalled him into silence.

'I think that on this occasion, a little tolerance and leniency may be called for, bearing in mind that you are new to the Academy… could you boys step outside for a few moments please?'

The two boys left the room and stood outside the door. Nicky could quite clearly hear the conversation which was taking place within.

'Young Piper needs to control that temper of his, he is getting quite the wrong sort of name for himself.'

'But Head, we cannot tolerate loutish behaviour from our boys'

'It has become common knowledge that Piper takes an unnecessarily hard line with other boys, Miss Piggott.'

'But Mr Goodwill, I scarcely have to remind you that Pipers' father does donate considerable sums to the upkeep of the Academy, and you yourself did promote him to prefect.'

'Ah Yes... Call the boys in please, Miss Piggott.'

Nicky and his adversary came back into the study.

Mr Goodwill took off his glasses and spoke. 'In the matter of the Academy uniform violation, it would appear that circumstance has done you a favour Mr Shepherd. However, I cannot have the unruly behaviours which are seen at other schools replicated within these walls. Mr Piper will construct a suitably mild punishment for you, during which you will have time to reflect upon the fact that prefects are an extension of the teaching staff – and should be respected as such.

'Thank you, gentlemen – you may now leave.'

In the corridor, the prefect turned to Nicky with a humourless smile which was nevertheless full of self-congratulation. 'Five to four – in the quad, Farmer's Boy,' he hissed, adding, 'Any smart questions now, eh?'

Nicky pondered for a moment, and then asked 'Yes – did your Mother have any children that lived?'

Dinner time in the big hall was not the joyous occasion of yesterday. The boys were chatting and swapping stories around him, but Nicky was still boiling up a kettle of anger inside. So, yet again he had been treated as a second-class citizen. Was this the way things were destined to go all the way through his school career? Just what was it about wealth that automatically bestowed upon you the right to treat other people like dirt? Was the cheque book really held in higher esteem than the library book?

It seemed to Nicky that this system mirrored the manner in which whole countries behave on the world stage – with the rich and fortunate treading on and abusing the less affluent nations. It was no wonder that the underdog became sick of being mistreated, and decided, 'Bugger doffing my cap – where did I put that sharp, pointy stick?'

The first afternoon lesson was English. They were reading and discussing some of the First World War poets. Nicky found it interesting, but even Mr Hyde-Jones' relaxed teaching could not coax him into participation. He had apparently done well with his Chaucer translations, but couldn't muster up much pride in it. He was now aware that he was his own Pilgrimage, and that the path was strewn with sharp stones – which the wealthy could afford to have removed by people like him.

The master reminded them about the auditions after school for the play. Maybe he could work his way up to be a famous actor – and then strike a blow for the Common Man on some television chat show where he would name, defame and shame.

Back into the Old Block and up the stairs, was the room where the boys were to be taught Religious Education, or "Divinity" as it was termed.

Nicky had always had an interest in the Bible, especially the more curious incidents as related by that great and noted Biblical scholar, Uncle Joe. Uncle had urged Nicky to seek out the story in the New Testament which featured the famous "Rubber Man", who in order to see Jesus preach, had tied his ass to a tree and walked to Jerusalem.

The boys entered the room, which was unnaturally dark. They found their desks and sat quietly, allowing their eyes to become accustomed to the gloom. The large arched windows were hung with black velvet curtains, only opened slightly so as to admit a grudging amount of daylight. Even the surround to the blackboard was finished in a blackened timber, and the whole room could well be compared to a serious and committed teenage Goth's bedroom (without the pizza box under the bed...). The door to the tall book cupboard was ajar, and from behind it emerged the master – who made his entry like the evil Grand Vizier in a pantomime.

This was the Reverend Felchingham. He had held the position of Divinity master at the Academy for many years, and was rather a mysterious and secretive figure. Instead of the more usual shirt and tie combination, he wore a black polo-neck sweater, with a cross hanging down in front. His pale, rat-like features and swept-back hair gave him the appearance of a low-budget version of a Dr Who villain.

All of the boys were immediately aware of the strong smell of incense that lingered in the classroom, and one or two of them had noticed some strange marks on the floor. At the four corners of the room were tall candles in wrought-iron holders.

The sombre vision addressed the assembled students.

'Good afternoon, gentlemen; I am the Reverend Felchingham. In my class we will undertake (possibly literally, thought Nicky) and study Comparative Religion. Without bias or favour, we shall investigate The Bible, Talmud, Koran, Hinduism, Shintoism, Buddhism, Shamanism and older Beliefs. I have made much study of ancient religions, and I hope to be able to pass on a little of my knowledge to you boys in due course.'

(In actual fact, the Rev. had not done spectacularly well at Theological College. From day one, students were taught "Disproval Philosophy" where they were encouraged to deny all previously held beliefs, doctrines, principles and creeds – I mean, can you believe that? He had taken to talking about religion with his pet cat – as he was not allowed to keep a dogma).

'We will begin our studies with the ancient religion of Wicca, upon which subject I do consider myself to be something of an expert,' said the Rev.

There followed an in-depth summary of Paganism in all its forms, and plenty of strange detail concerning "Mother Earth", "Moon Goddess" "Circles of Power" and other odd concepts. The Rev. also had quite a lot to say on the subject of ancient Stone Age circles, and various features left on the landscape by early Man. This led to one or two interesting questions which were posed by the more enquiring minds amongst the boys.

Merry, for instance, had asked if the ancient "Lay Lines" which he spoke of were in fact tracks worn in the earth by Early Man in search of the company of Early Ladies of negotiable affection. This had not gone down at all well with the Rev. The master had a very fixed and jingoistic outlook upon life – in his opinion, "Urdu" was what ladies of a certain age from Liverpool had on a Saturday.

His strange grip on life in general had to a certain extent been influenced by his father. At school, the only subjects at which he had excelled were mathematics and woodwork. This led to his father exclaiming in a moment of total exasperation –'Well I suppose I will have to get you a job in a ruler factory.' After some intense and lengthy family discussion, it was decided that he should study for the Priesthood. This had led to the Rev. leading a lonely and isolated life, with far too much time on his hands in which to find and follow his own personal calling. To celebrate his ordination into the Church, he had decided on a whim to indulge himself in a rare moment of extravagance, and buy himself a brand new high-class fountain pen. He made a special trip to town on Whit Sunday. In the stationer's shop, he perused racks of elegant writing implements laid out in their glass case. He settled on a superb gold-nibbed pen which cost him £95.50 (he had to admit that this was rather a lot for a pen to cost...).

He had found, and stumbled down the path of Alternative Religion, to the extent that he indulged in ritualistic attempts to contact discarnate entities. All he was really seeking was the guidance and support that were lacking from his Father, but was never able to achieve. He also began to question much of the advice with which he had been indoctrinated with as a teenager. (If playing with yourself did indeed stunt your growth, then why were all of the dirty magazines placed high up on the top shelf?)

His experiments in contacting "The Other Side" had not always turned out as he had hoped. Engaged in a ritual to contact and take guidance from Satan, he had temporarily forgotten about the mild dyslexia from which he suffered, and thus made contact with an angry discarnate spirit called Stan. This spirit was incandescent with rage, because that in order to pay some relevant penance, or teach some life lesson, he had been reincarnated as a rabbit. Stan was furious at this insult, and was apparently living in a state of permanent anger and fury at the situation in which he now found himself: - no, Stan was not by any means a Happy Bunny...

The boys left the lesson not exactly feeling enriched in the spiritual department. The agnostic element of the class reserved their judgement; until it could be proved that the man was a weirdo, and several members of the class secretly vowed to say their prayers only if answered by a confirming e-mail signed by the respondent.

What the boys were completely unaware of was the fact that Reverend Felchingham had been instrumental in setting out the weekly schedule for lessons. He had his own secretive reason for doing this. He had planned out the study schedule in order that the lessons, when placed sequentially, spelt out the words of an ancient Sanskrit curse. Taking the initial letters from the subjects for each daily period (i.e. – Biology, English, GEography, CHemistry, ARt, History, REligious Education and PHysics.) he was able to complete the Mystic Curse "BEGECH - AL-HI'REPH BENGE-ARTHIS-REPCHE-EAH-TWA-M'PINTA".

(This was an ancient curse discovered on a stone tablet from the tomb of the King Tela-M'Cawe in the Valley of the Kings, Egypt in 1922. The first part of the curse entraps the living soul of the intruder, whereas the last two phrases state "two pints of milk please". There is a very valid reason for this – insomuch that the stonemason who had created it had no problem with enslaving the minds and souls into eternal torment by carving out the ancient and enduring curse, but he was buggered if he was going to haul over another heavy extra granite slab, just to leave a note out for the milkman).

In Felchingham's warped plan, each time any boy consulted his weekly lesson schedule, he would be automatically reading out the ancient Sanskrit curse – and so spreading just a little evil out into the world, along with the chance of blackening his soul, and earmarking it for everlasting torment at some point in the future.

With ideas such as these, you may see exactly why he was not voted "Student most likely to..." in his college yearbook.

Feeling that he had probably exhausted the limits of concentration that his class could tolerate, the Rev. closed the lesson for today.

As the boys left the stygian darkness of the classroom, Nicky pondered just how bonkers the master must be not to have noticed that he was wearing his cross upside-down...

Chapter Seven

The last two periods of the day were given over to Games. The games field stood a little way away from the main Academy buildings, and was reached by means of a short walk through a quiet residential avenue. The column of reluctant sportsmen wound their way up to the fields, chatting, laughing and attempting to cause slight personal injury by means of tripping each other up. No weapons were involved during these scuffles, although a severe "Chinese Burn" was sustained, and a boy was inconvenienced by the injudicious use of a Custard Cream biscuit.

The changing rooms sat at the left hand side of the games field, amidst the sea of aerials which were the Rugby goalposts. Inside, there were the standard bench and peg arrangements for changing. The rooms had the familiar after-sport stench of changing rooms everywhere, mixed with "eau de chlorine" which emanated from the showers.

Boys changed into their unfamiliar kit quickly. There was much lacing and re-lacing of boots, and some hand-to-hand combat with athletic supports was in evidence. Finally, the boys clacked their way out of the changing rooms on their studded feet, and assembled in front of the steps where the sports masters were waiting to address them.

The sports masters were the epitome of fitness, and displayed all of the required homicidal and enthusiastic tendencies that their sporting status demanded. They were absolutely certain that physical exercise could never be fully enjoyed without the additional benefit of horizontal sleet being included. Their names were Mr Burke (immaculate fitted track suit, third-division footballers' hairstyle, sergeant-majors' voice, the caring attitude of a serial killer), and Mr Carter.

Mr Carter was similarly dressed, but his tracksuit had obviously seen action in various front-line sporting battles for years. It hung about his person as if it were embarrassed at any possibility of actually making contact with the body of the man. The most immediate and striking thing about Mr Carter (which had been noted straight away by every boy, oh my word yes...) was his ill-fitting and obvious toupee. It sat astride his head in ginger defiance of gravity, with a full drooping fringe, and wispy turned-up edges. When fresh out of the box, the wig may at some point have been the height of style and elegance for someone; but now, balanced upon the bonce of Mr Carter, it resembled tonsorial roadkill. With the surname of the former, and the mysterious hairpiece of the latter, these masters were known throughout the Academy as "Burke and Hair".

Burke called the boys to attention, and began a speech such as may well be given by an England football manager, to stir up, inspire, and gird the loins of his team just before they lose to Germany on penalties.

'Right – listen up... At this Academy we do not entertain the lame, cissy sport that you are no doubt all familiar with. I have got no time for pouting, preening, and the rest of the fannying about which we see from so-called professional sportsmen on a football pitch every Saturday. No, lads, here we play the noble game of Rugger. This is a proper game, which teaches control, strategy and teamwork. Now, we will divide into two teams and warm up on the main pitch.'

The boys followed the two masters at a run, over to the nearest pitch, and grouped in the centre, awaited instructions...

'Balls...' said Mr Carter.

'Arse...' said Weatherill.

'What did you say, boy?' snapped Carter.

'Sorry, sir, just joining in with the moment,' replied Weatherill.

'No, I mean we have no balls.'

'Well, sir, speaking purely for myself, you understand...'

'GO AND COLLECT THE BALLS FROM THE CHANGING ROOM!' the exasperated master demanded.

Weatherill and Nicky sprinted back to the changing rooms, and came back with a large string sack containing the rugby balls.

'Right, we will begin with handling skills,' said Mr Carter.

'Sir, If I may...' said David DeVere. 'Skills allude to dexterity, adroitness, aptitude and virtuosity in any given discipline, and by nature are subjective measures of any individual's competence, and as such are not capable of being "handled" in any physical sense as such...'

The boys stood open-mouthed.

'Thank you for that succinct observation, Mr DeVere,' said Carter. 'Any further interruption from you will result in a demonstration of just how specific and painful my own handling skills can be: in the meantime – once around the pitch please.'

DeVere set off on his run around the perimeter of the field as directed, with a strange self-satisfied smile upon his face. A casual observer would have noted that he was paying particular attention to the gates and fences around the field. He also seemed to take a specific note of gaps in the hedgerows and foliage. They may have even seen him make rapid notes in a small black notebook, which he quickly concealed about his person.

The boys were soon running up and down the pitch, passing the ball down the line as they ran. When the master seemed satisfied that the ball could be transferred from person to person without the loss of an eye, he gathered them once again in the middle of the pitch.

'Well done, lads. Now we will look at the tackle (he stared at Merry in order to stifle the expected comment). Our objective is to halt the progress of our opponent who has the ball. We achieve this by employing the poise of an Olympic gymnast, the fluid elegance of a swimmer, and the grace and poetry of a ballet dancer. We then grind their face into the earth with every ounce of strength which we possess...'

Carter then chose a boy at random, and demonstrated the flying posture for grasping the legs of the opponent and forcing him earthwards.

'Pair up, and I want to see some aggression from you chaps...' he announced.

Watching the half-hearted attempts of some boys, Carter demanded, 'GET A GRIP OF HIS THIGHS AND BRING HIM DOWN.'

'Shouldn't I at least buy him a drink first?' enquired Weatherill (a stickler for etiquette).

Mr Carter shook his head, and the toupee spun through ninety degrees in protest. This left Carter looking a little like a ginger version of one of the Beatles. He spun around and hastily repositioned the errant hairpiece with as much dignity as he could muster.

This was achieved without much interest from the boys. Their attention had temporarily been diverted to a figure way across the field who was slowly and precisely mowing the grass of the main rugby pitch. This was Mr Brooks the Groundskeeper. He took a fierce pride in the condition of all of the pitches, and kept them in absolutely tip-top condition.

He was mowing the "match pitch" with the concentration of a skilled craftsman.

He was using an aged mower which he kept sharpened for this very purpose.

He was also completely naked...

A boy called Hayman launched himself horizontally at speed, and caught his training partner squarely across the upper thighs – both dropping locked to the turf as the ball bounced away to the touchline. Mr Carter, wig temporarily restrained, was ecstatic: 'That is how it's done, boys! A textbook tackle, now remember what you saw just then.' He punched the air with glee, causing the toupee to make a bid for freedom, down over his left ear. 'Excellent Hayman. Well played, but now I think you can release the headlock...' he added.

The teams were then introduced to the mysteries of the "scrum", and the interlocking, skull-jarring clash as the two sides made contact. The ball was put into the scrum, was hooked out as directed, and the players stood up ready to play on. One player stood out from the rest, as he had reappeared from the melee of the scrummage wearing a top hat. 'What the bloody hell do you call that, Wetherill?' screamed the master.

'I don't call it anything, sir, it's just a hat...' replied the boy.

'Why in all the Buggering Hades are you wearing a top hat, Weatherill?' said Carter, slightly foaming at the corners of his mouth.

'You did say, sir, that Rugby is a game played by gentleman, did you not?' enquired a smiling Weatherill, 'I thought that it might lend a certain tone...'

Neither Carter nor his errant hairpiece had any credible response to this. There was a leaden silence, and an instruction given through gritted teeth –

'Remove it, boy...'

Remove it did he, and they attempted placing the balls in order to take a "conversion". This was partly successful, with Merry kicking high over the posts, and with Nicky only hitting Calderman twice. There followed a game of "touch rugby", where boys were touched and possession gained – but in a very manly and team-spirited manner.

Blowing the whistle to signify the end of the day's sport, Carter clutched at his head and directed the boys to the changing rooms for their shower. The showers were everything Nicky had dreamed about, usually after watching some horror film on late night television. The boys soaped, and ducked beneath the freezing jets, rinsing off quickly to prevent hypothermia setting in. Dripping in front of the benches, they hurriedly dried and dressed, with the predictable confusion as various boys put on their neighbours' blazer. Calderman, DeVere, Merry and the boys began the walk up the path at the side of the top pitch.

Nicky suddenly remembered that he had an appointment with the demon Piper, and so announced, 'See you at the play rehearsal later; I've got to go and see someone...'

He ran back to the Academy, with his satchel and games kit bag threatening to swing him off-balance. Back in the quad, Piper was waiting when a breathless Nicky appeared.

'Right then Mr Clever Dick...' Piper began, 'Look around the edges of the quad and tell me what you see'.

Nicky looked all around, but could not identify anything out of the ordinary.

'Well let me enlighten you, Village Boy – you will pick up every fallen leaf and piece of litter in the quad. I will be watching you, so you'd better get on with it, and no slacking...'

Nicky was handed a large black bin sack, and pushed roughly toward the School House wall. He began to scoop up leaves and pieces of paper, soon filling the sack by the time he had completed two sides of the quad. Piper took the full sack and thrust an empty one at him. He was thinking of the play auditions, and so tried to gather up all of the debris just as speedily as he could. He finished the onerous task at the end of the wall outside the toilets. Back aching, knees strained, and sweating profusely, he gathered up the plastic sack and turned around – to see a grinning Piper standing behind him.

'Here, I've finished...' said Nicky.

'I think all that ploughing must have affected your eyesight...' sneered Piper.

'What do you mean? I've done what you asked me to,' said Nicky.

Piper pointed to the other side of the quad, its edges and corners covered in leaves and litter, and said, 'I don't think you have – My My, it looks like you missed a bit.'

Nicky knew that whilst he had been clearing the bottom end of the quad, the Prefect had emptied the full sack out over the ground which he had already covered. He returned to the dining hall side of the quad and began to fill the sack again. Glancing across in the direction of the assembly hall, Nicky saw the crowd of laughing boys that spilled out of the double glass doors - obviously coming out of the audition. He knew that he had missed both his chance of catching the regular bus home, and any chance which he might have had of getting a part in the play. There was no point in rushing now, so he took his time, tied the sack, and handed it to the sneering prefect.

Too demoralised to be bothered to argue, Nicky collected his bags and strode off across the quad and out of the Academy gates. He sat in silence on the bus, and wondered just how he could ever rid himself of his tormentor. He really felt like a "peasant", and he knew that he could not afford Posh tears...

With her son uncharacteristically quiet at teatime, Mother asked if everything was alright, and how his day at school had been. He answered that he was just worn out from his session of rugby. She then asked how he got on at the play audition. Nicky told his Mother and Auntie exactly how it was that he came to miss the auditions.

'You need to stand up to him, Nicky,' said Mum.

'He is an odious little tit – you should break his knees...' advised Auntie.

Mum stated calmly, 'Well you know about Karma – what goes around comes around.'

Auntie described in detail her own personal and effective solution to the problem, adding, 'and it would be a good few minutes before he came around, believe me...'

In no mood for further discussion, the boy took himself up to his bedroom, toiled through his homework, and worked off his anger by miming every drumbeat played by Mr Moon on the album *Live at Leeds* by The Who. When the album had finished, he felt that something of the rebellion from the great rock band had seeped into his soul. He may not be a wizard – but by God, he would play mean and pin someone's balls...

It may have been the slice of cheese on toast that Mum gave him for supper, which made him dream of shapeless monster figures rising up out of piles of leaves and pursuing him through endless corridors – to the echoing sound of mocking laughter.

Today was Thursday. Well not Thursday everywhere on the planet, obviously; as there were still dark corners where Wednesday lingered sniggering, and a few islands where the inhabitants had already hung out the bunting on their huts in celebration of 'that Friday feeling'.

Nicky would find out today which 'House' he had been placed into. There were six Academy Houses. These were Foxe, Curteis, Moore, Newton, School House, and for some unexplained reason, "Beryl". The Houses were named after prominent bishops and noted scientists, apart from 'Beryl', who was someone's Auntie.

Foxe House seemed to attract boys who excelled at sports, and had cupboards full of gleaming trophies as testament to their achievements (not all were stolen). Curteis tended to have a quantity of boys who did well at art. Moore House was proud of its strong academic record from its members. Maths and science whizz-kids tended to be placed in Newton House. Beryl was the house for "all-rounders", boys who were not selected for other Houses, and those most likely to be turned down for credit in later life.

School House was the collective whose members comprised all of the boys who boarded at the Academy. They were an aloof and secretive group, who by nature of rich parentage considered themselves above the other students. They made no secret of their loathing of "Day Boys", and would readily seize upon any opportunity to vilify those boys who they saw as below themselves in the social strata. The exception to this rule seemed to be David DeVere, who his classmates thought did not fit in with the rest of School House, as he was friendly, funny and loyal – if a little secretive.

Nicky fed and watered Dave the Chicken, then collected his bags and made an uneventful journey to school. He felt less self-conscious now that the hated boaters had been banished. The decision to do away with the headgear was made by the governors, in response to the increasing incidents of a dangerous practice known as "rimming". This involved roughening up the brim edge of the boater with sandpaper, to leave a tough, abrasive edge all round. The hat was then used as a weapon when thrown frisbee-style (with unnerving accuracy from some boys) which had caused numerous cuts and abrasions to the faces of the unlucky recipients. Before the Academy was subject to a law suit from angry parents, the potential weapons were consigned to history.

Before the assembly bell tolled, all of the new intake clamoured around the notice boards in the quad in order to see which house they had been placed into. Merry declared, 'Oh... I am in "Rexel" House – what's that?' Nicky explained that Merry had been looking at a watermark on the paper, and that he was actually in with the 'Foxe' boys – or as Calderman termed them 'The Basil Brush Massive'.

Scanning down the list, Nicky noted that thankfully, both he and Weatherill were in Curteis House, so at least there would be one friendly face in house meetings.

Assembly came and went, and as usual managed to leave an indelible blank on the minds of the boys. The only incident of note was that some wag had taped a rubber chicken to the front of the lectern. This was obviously out of sight of all of the masters except Mr Newhouse at the organ – who said nothing, and thus gained credibility points from the boys.

The first lesson of the day was geography. The subject was taught by Mr Gerald Thwaite. He was a slight, pleasant man with a calm, if rather high-pitched voice. He welcomed the class to the lesson in a fussy manner, waving his hands to quieten down the boys. This gave him the appearance of a rather excited penguin.

In addition to his passion for all things geographical, he had also kept bees for the past twenty-seven years, and he still got a buzz out of it. His small and neat cottage in the woods of Rutland served as a library for his other passion, which was collecting maps. He had amassed an eclectic collection of documents which far surpassed those held in the town library, and included many rare and ancient copies drawn when cartography was a new science. He had Middle English maps, Saxon maps, texts from the Norman conquests, and two very rare Viking charts which were hidden in a concealed safe. It was a pity though, that Mr Thwaite himself had the amazing ability to become lost in a telephone box...

He called the class to attention, ran through the register, and began to introduce the boys to the marvels of the rocks of the Earth's surface. Most of the boys immediately warmed to the subject, and took a real interest in the specimens of Dartmoor Granite and other crystals which Mr Thwaite laid out for inspection. There were however, the usual diverse answers to the questions which he asked.

'Where are we likely to find the hardest examples of rock, gentlemen?' he asked.

'Usually at the Donnington Festival Sir...' came the reply from Merry.

The lesson progressed to the Earth in general, its formation, and place in the solar system. Nicky was on firm ground with this topic, and could make a positive contribution as astronomy was one of his hobbies. The boys soaked up all of the gory details concerning the earth's core, plate tectonics, and where the best place to be standing was, when the red-hot molten lava really hit the fan. When the master handed out homework sheets, Nicky noticed that the man's nails were long and manicured – not what he would have expected from a man who spent so much time digging up and handling rocks. There was something else that he could not quite put his finger on that was also different about the Master, a small detail that was shouting over the wall of his mind desperate to be heard.

DeVere had for some time been attempting to get the master's attention, with his hand thrust skyward, and a determined look set upon his face. Thwaite finally noticed the desperate limb raised in urgency.

'Do you have a question, Mr DeVere?'

'Yes. sir, I need to know, what sort of soil is this academy built on?' he asked.

'Good question, and an interesting one, young DeVere. We sit here on a basic topsoil of loam, edged with clay deposits. Deeper down are the heavy limestones which form the river valley. Good workable farming soils, you might say,' answered the master.

'Thank you very much, sir... ' said a pleased-looking DeVere.

Once again, out came the little black notebook. Information was written down hastily, as David poked his tongue out of the corner of his mouth. Satisfied, he snapped the book shut, and it was secreted somewhere about his person.

Mr Thwaite ended the lesson just before the bell rang, and his "troops" all seemed happy and animated – stuffed to the brim with information. He asked the boys to wait a moment before dispersing, as he had some 'Jolly good stuff on volcanoes' in the stationary cupboard, which they might like to have. He hurried smiling to the door and dived through it. At this point, he realised that his personal little "curse" had struck again – as he had gone to the wrong door, and was now staring down an empty corridor. Now – all he had to do was remember which room had he come out of...

Next on the timetable was a lesson that all of the form were really looking forward to. As with kids everywhere, there were many devotees of Dr Who, Star Trek, The Great Dr Steven Hawking, and space travel in general in the class. They couldn't wait to get all of the answers to life, the Universe, and Skegness (Oh come on...be honest with yourself, we all want answers as to who is responsible for that). The seekers of truth hurried into the physics lab and sat expectantly at the benches. When the master did eventually appear, pens were already poised.

The Physics tutor (Mere 'Teacher' would never do.) was exactly what the boys were hoping for. He looked for all the world like everyone's idea of the classic "Mad Professor". This was the legendary Professor Richard Strangler esquire. Now this man was regarded as strange – even by the skewed standards of the rest of the Academy Faculty. He was regarded as odd because he had an artificial leg. This would not normally be any cause for a raised eyebrow, but in the Professor's case it certainly was. Our dear professor did in fact have an artificial leg – but had a real foot...

'BANGGGGG!'

The professor shouted out at the top of his voice, causing the boys to jump in terror, loose paint to descend, pigeons to take flight, and two boys to suffer inclement underwear.

'That was the Big Bang, gentlemen... oh yes indeed. That is how the Universe began, and thus commenced its expansion and creation of stars, galaxies and lots of other sparkly things much beloved of Mr Spielberg, so I am led to understand. We shall travel to the stars and planets, boys, but first we must learn the rules that govern our Universe – not like that *Star Wars* nonsense, no by crikey – it's all a load of bloody ridiculous nonsense...' said Professor Strangler.

A voice at the back called out 'May the Farce be with you' at this point.

Now warmed up, the master continued, 'I shall learn yes, well, I expect I will, no doubt, your names – you do have them don't you? And erm... Ooh, cheese and pickle... (he had explored a pocket in his corduroy jacket, and located a forgotten item of yesterday's lunch). Jolly good, so we will sort out our basic units of measurement, and Ah... dead battery (the other pocket) we will discuss our friend gravity, and turning forces – damn, watch has stopped again.'

One boy in the centre raised his hand. 'Question, Professor? – oh no, that's me isn't it - Silly arse, sorry lad – what can I do for you?'

'You are quite wrong to suggest that there may be no conflict between other inhabitants and civilisations outside this solar system' said the smiling boy, in amiable tones.

'Well, ah... yes, I suppose, but err – difficult to see, and a damned long way too, you could well be right my boy...' answered the professor.

The master launched into an animated speech outlining some of the forces which act upon the planet, objects both stationary and in motion, and people in general. To the great amusement of the boys, this was liberally peppered with his little "excursions" off the beaten track as it were, along strange and uncharted pathways. His speech was confusing at first, but careful mental editing could be employed to extract all of the important facts. He may well appear to be a man who regularly got dressed in the dark, but once you had learned to avoid the meteor shower of thoughts that pushed their way into every conversation, it was obvious that the chap was a genius.

They had some fun demonstrating lifting forces by means of levers, demonstrated by means of brass weights of differing sizes, and a three-foot wooden ruler (Ha! Another one in the eye for the European fanatics). The boys worked out exactly what length of ruler was required in order to lift a weight of any given size. They also calculated the necessary force and angle of trajectory needed in order to ensure that the small weight achieved flight, and impacted upon the head of Lordsley. Unfortunately, the missile was deftly plucked from the air by the professor just before impact, but they were happy that an important scientific principle had been proven. DeVere in particular was fascinated by the "see-saw" effect, and the lifting forces generated. The little black book was much in evidence during this lesson.

So captivating was the delivery of the master, that none of the boys were aware of the time elapsing – and all were genuinely sorry when the professor called a halt to the class. He ended the session with a cheery, 'Now don't forget your homework. Blast, didn't give it to you, still, always next time… Ah! Time, now there's a thing, yes, must get the car in for its MOT… Sorry, forget my own trousers next. Thanks chaps – see you next time…'

Although considered by many of the staff to be as sensible as an ejector-seat in a helicopter, Professor Strangler had a firm grip on scientific principles, and had some of his more madcap inventions ever been taken on to their logical conclusions, they would have benefitted mankind. The governors knew this – and so were prepared to supply his physics department with the funds to continue his eccentric research into things that were probably best left alone. Such a scheme was the "Haddock Collider", which sat in the grounds outside the physics laboratory. Originally envisaged as a means of establishing 'metabolic and ionisation transfer between organic substances,' (i.e. something easily available – two of Westby the Fishmonger's finest) its planned purpose seemed to have been forgotten. It was however, now a means of producing absolutely first-class fish paste – thus making a regular and tidy sum of money for the Academy.

One very popular project designed and built by the physics department had been footwear fitted with an integral satellite navigation system, which gave pedestrians spoken directions to their destination, as well as weather conditions and shortcuts. These "Walkie-Talkies" had initially sold well, but a software glitch had caused mayhem.

It appears that the self-contained system within the shoe learned regular routes, but also learned the location of other Sat-Nav sandals in the immediate vicinity. Certain shoes developed a fiercely competitive element, and would seek to race the other shoes to their destination. This caused the wearer to be subject to sudden sprinting without warning, with many a groinal strain being suffered as a result. Certain styles of shoe developed a character of their own. These "personalities" began to manifest themselves in strange ways. Brogues were found to be aloof and poor mixers, Chelsea boots became attention-seeking nuisances, trainers were apt to kick over litter bins (and occasionally other pedestrians). Normally placid Dr Marten Boots began to nudge other footwear (and the attached wearers) off pavements, or stamp on passing moccasins. The unfortunate owners of hiking boots had found themselves propelled off the beaten track into the great outdoors, and taken off on some undisclosed quest. Sandals sulked and refused to budge in the rain, and would only go out if accompanied by a sock.

Not one of Professor Strangler's best ideas, I feel…

Chapter Eight

As lunchtime approached, war was breaking out on two battle fronts. It is fair to say that during the morning break, what could loosely be termed "an incident" had occurred in the staff room. Madame Dreadfell had purchased a large tin of assorted biscuits, of the type hidden away from the kids by grandparents everywhere. To demonstrate "Liberte, Egalite, and Frugalite" she had secreted the tin behind some packets of A4 copy paper near the coffee machine. Some Revolutionary had liberated some of the nicer silver-wrapped chocolate biscuits, and had carefully re-folded the wrappings to disguise the theft. She had scanned the room intently, seeking out the slightest look which might betray guilt on the face of the perpetrator. So far, no-one in the line-up had twitched...

Just prior to setting out the lunch service, there had been further uproar in the kitchen. This time, Betty's bottom had been pinched by some unseen hand. Now it was not only the disappearance of food and objects that was making the kitchen an unsettling place to work – now the phantom seemed to be helping himself to a large portion of rump that was not officially on the menu. Betty was furious, and this time Dr Goodwill had been summoned. He had adopted a kind, patient smile whilst a red-faced Betty had explained the circumstances leading up to the unwanted contact. He tried to defuse the nervy atmosphere by making light of the incident – 'Well, dear lady, I fear that in these trying times, we are all rather feeling the pinch... ' This was met with a stony silence, Betty's face resembling a souvenir bought from Easter Island. The Head attempted to instil logic and calm, but inadvertently added to the problem by using what he thought were helpful phrases – such as 'I am determined to get a grip of this situation,' and 'I shall attempt to get to the bottom of the puzzle.'

Doris didn't exactly help the situation when she stated (perhaps a little louder than she intended), 'She wasn't that worried – she went back to the same spot six times...'

Lunch itself had been a tense affair, and most of the boys in the dining hall could sense that all was not as it should be. There were constant nervous glances all around from the kitchen staff (much more than usual), and no-one noticed when DeVere pocketed two of the new knives. The students were used to feelings of foreboding, but today's atmosphere got eight and a half 'bodings' out of ten. Food was thrust out of the hatches at lightning speed, and the hatch doors slammed shut as if to lock out evil.

Today also marked the start of a new sport at St Onan's. Devised by the well-established firm of Calderman, Merry, Shepherd and Weatherill: the gambit consisted of seeing how much laxative could be introduced into the prefects' dinner.

Adjacent to the chemistry laboratory, and above the toilets (a fact that may well be significant a little later on, for various reasons) were the large rooms given over to metalwork and woodwork. Although St Onan's aimed for the very highest standards in academia, the headmaster saw no reason at all why the school should not be capable of turning out a first-class blacksmith or carpenter who was fluent in Latin.

These large workshops were reached by a narrow flight of stairs, and the boys trudged up them and made their way into the vast space that smelled of machine oil and hot machinery.

The laird of this technical estate was Mr Gregor Duggan. He was a tall, grey-haired dour Scotsman, with a pleasant Highland burr to his speech. He had earned the name of "Don't do it Duggan" from the boys of the Academy. This was because whatever high jinks you may be considering in order to liven up a lesson – don't do it in Duggan's classes. There was also a rumour that he cultivated some rather dubious friendships with persons of an unsavoury nature, but then we all know what rumours are...

The boys took in their new surroundings for the first time. On the window side of the room were the familiar long benches, and on their left was an extremely old and large blackboard. It looked as if it had been bought at an Elizabethan rummage sale, and was held together by wooden pegs at the corners – and a couple of large nails which looked like they had been hammered in by someone in a hurry. On a shelf above the ancient blackboard were various items presumably made by previous students, who by the look of the finished objects had constructed them whilst taking heavy medication.

On the opposite wall there was a wide rack, containing every type of tool that could ever possibly be required. Each tool hung on the wall like specimens in a trophy cabinet, and each was outlined in white in order to affirm its rightful position. This gave the appearance of a vertical murder scene with hundreds of chalk outlines showing the location of the victim. DeVere was scanning the racks intently, paying special attention to any tools for cutting, sawing and drilling.

At the far end of the room were the complicated-looking machines, all enamelled grey and looking threatening.

Mr Duggan welcomed the class in a pleasant tone. 'Hello, my lads. Ye are all verra welcome to my little studio. Afore we make a start, I really must tell ye to always take care of the tools. Ye may use any of the tools – but certainly not on each other. When ye have finished with it, any tool must be rreturrned to its home on the shelf. I have already drawn out today's project on the blackboard, and as ye can no doubt see, we will be constructing something which ye will find verra useful...'

The boys studied the item that had been illustrated on the blackboard, and none of them had any immediate ideas as to what today's "mystery object" might be. Nicky thought that it looked too square for a knuckle duster (which is what it did seem to resemble at first glance).

Mr Duggan now hooked his thumbs into the lapels of his immaculate brown dust coat, and gave the boys their instructions. 'Right, laddies... take the piece of metal that I have given to ye, and cut it to six and one half inches exactly. File all edges smooth, and at rright angles.'

The class followed his instructions exactly, although Davis did manage to file his index finger smooth, and Merry somehow shortened his tie by three inches.

'Now then, boys,' Duggan purred, 'we will now drill a hole three quarters of an inch from each end, and one hole directly in the centre of the metal.'

The boys queued up in an orderly line in front of the drill, and each pressed the pedal and brought down the handle to make the required holes in their metal strip.

'Ye now need to cut the heavy galvanised wirre which I have given ye to a length of five inches exactly,' Duggan instructed. 'We will now bend up the ends of the metal to one inch. When we have done this, we will push the wirre through the holes and bend over the ends flush and at ninety degrrees'.

The master walked between the benches, checking the objects which the boys now held in their hands.

'I shall now hand out your workbooks, lads, in which ye will make notes and drawings of how ye have constructed your project today,' said Duggan.

The boys were all highly delighted to see that the labels on the front of the books contained a superb printer's error. All were elated to discover that they were studying "Mentalwork and Crufts". Merry in particular could not wait to get home and have his mother's pet poodle, Trixie, sectioned under the Mental Health Act.

Duggan was delighted (and there had been no casualties today), and proclaimed, 'Well done, my lads... Ye have noo completed your firrst project.'

Merry raised his hand hesitantly, 'Please, sir... '

'Yes, Laddie, what can I do for Ye?' answered Duggan.

'Can I just check, sir... exactly what is it that we have just made?'

'Ye have in your hands, boys, an article which will prove to be verra useful to ye – ye have made your ain Tie Holder... '

'Gosh...' said Merry, without a trace of irony.

Calderman now held his hand aloft, to ask another question. 'Sir, can I just ask – what is the furnace thing with the bowl at the end of the room, and what are the covered blocks next to it?'

'That's the crucible and furnace, my boy, and dinnae fash yersel' about the other stuff on the bench there, I am currently pursuing a wee project of my own, in my own time, ye underrrstand. Righto… we will now clean up and clear up, and dinnae forget to put all of the tools away correctly please.'

Holding their self-constructed items with suspicion, the boys filed out of the room – smooth, and at right angles as instructed.

Things were beginning to take a nasty turn in the staff room. It had all begun to go wrong with the advent of "Biscuitgate" (as it would later come to be known). Madame Dreadfell was suspecting every member of the staff of the heinous crime of biscuit theft. She had failed so far to extract a confession from anyone, or identify the perpetrator(s). All were routinely subjected to a Gorgon-like stare, but to no avail. Now she had lost her Gallic composure in spectacular fashion – and had Mr Thwaite pinned up against the notice board at knifepoint. The threat was somewhat diminished by the fact that the knife still had a small piece of brie perched precariously on the tip of it.

Over the years, the staff room had slowly and inexorably become a powder keg of jealousy and petty rivalries. Rank and status within the staff of St Onan's were highly valued commodities (at least, to the individuals concerned). Some particularly juvenile bickering had been smouldering since last term – and these minor tussles were now beginning to escalate into open hostility. It would now take just a small push in order to throw these already unbalanced teachers completely off their academic trollies...

Madame was now angry (in English) and her face was contorted in the manner of one who has got a lot of issues to get off her chest, and by the Lord Harry, was going to go through the entire menu of gripes without pausing to consider the whine list.

'At the end of last term, you said that I was inadequate...' she hissed.

'No, Madam, I said that you were in Harrogate,' replied Thwaite

'You told everyone that my friend Sahandhi was a lesbian… ' she spluttered.

'I mentioned that she was Lebanese, yes… ' answered Thwaite.

'And you laughed and said that I put Beaujolais on my cornflakes,' Madame snapped.

'Absolutely first class idea that, man,' chimed up Matthews. 'Must try that myself.'

'Shut up you!' shouted the now incandescent Madame, 'You said that you would personally like to fill in the Channel Tunnel, in order to prevent rabid animals coming over here and terrorising decent people, biting innocent bystanders and urinating on everything wherever and whenever they feel like it...'

'I think he was referring to foreign football hooligans, my dear lady' said Thwaite.

'You must admit that you do have a somewhat Gallic fixation, Penelope...' said Rundell. If it doesn't small vaguely of garlic, you have absolutely no interest in it!'

'The French have class and breeding...' stated Madame.

'So does Crufts,' added a voice from somewhere.

'Please keep out of this all of you, this is a conversation between Thwaite and myself – it isn't a court,' demanded Madame.

'It is – Agincourt,' said the voice.

Whilst Madame gritted her teeth, and the piece of brie fell off the knife onto her French designer shoe, Thwaite suddenly rallied...

'And while we are on the subject,' he demanded then angrily. 'Why must you persist in referring to me as "The Viking", may I ask?'

As the room fell silent, awaiting the response, Dreadfell locked eyes with the man like a gunslinger at high noon, and answered, 'Because you have a face like a Norse.'

Her sudden outburst and personal attack came as a relief to the other members of the faculty, who were watching with nervous interest as to how the confrontation would progress. They were as a body mostly relieved that they themselves were not the chosen targets for Madame's attack, and so regarded the scene in smug fascination.

The attack upon Mr Thwaite was somewhat unfair. He was a mild-mannered inoffensive man who genuinely cared about the boys which he taught. His family history was a strange one, and the Thwaite family tree bore some very curious fruit indeed. His father had been a famous and incredibly skilled wizard in the truest sense. "Pater" was revered for creating objects out of thin air, and his manipulations of the universe around him. He had spent his days off from sorcery sitting in a local cafe – where he would scribble in a cheap notebook over countless cups of tea. He was writing a long story of a wizard boy who longs to attend Journalism School, and who then goes on to become a world-famous author. In his heart of hearts, he didn't think that the idea would catch on – he assumed that the public would think that it was a load of hogwash...

To this day, Father's pet unicorn, Colin, still works in the wedding hire and transport industry, where he still pulls the odd coach with the bride on board to the church. For some reason, possibly due to the conventions of the fairy-tale narrative, Colin still smells very faintly of pumpkin.

Madame's ire was not confined to any one individual. She considered that all of the male members of staff were deluded buffoons (with or without the standard issue red bottom) and way behind the times. She would regularly single out Mr Matthews for attack, as he could regularly be found behind *The Times* at break times, studying the obituaries in a state of happy intoxication. Since the majority of the masters were perhaps unsurprisingly divorced, and in the permanent grip of unceasing financial demands from their ex-wives, most were taking some form of medication in order to lessen the stress of the pressures under which they found themselves. When discussing them socially with friends, she would habitually refer to them as "The Prosac Posse".

The first lesson of the afternoon was Latin. Nicky's form arrived outside the ornate door to the classroom and elected a volunteer to knock on the door. The boys were summoned with the usual upper-class command from Mr Rundell.

'Today, dear boys,' he intoned, 'we will be reading and translating a little from the great works describing the siege of Troy. As I hope that you will all no doubt be fully aware, the great poet Homer describes the ten year war in his exquisite work the *Iliad*. At this point, Rundell noticed Trevill, who was chatting to Owen Money in conspiratorial fashion at the back of the room.

'Mr Trevill, I take it from your lack of interest that you consider yourself to be already something of an expert on the subject of the Trojan War, and so do not consider it necessary to pay any heed to my words?'

Trevill spun to face the front of the class at lightning speed. Having been caught out by the master, he spluttered out a response in the hope of avoiding punishment. 'No Surr, Oi don't consider moiself any koind of expert, but oi was just sayin' that oi 'ave read a book all about this sort of thing...'

'Then Mr Trevill, pray kindly stand and elucidate to the rest of the class upon your understanding of the subject, if you would be so good...'

Trevill stood up with an embarrassed yet determined look on his face. All of his new classmates really liked Trevill, and were praying that he would rise to the challenge and do well in front of Mr Rundell. He drew in a deep breath and began:

'Well, as far as oi sees it, you 'ad the Trojan King Priam see, and there was this woman called 'Elen who was supposed to be a bit of a looker. They must 'ave overlooked the fact that she 'ad a bit of a weight issue, 'cos she 'ad a face that could lunch on a thousand chips. Well Surr, she gets carried off to this 'ere town called Troy via Paris, and your bloke Manny Layus ('oo 'appens to be her Husband) is none too 'appy about it see... So this bloke Achilles, who sold eels I think, sets off on his flyin' 'orse called Peggy Sue to get 'old of this 'Elen lady and bring her back. Well Surr, see, them there Trojans were havin' none of it, and were lockin' the doors a bit sharpish. Then they all pretended that they were out – and wouldn't answer the door to 'em for ten years. Eventually Achilles and his mates comes up with this really great plan to get insoide. They builds a giant wooden arse, and loads of the warriors 'oides in it and keeps 'emselves dead quiet. Then they pretends that they'm 'ad enough of waitin' and the rest of the army makes it look loike they're goin' 'ome. Well, when the Trojans see this great big giant arse outside, they'm thinks, ''Ere, this must be a gift for us and no mistake,' and they opens up the gates and drags it insoide. That's where they'm gone wrong see, 'cos your great big wooden arse was full of soldiers just waitin' to do 'em harm and carry off that there 'Elen back to her Old Man, who was not happy with 'er antics, I can tell you. When it were all dark, they'm opening a hole in the wooden arse and came out an' did 'em damage. They all come out an' set the place on fire and then left – and I bet that the Trojans weren't insured neither, apart from that there Brad Pitt, 'cos 'eem could afford it...'

Mr Gideon Rundell stood open mouthed and speechless. The rest of the class sat open mouthed and speechless. Trevill gave a small, polite bow and sat down. There was a moment of complete and utter silent calm – and then spontaneous and thunderous applause broke out from the whole room, including Mr Rundell.

'Gentlemen... you have just had the great honour of hearing your fellow student recount what is (with just the odd minor adjustment necessary here and there) a complete and succinct account of the siege of Troy,' said the smiling master. 'I shall award you kudos and house points for your knowledge and delivery, Mr Trevill. For the remainder of the lesson we will read the translation of Homer's *Iliad*, though I doubt that it will inspire you as much as the account which we have just heard.'

The boys read through the translation of the classic work as directed, with many a grin and the odd muted chuckle in evidence. Rundell himself lit one of his Russian cigarettes, and paced between the desks, pausing to ruffle the hair of William Trevill Esquire as he passed the boy.

'Please read the texts in full in preparation for our next visit to the city of Troy, gentlemen...' said Rundell just as the bell signalled the end of the lesson. 'I thank you all for your most illuminating contributions,' added the master, laughing as he spoke.

As the boys paraded up to the Art rooms which were on the top floor of the new block, they all congratulated Trevill on his superb performance in the lesson. They piled into the vast art space and sat at the desks down at the far end of the room, where they were greeted by a master decked out in an extremely stained painter's smock and a battered panama hat. 'I am Mr Bell-Enderby, and I shall teach you all to express your innermost joys in the medium of painting, and how we may all enrich our lives by the appreciation of Art...'

Now this was more like it. Ever since he was a small boy, Nicky had loved drawing and painting. He had spent hours out in his favourite fields sketching trees and plants wherever he found something interesting. Some days he would take himself off to the big fields at the top of the village with sheets of blue paper, and lie for hours staring up at the sky, drawing the changing patterns of the clouds with chalk as quickly as he could. Obviously there hazards with this pastime, and he had often been harassed by the odd fox, an irate badger, and on one occasion (when his attention was so focussed upon his work) a combine harvester.

The master had painted an impressionist-style rendition of a local beauty spot near the river, which stood on an easel at the front of the class. He began to instruct the boys as to the best way in which to reproduce the effects and technique, by means of copying his example. Paints were mixed in plastic pallets, and suitable brushes were selected. Hardly any of the paint ended up on the walls, but several boys did appear to have decorated their classmates in the subdued colours of autumn. The exercise was well executed and enjoyed by all, and the results were surprisingly high in standard. Trevill had of course added the obligatory thatched cottage into the scene, but this was well received by the master. The one surprise was a rather strange painting done by a rather odd boy named Kendy. His painting showed what appeared to be a dimly-lit desert scene featuring low domed houses, with twin suns casting odd shadows across the landscape. When questioned by the master, Kendy had just stated that, 'he had painted something from memory – if that was all right?' The master was a little confused, but very happy with his technique. Just then, the boys noticed that a huge black cat appeared, walked in a leisurely fashion down the table, and leapt up onto the master's desk, where it gave them a brief nonchalant appraisal – and began to wash itself.

'Don't mind my friend Turner,' said Mr Enderby. 'That's just him introducing himself. Next lesson we will be using his talents as a life model for you to draw.'

Engrossed in their art, the time had slipped away unnoticed by the whole class. (Where it went to was never fully explained, better not to meddle eh?) They hung up their art work to dry across the large windows, like freshly-washed sheets on a warm breezy day and cleaned the equipment in the old pot sinks at the end of the room. It would be noticed some time later that some miscreant had managed to write the word "esra" on the back of Lordsley's chair in white paint. When viewed in reverse, the purpose of this little jape would become clear, as would Lordsley's status in the eyes of his new classmates.

As the bell sang out to call the end of the days learning, Nicky felt that at last he was beginning to achieve something. As they descended the stairs, the satchel was on top form again – hooking itself maliciously over the ends of the handrails all the way down, until Nicky caught it in a strong grip to prevent any further mischief. The gang said their daily farewells, and each headed off to their respective bus stops – each with one eye warily scanning the area for the dreaded Piper.

Nicky joined the queue for the bus back to the village, and after a few minutes, the asthmatic coach rounded the corner and wheezed to a halt at the stop. He paid his fare and looked around for a seat. There was just one vacant seat, next to a woman from the village whom he recognised. She saw Nicky and patted the seat at the side of her in a gesture of welcome. This was Mrs Jenkins, who lived at the very top of the village in a dilapidated old cottage with her dozens of cats. When the village children had been a bit younger, there had been much discussion between them, and she had gained the reputation of being a witch. If indeed she was a regular practitioner of the mystic arts was questionable to say the least, but what she did possess was the power to exude a strange odour similar to that of an open drain in high summer. Nicky smiled, sat down, and piled his bags and books on his lap like a talisman to ward off evil – all the while trying his best not to breathe.

'Well young Nicholas – how's your new school?' enquired the woman.

'S'fine, 'nk you..' answered Nicky through closed lips.

'I must say, you look very smart in your uniform,' she continued. 'I hope that your mother and the family are all well?'

'Yes, 'nk you.'

Nicky managed to edge one of his books off the top of his satchel and onto the floor of the aisle, and quickly dived into his pocket for his handkerchief, which he held firmly over his nose and mouth when he sat upright again.

'Do you have a cold? she asked. 'There's so much of it about at this time of year.'

''Tnk it mght be hayfvr,' Nicky replied, muffled.

'Do you know, you're the fifth person today that I've come across that is suffering from the same thing...' she said. 'But people are very kind, and don't want to come too near just in case they pass it on to me.'

''S ver'thtfl,' he answered.

Luckily, the bus had just about completed its arthritic struggle up the hill, and Nicky could see his bus stop approaching. With one hand clutching the handkerchief to his face, he gathered up his books and bags with his other arm, and prepared to make a hurried exit. He swiftly removed the "mask", smiled at the woman, and equally rapidly recovered his face – diving for the aisle of the bus. At that moment, the satchel saw that his concentration was distracted – and decided to strike. With the certainty of a televised football match action replay, the leather assassin swung out and caught Mrs Jenkins a glancing blow just above her right ear. Her hat became airborne and pinwheeled back down the aisle toward the back of the bus. In the ensuing commotion, Nicky made his break for freedom and fresh air. He didn't stop running until he was well inside his garden, and rounded the corner to the back door like an Olympic sprinter who really, really needed the lavatory.

Dumping his school stuff in the living room, he collapsed onto the sofa still gasping for breath. Mum called to him, 'You're in a hurry this evening – is everything all right?'

'Yeah. Sorry Mum,' he answered. 'I just had an attack of the Jenkins...'

'Oh dear, well, get a wash and we will have tea – and I think Auntie has got a surprise for you,' said his mother.

Nicky went into the bathroom and pulled the cord to switch on the light – but nothing happened. 'Bulb's gone in the bathroom, Mum...' he said.

'No, love, there's a power cut, but the electricity should be back on soon,' Mum replied.

He remembered their old house before the move. When he was a small boy there seemed to have been rather a lot of power cuts, which would regularly black out the house for long periods. Out would come the candles, which gave a lovely gentle light, and threw flickering magical shadows across the room. There would be no television, but that didn't matter, as this was the time when the family would all gather round and tell stories over the kitchen table – the spookier the better. Grandmother's oil lamp would usually be placed in the centre of the table, and the soft light would grow as the flame was turned up. To a small boy, these times were magical and happy. As he grew older and a little wiser however, he did begin to wonder how come the other houses in the street had managed to keep their electricity on, especially as there was no thunderstorm which may have "knocked out" the nearby transformer. As he got a little older still, he came to the conclusion that the electrical fault may have been caused by the lack of a shilling being put into the meter...

With power now fully restored (which he had to admit was rather a shame) he was able to get his homework finished. Auntie came into the kitchen bearing two large gift-wrapped parcels. She placed the boxes on the kitchen table, announcing 'Since you have done so well in getting to St Onan's, I thought that a little present would be in order.' Nicky picked up the first of the boxes, and noted the weight of the package. He began to unwrap it carefully, and the paper on the outside gave way to reveal a rectangular cardboard box underneath. Opening the end flap of the box he saw three rubber feet attached to something thin and chromed. A quick tip of the box caused the contents to slide out slowly – and revealed a brand new Premier snare drum stand and two pairs of drumsticks. 'I thought that I might help you get started on a drum kit,' said a smiling Auntie. 'To save you belting the hell out of the cushions in your bedroom.' Nicky glanced again at the other, larger box on the table, and prayed to the god of unexpected gifts that his guess about the contents of the box would be accurate. He tore at the paper like a madman, and levered open the second cardboard carton. What he saw inside gave him the same feeling that an archaeologist might experience having just found the Holy Grail in his other jacket pocket... It was a six and a half inch deep chrome Premier snare drum which shone out of its box like a diamond.

'Auntie, thank you so much – that's amazing!!' Nicky gasped, and hugged her in delight. 'How ever did you manage to afford it?'

'Well, let's just say that I had a bit of luck today, so I thought I would help you to make a start putting together that drum kit you have always wanted – we will have to see if we can get you the rest of it piece by piece, but this will do to get you going,' said Auntie.

The boy gently lifted the drum out of the box as if he were handling a religious relic. It was laid reverentially in the middle of the table, and he moved around the table admiring it from every possible angle. 'Are you going to try it then?' Auntie enquired.

With great ceremony, the prized drum was lowered onto the stand, and the gripping screws adjusted to hold it in position. It looked superb, and every word spoken made the eager snares gently buzz in response. Auntie took out a drum stick, threw it spinning into the air and caught it, spinning it effortlessly in her fingers like a professional – before bringing the stick hard into contact with the drum head. Everyone leapt back at the sheer explosion of sound which the single impact produced, and Auntie nodded sagely, declaring, 'Oh Yeah... Rock and Roll!'

'Not in the house until we work out how to quieten it a bit,' said Mum, still recovering from the rimshot. 'I bet they heard that right up the street.'

So with equal care, the drum and stand were put back in their boxes, and stored in Nicky's bedroom under the bed. When he got that call from a famous band that needed a drummer in an emergency – he would be ready (providing they already had the rest of the drum kit sitting around somewhere). He would practise until he had the official drummers' blisters – but tonight, he settled for Rock and Roll dreams...

Chapter Nine

It was by no means a fluke or freak of nature that Auntie had suddenly become the benefactor who had bought Nicky the great gift of the drum. Since she had retired, she had supplemented her income very nicely thank you by means of employing another of her hidden talents. She was in fact, or rather had become, a legendary "Horse Whisperer". When out and about in the town, she would discreetly edge into the local betting shop, approach the counter, and whisper, 'Twenty quid on Golden Gusset in the 3:30 at Kempton Park.' Her skill at choosing winning horses was now such that nearly all of the local bookies were considering imposing some sort of ban upon her – as she was having a critical effect on their earning potential on a regular basis. Secret meetings had been held in smoke-filled back rooms, in which ways of enforcing a ban on Auntie were discussed in hushed tones by very worried men. Could they actually prevent her from entering their place of business and fleecing them further? Somehow Auntie got wind of their scheming and placed a bet with 'Honest Harry' in the market place that they couldn't refuse her custom – and she ended up winning another £250.

Having selected her next batch of likely winners for the weekend, Auntie bided her time, and prepared to raise her stakes...

Meanwhile, Nicky was preparing for Friday at the "Funhouse".

For some nefarious reason, Uncle Joe had informed Mum that he could give Nicky a lift to school on Friday morning. Although this was always a treat for the boy, it usually meant that his secretive uncle was engaged on yet another of his dubious "missions". The trick was not to become involved – if you didn't know about it, then you couldn't give away any information, even under the threat of torture. Joe was apparently now acting as Business Advisor to "an old friend of his" called Tony. His full name was Anthony Curtis. He was in the throes of opening a kosher fish-and-chip shop. Joe had advised him that "Tony Curtis" was not a very Jewish-sounding name for a business owner, and pressed him to adopt a name more in keeping with his commercial plans. Joe had suggested the name of "Bernie Schwartz", which they agreed sounded a lot more kosher.

The planned premises were in the prestigious centre part of the market street. With Joe however, there was always going to be a point at which the advice he gave veered toward the unwise. After much deliberation (and research into take-aways in London) he had arrived at what he considered to be a clever and snappy name for the shop.

Joe supervised the design and fitting of the new shop front sign above the entry doors. The new sign was now in place, and both men had stood back (with the owner blindfold so as not to spoil the surprise). At the appropriate moment, Joe had turned his friend to face the doors. The blindfold was removed – and he read "YUM – KIPPER". (Fish that's too good to pass over.)

This morning had also proven the existence of the Chaos Fairy. It has long been suspected by Man that there may well be agents abroad who take delight in confounding our normal daily lives by stealing, moving, or hiding everyday objects which we need, urgently, no- right now, etc. Chaos Fairies see to it that your kitchen drawers contain spare batteries for any appliance that have been specially drained flat. They hide bottle openers from use at parties and birthday celebrations. They replace the refills in the pens on the hall telephone table with empty ones that look full. They carefully cut at trouser zips with tiny hacksaws, so that they snap off when halfway up (really well-trained Chaos Fairies will angle zip teeth in order to ensure that they jam fast, too). Shoe laces are the main source of training materials on which these little folk practice their malicious skills, and a Chaos Fairy that has studied well and trained hard can ensure that your new lace will snap just as you are five minutes late, and just about to go out of the door. Meanwhile, his partner will take out one lace from your other shoe, or if pressed for time, knot it solidly.

For fun and relaxation, these little buggers wear down the flints in cigarette lighters, as well as letting all of the gas escape. It is also an unconfirmed rumour that they may well have a specialist section whose job it is to pee on boxes of kitchen matches.

I digress...

Having more or less circumnavigated the various pitfalls created by the aforementioned wee folk, Nicky waited at the bus stop for the arrival of Uncle Joe. There was a squeal of tyres under protest, and Joe's car came around the church corner almost on two wheels. He screeched to a halt in front of Nicky, and swung open the car door. 'Mornin', son,' he said, 'I'm just rehearsin' for a part I've been given as a stunt driver for the new Mothercare commercial on telly.'

Nicky climbed in and hung on to the side of the door, preparing for take-off.

'So then... how's this school malarkey all goin'? Joe asked.

'Not bad thanks, Uncle – but I hate Maths and Latin,' said Nicky

'Well don't be worryin' about Latin unless you want to be a lawyer' said Joe, 'and Maths is just numbers made up for people who can't spell properly. Take your time, and if you don't understand – then ask, and if you still don't get it, then the answer is usually 47 or 53, or $Y=X-Zx2$. I could have bought a space shuttle you know, but I wanted any colour other than white – it shows too much muck.'

Joe sped down the hill, weaving in and out of the angry drivers who sounded their horns at him. The last car which he overtook was the local policeman, and Nicky shot his Uncle a look of dire panic. 'Don't bother about him, lad, I've already threatened to expose him as a secret lap dancer to the press – plus the tight bugger still owes me a pint,' laughed Joe. They arrived outside the school at a rate well in excess of the speed limit, and Joe made a terrifying handbrake turn outside the main gate.

'See you later, lad – I promised I'd give the Pope a ring later, must rush.'

With that, the four-wheeled warrior was gone.

Merry was standing aghast at the gate, watching Uncle fly off in a cloud of tyre smoke.

'Wow! Does he always drive like that?' he asked.

'No, sometimes he likes to put his foot down a bit,' Nicky replied.

The rest of the "mini-gang" met up, exchanged gossip, and trudged off to morning assembly.

The assembly followed the now regular pattern of stand/sing/stand/listen, etc.

Today the words "wrinkled winkle" had been written on a sheet of paper and affixed to the lectern front, out of sight of Dr Goodwill and Co. The head strode up to the edge of the stage and gripped the lapels of his gown.

'Gentlemen, on Monday of next week you shall have a rare privilege,' he announced.

'The entire Academy will be having a photographic likeness captured in the quadrangle at eleven o'clock precisely. I will expect every boy to be well-presented and groomed accordingly for the purpose. This photograph will record our number for posterity, and will be proudly displayed in the Honours Gallery,' said Goodwill.

He then handed over to Dr Chambers, who waited for him to exit the double doors before speaking to the assembled masses. 'Boys, you have heard what the Head has just said. Hair length will be measured on Monday, and uniform will be assessed. Any boy found not to be conforming to the required standards will be punished – do I make myself absolutely clear?' There was a general muttering on a theme of, 'Yes Sir'.

It was at this point that the unthinkable happened. In the silence immediately following the response, some boy broke wind with terrific ferocity. As the echoes died away, each boy looked at his fellow pupil on either side in order to identify the doer of the foul deed.

This was not just an insult to all of the high moral standards that St Onan's held most dear; this was trouser terrorism of the very worst kind. The shock was exactly the same as seeing someone moon at the Mona Lisa...

Dr Chambers reddened with rage, and spluttered, 'Right... whoever the own–whoever dro– whichever boy far– SEE ME AFTER ASSEMBLY IN MY STUDY THAT BOY...'

He stormed off the stage and let the doors slam behind him.

A small voice from somewhere piped up forlornly 'Pardon me...'

At this point, the whole assembled Academy collapsed with uncontrolled laughter.

The staff filed out off the stage, and the boys dispersed ready for registration and their first lesson. History was first on the agenda, and the boys hurried into their room, still speculating on the identity of the boy responsible for the act of anal ventriloquism. Calderman was somewhat philosophical about the whole incident 'All you need to do is spot someone with the arse ripped out of their trousers, and there you have your culprit,' he declared.

Dr Matthews greeted the boys in usual form. Well, he called the register for a completely different form to be exact. The boys let him get as far as 'Pargeter, Parker, Prenderghast...' before they pointed out the error of his ways. The Doctor decided to cut to the chase – 'Everyone here?' he asked. 'Good, let's make a start.'

Dr Matthews was in fact a pleasant enough man, once you acclimatised yourself to his funny little ways. He was married, and lived locally. He and his wife had three sons whom he had named Gordon, Gilbey and Theakston. These seemed like perfectly decent and respectable names to Dr Matthews. Theakston was still a pupil at the Academy, in the last year of his upper sixth form, and a sworn tee-totaller for some reason.

Weatherill was determined to "test the water" with Dr Matthews today – and decided to throw in a curve ball at the start of the lesson, to see if he could catch the master off-balance. 'Sir, I have a confession to make,' he began.

Matthews peered over the top of his half-glasses and almost focussed on the boy. 'Yes, Mr Weatherill, what is this confession?' he said.

'It appears that I have come to school today wearing odd socks, sir,' stated Weatherill. 'What is odd about that Mr Weatherill?' asked Matthews, rising to the bait. 'Well, sir, they're odd because they are made of wood... '

'Leave my classroom, Mr Weatherill,' Matthews said levelly, 'and return when, and only when, you have achieved some semblance of normality...'

Weatherill stood up and walked calmly out of the room, showing no expression upon his face. He carefully closed the door with its usual theatrical creak.

Matthews continued unabashed. 'Now that little distraction has been dealt with, we will continue with our studies, gentlemen. We will now look at early Stone Age burial customs and ritual, paying particular attention to long barrows and burial mounds. Fine examples of these may be found in many parts of the country, and are testament to the honour and respect shown to the individuals interred within. They have also been the source of some of the very finest examples of grave artefacts unearthed by modern teams of archaeologists. For your prep tonight, you will research and report on the location and contents of famous Stone Age burial sites in the British Isles.'

At this point, there was a knocking at the classroom door.

Matthews glanced over to the door and said with a trace of annoyance, 'Oh do come in, will you...'

At this point the familiar head and shoulders of a grinning Weatherill appeared around the door, and said, 'Oh. Thanks very much, sir, can I?' 'NO – GET OUT BOY... ' Matthews shouted, and the door was swiftly shut again to the great amusement of the class. The lesson continued with frequent glances by the master toward the door, expecting further attempts by the excluded pupil to gain re-admission to the class.

The boys were instructed to draw a typical long barrow, with the skeleton of the departed in situ. For reasons best known to himself, Trevill produced a superb sketch of a truly impressive long marrow. Whilst the class carried on with their task, the master edged his way over to the stationery cupboard and disappeared inside. There was a sound like the seal on a bottle being broken, and a hushed hint of liquid being poured into some receptacle. Matthews reappeared after a few minutes looking happy and a little flushed, like a newly-installed antique lavatory. He closed the stationery cupboard door (managing to grasp the handle at the third attempt) and strode over to the door. Yanking savagely at the handle, he was surprised to be greeted by an empty corridor, with no evidence of the grinning Weatherill in sight. He turned around and was startled to see the boy standing right behind him. With the shock, pens from his top pocket had leapt into the air, and were currently attempting to secrete themselves under the desks of the class. Matthews bent down quickly to retrieve his gold fountain pen, and struck his head on the end of the nearest desk with considerable force. He also caused the silver hip flask to leap out of his inside pocket and skitter across the floor like an upturned beetle. The master made a spectacular dive for the errant flask, and swept it back out of sight into his jacket. He righted himself, swearing incoherently under his breath, and rubbing his forehead, paced back into the stationery cupboard. The boys sat motionless, and again heard the sound of a cap being removed from a bottle. The master reappeared with a grin on his face, and the beginnings of a large lump trying its best to appear on his forehead.

'Well, bugger me backwards with a beech wood baseball bat...' quoth the teacher, 'Now, do pray remind me as to where we were...'

'You were explaining, sir, how Stonehenge was the Stone Age equivalent of Morrison's supermarket, sir...' said Merry, ever the opportunist.

'Quite so, Mr Merry,' said Matthews. 'As a meeting place for Stone Age man and his family, there was no greater meeting place with better parking. Beneath its trilithons I am sure that you will be able to imagine all manner of social interaction between families of early man.'

'Did the Druids get an extra ten percent off the Ritual of the Week with their Solstice cards?' asked Nicky.

'The "Heel Stone" may have been the express check-out,' added Calderman, helpfully.

'Druids indeed...' slurred Matthews. 'Load of silly buggers dressed in bedsheets waving mistletoe boughs around and hoping that the sun comes up over the right stone, just because their job might be on the line if it doesn't...'

The discussion continued until Dr Matthews, now seated behind his Victorian desk once again, began to lose the thread of the debate, and fell asleep cradling his head in one hand. With the lesson now satisfactorily destroyed, the boys waited until the bell for the next period sounded, then exited the room leaving the usual explanatory note for Dr Matthews.

So it was back to Latin class again. Nicky had the distinct feeling that no matter how hard he struggled, and for how long, he would just not get to grips with the subject. He had no interest in it at all, and that taking all things into consideration, there were much more productive things which he could be learning. Like everything else. At best it would sit gathering dust, and never again likely to be used – rather like Cousin Sheila's dating website profile...

The actual lesson had not turned out to be as stressful as Nicky had anticipated. Various members of the class had been chosen by the master to read out aloud from their homework on Latin verbs. He had attempted to physically shrink down into his school uniform, until he felt his ears touch his collar. By this means he hoped to render himself invisible to the teacher, and thus not available for ritual humiliation in front of the rest of the boys. He thought about his neighbour Mr Hill, who had experimented with what he had hoped would be a fully-functional 'cloak of invisibility' for the purpose of catching rabbits in the fields behind their houses. In practical terms, this had involved a bizarre system of pinning broccoli stems and cabbage leaves to an old overcoat, and lying very still in the long grass adjacent to the rabbit warren. The local rabbits however, were well used to the various deceptions employed by the locals in order to trap them. They had approached the recumbent Hill, (the man that is – not the local geographical feature) regarded him with a critical rabbit eye, sniffed the air suspiciously, and hopped off muttering the rabbit equivalent for 'bleedin' broccoli boy is up to his old tricks again.'

Undeterred by the lack of response, Mr Hill immediately went home and began work on an idea which he had just thought up for an animated film. It was an animated film all about a group of rabbits. It was an animated film all about a group of rabbits that always ate at a local motorway service station cafe. The working title for the film was *Watered-down Shit...*

'And what would the correct Latin phrase for that be, Mr Shepherd?' Nicky heard the master ask, jolting him back into reality...

'Casus Belli – the cause of war, sir,' he heard himself answer. Where the hell that had come from he did not know, but presumably two brain programmes were running in tandem within his head, and panic had forced an answer out of his mouth. He was just thankful that his reply had not included rabbits.

'Lucky shot there, Shep,' whispered Calderman.

The Master beamed, 'Good work Mr Shepherd, good work indeed.' They were given the normal sensory overload of verbs to conjugate and decline. Nicky wished that he could decline the lot of it, respectfully. All in all, he was coming to the conclusion that the only fact that he knew about Virgil, was the certainty that he was the pilot of Thunderbird 2...

Rundell bade them all 'Bene Facis'. None of the boys knew him from memory, but Merry made a mental note to keep a look out for Benny Francis in future.

French class today turned out to be a bit of a mystery – there was no French class. The boys had been directed up to the old library for a study period. It would appear that Madame was incommunicado, or some other expensive designer fabric. There was no sign of her small Renault car in the quad, there were no baguette crumbs to be seen on the staffroom floor, and the scent of Chanel was noticeably not wafting down the corridors. Madame was definitely disparu...

The lads sat at the long benches in the library, some already getting to grips with tonight's homework, others talking in hushed voices between themselves. DeVere was over at the huge black oak door. He seemed to be taking a great deal of interest in the intricately-carved ancient lock, and was pressing something into what looked a little like a bar of soap. When he was satisfied with the results of his labours, he carefully wrapped the soap in his clean handkerchief and stowed it away in the mysterious recesses of his blazer. An astute observer would then have seen him replace the large iron key back into the lock. Out came the little black book, notes were made, and it disappeared out of sight again.

Behind the masters' table at the end of the room were four steps which led down to a smaller oaken exit door to the outer walled corridor. The boys heard a key turn in the lock, and in through these doors came Mr Newhouse, the music master.

'Hi chaps...' he called out brightly. 'Sorry to mess you about, but it looks like Penny – sorry, Mrs Dreadfell, has gone AWOL today, so I guess we will have to amuse ourselves for this period. If it's okay with you boys, I will sit in with you and catch up on some marking.'

It certainly was all right with the boys. Mr Newhouse was utterly different to the other members of the faculty, inasmuch as he showed complete mental stability and an alarming degree of cool. The pupils looked over in awe as he took out his marking. It turned out to be this month's copy of *Classic Rock* magazine, which he began to scan through intently. He looked up at a sudden sound, and was surprised to see one of the boys high up on the stone cill of one of the far end windows.

'Hey there, Ashman...' he called. 'What are you doing up there?'

'I was looking for Isaac Newton's signature on the cill, sir' answered the boy. 'They told us that he carved his name into the cill somewhere on one of the windows.'

'Just be careful that you don't fall off, Ashman,' said the Master.

'Oh there's no danger, sir, 'cos the signature was written a long time before he discovered gravity,' answered Ashman.

The boy continued his searching, clinging perilously to the stone frame of the leaded window as he scanned for the name. After a while, Mr Newhouse looked up from his magazine and called out to the boy, who was now hanging dangerously from one of the iron window catches.

'Did you find it?' asked Mr Newhouse.

'Yes, sir, but there is a bit of a problem,' said the boy.

'What problem is that?' enquired the master.

'I've found four already, sir – all in different handwriting,' answered Ashman.

'Okay lads – game on!' said Newhouse. 'Let's get a team together; nominate four "climbers" and four more guys to take rubbings with a soft pencil on paper. We can compare the signatures and see which we think is the original.' The boys needed no encouragement to climb the tall book cases and investigate the stone window cills.

Several "Newtons" were collected, along with some splendid other names such as Tinkler, Wedgey, Manleigh-Parts and Scrottomley. It will come as no surprise to learn that three of these individuals went on to serve in the House of Commons, and Lord Manleigh-Parts was convicted and is serving time at Her Majesty's pleasure for an offence upon which we will not dwell. (Suffice to say that the Jury were made aware that the Police confiscated three bulldog clips, a pound of goose fat, two wooden spatulas, a leather 'device' and a moist copy of *The Times* from his Parliamentary offices.)

'Nice job, guys...' said the master. 'What we really ought to do is make some tee shirts using the signature – something with a bit of bite, any ideas?'

The boys thought for a moment, then Merry piped up. 'Yes, sir, we could have, "Newton was wrong – the Earth Sucks..."

'A bit harsh, I feel' said Mr Newhouse.

'Newton was dyslexic – he discovered gravy,' suggested Calderman.

'Isaac's favourite apple – Gravity Smiths,' said Nicky.

'Have you seen Mrs Newton's pear?' said Jackson.

'Now we're cooking!' said Mr Newhouse, rubbing his hands. 'Get your ideas down on paper, and we'll see if we can get a couple of the best slogans printed.'

With that, the so-called "study period" was brought to an unwelcome end by the sound of the bell. The boys thanked the master (leaving him a bit confused at the gesture) and marched off to their appointment with the odd world of the Reverend Felchingham...

All of the members of Nicky's form were extremely nervous about knocking on the door of Felchingham's room. For some reason, even the closed oak door radiated some sort of menace, and so the minimum of contact with it was adopted by boys and staff alike. As the class stood outside in the corridor, they could hear low chanting coming from inside, although the words could not be made out through the woodwork. They heard an alarm clocks shrill bell sound, and an oath of, 'Damn, blast and bugger it...' spoken by the master as he obviously knocked the clock to the floor in an effort to silence it. He opened the door to the class, who filed in slowly into the gloom within, and took in the scene. The room was full of the smell of rather pungent incense, and the Rev. had obviously just finished moving the desks back into order in rows.

'Welcome, gentlemen...' squeaked the master, who then coughed, and lowered the tone of his voice to its normal sepulchral level.

'Today, I thought that it might be interesting to discuss with you the subject of good, evil, and comparisons of both within religious teaching. In order to get a true and honest perspective upon the accepted divine texts, it is important I feel, to understand and appreciate "both sides of the coin" as it were. I thought that we might begin with the – Hang on… is Hopkins in this class? No? Good, well just checking-now where was I? Ah yes. Divinity teaches us the values of tolerance and acceptance of the point of view adopted by other, maybe stranger, faiths. Through the teachings of the Bible we are instructed to "Love thy Neighbour as thyself" and to "turn the other cheek" whenever anger would reduce us to beasts. I want us to consider, if you will, an opinion opposite to the one which you may currently hold, and (wait for it...) take the view of a practitioner of say, (here we go) an alternative religious practice. To truly understand godliness, we must first have experience (getting warmer) of the other end of the scale. To this end, we need to examine that which is classed as (nearly there) evil, and ask ourselves a fundamental question – is evil really as bad as we have been led to believe? (Bingo! Player is awarded a demonic black fluffy goat).

I will today ask you all to discuss the question "Lucifer – was he a bad egg? Or just a product of a poor upbringing and bad environment?"

Felchingham went on to explain that although Lucifer was indeed a fallen angel, he had to have been a true angel to begin with, and his inherent goodness could not have completely deserted him in the great scheme of ineffability. He seemed to be saying that there was good in everyone, and our failure to see it was a failure to scratch the surface hard enough. Calderman raised the point that the Spanish Inquisition had in fact made quite a career out of scratching very hard indeed on the surfaces of people who they wanted a confession from. The use of the rack on prisoners would seem to exclude the chances of finding any good or empathy. Felchingham thought that this was stretching the point.

'The mere mention of the name Satan,' said the Rev., 'conjures up images of a cloven-hoofed and horned beast.'

'With a celestial ASBO, sir, let's not forget...' said Nicky.

'But was he really as bad as his publicity would suggest?' asked the Rev., and broke into Shakespearean verse declaring:

"What's in a name?

That which we call a rose

By any other name, would smell as sweat..."

'The purges visited upon those who practiced Witchcraft during the Middle Ages sought to vilify the witch – and totally ignore the craft, gentlemen,' he said. These were caring elderly women with a passion to help the community.'

'And warts...' added Merry.

'And break dancing on the heath at midnight without any undercrackers on...' said Ashman.

'Yeah...' said Calderman – 'they get their kicks on Route 666...'

Nicky felt compelled to ask, 'Sir.. could you clarify please; is the bloke who lives at number 668 the Neighbour of the Beast?'

The Rev was now beginning to get extremely hot under the dog collar, and was toying with his inverted crucifix in a nervous manner. He attempted to regain control of the class before the lesson descended into complete anarchy.

'The point which I am trying to make, gentlemen, is to draw the distinction between a good deed done for what may well seem to be a questionable reason, and a seemingly evil act perpetrated by someone who believes that they are acting with the best of intentions...' he said. 'Religions teach us that we sometimes have to seek an alternative path or method in order to achieve a result for the greater good, and that an act that may be perceived as bad may have been perpetrated in pursuance of an outcome which is ultimately in the best interests of humanity.'

'What about Third Party Claims?' asked Calderman.

'What do you mean "Third Party Claims"?' asked the Rev.

'Well, I mean that when someone does some horrible murder, they usually come out and say that "The Devil made me do it", sir...' the boy replied.

'That would be wrong, as we all know that murder is a mortal sin,' said the Rev.

'Yeah... but what if the Pope got his hands on a time machine, and went back and shot Hitler – how would you class that?' asked Calderman. 'The Pope preaches that murder is wrong, but he commits an evil act in order to save millions of lives – is that good or evil, sir...?'

The teacher raised his eyes skywards, as if seeking Divine inspiration, and tried to give a reasoned answer to the question.

'Well, any act of wilful murder is obviously wrong and a bad thing. If a person should choose to perform an act of good for a good reason, then the bad aspect of the good act will be viewed as bad – even though the motive was to do good. Now the good thing about the bad act is that although it may be inherently bad, the outcome will be seen as good. It is erm... a bad thing that the err... good motive is perceived as bad, when in fact ahh... ultimate good is achieved by means of bad actions. If the bad action is seen in a good light, then this will be good, but err... it would be bad if the good act which is undertaken for the common good is seen as bad at the end of the day. The good, or rather bad, or ugly... no – not ugly, sorry... action is a bad act committed out of good motives – but would have been committed in the hope of taking action for the greater good, which is a good thing. The good thing was the act of eliminating the individual who went on to commit so many bad things, which was good. But this had to be done by means of doing a bad thing which was, err... not good. So the ultimate result was doing a bad thing which turned out to be a good thing, but the good thing which the good motive demanded was ultimately achieved by doing something bad, for the sake of good. Unless of course, it was done badly...'

There was a stunned silence, as the fog of confusion settled itself over the boys.

Merry turned around in his seat, regarded the rest of his class and asked, 'Anyone...?'

'Thank you, sir...' said Calderman. 'I am glad that we got that clarified.'

'And what about the Spanish Inquisition, sir...' said Nicky.

'What about it?' asked a now nervous Rev.

'Well, it turned out to be like a medieval version of *Deal or No Deal* but with better thumbscrews. I mean, "Let's see what is in box 13 – ooh look! Eternal damnation...' said Nicky. 'Was it such a "good cause" to go around torturing innocent people?'

Jackson raised his hand, 'Sir... can I just ask? If I was to borrow the Pope's time machine and go back in time and shoot my grandfather – would it be morally or spiritually wrong to keep the tenner which he gave to me for my birthday?'

The Reverend stood at the front of the class clenching and unclenching his hands, knowing that he could not give an answer that would satisfy the class. He assumed his "failsafe position", designed to win any argument, and cut off further discussion.

'We cannot presume to question God...' he said, 'His plans are ineffable, and not to be doubted by us mere mortals.'

'Plans can be questioned and refused, sir...' said Ashman. 'My Dad had his plans for an extension turned down by the planning department – and he said that they were a bunch of "ineffable idiots" who thought that they were God Almighty.'

'We have just had our loft converted,' said Weatherill conversationally. 'It's Jewish now...'

The Reverend felt the once-parted waters of the Red Sea collapsing down onto him, and he had forgotten to bring his swimming kit again...

He decided to plunge on with the lesson until he could once again get a grip on more solid ground. He made the choice to give the class a brief taste of Alternative Prophesy, whereby the future could be foreseen by means of reading the innards of a chicken. He produced the "star of the show" from his large desk drawer, and proceeded to demonstrate to the amused boys the precise technique required in order to accomplish the fowl deed. The class were of the opinion that a sacred dagger would have certainly been the desired weapon of choice – and not a small kitchen knife with the supermarket barcode label still attached (very mystic...). Looking at his finished handiwork, the Reverend made some bland and general "predictions" about the future.

In the eyes of the boys in the class, the Reverend's future would have been a good deal brighter, and the whole experience made rather more convincing if he had not chosen as his ritual sacrifice a piece of KFC bucket chicken...

Chapter Ten

There was much merriment among the masses at lunchtime (not just because there was an outbreak of "Ms") due to the fact that it was chicken for dinner. The boys chose to replicate their recent lesson, and all successfully predicted a future in which indigestion would be a significant factor.

Meals were now almost literally flying out of the hatches toward the waiting hands, before the hatch doors were rapidly dropped back into place. Nerves in the kitchen were obviously still on edge. Just to make sure that there was no unearthly interference with the kitchen (or her person, it would seem) "Devils on horseback" had been deleted from the menu on safety grounds. The tally of prominent crosses being worn had grown to epidemic proportions, and an observer might well assume that they were witnessing a cardinals' night out, or a cookery course being held at the Vatican. Mr Brooks, the groundskeeper and general handyman had been called in to fit locks to all of the kitchen cupboards, and so Betty Bradley was now forced to clink around her domain carrying a huge bunch of keys that would not have looked out of place on a Tower of London Beefeater. Despite the new security arrangements, she did not feel any more secure, and with good reason – as the boys were now plotting to further compound her problems by the use of some highly efficient magnets...

The dessert served was another "twenty questions" serving of an unyielding sponge brick topped with a bullet-proof icing of dubious parentage. It sat upon the plate and defied the taster to a) cut it, and b) digest it. Nicky thought that it looked like the white cliffs of Dover, and was not at all surprised to find that it tasted like it too. Even the usually paramilitary custard refused to soften the lump, and oozed off to hide around the back of the plate. As the uneaten puddings were safely returned behind the slammed serving hatches, the boys breathed a sigh of relief.

First lesson this afternoon was a new one for the class, it was double Biology. The boys were wondering what they might encounter behind those laboratory doors with the frosted glass panels. There were certainly rumours, and it was a fact that the Academy cleaning staff refused point blank to set foot anywhere near the laboratory during the hours of darkness.

The lads queued up in an orderly and strangely silent line down the corridor. Around the corner came a stocky, dishevelled man with a mop of wild hair flaring out in the manner of Albert Einstein. He bounded up to the laboratory entrance and produced a complicated-looking set of keys, with which he unlocked the doors.

'Right , chaps...' he boomed, 'grab a bench while I get my teaching kit on...'

The boys sat obediently in rows and looked around them. The walls of the laboratory were adorned with charts and diagrams depicting all manner of bodily organs, and the evolutionary route of several species. The cills of the windows were filled with what looked like exotic cacti and the odd orchid specimen. Nicky was certain that one of the orchids turned to look at him as he sat down, and he made a mental note to avoid this particular plant in future. The door at the rear of the laboratory suddenly burst open, and the master came into the room wearing a full-face protective helmet and hood, plus heavy cloth gauntlets. All of the boys shrunk back in terror, until the master lifted the heavy clear visor and announced, 'Sorry, lads, I just have to dust off one of the Madagascan cacti – only the little sod got me last time, and I ended up like a bloody pin cushion.'

This was Doctor Jonathan Darwin (no relation as far as we could prove so far). If ever there was a man obsessed with his subject, then Dr Darwin was he. He had a mission – and this was to ensure that he should become famous throughout the world for discovering cures for all of the deadliest of diseases which still afflict man. Ever since he had left Cambridge University, he had pursued his calling across the globe. He made frequent trips to Borneo, the Amazon Rain Forest, and any other uncharted wilderness in which he assumed that he might stumble over his own "Holy Grail". This had on several occasions led him to stumble over Pygmies, who had (as he described it) 'welcomed him as a God from the sky'. The National Geographic magazine actually printed a true account of how the Pygmies were pretty irate at his loud and sudden intrusion into their territory – and took great care to ensure that the "God from the Sky" left their village swiftly, with an arse liberally peppered with blowpipe darts.

Undeterred, he continued to scour the continents for rare and undiscovered new species, which he could name after himself. This is why there is now a small tree-dwelling lizard in Borneo which is known as Dick.

So far, his questing had proved to be unfruitful to say the least, and the only things which the dear Doctor had managed to bring back from his far-ranging travels had been Malaria, Prickly Heat, Dysentery, and an embarrassing rash which he had picked up during a short stop-over in Thailand. For the time being he had decided to "rest" in his teaching post at the Academy, until his next globe-trotting challenge presented itself.

Two years ago, Darwin had made the decision to extend his expeditions to include the American North West, and was delving deeply into the forests and crowded woodlands in the feverish hope of discovering some natural wonder which would make his name famous. Following a particularly violent thunderstorm, he had become lost in the dark woods. Seeking shelter from the deluge which still hammered down from the heavens, he sighted a small rough-hewn log cabin in a clearing. He made tracks for the simple dwelling and tentatively knocked at the door. The door opened slowly to reveal the largest man that Darwin had ever encountered, standing at what he estimated to be well over seven feet tall. The man gave Darwin a pleasant grin, and gestured with one of his long, huge arms for the traveller to enter.

Giving his apologies for the interruption, Darwin explained to the big man the reason for his travelling in the region, where he was from, and what he did for a living. The man listened intently with his head on one side – always with the same friendly and curious smile on his face. He unfolded himself from the handmade stool and went into the back of the cabin, reappearing a short while later with two mugs of what Darwin assumed was steaming tea.

A wooden plate was placed in front of the visitor, upon which were a variety of fruits, nuts, and other vegetables which looked both familiar and appetising to Darwin.

'Do you live here, sir?' enquired Darwin, sipping his tea.

'Here... Live... Yes... ' replied the man.

'May I ask your name, my friend?' said the teacher.

The reply was a low rumbled growl, out of which Darwin picked up what he presumed to be the name 'Bernie'. Now feeling a little more settled in his surroundings, Darwin began to tell (with much use of sign language and badly-executed mime) his companion all about the Academy in England, and about his friends. (This was an outright lie – Darwin had never managed to get the hang of keeping friends for very long, and even casual acquaintances always seemed to remember some urgent pressing engagement seconds after meeting him.)

This was different, for now he felt that he may actually have met a potential friend who did not want to pull off his head – although from the look of Bernie, he could achieve this with the bare minimum of effort being required.

The huge man opened the door, looked out into the dense, rain-soaked forests, and declared, 'Still Water... Not leave... Stay for time if wish...'

This seemed to be an invitation to further enjoy the hospitality of his host, and Darwin was only too happy to take up the kind offer. Hours became days, which became weeks, then months. The two spent hours deep in the forests, with Bernie showing Darwin many new and exciting species. One evening, on their way back to the cabin, Bernie paused and held out his long arm, as if to prevent Darwin from walking forward any further. The teacher looked at his friend, who hung down his head sadly and said in a soft, low voice which was barely audible, 'Not go here... Sacred place... Saskalia – she sleep...'

They returned to the clearing, and over another meal of forest food, Darwin attempted to find out exactly who Saskalia was, and why Bernie had turned them away from that particular spot in the forest. As Bernie related the tale, it seemed that the smile faded from his huge face, and was replaced by a deep sadness which rose from his very soul.

Saskalia had been Bernie's wife. They had lived in secluded happiness in the shack for many years, untroubled by the outside world and happy to enjoy their life as just two more of the creatures of the dark forests. Their idyllic life had been shattered when Saskalia had been killed by what was (as far as Darwin could make out) a stray bullet from the rifle of a hunter. Her resting place was the patch of hallowed ground which Bernie would allow no-one else to stand upon, and his beloved had returned to the forest once again as nature intended.

One amazing fact had emerged though, because despite having hands of incredible size, Bernie had somehow miraculously gained superb skills as a watchmaker. With gold and metals obtained from who knows where, he fashioned the most beautiful and delicate timepieces on the bench at the rear of the shack. He would lovingly inscribe each of the faces of the watches with the name "Sask", in memory of his lost love. When he chose to do so, Bernie would sell these items at the nearest local towns, and they would sell commercially for very high prices indeed. They became highly prized by collectors worldwide – especially in America. Such was the beauty and legendary reputation of these objects (not to mention their rarity) that very few people indeed could ever lay claim to owning, or even to having seen a Sask Watch.

Bernie had somehow been persuaded over time to accompany Darwin back to England, and take up a position at St Onan's as his laboratory assistant. The huge man was very happy in his job, and Darwin had an enthusiastic helper on tap. There had been some scandal over questionable Immigration and residential laws being flouted, not to mention the lack of job advertisements for the Academy post (several staff members thought that Darwin had put his Big Foot in it again...) but the matter had resolved itself with Bernie moving into the position quietly and efficiently.

'Okay, boys, we will start at the very beginning,' said Darwin. 'There are a large number of living things on the planet. As well as those alive today, a great many have become extinct. It is important to sort these living things into groups – so that we can identify them and relate them to one-another. So, we will start with Classification.'

Soon the boys were doing their best to copy down into their notebooks all of the information which the master was scribbling furiously onto the blackboard. Nicky did his best to copy down Kingdom, Phylum, Class, Order, Family, Genus and Species – (adding Lordsley on the end as a separate subdivision of humanity, which seemed fair). There was a fair amount of discussion concerning the Animal and Plant kingdoms, and a mild uproar as Calderman, Merry and Ashman all argued that man was the direct cause of the extinction of so much of the Animal kingdom. Darwin calmed down the situation by stepping neatly sideways into the process and scientific method for proving a hypothesis. He described how the class would be performing various experiments in the course of their studies.

Throughout the master's enthusiastic ramblings, there was one boy at the rear of the class who was paying particular attention to each and every word which came from Darwin. This was a boy called Kendy. He was extremely friendly, polite, and seemed curious to find out about all of his new classmates and how they lived. He spoke with a curious precision, and often punctuated his sentences with a short rasping hiss, as would be made by someone clearing their throat. Some of the boys found his mannerisms a little alien – but were completely unaware of how entirely correct this assumption would prove to be.

At the Academy in the 1950s, the Physics department had constructed a large and powerful radio transmitter as an Electronics Club project. The object was to interest the boys in electrical engineering, and to make contact with other schools across France, Belgium, Holland and Germany. When the transmitter was completed, and the massive aerial put into place on the roof of the Physics laboratory, pupils would regularly make contact with other radio hams from schools across Europe. This could be used for increasing their language skills (cheating in exams) and for arranging student exchanges which were a new idea at St Onan's. Since the generator which provided the power for the transmitter was rather unreliable, a senior student at the time (to whit – one Richard Strangler Esquire) had managed to harness the electrostatic generating power of an underground stream which ran beneath the Academy. A fiendish and rather baffling amplifier and current booster had been linked up to the transmitter, which had its own independent power supply capable of hurling out radio signals for incredible distances.

During the early 1960s of course, came the events of the Cuban Missile Crisis, and the threat of impending 'Kabloweee!' for mankind. At the Academy, the perceived threat from Soviet Russia and Communism was taken with a pinch of panic. In case their signals of fraternal welcome should be intercepted by "Ruskies" with good quality headphones, and their location pinpointed for chastisement of the nuclear variety, the transmitter aerial was hastily dismantled and stored in the vacuum of the loft space above the laboratory. The power supply input was papered over and forgotten. Forgotten that is, until fate took a hand in events many years later...

To celebrate the large cash infusion given to St Onan's by the father of one of the pupils, the Physics department (now under the direction of one Richard Strangler Esquire) decided to build a huge dish on the roof of the laboratory for the purposes of studying Radio Astronomy. The mammoth concave structure sat on the ancient tiled roof, staring up into the heavens. When it came to connecting the power supply however, a very resourceful workman (Biggley's Electricals – no fee too small, no job we can't bodge up) found a most convenient power supply already wired in. He connected up the dish to the electricity point (no-one would ever look up here anyway...) and claimed his astronomical fee for installing the astronomical equipment. In doing so, he had inadvertently hooked up the radio dish to the old transmitter which lay directly below it in the attic space. This now acted as a booster which pre-amplified and supercharged the signals out through the dish. When a smaller radio set was installed downstairs in the laboratory, the old power point was uncovered, and the set plugged into this.

Following all this so far? Good.

Now the pupils still sent out their messages to other schools across the Continent, but with the huge boost in transmission power going out directly from the dish – their requests for "Exchange Students" were sent out and received a little further than anyone could ever have anticipated...

It was on a Wednesday that the Academy Physics Society received their first message from the Pegasus star system. In true sci-fi film fashion this message sat blinking away merrily to itself on the electronic display board, whilst the "technician" Julian sat deeply immersed in the pages of *Jugs* magazine. (Not what you were thinking, wicked people – he was an avid collector of antique pottery. There were however, a smashing couple of full-frontal tea cups on page seventeen.) This was a communication sent in binary code, which was hurriedly sped off by the panicked Julian to the Maths department, for decoding on their rather ancient computer (a steam-powered leviathan which gasped, wheezed and farted out answers by means of text punched out of small cards). The message was full of praise for their invitation, and stated 'We will be happy to send one of our adolescents in order to facilitate a mutual exchange of culture and knowledge.'

(Actually, the first card produced had said, when translated, 'Is this bloody thing on? One-two One-two.')

So – regular and secretive contact had been made with intergalactic pen-pals.

Now that lines of communication had been established, it was time for the important questions that would cement the link between races living in star systems many light years apart. Excited but rather anxious faces clustered around the transmitter in the attempt to formulate a message to the people from the stars. Eventually, after much deliberation, and a nosebleed caused by a lucky blow from an elbow, consensus was reached. The questions were beamed out. 'What do you look like?' 'What do you want?' 'Do you have ample parking?' and that sort of mundane nonsense essential to establish cosmic harmony.

Due to the usual errors committed by administration assistants everywhere, the replies were sent out in completely the wrong order. When the complex signals were translated, it would appear that the Pegasus people looked exactly like cabbages. Picture two gave the impression that what they desired were creatures very similar to ourselves. The third question was never satisfactorily answered, as the poor alien scientists had no idea at all what 'Apple parking' was, or why they should require it. Nevertheless, this was the beginning of a regular "courier" service between the planets. Despite the attempts to maintain a decent level of secrecy, the visiting ships from the Beta Pegasi star system were spotted from time to time, and caused many a 'UFO flap' across the country. It was on one such mission such as this, that a young Pegasian stowed away onboard a craft, and after some hurried and embarrassed negotiation, had been accepted as a student at St Onan's. He had been placed with a dotty but loving couple out in one of the villages – who could care less where he came from, as they finally had achieved their dearest wish of having a son.

Back on his home planet, his people had been picking up television signals from American news broadcasts since 1963. It was decided that this boy should be given a name that they had picked up from just such a transmission. It seemed to be a very popular name, as it featured heavily in all of the broadcasts which they had received at the time – hence the boy had been "christened" by the Earth name of Jonef Kendy.

Darwin was now striding around the classroom waving his arms in wild and descriptive abandon, whilst describing the distinctions between vertebrates (animals with backbones) and invertebrates (various – including Lordsley). Whilst enjoying the enthusiastic descriptions of Jellyfish, True Worms and Flatworms, the boys could not help but glance at the laboratory prep room' door, and saw a huge smiling face grin back out at them from behind the thin glazed vertical slats set in the door. Bernie liked children, and was sorry that he had not had the opportunity to have a family of his own. For the sake of discretion however, he leaned back out of view and carried on with his work.

'For your prep work, boys...' said the master, 'I would like you to classify six members of the animal kingdom, one of which may be extinct if you wish.'

As the class put away their workbooks, Nicky again noticed that one or two of the exotic orchids on the window sills turned to look at them. The boys filed out of the laboratory with a casual glance back at the prep room door – and were rewarded by the sight of a huge hand giving a quick wave...

Last lesson of the day was English, which for the double period was Drama in the assembly hall with Mr Hyde-Jones. All of the boys were looking forward to his lesson, because the man had none of the rigidity of the other teachers, and taught in a relaxed and conversational style. He was in fact an out-of-work actor, who had appeared in a wide variety of West End productions, as well as film and television. When he was working as an actor, he was obviously an out-of-work teacher, but didn't seem to mind.

'Hi guys...' Hyde-Jones said in his usual bright manner. 'For today's session, I thought that it would be fun to improvise a short play based upon your own family history. I am looking for something really impressive or better still some heroic incident which may have happened to your folks. We will split into groups of five, and spend a few minutes working on a script, and then we will act out the story for the rest of the class.'

The boys divided up as asked, and began to talk over ideas for their short dramas.

Calderman had been quick to conscript Nicky, Weatherill, Merry, and Trevill into his group.

'Right, chaps... does anyone have any heroic story which we can act out?' he asked.

'Oi think that Oi moight 'ave somethin' roight up your street,' said a smiling Trevill.

Trevill went on to explain about a relative of his that had played a key role in the French Resistance during the Second World War, and had been parachuted in behind enemy lines to engage the Germans in hand-to-hand combat under fire. This sounded great to the boys, who eagerly allocated character roles to each, with Trevill taking the part of Narrator. When lines and actions had been agreed and rehearsed, the group waited patiently for their turn to perform. Eventually, it was their turn to act out their play. Trevill took his position to the side of the group, and assumed the posture of what he hoped looked like a great actor about to deliver an Oscar-winning speech....

'Twas in the winter of 1940...' he began, 'when moi Auntie Brenda was secretly dropped by means of a parachute out of a plane above the forests of darkest Frrance...'

Nicky had been chosen to play the role of Auntie Brenda, and began the mime of leaping out of an aircraft and opening a parachute whilst scanning the ground below for danger.

'Now see, shee'm comin' down towards the ground under cover of darkness, and she be a-lookin' all around 'er for them German buggers in case they'm seen 'er, or maybe seen 'er parachute openin.'

(The other three boys grouped together, and began looking and pointing up to the sky, one of them grinding an imaginary cigarette out under the sole of his imaginary jackboot). Trevill continued...

'Now Auntie has spotted three German soldiers wot 'ave seen 'er on 'er way down, and she ain't too 'appy about that I can tell ee. She knows by crikey that she'm in for some rough stuff when she'm gettin' to the ground – so she'm beginin' to get ready for 'em.'

(Nicky was now performing a complicated mime involving searching for something about his person, whilst holding the parachute strap and looking down at the ground...)

'She'm takin' out 'er large hip flask wot she'm had in 'er pocket see, and she'm be whippin' the top off and guzzling down ev'ry last drop of brandy in the flask.

She'm be thinkin' that if she'm be goin' to get shot, then she'm takin' a few buggers with 'er.'

(The "troops" now pointed imaginary rifles up at the sky, having fixed bayonets...)

'Well I tell 'e, she'm comin' down a-lookin' at these 'ere Germans lookin' up at 'er and grinning.' And she lands on the ground and rolls, throwin' the hip flask at the first soldier. She'm pullin' out her pistol and shoots one of them, then kicks the other one dead 'ard in the goolies when 'er gun jams...

(The mock fight portrayed was quite impressive, although the glancing strike to the nethers did rather cause Merry's eyes to cross somewhat.)

'Now she'm out of ammo, well there's only one thing that she'm able to do – so she beats the last German to death with his own rifle before 'ee can grab 'er. Then she'm stormin' off still in a foul mood, and went off to join up with the rest of 'er comrades in the Resistance.

When she'm finally comin' 'ome loike, they'm givin' 'er a great big medal for 'er 'elp with the war and suchloike...'

(The defeated troops lay prone on the hall floor.)

Trevill bowed with great dignity to the audience like a seasoned professional, who burst into loud applause

'Gents – that was really fantastic!' said Hyde-Jones. 'I'm sure that we all really enjoyed that. Before we move on, who can tell us the most important thing about that story?'

Ashman raised his hand and answered, 'It proves that you don't piss about with Trevill's Auntie Brenda when she's had a drink...'

Chapter Eleven

Standing at the bus stop awaiting the good old "Mission Impossible" bus up to the village, Nicky was thinking about the friends which he had made during what was nearly the first full week at the Academy. He had made a pact with the little group of five that if they all stuck together, then there was an outside chance that they might actually get to survive their time at St Onan's. There were such a lot of issues which his inexperienced mind was unable to resolve, such as why there was such hatred displayed toward the poorer boys from the pupils whose parents enjoyed the trappings of wealth. There were times during the day when he longed to be back at his little primary school, with its happy children and comforting surroundings, and where education seemed to settle on the children like the blown petals of apple blossom. He knew that he was growing up now – but he was determined that however tall he might grow, he would not look down on people. His target was to achieve just enough height to enable him to poke Piper the prefect in the eye. Hard.

As he stood contemplating social justice, there was a squeal of tyres cornering under protest, and around the corner came the familiar shape of Uncle Joe's Zodiac. The car screeched to a halt just past the bus stop, then reversed back hurriedly mounting the kerb with a back wheel, and sending members of the public scurrying away in fear of their lives.

'Hey up, lad… sling your gear in quick,' said Uncle Joe.

Nicky did as he was told, and just as he managed to get the car door closed, Joe took off at supersonic speed, unnerving drivers behind him, and causing a vicar on a bicycle to double the cost of his weekly laundry bill.

'How are you doing, Uncle – What's the hurry?' asked Nicky.

'I'm being followed again by the bloody Gay Russian Secret Police – you know, the KYGB,' answered Joe with his usual grin.

Joe continued his regular "speed limits are merely a serving suggestion" style of driving up the road towards the big hill. As they reached the very top of the hill, Joe violently swung the car through an open farm gate and into the field, quickly turning off the engine and ducking down – but peering over the rear seat back at the road. A Morris Traveller laboriously climbed the last few feet of the hill and passed the opening to the field, with two elderly ladies in the front seats.

'Hah! Buggers missed me again...' laughed Joe.

'But that was just two old ladies, Uncle...' said Nicky.

'They were two men with beards when they followed me into town,' said Joe. 'They're a devious lot of buggers – but I'm onto 'em all right...'

'But they were women, Uncle, I could tell,' Nicky said hopefully.

'Still 'ad the beards though, didn't they Lad!' Uncle chuckled...

Reversing out of the field carefully, Uncle adopted a quizzical look on his face. He pulled out onto the main road without reference to personal safety or mirrors, and drove up to the bus stop outside Nicky's house.

'Now you're a man of wisdom and learning lad, I need to ask you an important question,' said Joe. 'Do you learn about medical science?'

'Well, I've only been at the school for a week, Uncle, and we've only had one real Biology lesson...' Nicky answered hesitantly.

'Good, that'll do for me – now, I need to ask you a personal and medical question,' said Uncle with a serious tone of voice. 'How far up is a rectal thermometer supposed to go... ?'

Nicky was both horrified and embarrassed at the question, and felt himself going red.

'I don't really know, Uncle....' he stammered, 'But I supp–

'Because the one that I've got only goes up to 80 degrees...' said Joe.

'I will try and find out for you Uncle,' said the relieved boy, and he gathered up his school stuff and shut the car door swiftly before Uncle could quiz him on any other medical topic.

As he watched the car disappear up into the village, he had a horrible vision of Uncle Joe involved in experiments with various kitchen thermometers, and made a mental note to remember to refuse a chicken sandwich at Joe's house if it were offered in the future.

Mum was in the kitchen preparing their dinner. Tonight it was one of Mum's world-beating stews, and it already smelled wonderful. Auntie was out in the garden, sitting on the bench side on the side lawn and selecting her latest batch of four-legged financial benefactors.

'Hello, love...' she smiled. 'How was today then?'

'It was okay, Auntie, but I just got a lift up from town with Uncle Joe, and he seemed a bit weird.'

'What – weirder than usual?' Auntie laughed. 'I think that might be because he has been in court again today...'

She explained that dear uncle had once again been summoned to attend the local Magistrates' Court. It was something that happened every so often, and usually as a result of Uncle's insistence that laws were only to be strictly applied to other people. This time his call to face the music had been the result of a hunting trip. He had appeared in front of an elderly and severe magistrate accused of deliberately shooting a Golden Eagle. This had sat very badly with the magistrate, who was quite a keen ornithologist in his spare time. Auntie recounted the details of the trial (as far as she could verify) which were as follows:

(Magistrate) 'You are accused, Mr Prentiss, of the wilful and premeditated killing of a species which is protected under the English law; that is, on the day of Saturday. 20 December you did knowingly discharge a firearm leading to the demise of one Golden Eagle. This event took place on the Vale marshes at approximately 07.40. What have you to say for yourself?'

(Uncle) 'I were out huntin' for duck, yer Honour. I was after a bird for our Christmas table – me not being able to afford the extortionate prices what them butchers and supermarkets is after chargin'. I was laid out in the marsh yer Honourship, at great personal risk as I am a martyr to me rheumatism. I sees this flight of ducks take to the air, and sails right over me 'ead. I raises me gun, your Warship, and takes aim at the back end of the group. Now just as I gets ready to shoot, I sees this dirty great big bugger (pardon my Greek) fly right up behind them at a good speed, so I thinks 'I'll 'ave you matey' – and I fired at it.'

(Magistrate) 'And you shot it?'

(Uncle) 'Right up the ar– at the rear, sir, your Honourship.'

(Magistrate) 'Were you aware that it was an eagle – and hence protected under law?'

(Uncle) 'No sir, your Majesty – I saw it had a different coloured head, and assumed that it was one of them foreign species of duck what is comin' over here, and taking the bread out of the beaks of good honest British ducks on their ponds.'

(Magistrate) 'You thought it was a duck...?'

(Uncle) 'Yes, Mallard, I did.'

(Magistrate) 'And may I enquire as to what you did with the Eagle in question?'

(Uncle) 'We ate it, sir, Honour...'

(Magistrate) 'You actually plucked, cooked and ate a Golden Eagle?'

(Uncle) 'Well the lamb chops were out of date your Sirship...'

(Magistrate) 'Well I am astounded. The killing of a protected species is a very serious matter indeed, but I am mindful that your actions may have been somewhat born out of domestic necessity, and not malice. Before I consider what penalty I am to impose upon you, I am forced by curiosity to ask one more question – what does Golden Eagle taste like?'

(Uncle) 'A little bit like swan, your Honour...'

Auntie was unable to verify what penalty the magistrate had imposed on Joe, but just the story had the pair of them crying with laughter for a good fifteen minutes, until Mum came out to ask if everything was all right.

With tears of merriment still marking their faces, Auntie and Nicky went back into the kitchen and sat at the table, and tried to eat without laughing. All went reasonably well until Mum said, 'I thought that I might roast us a duck on Sunday...' It would take a while to clean the wall and remove all traces of airborne stew...

In a rare moment of conscientious planning, Nicky had decided to get all of his prep work done as soon as dinner was finished. Auntie took a particular interest in helping him with the various tasks set – and displayed an impressive knowledge on a vast range of subjects. He was deciding which extinct animal to classify as part of his Biology work, and asked Auntie for advice.

'Mrs Jenkins...' she replied. 'No question about it.'

'But she isn't extinct, Auntie,' said Nicky.

'Sorry, dear, I thought you asked me to suggest something that stinks... I don't think that she needs to be classified – probably sanitised would be better.'

He settled on a dinosaur called Ankylosaurus, drew the creature with extreme care in his workbook, and wrote a classification for it. Five more to go – so he added a horse, dog, next door's cat, a goldfish, and Dave the chicken (who had mysteriously managed to peck and undo his shoe laces under the table) (that's Nicky's shoes – not Dave's by the way). Since it was now late in the evening, and there was nothing much in the way of entertainment on the television, he decided to read the book which he had been given for his birthday, on the subject of interstellar travel, other planets, and UFOs. He didn't remember falling asleep, but obviously must have been dreaming, as the female inhabitant of the distant planet with three suns asked him, 'Would you like a cup of tea, dear?' In the dream he had been attempting to classify the strange plant which had crept up to his side, and tried to snap at his gloved fingers as he wrote.

'Don't be too late out of bed Nicky – remember you have school in the morning,' his Mother reminded him.

'Can't I tell them that I can't go?' he asked.

'What excuse would you give?' said Mum.

'I could tell them that Saturday school is forbidden – because I'm Jewish...' he answered.

'Well, it's no skin off my nose...' Auntie helpfully added.

As it turned out, there was an old Hammer Horror film on the television a little later, starring dear old Christopher Lee as the evil Count Dracula, and the wonderful Van Helsing as his nemesis, played by the true gentleman – Peter Cushing. Crosses were waved about, stakes were poked into deserving victims, ladies in wispy night dresses were duly nibbled, canine teeth were displayed prominently and old Drac' dissolved into a kind of smoky soup at the end – all in all, a great night's entertainment. Good triumphed over evil, and we could all sleep safely in our beds once again. For a few minutes, the film distracted Nicky's mind from the fact that he would have to go back to school in the morning. As the dramatic closing music played out, and the credits rolled, he kissed his mother and Auntie, and made his way up to bed. (He did however, take a few moments to ensure that his bedroom windows were locked, well, you can't be too careful...)

The bright new day dawned, and it also dawned on Nicky that he could well do without it. There was something deeply unnatural about having to attend school on a Saturday morning – even if it was only until lunchtime. He felt that a part of his comfortable life had been stolen by posh people who could well afford their own Saturday mornings- so they should keep their upper class hands off his. It felt a bit like getting up earlier than normal when you were setting off on holiday, but he knew that this morning was certainly not going to involve any paddling. There were, however, quite a few donkeys in evidence at the Academy.

Nicky got himself dressed very reluctantly, and got his school stuff together whilst he munched grudgingly on a piece of toast. Dave the chicken followed him as he meandered around the kitchen, picking up any stray crumbs that had made a bid for freedom. The bird paused, and regarded Nicky with the contented (and a little smug) look of chickens everywhere. Nicky saw this, and said to Dave, 'And what do you plan to do with your free Saturday morning eh?'

Dave answered, 'I shall preen, I shall exercise, I shall eat breakfast, but mostly I shall bemoan the fact that I do not belong to a highly-evolved species which can enjoy the benefits of civilised education and learning available to all...' (This is what Dave actually said, whereas Nicky only heard the usual clucking of a domestic fowl under the table.)

Mum called out to him, 'Are you ready to go? You don't want to miss the bus...'

'It's okay, Mum, I'm getting a lift with Gerry's mum – they come through the village on their way into town,' he answered.

He gathered up a couple of stray books, and carefully picked up the Ninja Satchel, taking care to avoid being garrotted by the shoulder strap. He kissed his mother, shouted 'See you later, Auntie' out of the back door, and slouched up the garden path. Even though (as far as he saw it) his morning had already been ruined, there were other garden inhabitants who were already enjoying the sunshine. Butterflies were skittering from flower to flower all the way up the path. Birds were singing loudly from their perches on the telephone poles, although Nicky could clearly see that some of them didn't actually know the song, and thus were miming along just for the look of it. At the top of the pole nearest the bus stop, he noticed a large black bird with what looked from this distance like a small Gibson Explorer guitar slung casually around its neck. Rook and Roll.

After a few minutes, a small car came around the church corner, and pulled into the bus stop in front of him. As the car came to a halt, he could see several faces, all pressed up against the rear windows. The front door of the car was opened for him, by the driver – Gerry's mother. In the back of the car were Gerry, Jim Jackson, Gerry's younger brother, Danny, and Alfie, their rotund black Labrador dog. This was not a dog that could be used as an excuse for not handing in homework, ('Sorry, sir – the dog ate it') but looked very much as if it may well have eaten another of Gerry's siblings. Nicky said, 'Good morning, all,' to them, and climbed into the front seat- with the satchel making a last gasp attempt to restrain him as it hooked itself over the open door. He put on his seat belt just as Gerry's mother swung out into the road at speed. He was immediately terrified in case Uncle Joe should be coming in the opposite direction – this was one meeting which could prove catastrophic.

Gerry's mother tried talking to Nicky, but was all but drowned out by the sudden cacophony of sound which came from all angles as all of the occupants of the car tried to talk at once. Even Alfie the dog joined in, barking loudly and happily, whilst slobbering over the back of the seat into Nicky's ear. Young Danny was insistent in showing Nicky his model aeroplane and this was thrust in front of his face almost taking out his right eye in the process. How the very tall figure of Jim Jackson had managed to fold himself into the cramped space in the rear of the vehicle was a complete mystery. He was bent over like a paper clip, and was pinned back by (and under) the weight of the exuberant dog. With the bombardment of noise from the people in the car, constant airstrikes by a lone fighter plane, bumping from Jim's knees in his back, and attacks from the Hound of the Basketcases, the car weaved its way down to the town. As they pulled up outside the Academy, the noise abruptly ceased. Nicky flung open the front passenger door, and released himself from the Bedlam within. The other boys squeezed themselves out of the rear seats, looking like the ten or more clowns at the circus who emerge from a car clearly built for two. Gerry's mum called out 'I'll be back later to pick you all up...' but Nicky had already planned to avoid another nightmare journey, and walk home if necessary. He thanked Gerry's mum for the lift, and tried to force Alfie's huge head back into the car before he closed the door. The walk across the road to the Academy gates was almost relaxing....

There was no assembly on a Saturday, so it was into the form room for register, then on to their first lesson.

The boys sat in the Geography classroom for a few minutes, staring at the empty master's desk at the front. Since there was no imminent danger of education taking place, conversations began around the room. Nicky was busy telling Calderman, Merry and Trevill just how bad it was to have to attend school on a Saturday. At this point, Lordsley spun around in his seat and pointed at Nicky, declaring, 'Well I do not for one moment expect a Day Boy to acknowledge the benefits of a full programme of top-grade education, some of us are only too happy to realise the advantages which an extended academic week presents. I intend to use my education to ensure that I get a good job, perhaps in the banking sector – whereas you will probably not aim any higher than working in a local factory; but I am sorry if it has disrupted your potato-picking...'

He turned back to face the front of the class, smirking as he did so, expecting his fellow classmates to join in the verbal attack.

Calderman was having none of this, and jumped up angrily. He turned to face the smug pupil, leaning over and placing both his hands flat on the desk.

'You could do with an extended programme of manners – you pompous little tit,' he began. 'It's people like you with that attitude that have caused revolutions, and driven a wedge between the Haves and Have-nots. When Daddy was writing out the cheque to pay for your fees to come here, he should have invested a little more cash and bought you some bloody humility. Why don't you save up your pocket money and buy some?'

'I do not get pocket money,' said Lordsley, shrinking down into his desk.

'Are you saving up to buy a chin then? said Calderman.

'Shallow chins are a sign of good breeding...' replied Lordsley.

'A sign of bloody inbreeding more like!' said an angry Nicky.

At this point, Trevill stood up and spoke. 'Oi reckons that Ee reminds Oi of the fittins on one of them there Chipp-en-dale antique soideboarrds...'

'What, unique and worth a lot of money?' said Lordsley, grinning.

'No – I mean you're a knob...'

When the gale of laughter had subsided, the class were surprised as the door opened, and Mr Thwaite came into the room looking somewhat flustered.

'Sorry I'm late, boys, I was sitting waiting in the wrong classroom,' he said.

'Now, I have marked your prep work – and very good some of it was too. This morning we will begin to look at rock folding and faulting – as well as briefly touching the subject of volcanoes. Did I miss something?'

The master could sense that he had just missed some event in the class, and whilst noting the grins on some of the boys' faces, he could also pick up on the looks of contempt which were directed in the general direction of Lordsley.

'Right then, chaps... I've got some printed sheets for you to look at which will tell you all about rock faulting and locations of the great valley faults – if I can find them...'

Thwaite walked over to the door, and before any of the boys could warn him, had disappeared out into the corridor gain. He reappeared looking baffled, then successfully located the stationery cupboard, and went inside. Shortly, there was a thud, and a large globe of the world rolled out of the door, until it was deftly fielded by Merry. The master emerged with a puzzled expression declaring, 'I'm damned if I know who keeps moving this stuff around.' Undaunted, he strode to the blackboard and began to draw diagrams on it – at least he would have done, had the stick of chalk not actually turned out to be a white plastic pen top.

He turned back and sat in his desk chair. Pulling out each of the drawers in turn, he hunted for the errant chalk. There was soon a pile of items stacked up on the desk, which more closely resembled the products available on the cosmetics counter at the local pharmacist – with nail polish, lip gloss, blusher powder, bottles of face cleanser, lipsticks (of various violent hue) and hairsprays all on full view.

'No... Not a useful thing in the whole drawer,' said Thwaite. 'We'll just have to discuss the subject between ourselves until I find some more chalk – sorry.'

He paced between the desks and handed back each boy his prep workbook. As he passed, Nicky noticed two things. One was how the master's nails were shaped and polished in a very similar manner to his mother's, and the other thing was the smell of a perfume with which he was familiar. It was pleasant, but not what you might call a 'manly' fragrance. Still, it was probably one of those ridiculously expensive new aftershaves which they were always advertising? If he wasn't very much mistaken, he got the distinct impression that Mr Thwaite was wearing mascara...

Much embellished in the eye department as he was, Mr Thwaite kept the boys spellbound with his very detailed descriptions of volcanic activity, and the havoc that Mother Earth could wreak upon her children seemingly at will. Absorbed with horrified interest were the examples of the 1902 Mont Pelee blast, and the more recent fury of the Mount St Helens eruption. There was a slight confusion when the difference between "Pompeii" and 'Pompey' had to be explained in a bit more detail to Trevill, but apart from that, the class hungrily absorbed all of the gory details concerning vulcanicity. There should really have been a slide presentation with which to illustrate some of the features discussed: however, true to form, Mr Thwaite had a) mislaid the slides, b) somehow lost the projector screen, and c) had absolutely no idea where he had put the spare bulb for the projector. Had he been born a chicken, then Nicky suspected that the man might well have been able to mislay his own eggs.

The class had enjoyed the lesson, which was over far too soon for them. Mr Thwaite dismissed them at the sound of the bell, and they left the room with the sight of him desperately patting himself down in order to locate another missing item.

For their English class, they were back in the classroom, where Mr Hyde-Jones was sprawling in his chair in jeans and rugby shirt. He looked slightly pale, and was about to swallow a glass of something fizzy.

'Hello. guys...' he declared. 'Bear with me, we had a bit of night out with an actor friend of mine, and I ended up like Sir Toby.'

Nicky couldn't resist it – 'Was it your twelfth night, sir?'

Hyde-Jones smiled at the boy, and said, 'Nice one!'

'Okay, chaps, I think today we will begin to look at poetry. Now before you all start groaning, poetry can be a very forceful and beautiful medium – it's not all about roses, daffodils and lacy shirts. Does anyone know any famous poems?'

Ashman stood and impressively recited a part of "The Rime of the Ancient Mariner" by Samuel Taylor Coleridge.

Jackson arose and treated the class to Walter De La Mare's "The Listeners".

Merry went for one of Spike Milligan's finest nonsense poems.

Trevill (not wanting to be left out) stood, cleared his throat, and beautifully enunciated, 'There once was a man from Nantucket, whose –

'Yes, well, Mr Trevill, strictly speaking that's a limerick- which we haven't got onto yet, but thank you for your contribution,' said the master hurriedly.

'See, we all know some poetry. When the poet does his (or her) job correctly, the words reach into our mind and soul. Poems can be about the man in the street, or the man in the moon, but if it stirs something in the reader, then it works. Whilst I try and get my head to calm down, I want you all to attempt a short poem on any subject that you like – and don't be afraid of the spelling; I want to get the feeling from what you have written.

There was much rustling of paper and frowns of concentration from the boys as they searched for the muse which would inspire them to compose their odes. Pen tops were chewed, and windows were stared out of, in the hope that inspiration might be written in the clouds in rhyming couplets. For some time, the loudest sound in the classroom was the fizzing of Hyde-Jones' hangover cure dissolving in its glass on his desk.

Having drained the magic potion and returned to the world of pain-free sobriety, Hyde-Jones called the class to attention.

'Okay, My Little Shakespeares; let's see how you got on.'

There were one or two quite passable attempts from the boys. A couple of the sonnets were obvious "lifts" of song lyrics, and some seemed to be thinly-disguised parodies of current television advert jingles. The master paced around the room whilst he studied the individual writings which the boys had submitted. Nicky had written nothing. He was still smarting from the comments which Lordsley had made earlier, and could raise no enthusiasm for the task in hand at all. Hyde-Jones did not show any emotion at all as he viewed the blank piece of paper which Nicky had handed in, and merely turned over to the next boy's work.

'Well done, boys, we've got some really good work here,' said Hyde-Jones. The master put all but one of the sheets of paper on his desk, and held up one particular offering.

'I like all of your attempts, but this one for me captures everything which I asked you to consider when writing your poems. It contains humour, tragedy, and is concise enough to make an impact upon the reader. Mr Merry – perhaps you would do us all the honour of reading out your work to the class?'

Merry stood up, rather embarrassed, and took back his paper from the master. He looked around the class, and then read:

'It is an ill wind that blows nobody any good-

And that is why we don't stand behind Granddad.'

'Now that, Gents – is poetry' said Hyde-Jones.

Looking at the clock, the master said, 'Well now that time has beaten us, we will carry on with some more in our next lesson. Have a think about which poems you find really interesting, and don't be afraid to try some more of your own! Thanks for your efforts, and I will see you on Monday.'

The boys began to pack away their books. They filed out of the room in an orderly manner, and Nicky was trying to hide himself away amidst the throng. He had almost reached the door when the inevitable happened – Hyde-Jones called him back.

In a calm voice, Hyde-Jones asked him, 'Not able to come up with anything today, Shepherd?'

'No, sir, sorry, sir, I just couldn't do it,' Nicky answered.

'Didn't see you at the play auditions – did you not want to be in it?' asked the master.

'Something came up, sir – I couldn't get there on time,' Nicky responded.

'That's a shame. Can I just ask – is everything all right; is anything worrying you?'

'No – I'm okay, sir; I just had a bit of a row with Lordsley, sir...'

'What was all that about then?'

'I've only been here a week, sir, and I'm already sick of being treated like a peasant by the snobby kids. I didn't even want to come here in the first place. I probably will end up in a factory – like they keep telling me.'

Hyde-Jones slowly shut the drawer to his desk. He took a piece of paper, and wrote four names on it. He pushed the piece of paper over the desk to Nicky. 'Have you heard of these chaps?' he asked.

'Dickens, Defoe, Shakespeare and Einstein? – Well yes, everyone has.'

'Right... Dickens – son of a newspaper reporter: Defoe – was a hosier by trade, Shakespeare was the son of a wool-stapler, and Albert Einstein was a patents clerk. Where you have come from is not who you are – and certainly not who you may turn out to be. Boys like Lordsley need their butler to tell them which end to wipe, so don't pay any attention to them. Just be yourself, and try your hardest. Try to turn the other cheek, and if that doesn't work – then kick them so hard that they end up with three Adam's apples! Go on, lad... get to your next lesson.'

Nicky hurried over the quad to the music room. He caught up with the tail end of his classmates as they filtered into the large, airy space. There was the usual huge blackboard at the front of the class, but around three of the walls were a variety of various shaped cases – no doubt containing exotic and interesting musical instruments. Into the room came the master which all of the boys now recognised as Mr Newhouse.

'Hi, boys...' he began. 'Grab a chair and get settled in. I will run through the register, so those of you that are here can answer to your name, and anyone who is absent needn't bother!'

Now this was more like it... Nicky thought that this might prove to be a good lesson.

'We are going to start today with a listen to some Classic music,' said Mr Newhouse.

'I presumed that we would be learning Music Theory, sir?' said Jackson.

'That's right, we will do all that quavery, crotchet and minim stuff later, and I can assure you, when I've finished with you, Jackson, you will be able to sight-read fly shi – droppings...'

'Can I ask a question, sir?' Lordsley said, hand raised. 'What is the instrument sticking out of the tall case against the wall over there?'

'I call it the great big wooden tube with the pipe sticking out of it,' replied the master.

'I think it is a bassoon, sir...' smarmed the boy.

'You may well be correct, Lordsley, or it may be a bong belonging to a very tall Hippie' said Newhouse.

'Papa said that I may well be getting one for Christmas, if I do well with my reports,' Lordsley stated without any trace of embarrassment.

'Then you will be an extremely fortunate fellow,' said the master 'I can assure you that there is no finer instrument for gaining the attention and respect of the opposite sex, than the bassoon. You will be guaranteed to be beating them off with a stick; mark my words.'

All but Lordsley appreciated the intended humour. The master continued,

'Okay – now we are going to listen to, and appreciate a recording of supreme musical ability displayed at its very highest level.' (Mr Newhouse crossed over to the large wooden-boxed record deck, and carefully placed an album onto the turntable).

'I am sure that you will agree that this is one of the finest recordings ever produced. It displays orchestration of the highest quality, and subtle usage of diatonic and harmonic scales. This recording is one of the most perfect and grandiose compositions which it will ever be your privilege to hear. Gentlemen, I shall now play for you the album entitled *A Night at the Opera* by Queen...'

Nicky had to pinch himself, and there was much head-nodding with respect from Calderman, Merry and the gang of five. His faith in the God of Saturdays had been restored – at thirty-three and one third revolutions per minute.

Their teacher was taking full advantage of the music, which was being hurled out of the massive classroom speakers at the volume which Mr Mercury and the boys would approve of. There was much "air guitar" in evidence, with Nicky and several of his friends joining in on the old "Gibson Glenn Miller" model.

They admired the arrangements, they joined in on the complex and multi-layered harmonies, and there was the head-banging which is compulsory by law during the end section of "Bohemian Rhapsody". When the album ended with Brian May's arrangement of the National Anthem, the boys as one, stood to attention and saluted. So did Mr Newhouse, who raised one arm in a Freddie-type gesture as the music faded out....

'I am not going to make any further comment, guys...' said the teacher, 'but for your homework, get your ears wrapped around as much Queen as you can, and write me a small review on what you have listened to. I will see you all next time, so until next week (he turned, deftly slipped into his leather biker's jacket, and paused at the now open door), Ladies and Gentlemen... Newhouse has left the building.'

Mr Newhouse smiled to himself as he walked down the corridor to the sound of applause from the boys in the classroom.

So he had managed to survive a whole week at St Onan's, give or take the odd incident, without loss of life or limb. As the boys made their break for freedom out of the gate, the relief that Nicky felt was almost physical. There was a lot of Saturday still to be used, and once he had rid himself of his "prison uniform" he intended to do just that.

Little did any of the boys know, that one member of the class had already made his own personal break for freedom. DeVere had "borrowed" one of the long climbing ropes from the gymnasium, and had let himself into one of the unused classrooms which faced onto Church Street. Climbing onto the window cill, he had gently levered open one of the leaded windows, secured the rope around the cast-iron handle, and lowered himself down to street level. He was at this moment planning his route homeward, whilst sitting munching a packet of crisps on the top deck of a local bus heading out toward the city of Lincoln. His school jacket turned inside-out; he gave no indication of his fugitive status. Certainly, his disappearance would be noticed soon, but by that time he would be well on his way home. He would miss his new friends, but that gloomy, draughty, spooky old boarders' dormitory could kiss his escaped arse goodbye...

Nicky pretty much sprinted to the bus stop and dived onto the bus. The climb up the hill seemed to take ages, and he was praying that today would not be one of the days when the old charabanc decided to have an asthma attack and halt in the road. Miraculously, the rusting red coach climbed the hill with ease, and he ran down the garden path and round to the back kitchen door. Books were hurled onto his bed: school uniform was replaced by tee-shirt and jeans, and the still stiff school shoes were flicked off unceremoniously to a position somewhere in the shadows under his bed.

Auntie was digging in the back garden. Actually, she was having a cigarette and chatting to her friend the robin, who habitually came to perch on the handle of the spade every time she tended to the vegetable patch.

'How was Saturday school then?' she asked.

'Well it was as rubbish as the rest of the week, until we had the music class – then we got to listen to Queen, at proper volume, Auntie,' he replied.

'Great – right then, let me finish off here, and we'll have a cuppa,' declared Auntie.

Over a very welcome cup of tea, Nicky asked Auntie if there had been any further developments in the "Joe versus an Illegal Eagle" saga. It transpired that the magistrate had requested time to deliberate before passing judgement and handing down a suitable penalty to Uncle. At some point soon after, the gentleman was visited in his chambers by a heavily disguised figure in a trilby hat, dark glasses, and overcoat. The visitor claimed to be a member of the Wildlife Protection Agency (covert operations division), and would only identify himself by the codename of "Deep Stoat".

Certain grainy but unmistakable photographic images had been revealed to the magistrate, which appeared to show the gentleman himself engaged in, shall we say, practices of an exotic and highly specialised athletic pursuit (certainly for a man of his advanced years). It was inferred that there was a very real danger of these images coming to the attention of the local press. This could of course, be avoided, and the whole matter hushed up by Agency intervention – in return for the dismissal of charges relating to a certain legal case which was ongoing at this present time.

Uncle had been released by the court shortly after this clandestine encounter, and had been told by the magistrate that he considered that 'the whole incident had been caused by a case of mistaken identity'. No charges were brought, and the case was dismissed.

Chapter Twelve

There would be no visit to the town to see the local football team play today. The "Chessies" were playing away at the ground of some smaller town further north. His home side, whilst enjoying incredibly loyal and vocal regular support, were to be perfectly honest a bit of a let-down in the results department. They were suffering a bit of a spell in the doldrums at the present time, and could often be seen taking part in the goal celebrations of the opposing team. Things had got so bad, that the team had taken to doing a lap of honour if they won the toss.

'Don't forget that it's the Late Goose Fair up on the green tomorrow,' Auntie reminded him.

'Not sure I'm going this year, Auntie...' Nicky answered.

'Why not? Remember the fun we had last year when we clamped Mr Wragley's mobility scooter?' said Auntie, with a wry grin.

The "Late Goose Fair" was a village event which took place up at the top of the village on the playing field-cum-football pitch. It was a remnant of an ancient farmers' market ritual from a long time ago (as were some of the locals). It was usually very well attended; even when wind or horizontal rain sent objects sailing past (like some of the locals). There were a variety of stalls and rides to try, as well as the usual tents where prizes were awarded for the best flower display, best cake, and best garden produce- with a special award for the most humorously-shaped vegetable (again, possible mistaken for one of the locals). It was a guaranteed meet-and-greet hotspot where you could catch up on all manner of local gossip, or perhaps start a few rumours of your very own after visiting the beer tent. Uncle always told the story of how he met his wife amongst the fragrant blooms of the flower tent: after which they spent hours walking and talking as they browsed amongst the stalls and rides. He always insisted that it was fete that had brought them together...

Auntie was back in the kitchen, scanning the racing pages of the daily paper as she checked her latest equine earners. She had obviously had a busy morning dealing with her latest "little project" which was housed in the shed. Because the elderflower crop had been so prolific this year, Auntie had decided to branch out and go into the production of elderflower wine. This variety would grace the shelves of the shed along with potato, parsnip, and a particularly lethal damson wine. Until the bottling process had been refined and perfected, there had been several disasters. One such recent "hitch" had been when the bottles containing the dangerous brew had not been able to contain the gases produced by the latter stages of fermentation – and had blasted their corks (and necks) skywards, punching several ragged holes in the corrugated plastic of the shed roof.

Placing some bottles of her finest potato wine in the fridge (to cool for after dinner) had inadvertently led Auntie down the road of freeze distillation. Having suddenly remembered the chilling wines in the fridge, she was forced to pour off the fluid which had not frozen – and bless my soul! It was a big hello to the world of homemade Schnapps... One small glass of this lethal liquid would ensure that Language was no longer your first language.

'They'll be setting up for the Goose this evening – are you going to help?' she asked Nicky.

'I might have a wander up later, and see what they are up to' he replied.

'It starts at eleven o'clock tomorrow, and don't let me forget to take half a dozen bottles of my "Chateau Shed" up with us – I'm entering it in the Best Local Produce contest.'

'But Auntie, you know that what your wine produces is unconsciousness...' said Nicky.

'Oh yes... but we won't tell 'em that just yet, will we?' laughed Auntie.

Nicky sat on the back door step gazing absent-mindedly at the end of the garden. Beyond the old wooden fence which marked the end of their lawn was the big field. He could see right across to the edges of the bomb crater, and he remembered the long summers when the gang had played there until dusk. He was tapping out a rhythm on his knees without really thinking, when suddenly, Dave the chicken landed in his lap. Auntie passed him out a cup of tea, which he placed at his side on the stone step. Gently, he stroked Dave's feathers, and the bird settled contentedly.

'It's a pity that you can't talk, Dave' he said. 'Sometimes you need to talk to someone who isn't family. If you can understand me, Dave – it's one peck for "no", and two pecks for "yes".

Great, he thought, now I am talking to a chicken. Maybe I should take you up to the fair and enter you in the "Cutest Pet" contest...Dave climbed off his lap, and began to scratch at the grass.

He stood up and took his tea into the kitchen. He sat at the table wondering what sort of welcome he might expect when he encountered the village kids. From the front room he heard the sound of the first of Auntie's horses winning at Doncaster. Soon, he became aware of another sound which grabbed his attention. After a few seconds he was astonished to discover the source of the tapping. Dave the chicken was busily pecking out 'one-two one-two' on the kitchen door...

Nicky called in to his Aunt, and told her that he was going to walk up to the top of the village, to see how the setting-up of the Fair was progressing. She called back,

'Okay – but if you happen to see Seaton's van parked up in the lane, don't forget to let his bloody tyres down.' Mr Seaton was an employee of the Water Board. There had been a severe disagreement over alleged damage to his van when it was parked in the lane behind their house. A thoroughly miserable individual, Seaton was now on the "wanted" list as far as Auntie was concerned – and a state of war between them was now in existence.

Setting off at a leisurely pace toward the Fair, Nicky heard a car sound its horn. Turning around, he saw Mikey leaning out of the passenger window 'Shep – we've lost Granddad.'

'Oh Mikey... I'm really sorry, he was a lovely bloke,' said Nicky.

'No, I mean we can't find him – he's wandered off again, so if you spot him could you see if you can get him to my house?'

Relieved, Nicky assured his friend that he would look for his grandfather.

'Thanks, mate, see you later... ' called out Mikey – and was gone.

Well that didn't seem so bad, thought Nicky, and with any luck, if I can find the old boy, I might actually get the lads to speak to me again. He decided to take the longer route up to the far end of the village. His walk took him up the long and leafy Church Lane, where the trees were now heavy with foliage, and formed a pastel green canopy overhead. It was only a short way up to the wooden bench seat at the brow of the small hill, where he had spent many hours sketching, or simply admiring the view out over the Vale of Belvoir and into the distance. Already sitting on the seat was a lone figure wearing a familiar cap.

Nicky approached the man and sat down next to him, a little distance apart, so as not to startle the gentleman.

'Hello, Mr Morris. How are you?' he asked.

'Fine, lad, fine...' came the reply from the smiling man.

'Enjoying the view?' Nicky enquired

'You know, lad, when I was a boy, all this was fields...'

'It still is all fields...'

'Cheeky bastard: I meant the new estate behind us...'

'Err... Sorry Mr Morris,' said Nicky. 'You know that your family are all looking for you?'

'Well they can keep bloody lookin' as far as I'm concerned,' he said. 'When you get to my age, lad, you get fed up to the back teeth with people talking at you- and not to you. I've probably forgotten more than that lot of buggers will ever learn, and they still treat me like I've lost me marbles,' said Mr Morris, now leaning on his walking stick.

'It's just that I've just spoken to Mikey, and he and his dad did seem really worried about you. I could walk back home with you – if that would be all right with you?'

'Aye, well, they'll be more worried still when they find out that I've booked up next week to go sky-diving...' said Mr Morris, with a satisfied grin on his face.

'Are you sure you will be okay to do that?' asked Nicky.

'Lad... I'm ninety-two, so what's the worst that can happen?' laughed Mr Morris.

'Then do it, enjoy it, and when I get a bit older you can show me how it's done!' said the boy.

Nicky knew that he had found a new friend in the old man, and was happy to convince him that he didn't need to be old if he didn't want to. They spent a long time sitting on the bench, laughing and talking until Nicky saw Mikey coming up the lane in the distance.

'Quick, Mr M – up the tree!' Nicky said (with no other 'cover' available).

The man seemed only too happy to oblige, and the two sat up in the branches stifling giggles as Nicky's friend passed right beneath their feet. When Mikey had gone to a safe distance, Nicky helped Mr Morris down from their hiding place.

The man was grinning like a Cheshire cat, and told the boy, 'Bloody marvellous, lad – I haven't done that in years!'

It was mutually agreed that a protest had been officially made, and a stand definitely taken. Nicky and Mr Morris began the walk back to Mikey's house on the new estate. As they rounded the corner and approached the drive to the house, Mr Morris swore Nicky to secrecy about their arboreal excursion, and his planned leap from a plane. They shook hands, Mr Morris straightened his cap (pulling a few stray leaves out of the brim) and winked at the boy as he strode defiantly back up to his front door.

Nicky thought that some things were so much better than seeing people putting up a few old stalls...

Saturday evening was proving to be quite peaceful. Uncle Joe was suspiciously quiet, none of their neighbours were engaged in family warfare, and Cousin Sheila had not been arrested (as far as anyone could ascertain). There was no need to do any of the homework given to him by his music teacher, because he could review note-for-note all of the songs ever recorded by Queen, and he bet that his Mum would be able to do the same.

After dinner the family settled down to watch a spot of television, but the fare on offer was the usual bland and uninteresting catalogue of game shows, so-called "trials" on a desert island involving neurotic z-list celebrities that no-one had heard of, and "talent" shows, where the performers' only skill was to get totally and utterly on one's tits. There was some fun to be had as a unicycling juggler set fire to his own bum, but all in all there was little to captivate the imagination. Even Dave the chicken was asleep on the other armchair. Nicky decided to set up his telescope on the side lawn and explore the heavens for an hour or two. He had only just set up the equipment, when a familiar head appeared around the hedge.

'Hey… ' called Mikey. 'Mind if I join you?'

The boys took turns at the eyepiece of the telescope, with Mikey acting as "navigator" using a red torch, so as not to ruin their night vision. He thanked Nicky for finding and bringing home his grandfather, but was not given any of the true details about what was said or done by the two of them. Mikey brought up the subject of tomorrow's fair, and asked if Nicky was going to be up at the fields. Uncharacteristically, he then apologised on behalf of the rest of the "gang" for tormenting his friend about his new school. 'I'm not a snob you know...' said Nicky, testing the water 'I was just lucky that I got into St Onan's.'

'No problem, and well, I just wanted to say, well done,' said Mikey. 'I know you've not gone all posh on us.'

At that moment, Mum came out and said, 'Oh hello, Michael. Nicky – your friend, Gerry, is on the phone, and he wants to know if you want to go horse riding with them tomorrow?'

Both of the boys burst out laughing, and Nicky replied, 'Tell him thanks, Mum, but I'm going up to the fair with my mates.' Mum disappeared back inside. Mikey smiled the smile of someone who has just witnessed a difficult test being passed.

Nicky asked Mike if he wanted a quick biscuit and a drink, and added, 'Why not try our house Cola – it's a particularly fine vintage, so Mother assures me...' More laughter, and the bond was re-established. The two boys continued to gaze in wonder at the stars for hours, until Mum came out and indicated that it had got a lot later than either of the boys were aware of. Mikey leaned over conspiratorially, as Nicky began to pack away the telescope, and whispered, 'I wanted to ask you something else...' Intrigued, Nicky paused and asked his friend what the big secret was. 'We want you to become a member of the PLO,' said Mikey. Now Nicky knew that the village gang were involved in a lot of scrapes and schemes around the area, but he had no idea that their influence had extended out as far as the Middle East... 'No, you twit, not them... I mean the Pig Liberation Organisation.' Mikey laughed.

'And that would be?' asked Nicky

'All will be revealed tomorrow, Comrade Shepherd... ' was his cryptic reply.

'Right – I'm in,' Nicky said without hesitation.

Tapping his nose to indicate secrecy, Mikey told his friend that they would meet up at eleven precisely, and all would get their orders then. Nicky waved to him as he left, and wondered what undercover mission he had just agreed to take part in. He went to sleep that night and dreamed of black-clad agents creeping silently through corridors, following the scent of cooking bacon which was wafting through the tunnels of the evil organisation's secret base.

He awoke early, with a lazy sun yawning its way above the horizon. Sundays were the day when he and Auntie would trawl the big fields and return with a haul of fresh mushrooms. They returned and enjoyed their free breakfast. These early mornings had a lovely "unused" feel to them, and the whole village was quietly waking up and yawning its way into the day.

Nicky had asked Mum if she was intending to take some of her excellent bread up to the fair and enter it in the cake competition – but she said that 'There was no way that she was having the whole village scrutinising and prodding at her buns...' Who could argue with that. Auntie however, had elected to bake a cake as a competition entry, although there would be a few raised eyebrows when the villagers saw the shape of it. (The answer is yes, before you ask, it was indeed what you were thinking). Nicky told them that he would head off up to the fairground, and would see them both later. He took his pocket money with him, and set off up the village.

The organisers of the fete must have worked since dawn broke, because all across the field there were various stalls and rides either fully completed, or in the latter stages of construction. Most impressive in the centre of the field was a huge merry-go-round. The vast mechanical ride shone with the gold, red and white fittings which were much in evidence all around it. Proudly painted in flowing script around the top of the ride was the legend "The Tattershall Flyers", and at the side of its mighty motor unit sat a gleaming, polished pipe organ. Nicky was fascinated by the huge carved animals on which the riders sat: there were of course horses, but also cockerels, ostrich, seahorses and zebra. Each was transfixed by a twisted golden pole, and even before it began moving, the open mouths of the collection of animals gave the impression of a stampede in progress.

At the very bottom of the field was a huge Victorian-type steam boat ride bearing the title "Cutty Sark". The vessel hung from an enormous iron cradle, and presumably swung on its armature to treat the riders to a significant amount of gravitational force. It looked like great fun, and Nicky couldn't wait to try it out later on.

Around the outer perimeter of the field stood a motley assortment of small tents and stalls which would soon be selling food, novelties and bric-a-brac to the unsuspecting villagers. One particular tent caught Nicky's eye as he passed. On a large placard which hung from the guy ropes of the tent was a sign proclaiming "Madam Jenkinski – Fortunes Told: She sees All – Tells All – and Knows All". According to Auntie, there was a word missing from that last statement, one which was certainly not going to appear in any of his Latin translations. He shuddered at the thought of being trapped in any confined space with the malodorous Mrs Jenkins...

Bland pop music began to blare out of the public address system set up at the field edge, and to his horror, Nicky noticed that the DJ was none other than Mr "All the charm of an open grave" Seaton. He noticed that the microphone tent was visible from all around the field – oh dear me...now all Auntie would need is a decent telescopic sight.

Before he could investigate any of the other offerings on show, Nicky was surrounded by the gang. They were all happy to see him, and Mikey led the group off to one side of the main show tent. They huddled round as nonchalantly as they could, and the mission was explained. 'In this tent...' whispered Mikey, 'will be housed the object of our undertaking. Later, Lowell the Butcher will be hosting the "Guess the weight of the pig-and win her weight in sausages" competition. This contest will feature as its star one Betsy, the pig. Our aim, gentlemen, is to liberate Miss Betsy from her shackles, and (when the tent is full to capacity) release said captive amongst the horde gathered within. We shall then observe what chaos may ensue, and piss ourselves laughing from a safe distance...'

The boys all nodded gravely. Mikey continued...

'Stewart, your role will be tent flap control and access.'

'Peter, you will be responsible for decoy and distraction.'

'Squid, you and your mission partner agent, Nicky, will deal with stake removal.'

'Agent Richard and myself will take care of tent flap sealing and covert photography. Mission will commence at 16.30 hours precisely. Is everyone clear on their duties?'

The boys nodded in assent.

'Good. We will reconvene here at 16.20 hours. I do not need to remind you that the details of this mission must remain absolutely Top Secret. Thank you gentlemen...'

Their orders received, the boys split up and blended in with the already swelling crowd (swelling in numbers that is, not in volume – well, mostly). Nicky was accompanied by Mikey and Squid, as they met up with Nicky's mum and Auntie. For some reason best known to herself, Auntie had brought Dave the chicken with them, and he sat cradled in her arm looking around in rapt fascination. Auntie enquired if there was the usual barbeque being held later on, and received what can only be termed as "a look" from Dave.

Over at the mystic tent of Madam Jenkinski, one brave soul had opted to put her psychic abilities to the test. This kamikaze punter was the local "Knight of the Roads", or colloquially, Edgar the tramp. He entered the tent cautiously and sat down on the threadbare padded armchair provided. Madam J swept in from behind a curtain, sat opposite the dishevelled figure, and without any trace of disapproval went immediately into her rehearsed speech.

'Good day, sir... I see that you wish Madam Jenkinski to help you see the future beyond the veil? Please grant a token that I may avail you of your future to come...'

'Yer what?...' grunted Edgar.

'A small boon that I may enlighten you, sir...' she said.

'What are Ye after Wumman?' said the as yet unenlightened Edgar...

'Two quid mate...' said a distinctly un-mystic Jenkinski.

A coin was passed from Edgar's greasy overcoat pocket, and was swiftly pocketed by the potential psychic. Rather than risk reading Edgar's palm (not a task to be undertaken by the faint-hearted) she opted for the good old crystal ball, and whipped off the silk cover in theatrical style.

'I see a man...' she intoned. 'A man who has set off on a long journey... I see this man walking a long distance over many roads toward his goal... He will traverse a great many streets in his search for happiness. Many will ask the reason for his wandering, and yet he will answer them not... For he must continue his questing until he shall find that which he most desires... '

'The bog... ' said Edgar. 'I come in 'ere lookin' for the bog. Where is the kharzi?'

'Big tent opposite the main gates,' Madam J instructed.

'Ta very much,' said Edgar, and thus enlightened, set off to enlighten himself a little.

It was always a mystery to the people of the town and village just how come Edgar managed to support himself. Although never actually employed, and certainly of shall we say, a somewhat advanced vintage, he always seemed to have about his person the wherewithal to feed himself and others (if he took a liking to them). He didn't swear, dribble or mutter, and if you were able to peer closely behind the grey bushy beard, seemed quite a decent sort of fellow. Few people knew that he was in fact a multi-millionaire, who had one day had a "Damascus Moment" at his desk in his plush London office, hurled his heavy inkwell at the wall, shouted, 'I've had about enough of this bollocks!' and had grabbed his overcoat and set off to walk home. Since that day, he had become a well-known feature and tourist attraction for the area. Approximately sixty-three per cent of all photographs taken in the town centre would be guaranteed to contain an image of the smiling Edgar somewhere in the frame. Local farmers would make sleeping places for him during the summer months in their barns and haystacks – and these were known as "Ed-Beds".

It is thus that he survived the Jenkinski incident, thanks to total anosmia. Emerging from the "little boys tent" Edgar was greeted warmly by several of the local children. He was incredibly popular with all of the kids, and you would be very hard pushed indeed, to find an adult who wasn't fond of "Uncle Edgar". He would often be seen chatting to children and ensuring that they were playing safely, and had the additional attraction that he could usually be found with a kitten in one of his deep pockets. Cats would home in on him when he came into view, and he would talk to them like old friends. In the towns and cities, he found that he soon became the same as other homeless souls on the street – invisible, and regarded as part of the everyday street furniture. Here in the countryside and the villages, he was not moved on, but welcomed and respected (not to mention cherished) by the people who knew him as a free spirit.

Spirits of a different description were disappearing down the necks of quite a few villagers in the beer tent. Uncle Joe was busily engaged in an animated discussion with a friend, whilst sipping merrily on a pint of 'Chateau Youpay' as was his wont. He had obviously been offered meat from a local poacher, and was not happy at the price which he had been asked to pay.

'So he offers me eight legs of venison for £70...' said Joe.

'What did you tell him?' asked his confidant.

'I told him that I thought that was too dear...' answered Joe.

Joe's immaculate car was parked at the side of the beer tent (just in case). Such was his fearsome reputation for "little modifications" to the security system, that it remained untouched by any inquisitive hands.

Mum, Auntie and Nicky had just thoroughly enjoyed their ride on the big carousel, which felt like riding in the Grand National. They climbed down laughing and happy, ready to move on to the next treat. It was at that point that Auntie spotted Seaton...

However the stall-keeper had managed to persuade him, Seaton was standing in a set of mock stocks, with his head and hands poked through cut-out holes in the frame. The victim was then pelted by soaking wet red sponge balls for two pounds a go by the public. Before the man had the chance to be released from the device which held him captive, Auntie quickly paid her money and dipped her hand into the bucket of water to soak her missiles. The first two direct hits had answered the question for Nicky, as to why Auntie had insisted he buy six of the rosiest red apples which he could find. The now unconscious Seaton was unchained, and Auntie politely asked to move on...

Joe meanwhile, had prised himself out of the beer tent and joined the long queue for the swingboat. There had been a furious argument between himself and Mr Norman Butterley, the owner-manager of the local "Save-U-More" supermarket. Butterley had commandeered the swingboat for the purposes of having a publicity photograph taken. All of the staff from his village store sat embarrassed in their full store uniform (designed by Butterley) in the rows of seats on the ride. The man himself demanded that the rest of the queue should wait until he had enough publicity shots taken (with Butterley in the middle of course). Joe had taken great exception to this, and the conflict was nearly at the coming-to-blows point. Butterley stamped to the 'bow' of the ride, and instructed the operator to set the ride in motion to get in some action shots of his team. Joe had disappeared around the back towards the motor, and unnoticed, had made 'a little tweak' to the mechanism.

Seeing Joe still in his field of camera shot, Butterley angrily confronted him, and the two men stood toe to toe shouting at each other as the ride began to pick up speed. Joe had mentally calculated exactly what he needed to do next. As the boat completed its upward swing and began the downward descent, he leaned forward into Butterley's face with a dangerous look in his eyes. Butterley leaned back to avoid the irate Joe, just as the end of the bow approached. Joe's calculation had been perfect. The very end of the bow caught under the collar of Butterley's coat, and he was lifted into the air on the upswing. Flailing his arms around in panic and terror, he managed to unhook his coat from the end of the ride, but the rising force now carried him high over the adjacent hedge and into the next field.

Which was unfortunately where the week's pig manure had been carefully heaped.

Joe, the ride operator, the assembled queue of villagers, and the entire staff of "Save-U-More" heard the sound of their manager impacting onto something soft, wet and unpleasant. In seconds, Butterly had freed himself from the mire, and came through the hedge toward Joe looking like the Creature from the Black Latrine. 'You bastard.,' he squealed, 'I'll bloody kill you for this.'

He never got the chance. As he got within striking range, Joe swung his polished brogue up with considerable force and caught the man squarely in the groin. As he fell clutching his injury, Joe informed him 'unexpected item in shagging area....'

There are certain immovable laws which govern any celebratory gathering of English people the length and breadth of the land. One of these laws is having a large poster advertising the outdoor event which prominently states that there will be an appearance by The Red Arrows, and then states "indoors if wet". Apart from tropical rain, which will sneak up to the site of any event and instantly transform the area into a paddy field, there is one other compulsory feature which strikes fear into the heart and soul of all who are forced to endure it. I refer to the scourge of an English summer... Morris Dancers.

Now there are great historic and traditional Morris dances (such as the Lancashire Nutty Dance and the eerie Black Morris) which are perfectly acceptable as illustrations of thousands of years in rural culture and folklore. A bunch of ill-rehearsed twats in bowler hats, waistcoats, loose white cricket flannels, and bells do nothing to recreate years of cherished English folk tradition. Having Kevin from the HR department ponce around waving a bladder on a stick makes him no friends whatsoever. Let's be honest with each other shall we? The only reason that we pay the motley crew of middle managers any attention at all is in the hope of seeing them fracture each other's fingers when they do the "cross staves" move.

As the assortment of college lecturers and library assistants prepared to take away the crowds' will to live, Auntie was already toe-to-toe with one of the participants.

'Madam... (oops – bad start son...) we are recreating some of the dances which have been performed in these parts for hundreds of years – it is an old tradition,' said the man

'So are rickets and the Plague... ' answered Auntie.

'We must keep history alive...' he pleaded.

'Which local historic tribe wore Nike trainers then eh?' she countered.

'Dear lady... (I would duck now, if I were you mate.) this is a dance performed by local agricultural workers from hundreds of years ago,' he stammered.

'Listen, mush, go back a couple of hundred years, and you would find that the only people who wore bells were lepers. We've all come up here to have a good day out, not to hear what you did on "The Merry Morn of some Rilly-Dilly Day-o". Chances are that if you did indeed "Espy a fair Maiden" then she would have seen you for the prat you are, and kicked you squarely up the "Fol-De-Wack-De-Fiddle-O".'

Distressed and defeated, the fellow jingled off toward the beer tent to hurl one down his Neckie-o.

(Historic note: The local tradition of dancing in this fashion stems from a harvest supper dance reputed to have been held in the village in around 1604. There were two of the village girls engaged deeply in conversation as to who they should select as their partner for the evening. There were two unaccompanied males to choose from – one was the local vicar's son, and the other a Morris dancer. One of the girls was not certain that the clergyman's offspring would provide all of the "entertainment" which she was seeking, and so was urged by her friend to 'Pulle thee other wonne – iyt haf gotte bloody bellf on...')

Zero hour for their mission was fast approaching, and across the field the boys were casting furtive glances at each other. Mikey and Nicky were over with Mum and Auntie, watching the finals of the children's fancy dress competition. This had in fact been won for the last two years running by Peter and Squid, who would enter the contest as the racehorse, Shergar, and then fail to turn up. Isabella Hislop had of course won the contest hands-down, dressed in some strange and multi-layered costume reminiscent of Marie Antoinette. Nicky was looking around for a guillotine, and Auntie had won £25 betting on the outcome.

As the time drew near, the gang began to drift off individually toward their rendezvous point. Mikey gathered them all behind the tent.

'Okay, gentlemen... on my signal, we go in – three, two, one – GO!'

The boys spread out like the Red Arrows (out of doors – it wasn't wet) and went about their allotted tasks. Mr Lowell the butcher was standing on a small stage resplendent in an immaculate white coat. At his side was the captive, and the prime objective of their mission. He was explaining that entrants into the competition should now write on the back of their purchased ticket, the estimated weight of Betsy the pig. The nearest guess (to within a pound) would win the weight of the pig in free sausages for a year. Stroking Betsy's ear, he felt at the lead-lined collar that would ensure that no-one would accurately guess the correct weight. A large set of tall scales sat at the side of the stage, on which the pig would later be weighed.

'Good luck everyone...' Lowell boomed. 'Let the guessing begin!'

There was much scribbling on the back of tickets, whilst some serious estimators came up to the front of the roped-off stage in order to visually assess the weight of the dozing Betsy. Arguments broke out as entrants tried to borrow a pen that was in working order, or fought to inscribe their mark on their ticket using lipstick or eye pencil. A shoal of small blue biros leapt out of the handbag of one contestant (such as are found in betting shops and stores where you pay first, and collect later) and immediately caused a melee as pen-deficient punters made a grab for them. When the frenzy appeared to have died down, Lowell the butcher dispatched assistants to gather up the tickets from the audience. These were scrutinised at a table in front of Betsy's enclosure, by some of the more severe members of the Women's Institute (hairborne division). After the bids had been whittled down to the last half dozen entries, Lowell stepped up to the microphone and raised both of his arms – signalling for silence in the room.

At that moment, Peter set light to helium-filled balloons which were dancing gaily in the breeze at the rear corner of the tent. There was a thunderous explosion as the gas within the decorations exploded. All heads in the audience either crouched in terror, or turned terrified to see what had caused the eruption. The boy had now rolled several small balls under each of the tables. These objects were composed of a mixture of bran, pig swill, and carrot.

Betsy was immediately alert, and her porcine radar had picked up the unmistakable aroma of her favourite treat. She stood and strained against the leash which tethered her on the podium, and as she did so, Squid and Nicky grabbed the short metal bar which was pinned to the ground to anchor her – and lifted.

Realising that she was now free, Betsy took off like a bullet and headed for the first carrot-ball under the nearest table. Making rather a pig of herself, she swallowed the treat and headed for the next free delicacy. At this point, the bar on the end of her now trailing leash made contact with the legs of the table, and dragged it into the air with the force of her exertion. As she darted from table to table in search of further titbits, she pulled behind her an ever-growing collection of buffet tables, which lurched after her in a frightening mass. The crowd were now in full panic mode, and ran as one to the far end of the tent toward the large flap "doors". (More to the point, to escape the mad pig loose inside, and the tower of animate tables careering their way.) They found their way out closed, with Stewart already having reef-knotted the flaps from the outside. At this point, he carefully lifted the bottom of the tent flap, and rolled three more balls back up toward the stage area.

Betsy saw them go, turned around, and darted back the way that she had just come. The mound of badly-damaged tables swung around in a graceful arc, and followed her at speed. No-one was in any condition to notice, but a series of flashes indicated that Mikey and Richard were busy capturing the moment for posterity on a small camera. This time, the crowd decided that they were not taking any chances – and ran at the end of the tent, tearing through it by sheer brute force and weight of numbers.

Mum and Auntie were outside, casually chatting to Uncle Joe, when the big tent erupted and spewed out a fleeing horde of frightened, battered and bruised villagers – followed by a huge sow pulling a mass of twisted metal and wood (also now including a large marquee tent). Betsy had now got a real taste of freedom, and screwed up her piggy eyes to the distance, stuck her head down, and set off at tremendous speed with her legs pumping like piggy pistons. As she careered across the field, the dragging tent swept up the last of the slower Morris dancers, who pin wheeled into the air like skittles. Joe, Mum and Auntie watched as the speeding collection of pig, tables, tent, and unwitting "passengers" headed off into the distance.

Mum turned casually to Auntie, and said, 'Well, that's something you don't see every day.'

From the ragged remains of what was left of the tent came a groan. Very shakily, a head appeared from under the debris, plus an arm which was holding a very crumpled ticket. Lowell the butcher slowly raised his head, held up the torn paper in his hand and said, 'And the winner is...' before collapsing face down in the mud.

Chapter Thirteen

The family had made their way home in the evening, munching on toffee-apples and clutching a large bag of unsweetened popcorn for Dave the chicken. Mum was proudly wearing a rosette which Dave had won in the "Cutest Pet" contest. He had behaved impeccably, and had thoroughly deserved his win. Mum thought that it was rather ostentatious of him to have begun moonwalking for attention, but she would forgive him this once, as the rosette would look so nice on her dresser. Nicky decided not to fill her in on the finer details of the Betsy incident, and wondered if he might be able to blame it on Swine flu. Auntie saw Seaton in the passenger seat of a car which passed them as they strolled past the church, heavily bandaged and interestingly bruised. She gave him a cheery wave, but to save on energy she just used two fingers.

Flopping into the sofa and armchairs in the living room, they discussed this year's Goose Fair.

'I thought it was a bit quiet this year...' said Mum.

'I enjoyed the somersaulting Morris Dancers,' said Nicky.

'I'm taking cricket balls next year – just in case,' stated Auntie, ever the forward planner.

Sunday nights were strange. There was still a feel of wanting to squeeze in something in order to make the best possible use of your remaining free time, and yet you were aware of the spectre of Monday waiting in the shadows to leap out on you and shout 'Boo!'. If you were not careful, the soft foreboding could settle upon you, and you could be consumed by the feeling of unease. The last hours of every Sunday seemed to slip away like sand, and it would take another seven days for another dune to build itself high enough to protect you from Monday morning.

With no homework to worry him, Nicky could sit back and watch television with Mum and Auntie, if their rather ancient set didn't decide to have an early night of its own. There are children throughout the land who always want to go to bed early on a Sunday night so that they can be ready bright and early to get back to school and start another week of education. These children are not normal.

Mum reminded him that he should have an early bath, as he was having his photograph taken in the morning at school. Auntie added, 'You do want to smell nice in the photo, don't you.' It was a few seconds before he realised that dear Auntie was in fact taking the piss. Mum was already eyeing the wall above the dresser, in contemplation of where the Academy photograph might best be placed – maybe the plaster ducks could be persuaded to migrate south for the winter to the opposite wall? Just as she was deep in thought, the telephone rang.

The telephone had been grudgingly installed by Mother 'just for emergencies', and its use was restricted to urgent need under pain of death. Because money was always tight, the family shared a "party line" with their neighbours. To make a call, you had to depress a large plastic button installed on the top of the phone, but you took pot luck as to whether or not you could achieve a connection. On the rare occasions where Nicky had been granted Royal Assent to use the phone, he had lifted the receiver only to hear their neighbour Mrs Burton engaged in animated conversation already. He heard the phrase, '… and by the time I had managed to change the batteries, he had fallen asleep anyway...' before he gingerly replaced the receiver, trying not to let the phone make a click which might betray his eavesdropping presence.

This time it was an excited sounding Uncle Joe on the phone. He handed the phone over to his Mother, and watched as her expression changed from slight annoyance, to surprise. Nicky could just make out the tinny scritching of the voice on the other end of the line, but could see his mother's shoulders shaking with laughter. She eventually ended the call with a polite, 'Thank you for calling Joe – I will speak to you soon, and thanks for your news.' Nicky asked what had prompted Uncle to call them this late on a Sunday night. Mum tried to keep her face straight, as she informed them, 'He said that he has finally discovered a way to prevent cancer.' Both Auntie and Nicky were shocked into silence, and sat aghast at this information.

'What did the daft bugger say then?' asked Auntie.

'He said that he had done months of work, and now had discovered a foolproof way of avoiding cancer,' said Mum.

'Is he serious?' Nicky asked.

'Perfectly serious. He says he has finally got the answer he's been searching for,' said Mum.

'But he's not medically qualified, is he Mum?' asked Nicky.

'And this is the same Joe that insisted that "erudite" was posh glue, is it?' Auntie queried.

'Well, you can never be sure with Uncle Joe. He claims that he done his research, and checked and double-checked all of his results – and he's sure that his findings are correct, so he is really over the moon...' answered Mum.

'My goodness, well if that's true, then he's finally done something useful at last – he might end up as a millionaire like he has always planned...' Auntie said in a serious tone. 'How did he say that we can all avoid it then?'

They waited with baited breath for Mum's reply...

Mum hesitated, and answered completely deadpan: 'He said that the way to avoid cancer is not to get yourself born between twenty-first of June and twenty-second of July...'

Sometimes with Uncle Joe, you had no option but to take what you were given.

Having laughed to himself all the way through his bath time, Nicky decided that perhaps he would go to bed a little earlier than would normally have been the case on a Sunday night. He hoped that in time, the feeling that Monday morning was approaching would stop feeling like a planned visit to the dentist. Maybe Uncle could find a cure for that...

He needed some soothing music to help him drift off into a peaceful sleep, something calm and restful to round off the chaotic day. He took out his headphones and selected a disc to play. Yep – AC/DC would do just fine.

Nicky awoke early with his headphones still on his head. He put them aside and began to get dressed in his uniform. He checked himself in the big mirror, and not seeing any more than the usual obvious flaws, made his way downstairs. As he came into the living room, the satchel from hell caught his foot in the strap from its lair behind the sofa. Maybe somewhere there was a military-run training school to which he could take the satchel, and try to have some of its homicidal tendencies beaten out of it.

Breakfast finished, Mum was scrutinising his appearance through the microscope. Stray fibres and fluff were removed, and creases checked for neatness. 'Do try and do something with your hair,' Mum advised. Nicky enquired if his hair and he could put themselves onto the sofa – and stay there for the day. Surprisingly, the answer was in the negative.

'Don't forget to find out how much the photos will cost, and how soon we can get one,' insisted Mum.

Nicky knew that once his image had been captured on film with "The Posh Boys" of St Onan's, the standard excuses of, 'It wasn't me, I wasn't there, it must be someone else,' wouldn't work anymore. Any callers or (God forbid) relatives who called at their house would no doubt be marshalled up to the photograph, and he would be singled out and identified. Any of his friends that came to the house would easily be able to pick him out of the line-up, and he wondered if there would be time to fix himself up with some sort of cunning disguise.

With seemingly no possible excuse or "get-out" clauses available to him, all Nicky could do was put his nose to the grindstone, bite the bullet, shoulder the burden, and put in a written complaint about the over-use of common metaphors. More in anger than efficiency, he stuffed the deadly satchel with books until the leather creaked in protest – if he did manage to choke it, then it was at last positive proof that too much learning was indeed a dangerous thing. Waiting at the bus stop, he pondered just how invisible it was possible to become without any scientific aids. His planning very nearly came to fruition, as the bus attempted to sneak past him, and only frantic arm flapping halted its stealthy progress. He boarded.

'I didn't see you,' said the driver.

'I was the one flapping their arms like a demented albatross,' said Nicky.

'Never seen one of them, neither...' said the driver.

It was beginning to look like another glorious day in paradise.

The ride to town was uneventful. The bus was quite empty – and more to the point, was mercifully empty of Mrs Jenkins, so at least he would be able to breathe in comfort for the duration of the journey. As he got off the bus, he noticed that Gerry was walking up the path to join the pack of Academy boys on their way to school. This seemed unusual.

'Hey up, Gerry!' called Nicky. 'How come you're on foot? Has your mum had a problem with the car?'

'You could say that... ' answered Gerry, frowning severely.

'What's up then?' asked Nicky.

'She's been banned from driving,' Gerry answered without emotion.

'Wow! – what happened then?' Nicky just had to ask.

Gerry lowered his voice a little, to ensure that the details were not overheard by the other boys. Any juicy gossip such as this would certainly be spread around the Academy in minutes, and he would have to endure the taunting and mockery of the boys who were only too happy to pounce on any sign of weakness. The boy continued...

'Well, Mum had been out with her friends from the yoga club. They had been to the Duck and Puddle after their class, and Mum decided to drive home. She called the police, 'cause the car had been broken into. When the coppers turned up, Mum explained that someone had gotten into the car and stolen the steering wheel and gearstick out of it. The policeman breathalysed her straightaway, and she was arrested for drunk driving.

Nicky was horrified. 'Why was she arrested if the steering wheel and gear lever had been pinched?' he asked.

'She was arrested because she was so pissed that she didn't realise that she had got into the back seat by mistake...' Gerry confessed.

Arriving at the Academy gates, the boys were forced to walk cautiously past the line of prefects who scrutinised them for any uniform misdemeanours. The threatening glares followed them as they made their way across the quad and up to their form room. The register was taken, and they walked down to the assembly hall. The crowd of boys rose as the Headmaster entered, crossed the stage, and straightened the lectern as per usual. Today's point of interest would be the large pair of plastic comedy breasts which had been fixed to the front of the lectern...

The head began...' Good morning, gentlemen.'

'Good morning, sir...'

'Now this morning, we are shortly to proceed into the quadrangle, where Mr Egdon Heath of Heath and Company, photographers, will be securing the image of the Academy for posterity. First periods will thus be cancelled for today. We will arrange ourselves on the stepped seats provided, with Year One at the front, and the Upper Sixth and prefects on the upper tier. This process will be conducted with speed and dignity, and I expect no horseplay from any boy. DO I MAKE MYSELF CLEAR?'

'Yes, sir.'

'Good, now there is one more matter which I wish to bring to your attention. We have a new trainee teacher with us for the duration of the term. I do not want, and will not tolerate, the same levels of ridicule and barracking that certain staff have had to endure from boys in the past. There will be no mockery of the surnames of masters.'

(This had come about due to the ribbing suffered by the German master- Mr Goerling. To make matters worse, he had been temporarily replaced by another fresh-out-of university teacher. His name was Littler. A former maths assistant named Scrotem had disappeared without trace, and dear old Mr Purvey from the History department was still taking heavy medication.)

'The mockery will cease immediately, gentlemen. I will not tolerate members of the Faculty being subjected to scorn. There is nothing even vaguely amusing about a surname – which may well trace its origins back to a link with land and title. We will treat all members of the Academy with dignity and the respect to which they are due. Now that we are clear on this point, I will, without further ado introduce the latest addition to our Languages Department. Gentlemen, may I introduce Mr Nathaniel Phuctrumpet...'

After a rather strange and somewhat strangled version of the Academy song, the boys all made their way down onto the quad. Standing in a half-circle was a bizarre construction intended to present the boys of the school in rows for the benefit of the camera. The bottom row consisted of gymnasium benches, the second tier were chairs, and the upper levels were achieved by means of ascending levels of scaffolding, for the older boys to sit on. The whole arrangement was placed to ensure that the camera could sweep around 180 degrees from end to end, thus capturing the whole school in one long exposure. This would place the subjects in front of the background of the historic school buildings. (Which is why an irate Hyde-Jones had been forced under protest to move his E-Type Jaguar out of shot of the camera.)

Prefects were gathered around in small groups, all preening themselves to perfection in their summer "House colours". The new entrants and younger members of the Academy were being shepherded into position by four of the masters.

'Yes – sit at the front, Blake, no, not that way, facing forward for goodness sake, boy...'

Fussing around in front of the entire mass was the photographer Mr Egdon Heath (a native of the area, who had recently returned). He was busy testing light levels and adjusting his equipment (not a euphemism). His manner of dress seemed a good forty years out of date, and may well have originally included spats. As the boys began to fill the lines of seats, he began ushering them into shot, and "framing" the scene with his hands, one held above the other to form a rough rectangle. The pupils were now all in place, and the staff had settled in vertical rows at the side of the gathering.

A hush now descended, and for a moment the only sound was Heath muttering, 'Nice... Nice... in just a bit... nearly there... oops, bugger... back a bit... Nice... okay.' With his head under the black cover which covered the panoramic antique camera, he was completely unaware of the commotion which came from the far side of the quad. All heads turned to see what the cause of the disturbance was. DeVere was being led back across the quad toward the boarding house by two burly housemasters. He had a sorrowful but still incredibly angry scowl upon his face, and kept his head down to the concrete.

As he was marched into the School House entry door there were calls of, 'Bad luck, old chap...' and, 'Nice try, DeVere... ' as well as, 'Welcome 'ome, Davey...' Several of the boys began to whistle the theme from the famous war film *The Great Escape* – and were swiftly silenced by the headmaster, who leapt up and faced the assembled boys, daring them to continue.

'Mr DeVere will be joining us shortly', he announced.

DeVere was indeed quickly escorted back out of the School House doors, and taken to a space left for him on the front row. He shrugged off the hands that forced him into place, and sat with arms folded in defiance. 'You may continue, Mr Heath...' called the head.

'This process will take approximately one hundred and twenty seconds to complete,' said Heath. 'Please remain absolutely still until I give the signal – thank you.' With that, he again ducked his head under the black cover, re-emerging with both thumbs in the air to signal that the process had begun. As the camera panned from left to right, the boys stood or sat stock still, watching the slow progress of the camera as it carefully edged its way around the assembled throng. Heath studied his stopwatch, and when he judged that the camera had completed its allotted task, said, 'Right, gentlemen, we will allow ourselves one more exposure just to make sure...'

Out of the corner of his mouth, Mr Hyde-Jones said, 'Merry, pull your zip up – you know very well what he meant.'

Another two minute session of unmusical statues was enacted to satisfy the ever-enthusiastic Mr Heath. At the completion of the second run of the camera, he announced, 'Very well done, one and all – thank you for your patience, and please do inform your families that Heath and Co. do a very competitive rate for all your family photographic needs...'

Slowly and carefully, the boys clambered down from their perches, having been immortalised on film, or as Trevill succinctly observed, 'We'em bin captured for posteriors...' They dispersed, allowing the "volunteers" to remove and replace the chairs which had been loaned for purpose. As they made their way to the next class, all the boys were eager to hear the tale of how DeVere had been recaptured.

'I was sitting at home on the sofa on Sunday morning,' he said, 'when there was a loud knock on the front door. My stupid sister opened it – and there were two of the housemasters come to take me back. Before I could scarper, my dad grabbed me and demanded to know what was going on. I had told them that the school had to be urgently closed due to an outbreak of Russian 'flu, and that's why I had to come home without any luggage – cos' it had all been placed into quarantine. Dad was having none of it, and forced me into the car to come back to this rat-infested hole.' Tears began to well up in his defiant eyes. 'I'm not staying – first chance I get I'm going to leg it. I hate the place, I hate the stupid toff kids who steal your sweets and stuff, I hate the crap food, and I hate the stupid lessons. They won't keep me locked up here – and next time they won't catch me neither...'

His friends knew just how he felt. Most of them had experienced bullying and abuse from the wealthier boys during their first week at St Onan's. They too felt like cutting their losses and making a break for freedom. This was an option for some of the 'Day Boys', but most of the parents of the boarders were overseas, or working a long distance away. None of these factors were going to deter our Mr DeVere however, who everyone now knew was sworn to achieve his own liberation at any cost.

It was no wonder that DeVere and others had an issue with the Boarding House. This Victorian edifice loomed over the quadrangle, with its crumbling stonework and dark, supernatural shadows. The dormitories were spacious, but with the high ceilings and ancient windows, were permanently in a state of unnatural chill. The breezes that blew through them did so quickly – because they didn't want to hang about in that place for long. The food given to the boys was regular and exceptionally tasteless. No doubt "flavour" was written down as an "extra" somewhere on the list of items to be paid for by parents. Some boys thrived in this environment however, and not only saw themselves as a cut above the rest of the pupils, but also trained and studied very hard in order to become some of the biggest bastards ever produced by the Public School system. Thus the boarders were not universally popular with the other boys, but those few that were perceived as "normal" were treated with a good deal of sympathy in view of their plight.

Nicky also liked DeVere after he found out that they had something in common – plastic surgery. Although a somewhat tenuous link, they both had experience of family members who had made the great mistake of attempting to augment themselves artificially. DeVere's sister had an extremely sad story to tell. Never happy with her imagined deficiencies in the chestal department, she chose to opt for enhancement surgery. Not having the cash to achieve her goal, she borrowed money for the operation from a Mafia loan shark. She was immensely proud of her new "acquisitions", and showed them off far and wide. Unfortunately, she was unable to keep up the exorbitant repayments, and not very long after she defaulted on payment, heavies from the Mob came round and repossessed her tits.

Nicky's cousin, Sheila, had an ex-husband called Clive. He had always hated his short legs, and vowed to have surgery on them if he could ever afford it. Thanks to a win on the Lottery, he travelled to America and made arrangements to fulfil his dream. However, in true Clive fashion, he elected to have the surgery done on the cheap. When he came round from the anaesthetic he found to his horror that one of his new legs had been put on back to front. When Mum had heard about his plight, she had exclaimed 'Oh... The poor man – I bet he could kick himself.'

The day's educational assault course would now begin with a visit to the top floor of the new building, and an appointment with Miles Bannister and his amazing split personality. Although some of the boys (even if they would not admit to it) had difficulties with mathematics in general, all of them enjoyed the entertainment which the master's odd behaviour provided.

Bannister sat at his tidy desk surrounded by various large plastic triangles. In large letters on the blackboard was written the name "Pythagoras". Nicky thought that this was a very nice name for a blackboard. The class filed into the room and sat in eager expectation at their desks. Bannister seemed to be in a very cheerful mood, and actually smiled at the boys.

'As you may deduce from the name which I have written on the board, chaps, we will today be examining the wonderful subject of geometry,' he stated.

'Haven't we forgotten something?' said a female voice in a questioning tone...

'I don't think so, Madam,' said Bannister.

'Perhaps something to do with our last little chat?' asked the voice.

'May I have a clue?' asked Bannister.

'Possibly something which we agreed, concerning the subject of manners?'

'Ah... Yes... Indeed. Good morning, boys. I hope that you are well? How was your weekend? Are all of your families thriving?' he said, smiling manically.

'That's better, Miles. (Miles better – He He!). But a little bit over the top, dear...' said the female voice.

The class were happy that there was no "warm-up" act, and it had been straight into the main performance. They all settled back to enjoy the show.

'Well, if I may be allowed to continue without any further interruption.'

'Sorry, lovey, but I'm helping Mrs Meeks with a crossword. Do you know if there is another word for Thesaurus?' asked the voice.

'Madam, I would suggest that you make use of a library?' said Bannister.

'I would do, dear, but there is always such a queue, and Lavinia does get a bit fretful if she gets stuck on a particular clue for a long time...'

'Well I suppose you could try "Lexicon" if you are stuck?' said Bannister.

'What, like at *The Alamo*?' asked the voice.

'No, madam – I said "Lexicon", as in "wordbook" or "glossary", replied Bannister.

'Thank you, Miles – I will speak to you later,' she said.

'Much later, if you please...' whispered the master.

Miles' seeming split personality was not a situation of his own making. There was a perfectly reasonable and acceptable cause for all of the little interruptions. When Miles had been a young boy, curiosity and bravado had led to him climbing up onto the window cill of his bedroom (in the guise of Batman). He had fallen out of the open window and landed heavily in the flower bed (in the guise of Unconscious Man). The first person on the scene had been the very concerned former occupant of their house – Mrs Elsie Noakes. Mrs Noakes had stayed with the boy until help had arrived. The fact that Elsie had passed over to the spirit world had nothing to do with her need to care for an injured child.

When the young Bannister had regained consciousness, he found that he had the voice of an unseen but very kindly Elsie Noakes chattering away in his ear. Occasionally she would introduce him to her vast legion of similarly gregarious friends- who were also on "the other side". As a child, Miles had absolutely no aptitude for anything to do with mathematics, and was what might be politely referred to as a bit on the thick side when it came to numbers. Elsie saw it as her spirited duty to help and assist the young Bannister with his education. She set about enlisting the help of various "specialists" to make this happen. So throughout his early years, Bannister had the advantage of being tutored by the finest late mathematicians that Elsie could lay her spiritual hands on (the arrangement was this – Elsie would sort out their laundry and darning, in return for their help with the young Miles). And so the lad had the advantage of some awesome minds looking over his shoulder as he tried to get to grips with figures. She had enlisted the help of Descartes, Newton,

Fermat, Pythagoras, Einstein, and the undiscovered genius that was Mr Alf Pinner (ex-newspaper vendor from the 1930s who was a wizard with numbers).

Miles never had to revise for a single examination, because he always had a battalion of brain power at his disposal. He had sailed through each and every one of his school and college tests, and was hailed as something of a genius at his university. The payback for this was that Elsie would use Miles for her own A to Z of anything which she wanted to know – often quite mundane or bizarre information. The one thing that Miles could never work out was exactly when Dear Mrs Noakes would put in an appearance, and she could never calculate the probability that her constant interventions would most likely drive the poor man insane...

'Geometry, gentlemen...' began Bannister, 'the science of properties and relations of lines, surfaces, and solids...'

'Sorry, love...' came the voice again. 'Do you spell "Water Works" with a hydrant?'

'OH FOR GOODNESS SAKE MADAM – HOW CAN I BE EXPECTED TO TEACH WITH ALL OF THESE CONSTANT INTERRUPTIONS?' shouted Bannister.

'Sorry, Miles – only asking...' said a voice which quickly faded away.

Bannister looked furtively this way and that, wiggled his little finger in an ear, and sensing no further intrusion, continued. He walked nervously down the rows of desks, still looking around for as yet unseen interlopers, and handed various boys the plastic triangles which they had seen on his desk earlier.

'Now, fellows...' he proclaimed to the class. 'Those of you that I have given a triangle to, will stand and tell the rest of the class what kind of triangle they are holding: what is special about it, and what angle it describes.'

Lordsley was first on his feet. 'My triangle, sir, is a right-angle triangle. From the adjacent sides we may deduce that the square on the hypotenuse is equal to the sum of the squares on the other two sides...'

'And what have you in effect, just described, Lordsley?' asked the master

'Why I am such a nerdy little dick...' came a hushed, yet still very audible reply.

'That's right – I mean no, I mean err... You have described Pythagoras' Theorem,' said Bannister.

Calderman leaned over and whispered 'He's a square, and hypernuisance, and a dick from all sides.' This caused a ripple of laughter from the boys who heard his remark. Bannister scanned the room in order to spot the cause of the jollity.

At that point, a voice with a very obvious French accent spoke up, 'A leetle deek from all sides – tres humereuse!'

It would appear that Monsieur Fermat had formed an opinion of Lordsley already. Random attacks of Frenchman were the last thing that the already unsettled Bannister had wanted, and he immediately clamped a hand over his mouth to prevent further Gallic ad-libbing. The class regarded the spectacle of their mathematics guru as he stood at the head of the class, with one hand holding a large plastic triangle, and the other held tightly over his mouth. It looked like a vision of a man who had suffered a bout of acute angle poisoning...

As the bell rang, Bannister kept his hand clamped to his face. He waved the boys out of the room with his other arm, deftly flinging the triangle which he held at the notice board – where it stuck and vibrated gently. 'Wow!..' said Merry. 'Ninjometry!'

The staff room was its usual melting pot of petty jealousies, suspicion and scurrilous rumour during the morning break. Some of the more juvenile bickering would take place over the injudicious use of the chairs. Over a long period of time, the various staff members had brought in or acquired their own personal seating – strangely applicable to their teaching subject. We can thus observe the high-backed leather Art Deco chair of Gideon Rundell the Latin Master, and adjacent to it, the battered and sunken cord fabric covered seat of the English teacher. The (as yet empty of La Bum Gallic) chair of the French mistress was an ornate and elegant chaise longue, whilst the chair of Matthews the history man was rather war-torn (as was its usual incumbent), and if not afflicted by the ravages of time, was certainly under the influence of it (as opposed to Matthews – who was merely under the influence).It bore the obligatory and permanent wine and beer stains in keeping with his favourite off-duty relaxations.

Biology and Physics posteriors were catered for by means of a very modern sofa of square design, whereas the Chemistry master opted for a hard and uncushioned chair of Scandinavian design. Our man from the Divinity faction had a severe and unforgiving chair of a folding nature – and this may have well been some self-inflicted penance which included splinters. The "Craft" team of Metalwork and Woodwork had chosen to construct their own chair and stool, which bore all of the hallmarks of having been constructed by hands which were wearing boxing gloves during the process. To prevent the misappropriation of their seats, a cunning locking device had been incorporated into the design – without the operation of which the items would collapse under any would-be user. Matthews had several times found himself prostrate of the staff room carpet, and with no pressing duty, had decided to have a nice forty winks. The Art Master exercised his rights as a free spirit, and was not willing to be tied down by the system by having to conform to a chair. He would lounge or lean casually wherever he chose to do so, but on the odd occasion would flop onto a luridly-patterned bean bag in the corner of the room, and give off an air of artistic detachment. He was casually lounging in just such a manner, when the door to the staff room was flung open – causing alarm, and waking up the dozing Matthews...

Into the room strutted the mislaid French mistress. To be absolutely technically correct, what came into the staff room was the chest area of Mrs Dreadfell, the rest of her following on sheepishly behind somewhat later. Apart from the now snoring Matthews, the rest of the staff looked over at her as she made her grand entrance. It was open mouth season...

It was blatantly obvious that Mrs Dreadfell's elegant blouse contained a) significantly more Dreadfell than had previously been the case, and b) more than the fabric of the garment looked physically able to keep under restraint. Madame herself strode to the coffee table area, and swung her fake fur coat off her shoulders – causing structural movement and light damage to the building foundations.

'Bonjour, mes amies...' she said.

Hyde-Jones nudged the leg of the sleeping Matthews in an attempt to wake him. He spluttered back into consciousness, straightened his tie, replaced his glasses onto his nose and peered intently across the room at the latest arrival. Not able to fully focus, he quickly replaced them with his distance spectacles.

'Great Bloody Purple Pansies!...' stammered Matthews. 'I mean to say... just look at the... She's had 'em... They're both... My God – it's the Bloody Hunch-Front of Notre Dame!' There was much stifled giggling from the other staff members, not to mention a couple of titters.

Rundell was impressed.

Strangler was confused.

Brayfield was outraged.

Thwaite was busy taking notes.

Duggan was busy taking approximate measurements.

Hyde-Jones was aghast.

Dr Chambers was aghast.

Darwin was aghast.

Stan was a ghost (and also stunned).

Bell-Enderby was staggered.

Newhouse was grinning, nodding sagely in admiration.

Felchingham was still covering his eyes.

Miles Bannister was first to break the silence... 'I notice something a little different, Penny?'

'Very nice too, dear...' came the admiring female voice of Mrs Noakes.

'Looks like a dead heat in a zeppelin race...' said Matthews.

'Bad taste, that man,' answered Brayfield. 'I am sure that it is nothing for any of us to get excited about,' he said.

'Bit of a storm in a D-cup then?' asked Mr Newhouse, giggling.

Madame Dreadfell rounded on them. 'I have merely made a choice to enhance my femininity,' she answered them haughtily. Yes, I have had a little work done.'

'Must have been some impressive scaffolding for that job then... ' said Mr Newhouse.

'If it isn't impertinent, may I ask where you had the "work" done, Penny?' asked Thwaite.

'I flew over to see the finest surgeon in Monte Carlo,' answered Madame.

'Monte Carlo or bust...' chipped in Matthews.

Dreadfell glared at him. 'You stupid man – have you never seen breasts before?'

He answered in Churchillian fashion. 'Madam, I have seen photographs of the Himalayas, but I am sure that they would seem much bigger when one is standing beside them...'

'Well I for one like them, Penny,' stated Rundell.

'Yes – you ignore the knockers...' added Strangler.

'Were they – I mean was it expensive?' asked the curious Thwaite.

'Well yes, rather, but I think that I got value for my money,' answered Madame.

'And the ability to be able to breastfeed Cornwall...' said Mr Newhouse.

'It looks like inflation is much worse than we feared...' chuckled Matthews.

At this point, the majority of the male members of staff were reduced to helpless laughter. Madame fixed them with a Gorgon stare, and Dr Chambers firmly stated that 'enough was now enough, and Madame's choice to augment her bodily shape was not a matter for general concern or further comment.'

Mr Newhouse agreed: 'We don't want her knockers to be blown up out of all proportion.'

'She obviously did...' said Darwin. He was silenced by a look from Dr Chambers.

The matter now exhausted, the staff drank their tea in silence, punctuated by the odd guffaw or sneaky chuckle here and there. 'Righto then...' said Matthews, levering himself out of his body-moulded armchair 'I'm off to class – see you all later.' He veered off unsteadily toward the door, but stuck his head back in and said to the Maths teacher, 'Oh, do me a small favour will you, dear chap – please let the younger boys know that the bouncy castle has arrived...'

Madame's teacup hit the door just as it closed with a bang.

Chapter Fourteen

French class for the boys was nothing out of the ordinary. Only Weatherill seemed to have taken more than a passing regard of Madame's pneumatic enlargements. Nicky was far too busy keeping his head down, so as not to be called upon to demonstrate his ever-growing lack of grip on the French tongue. Today, they were learning what seemed to be an endless list of the shops and trades – including (as pronounced by the noted linguist Trevill, some bloke called "Pat Tissery", and not forgetting the geezer, "John Darm"). There was a supposed 'fun' exercise involving role play, where the boys would take on the persona of shopper, or shop keeper. Weatherill angered Madame by refusing to serve Merry (as the irate customer in his butcher's shop) claiming that he was 'observing the usual French custom of knocking off early for a two-hour lunch.' In the baker's premises, Calderman's Gallic shrug when asked for a fresh loaf had been inspirational. Lordsley was given the part of a local trying to procure the services of a village taxi to get to the railway station. DeVere cleverly thwarted his request by expertly playing the role of a Japanese taxi driver who was fresh into the country. Mark Davis was very well prepared in the planning department, and perfectly executed the role of a deaf newsagent.

With her hopes of portraying typical life in a French town destroyed by the boys, Madame turned to the vocabulary books for solace – and only just retained her composure when for a dare, Weatherill asked her what the French word for "serviette" was. She stared down at the textbook on her desk, and made the stark realisation that due to her recent improvements, she could no longer see the book which was now shadowed by her twin balconies. She vented her anger by handing out a list of required learning and translation which was considerably more than usual. Instructing the class to read from their books until the bell, Madame began to think about the book which her husband had just written. He was a specialist craftsman in the woodworking, cabinet making and veneering trade. He had also found out that far from being a boring or mundane occupation, there were certain elements within his profession which indulged in shall we say, a more exotic type of leisure pursuit. He had taken two years in which to research and write a book outlining the incidence of bondage and sado-masochistic practices within the woodworking trade. He had titled this work *Nifty Shades of Grain*. According to the information written on the inside cover; the term 'French Polishing' was given a whole new meaning...

Leaving Madame and her new European mountain range in contemplation, the boys made their way across to the door of the reverend, for some more uplifting spiritual spring-cleaning.

Welcoming the class into the room, Felchingham ushered the boys to sit in one of the chairs which had been placed in a wide circle within the room. 'Today, gentlemen, I thought that it might be interesting if we attempt to disprove the negative opinions concerning necromancy. To this end – we will attempt our very own Victorian séance,' said the rev., with a little too much glee. 'I shall endeavour to illustrate just how unscrupulous mediums would engage in stage trickery in order to extort money and respect out of their gullible victims.' (Felchingham himself had often had to endure the taunts of fellow teachers and students alike, who would openly refer to him as a 'Dabbler in the Unknown', and on one occasion, as a 'Cult'.) 'I assure you that no harm whatsoever will come to you boys...' he declared. 'I merely ask that we open ourselves up to other facets of worship and divine contemplation.'

With that, he began to lay out cards in a circle in front of each chair. Each individual card had a large letter of the alphabet written on it, as well as the words 'Yes' 'No' and 'Goodbye'. He asked that the boys all link hands, and instructed Lordsley to draw the curtains shut. The room was now plunged into a muted half-light, as the circle of boys looked nervously at each other. Felchingham joined the circle and sat down.

'Firstly, boys... we must clear our minds,' he stated.

'Shouldn't take Lordsley long to do,' came an anonymous voice.

'Please try and concentrate, chaps...' insisted the rev.

After a minute or so of silence, the master opened his eyes and asked, 'Is anybody there… ?'

There was no reply, or any movement from the glass which the Rev. had placed in the middle of the circle of cards. He called out again... 'Is anyone there...?'

'We could just leave a message?' said Merry, helpfully.

'Quiet boy, I am trying to establish contact with the other side.'

'I'd try contacting reality if I was you...' came the voice.

'I heard that...' said the rev. 'Look, four of you place a finger on the glass, and see if we can get a message to come through,' he insisted.

The boys reluctantly laid a finger on the upturned glass as instructed, and the rev. again asked, 'Is there anyone there who has a message to give us?'

To the horror and fascination of the boys, the glass firstly gave a shudder, and then inched its way over to the card which bore the word "Yes".

'Do not push on the glass at all,' said Felchingham. 'Let the message come through straight from the spirit realm. Have you a message which you wish to deliver to one of us?' he asked again. The glass retreated slightly, then nudged insistently at the Yes card. 'Then please, in a spirit of light and love, give us the name of the person for whom the message is intended,' he said. The glass moved smoothly this time, spelling out the letters Y-O-U. 'For me?' queried the now worried Felchingham. 'Are you sure?' Again, the glass glided over to the Yes card. 'Then please may I have the message, friend?' said the rev, with just a trace of a tremor in his voice. The glass began to spell out the message. The glass went over to the K. It retreated and slid over to the letter N. The next letter selected was O. Finally, the glass came to rest opposite the letter B.

'What the hell does that mean?' said the rev., confused.

The glass shot over to the letters U, R and A in very quick succession, and returned to Yes.

'URA, KNOB?' asked the rev, now a little suspicious. A horrible feeling of recognition was beginning to form itself in his mind. Suddenly, he knew with crystal clarity exactly from whom the message was coming.

'This is you Stan, isn't it?' he demanded. 'You've ruined everything now, you spiteful old sod...' The boys were a little shocked at the irreligious language used.

The glass hovered repeatedly between the letters H and A, until it flew up into the air and landed upright on the desk of the now irate master. The lads thought that this was a brilliant trick, and Merry insisted that he show them another one – with a top hat and a rabbit this time.

As the rev gathered up all of the cards from the floor in temper, everyone heard the distant sound of throaty cackling laughter, as it faded to silence. The master was beside himself with rage, and told them, 'Take an early lunch, boys, and we will explore another alternative theological mystery in the next lesson...'

The class packed up their books and hurried out of the room. The rev. opened the curtains to re-admit the daylight, and began to move the desks and chairs back into rows. He would get even with Stan, if he could only work out a way to do it. Whilst he was contemplating spiritual retribution, he became aware of a persistent sound which was trying to gain his attention. It was the repeated rattling and knocking of wood against wood, but was seemingly being made by some small object jumping around making contact with a larger surface. He stood stock still, and tried to locate the source of the sound. It appeared to be emanating from his own desk – from the one of the drawers in his desk to be more precise. He approached the desk with trepidation, and all the while the rattling continued. It sounded as if something were alive within the top drawer, and was desperately seeking to make its escape. Strangely, he noted that the fitting which opened the drawer was missing, and he feverishly searched another drawer until he found his Tesco "Sacrificial dagger". As he inserted the end of the knife into the top of the drawer to prise it open, the noise seemed to increase in urgency. Suddenly, the rattling ceased, and the rev. paused in shock.

With the caution of a bomb-disposal expert, he cautiously eased open the desk drawer, then leapt back, covering his face with both of his arms in case of attack. No rapier-clawed demon was forthcoming, and so he gingerly bent over and peered into the now open drawer. There, in the middle of the drawer, alone and still rocking gently – was the source of the sound. It was the knob.

'Damn you, Stan!' he shouted, waving a puny fist at the sky.

From far off, he heard again the throaty chuckle of his ghostly Nemesis...

Right then... if it was games that the old bugger wanted to play, then the rev. was going to make sure that he passed "Go" and collected his £200. He would teach Stan a lesson which he would not forget this side of purgatory. He knew exactly what he would do. He would "cleanse" the classroom spiritually, and thus banish the curse of the Stan. Now, what did he need? Ah yes, where had he put the holy water? A liberal dousing and a good hellfire prayer session should frighten the hell into the tormenting old git. He began a desperate and frenzied search for the holy water which he always kept in his stationery cupboard, along with the emergency disposable vestments and fold-away altar. Papers and various artefacts flew into the air as he ransacked the store area for the vessels containing the precious liquid, but his trawling of the cupboard could not locate what he was looking for. Just then, a thought occurred to him – hang on, any liquid can be holy if I consecrate it with a blessing, surely? So another search began, this time involving a rummage through the contents of his desk. With a shout of triumph he located a bottle of holy Ribena, and held it aloft in the style of the early biblical prophets. Falling to his aching knees, he blessed the fizzy, fruity drink in preparation for the ceremony which he had planned.

Walking slowly and deliberately around the classroom, he anointed each of the walls with a healthy coating of holy pop, whilst intoning a blessing designed to act as an exorcism. When he had finished, he found himself gasping for breath, but feeling calmer. He closed his eyes and took in a long, deep lungful of air. Upon opening his eyes again and looking around the room, he saw that all of his nightmares had come true... The walls of the room appeared to be dripping with watery blood, which was running down in alarming streaks. Terror and panic now gripped at his soul – was this Stan exacting a terrible revenge upon him? He knew that he had to get rid of the vision of the housewarming held in the home in Amityville. Like a man in a trance, he leapt out of the door and into the corridor. Seeing no-one in sight, he savagely yanked the chunky fire extinguisher off its bracket, and sped back into the classroom. Not bothering to attempt reading the instructions, he tore at the "safety catch", released the hose of the appliance, closed his eyes tightly, and began to spray the walls.

When the hissing from the extinguisher had diminished, indicating that he had emptied it, he risked opening his eyes again. Oh Shit... what he had thought to be a water extinguisher had actually held foam. The room now resembled an outdoor scene from that great Christmas classic, *It's a Wonderful Life*... only for him, it wasn't. Glancing down at the floor, he noticed what appeared to be small footprints in the foam – footprints resembling those which might have been made by... a rabbit. In utter despair and frustration, he fell to his knees as the slushy coating of foam and fruity refreshment (not forgetting the added vitamin C of course) oozed its way down the walls according to the instructions of gravity. He fell forward onto all fours and looked at the frothy wall. Right in front of his face at eye level, sliding lazily down the vertical surface, was a word which was written in large capital letters – and still clearly readable as it slid floorwards. The word was "KNOB"...

Before they were required to line up in the queue for lunch, the boys had plenty of free time in which to indulge themselves in a few games. The glorious season of autumn had once again provided some free bounty with which the boys could amuse themselves. Taking place in the far right corner of the quad was a contest which has been played out at this time of years for centuries (or certainly since the invention of proper string). The motto for this brief championship had been helpfully translated into Latin by Calderman, and consisted of the phrase "Veni, Vidi, Horse Chestnuti" – "I came, I saw, I played conkers..." The sport had progressed to the badly bruised knuckle stage, and Merry had suffered an attack of badly frayed string, and so retired undefeated on the advice of Nicky, his trainer. Jackson had won the contest outright, shattering the conkers of all challengers with ease. The beaten opponents were completely unaware that his prized conker had in fact been carved out of hard wood, then varnished with several coats of a nautical paint designed to keep the hull of a yacht safe from attack by giant squid. The group suddenly found themselves subject to an attack by a familiar invertebrate.

'What the hell is going on here?' sneered Piper the prefect, hands on hips. 'You know that conkers are banned in school – so what do you peasants think you are playing at?' he said.

'Would you take "Lacrosse" as my final answer?' said Nicky.

'Oh... I thought that you would be involved in this somehow, Farm Boy,' said the prefect. 'Right – come with me to the head's office now...'

The smirking prefect marched Nicky up the narrow winding path to the headmasters office. Without looking at his prisoner, Piper knocked at the door, waited for the command to enter, and then pushed his captive into the head's office. Goodwill was sitting behind his desk, and was just replacing the ornate glass stopper into the sherry decanter. He regarded the two boys over his glasses.

'Right then, what is going on here?' asked Goodwill.

'Shepherd was caught by myself disregarding Academy rule 46c (subsection 12), sir, in that I caught him playing with his conkers in the quad.'

(Miss Piggott, who was carrying in a tray of tea and biscuits, suddenly began to choke when she heard this, and hurriedly put down the silver tray and rushed out into her annexe.)

'Why do I seem to be seeing Mr Shepherd with such alarming regularity?' asked the head.

'Because he disregards the Academy rules, sir,' answered Piper.

'But we are not talking about multiple murders being committed here, are we Piper?' said the head levelly.

'Maybe not, sir, but this is how his sort start to break down the system, sir, by taking no notice of rules which are put there for their safety. We have to keep up standards, sir, otherwise we will end up just as bad as the other schools – which, in my opinion, is where he should be.'

The head took a long, hard and penetrating look at the prefect. He then turned to Nicky, who noticed just the slightest hint of a smile playing around the corners of the head's mouth.

'Mr Piper, regard if you will, the objects placed upon the mantelpiece,' began the head. 'Pray tell me what you see slightly left of centre, near the candlestick?'

Both boys flicked their eyes up to the fireplace, and Nicky had to stifle a grin when he saw the object that the head had indicated. There on the mantel shelf was a small glass case. Inside the case, set on a small pedestal was the instantly recognisable object known to all as a conker. In front of the plinth was a card which bore the inscription "Gerald Ibsen Goodwill – Conker champion 1950-55 St Onan's Foxe house".

'Mr Shepherd, for your personal safety and that of your fellows, I would be obliged if you would pay heed to the rules forbidding the playing of any game likely to cause harm or injury,' said the head. 'However, I feel that no harm has been done on this occasion, and will take no action in the matter.'.

'But, sir... he...' began the prefect.

'I will speak to you about the matter privately, Mr Piper – Mr Shepherd may now go about his normal duties,' interrupted the head. Nicky turned and left the office, passing the ever-scowling Miss Piggott on the way out. Whatever was being said to the prefect by the headmaster was being stated in an angry-sounding voice. Whatever the outcome, he was certain that Piper would now redouble his efforts to persecute him even more.

When he rejoined his friends, they quizzed him as to what had gone on in the mysterious realm of the head's office. Nicky explained the conversation word for word, and the boys now had a new found admiration for Mr Goodwill.

'Two champions then...?' asked Calderman.

'Sorry – how's that?' Nicky asked his friend.

'Well, one champion at conkers- and one champion tosser,' laughed Calderman.

At that point, Merry called out. 'Look out, here comes Piper now, and he doesn't look happy.'

Indeed, the angry prefect was striding across the quad in their direction. He began to shout at the group of boys, 'Right, you peasants – give me those conkers immediately!'

Merry turned away, and then turned back with his hand full of the banned nuts.

'Hand them over now,' said Piper, holding out his hand to receive the conkers from Merry. 'And I will not be letting go of these, so don't expect to see them again...' He stamped off across the quad, back toward the prefect's common room.

Merry spoke first. 'That's quite right; he won't be handing them back any time soon.'

'What do you mean, Gerry?' asked Nicky.

'Well, he won't be letting go of those conkers, because I gave them a good coating of Super Glue just before he took them off us!'

Lunch was a rather tense affair, and not merely because of the seething looks directed at the boys from Piper – who appeared to be eating one-handed for some reason. Today's fare was roast chicken, but once again there seemed to have occurred some interruption in the food delivery system. Chickens had been prepared, plated, and passed to the serving hatches. Where they were disappearing to from that point had given Betty Bradley cause to take two of her tablets urgently.

The problems had started again just the other evening. Rehearsals were being held in the assembly hall for the upcoming play, and Betty thought that it would be a nice gesture to deliver a cake in order to celebrate Mr Hyde-Jones' birthday. She and Alice had wheeled the large iced beauty up to the hall on the tea trolley, and had placed it on the front of the stage, ready to surprise the teacher when he turned up with the cast of boys. They had returned to the kitchens to collect knives, plates and napkins, which had not taken them more than three minutes. On their return there was no tray, no cake, and no candles. Betty had searched the hall in case one of the boys had hidden the cake as a prank, but there was no sign of it anywhere. All she found were small almond-icing fingerprints on the doors of the stage front. This was now all too much for her, and she had to go and have a lie down, covering her face with a damp tea-towel until her migraine subsided. She was now more convinced than ever that the

Academy was haunted, and that she should approach the Reverend Felchingham for his advice on how to deal with the problem. She sat bolt upright in her chair. The cake had been a large one-big enough to serve the teacher and the entire cast of boys. For the briefest of moments, she had the vision of a very overweight ghost looming out of the store cupboards towards her, a fork held hopefully in its podgy spectral hand...

'So Goodwill's middle name is Ibsen then, is it?' said Calderman.

'Yes, apparently his father was a bit of a reader,' said Nicky.

'My middle name is 'Pendragon,' said Mark Davis, sulkily.

'Was your dad a bit of a fan of King Arthur then?' asked Merry.

'No, he was just a bit of a dickhead...' answered Marcus Pendragon Davis the First.

Lordsley had obviously received news of their skirmish with Authority on the grapevine, and hurried over to the group to give them the benefit of his worldly wisdom. 'I hear that you had your conkers confiscated?' he asked smugly. 'Well I think that the prefect did the right thing, because you know that it's not allowed in the Academy rules, and you could have caused a serious injury to someone,' he added.

'There was no risk of anyone getting injured – because we couldn't find you, you little turd,' said Calderman.

'Just the sort of stupid attitude that could have earned you a trip to see Matron...' advised the expert on health and safety a.k.a. Lordsley.

Even accepting the fact that Lordsley had all the social grace and skill of a small soap dish, his implied threat of a visit to the Matron did hit home. The boys were all quiet for a few seconds, as various images fought with each other in their heads.

When the Academy had reluctantly had to allow the previous holder of the post of Matron to go (the lovely and caring Gladys Juggs- who retired under protest at the age of 85) it had been forced to advertise for a new member of Boarding House staff. Various candidates had presented themselves for interview, and most had proven themselves to be a) unsuitable, b) mentally unstable, c) unnaturally interested in bodily injury, or unbelievably d) Gladys Juggs re-applying for her old job. At the point of both giving up, and nervous collapse, the interview panel had witnessed the arrival of one Lucretia Dipper...

The panel were immediately struck by her fiery red hair, and her six-foot-four stature (aided and abetted by six-inch stiletto heels). She resembled for all the world one of the Valkyries from the Old Norse legends. She stood in front of the interview table and declared, 'I find myself in need of employment. I am willing to take up any position which you gentlemen may require.' At this point Dr Goodwill nearly choked, Dr Chambers was struck dumb, Bannister failed to see the double-entendre, and poor Mr Thwaite fainted. With no other candidates seemingly available, "Miss" Dipper was welcomed (carefully, at arm's length) to the Academy staff, and permitted to establish her very own "Valhalla" in a cellar room of the Boarding House. She was soon known as "The Big Dipper" by the boys (please don't do the joke – she might be listening...).

Once settled in to the Academy, it must be said that she carried out her duties with great enthusiasm. Any boy with any kind of sporting injury found himself whisked off to Matron's quarters for treatment or massage. Whilst her somewhat striking appearance made the lower school boys rather apprehensive, her services were in ever greater demand from the pupils of the Upper School, several of whom were on rather familiar first-name terms with her. Nicky was convinced that she was in fact performing a second job in the evenings, as he had once or twice seen her (or someone extremely similar in appearance) in fancy dress – on a card which had been left in a telephone box in the town.

Hyde-Jones was in no doubt at all as to the actual credentials of the new matron, and freely stated as much to his friend the geography master during one coffee-break. Thwaite listened horrified, but ended the conversation much enlightened. He was a little unsure of what the term "Dom/Sub" meant or implied – but in his own mind he pictured a long roll which one might have for lunch – made of leather, or perhaps an underwater vehicle owned by the Mafia boss? There was talk of her concern for the wellbeing of some of the gentlemen who lived in the town. The Boarding House had its own entrance and exit doors to the rear street, which were reached by means of a short cloistered corridor. Such was her worry for the health of the male townsfolk, that she regularly admitted them through the corridor and into her treatment room "out of hours" for one of her medicinal "sports massages". Such a commitment to the general public was to be applauded – however, there were rumours...

As the boys made their way out of the dining hall, the Matron catwalked past them with a clicking of her towering stiletto heels, and gave them a smile, the meaning of which none of them could comprehend.

Geography lesson began in the usual fashion. Mr Thwaite could always be relied upon for one thing, and that was complete and utter geographical displacement. At any given moment, he could not say with any degree of certainty where he was, or where the item might be that he was looking for, or where it was that he had just left it, or where he was when he realised that he had lost it. (You get the general idea.) If he had written the words arse and elbow in capital letters on a large piece of paper, it would be a matter of seconds before he had misplaced it. Nicky and the boys noted that this afternoon, their teacher looked a little flushed with colour around the cheekbones, but put this down to the warm weather.

'Good afternoon, boys...' Thwaite said cheerily. 'I seem to have temporarily misplaced the key to the stationary cupboard, and so I cannot give you the rest of the materials which I had for you on volcanoes. Instead, I thought that we would make a start on the fascinating subject of Plate Tectonics.' This sounded good to the boys. Thwaite was obviously something of an expert in this subject, and kept the class enthralled with descriptions of who lived on which great plate, where they collided on the surface of the Earth, and what mayhem their collisions would likely cause.

Trevill was fascinated by the thought of gigantic plates of rock moving along the surface of the planet. He felt compelled to ask, 'Surr... so if I dunt feel loike trailin' all the way down to the shops, then all Oi 'as to do is sit it out, and the supermarrket will eventually come past me front door?'

'Well in theory, yes, Trevill...' answered Thwaite, 'but you might be in a bit of a pickle if you have run out of milk. I would recommend that you perhaps invest in a very thick book!' Moving over to the blackboard (having found the chalk, lost it again, rediscovered it and then forgotten where he had put it) Thwaite drew a map of the world showing all of the great tectonic plates, and instructed the class to copy it into their workbooks.

Kendy asked. If. 'any attempt had been made to stabilise the plates, or make use of the geothermal energy available at the intersections so as to prevent further strata diversification or displacement – which could be achieved by "Terraforming" the sites on a local level?'

In order to ignore the fact that he had failed to understand one quarter of that sentence, Thwaite told the boy, 'No...'

'Then can I ask another question please Sir?' Kendy enquired.

'Go ahead Kendy...' said a nervous Thwaite.

'Well; sir, I was just wondering, and it is a geographical question; why half of the planet produces far too much food for them to eat, and the other half seem to be starving. Surely if we just share out the food we have between all the inhabitants of the Earth, and focus our energies and skills on lessening the effects of climate upon the availability of domestic food production, then we could have a world where famine was a word consigned to the history books. Why do we spend so much money on weapons and technology to kill people that we have never met, instead of investing that finance in food production and saving lives?'

'Wow! That's a bit of a political question, Kendy...' said Thwaite, taken aback.

'It's not political – it's bloody criminal...' said Calderman, with feeling.

'I mean, sir, at some point it makes more sense to realise that it really is a very small planet, and all of its inhabitants need to be given the same chance of life. It's utterly ridiculous that those who have plenty disregard the plight of those who have nothing, and yet waste their money on possessions and things which they do not really need, instead of investing a little of that wealth to help their fellow humans in need. It would be a start if you stopped treating other species as unimportant, and acknowledged the whole of the ecological cycle as an organic self-regulating mechanism with which Man should not interfere... An outsider from another galaxy would be horrified at the way that this planet has been plundered, and species rendered extinct by the arrogance of a so-called "higher animal".

Thwaite did not attempt to answer the boy. He had the uneasy feeling that he was dealing with a mind equal to (if not vastly superior to) his own. What troubled the master was the way in which the boy had delivered the passionate speech with such a benign look of pity on his face. He would have to keep an eye on young Kendy, that much was certain.

Thwaite was relieved when he heard the bell sound to end the lesson for today. For some reason the boy had unsettled him, and also his mind kept turning to the principality of Monte Carlo. He could see a hazy choice shimmering as it hovered in the distance. One of these days he was going to have to stroll straight up and confront it. Now... where the hell had he put his pen again? His leg injury was bothering him. He had attended a village fete at the weekend, but the performance of his troop of Morris Dancers had been unexpectedly devastated by the sudden appearance of a huge sow attached to a rope, trailing a battered collection of tables, and the ragged remains of a tent. He had been catapulted into the air, and upon landing had suffered a particularly unpleasant graze to his leg, and had badly bent his bells...

There was a curious song emanating from the history room today, the purveyor of the melody was Mr Matthews. The content of the song was a ditty about somebody (whose name wasn't clear) only having one (bodily part – again, indistinct) and some other poor unfortunate soul who it would appear had none at all.

The boys knocked at the door and entered on command. (Not all of them knocked, obviously, otherwise the door would possibly have suffered considerable damage.) Old "Matthewselah" was sitting at his desk with the rosy glow of imbibement all over his happy face.

'Thought that we might do a little personal hist'ry today fellows...' he boomed. 'We can have a gander at some old parish records, and see if we can trace some of you back to the time of Welcome the... of Wilbur the... Will the Cucumber... William The Conqueror'.

''Scuse Me – dry throat,' he said, belching politely as he did so.

The master took a loud slurp from the oversized mug on his desk. Even from as far back as the middle row of desks, it was obvious that the contents were more usually found in close proximity to tartan and haggis. He stood up abruptly, and picked up the bundle of papers that lay on his desk. With his other hand, he swept up the mug like a pirate, and set off to distribute the papers to the boys. With his second step, he found that against all odds, he was attempting to stand on fresh air, his foot having extended over the edge of the raised dais. In a quite beautiful and graceful slow-motion arc, he turned a complete somersault and sat heavily down on the classroom floor. The boys were impressed – not only did Matthews not turn the air blue with curses, but he had performed his impromptu acrobatics without spilling a single drop from his mug.

From the back of the class, Jackson called out, 'Ta – Daaaaahh!'

Rather than admonish the boy, Matthews merely stated, 'I Thank Yew...' and giggled.

'Now then, where was I?' asked the bemused Matthews.

'You had just fallen on your arse, sir' replied Nicky, helpfully.

'Oh, yes – right you are... Ha Ha! So I have, well I never...' The still amused Matthews eased himself up from his unplanned point of impact and straightened his clothing. He managed to place the mug onto the desk at the third attempt, and then picked up some large sheets of paper, which he brandished triumphantly in the air. 'I hold in my hand some of your hiss... hypno... hysterical... erm – histories, my lads' he declared with a great smile. 'I have managed to place... no, erase... err, trace, yes, trace some of your ancestries back to the 1600s. So let's start with you Mr Shepherd...' The master strode (rocking slightly) over to Nicky's desk, and laid one of the large sheets down on the desk top. Carefully and patiently drawn out on the paper was a long family tree tracking back through five generations. Good old Matthews had obviously spent a great deal of time and effort on these ancestral histories, which despite his seemingly constant state of inebriation, were written out in immaculate italic script.

'Nicholas Shepherd: current youngest son of Mary and William – Grandfather, Jack, railway maintenance worker, (at this point there was a loud guffaw from Lordsley.). Great grandfather Charles Victor Avery, Army officer in India. Great-great grandfather Ronald Avery, farmer (another sneering laugh from the back of the class). And if we go even further back, we find that one of your ancestors lived a most colourful life indeed. You have an ancestor named Llewyn Avery who it would appear inherited a large amount of land around 1770. If we go back further still, you will all be interested to hear that we come across one Captain Jack Avery. This gentleman was a "privateer" – what you lads would call a pirate, operating in the South Seas. Alas, I cannot determine the ultimate fate of Captain Avery: but I hope for Mr Shepherd's sake that he managed to bury a vast hoard of gold and jewels somewhere beneath a tropical beach, and evaded the harsh justice of those times... You may well be the heir to an undiscovered fortune my boy!'

All but one of the boys burst out into spontaneous applause, and there were many pats on the back from his friends. Nicky looked a bit embarrassed, but in his mind's eye could see Captain Jack sitting on an upturned rowing boat on silver sands. He was leisurely puffing on a huge cigar, smiling hugely, and making a very graphic gesture in the direction of Lordsley. Sitting on the handle of the spade which he had obviously just used to bury his looted treasure, was an avian specimen bearing an uncanny resemblance to Dave the Chicken...

Lordsley could wait no longer... 'So, your family tree is full of criminals, then?' he said, folding his arms and adopting an air of superiority.

'What a coincidence that you should mention criminals, Mr Lordsley...' said Matthews, walking over to the smug boy at the rear of the class. 'Let us examine your own genealogy and see what we may find. In the 1700s we find Mr George Bumsby – who marries a Miss Alice Tredge, his given occupation is "pig farmer" I see. The next generation records their son Arthur marrying a Miss Marjorie Lawksley, and he was I see a "flitch carter" by trade. It would appear that your forebear, Wilfred Bumsby, seems to have adopted the name "Lawksley" to avoid the attentions of the authorities who were eager to speak to him over allegations of meat theft: and his son, James, narrowly avoided transportation to Australia over the matter of malicious wounding and charges of arson. It was James that appears from record to have changed his surname to "Lordsley" in an effort to further distance himself from accusations of the misappropriation of land and title in 1852. I would be very much surprised if any of us do not find the odd nut in our family trees, gentlemen...'

Lordsley had become strangely silent. Calderman leaned across the aisle and whispered, 'So what have you got to say now, 'Bumsby'– me old pig carrying mate?'

'Yeah – we don't want any more arson around...' added Merry.

Matthews rounded off the lesson by asking all of the boys to research their families as far back as they could, and this would count as prep work. As the bell rang out to end the school day, the master raised his mug high into the air in salute to his young charges. He moved to strike what should have been a heroic pose with one foot upon the raised dais, but once again he miscalculated the distance, and spun into a heap behind the desk. With the dear old boy now snoozing happily with a contented smile upon his face, the class quietly left their tutor to his ancestral slumber...

Having said his goodbyes for the day to his classmates, Nicky found himself deep in thought as he walked out of the Academy and headed for the bus stop. Had he actually managed to absorb any education in his first few days at St Onan's? His academic life so far seemed to have consisted of marvelling at the erratic and unpredictable behaviours of his teachers, and trying by any means possible to avoid the attentions of Piper the dreaded prefect. He still felt the same initial panic as he had on his first day at the Academy, and continued to ask himself if indeed he did actually belong there, amongst boys who were very clear that they thought he didn't. How had his Uncle Joe managed to survive the place, and come out "normal"? He banished this particular thought immediately, as he couldn't find any measure of "normality" into which he could comfortably fit his dear uncle.

The bus spluttered and coughed its way up to the stop. The automatic door was not so automatic today, and had to be manually assisted by the driver- who had some very interesting points to make about the capabilities of the mechanics, some suggestions being biologically creative, to say the least. Finally getting to a seat, Nicky discovered a copy of the local newspaper which some passenger had discarded. Emblazoned across the top of the front page was the headline "LOCAL POLICE RESCUE SHEEP USING JET SKI". Nicky thought that sheep were obviously a lot more technically resourceful than they were given credit for. He wondered what mayhem could possibly ensue if the woolly lads got behind the wheel of their farmer's tractor...

The journey home was uneventful, and no quicker than usual, with the bus driver playing a game of "Blind Man's gear change" at every opportunity. Nicky opened the front door and entered the living room – carefully placing the satchel on the sofa in case of attack. He took off his tie, and was pleased to hear the urgent tones of Uncle Joe's voice issuing forth from the kitchen. Mum, Auntie and Joe were sitting at the kitchen table. Uncle was busy demonstrating his part in the D-Day landings by inventive use of cups, plates and cutlery. He was at present trapped behind the cruet set, with grenades at the ready. He demonstrated how he had crawled behind a damaged tank, spilling salt out of the pot in the process.

'Quick, throw some over your left shoulder, it's unlucky,' said Mum.

'It was certainly unlucky for the buggers that I came across then,' chuckled Joe, doing as he was told. He noticed the boy who had come in to the kitchen, and greeted him cheerily 'Hello, lad! I was just showin' how I helped our boys win at Dunkirk. I lobbed them grenades over at the German tank usin' me skills as a bowler. Did you know, I once had trials for Yorkshire?'

Auntie corrected him – 'No Joe, you were once on trial in Yorkshire...'

'Anyway...' Joe continued (with a chastised look), 'there was bits of German Pansy tank flyin' all over the place when I had finished.'

'What brings you here, uncle? Is everything okay?' Nicky asked.

'Oh yes, no problems. I just called round to check some details about the family with your mum,' he answered.

Rather than run the risk of Joe taking off on another of his detailed flights of fancy, Mum explained the situation. It would appear that Joe's brother Reginald, had gone off on one of his frequent foreign explorations. Ever the seasoned "joiner-in" with the local culture of any given area in which he might find himself, Reg had taken part in some colourful ceremony. In a bizarre incident involving several bottles of Tequila, a large roll of sellotape, two packets of sunflower seeds and a rubber sink plunger, he had inexplicably found himself to have become engaged to one of the Leeward Islands...

Rather than risk even the slightest explanation for what he had just heard, Nicky asked Joe if he could help him with his homework on Genealogy. Mum leapt in quickly. 'I'm sure that Joe will help you, but wait until we have eaten?' she insisted.

Uncle was now busy explaining how he had been brought in as a historical consultant for a book on local legends, which another friend of his was in the process of writing. This was a collection of some of the more terrifying legends pertaining to their locality, on which subject (would you believe it) Joe considered himself to be something of an expert.

'What story are you working on, Uncle?' asked Nicky.

'Well, lad, it's the tale of mystery which centres on a spirit which has attached itself to an ordinary household object,' explained Uncle. 'The story is titled "The Haunted Comb of Lord Belvoir".'

'Is it really scary?' Mum ventured.

'Well it certainly made my hair stand on end, I can tell you...' said Uncle.

Chapter Fifteen

Following a quite animated and boisterous evening meal, the topic of conversation turned back to the subject of Ancestry, and which distant relatives had achieved anything spectacular or heroic. Nicky told Mum, Auntie and Joe all about the distant link with piracy that Mr Matthews had uncovered. Mum and Auntie were able to supply a wealth of detail concerning Uncle Charles, who had seen active service in Burma during World War Two as a sergeant in the "Chindits", fighting alongside fearless Ghurkha troops. Joe asked if the boy was going to write about Cousin Maurice and his escapades.

This comment earned him a stern look from Mother, and Auntie told him, 'I think that particular tale is best left untold, don't you?'

Nicky's curiosity was now on high alert, and so he asked them to tell him all about Cousin Maurice. Had he been a military hero? Was he another pirate?

Over a cup of tea, Mum began to explain about the cousin in question.

Being an orphan, Maurice had hated the institution into which he had been placed. At the tender age of eleven he had run away. He had somehow kept on running until he found himself at the coast, where by some means he was able to get aboard a small ship destined for Portsmouth. Once at this great harbour, he gained access to another ship which was setting off for distant lands. He continued to travel the high seas on board a variety of ships until he was about eighteen years of age, when he returned to England and signed up for the Royal Navy. During the war, he saw action in several violent sea battles, and was apparently decorated for his bravery (Auntie said that having seen his wife – it was she that needed the decorating...). During a period of shore leave, he had met and wooed a young lady from the town, and the pair were married during his next period of leave.

Having settled back in the village, all seemed to be a picture of domestic bliss – but moves were afoot which would blast Maurice's ship out of the seemingly calm waters. There were rumours circulating around the village concerning the fidelity of his wife (or to be more specific – the lack of it...). She was found to be engaging in a torrid affair with the local coal merchant – to which she confessed when Maurice confronted her. She packed a bag and left the house, leaving poor Maurice hurt and confused. Such was his anguish that one night he picked up his service revolver, loaded it, and placed it against his head. As he pulled the trigger however, an unexpected sneeze ended up with Maurice being left with part of his ear blown off, and permanent hearing loss. Once out of hospital, he became a recluse, rarely venturing out into the wider village. Fate took a hand however, and one stormy night he was shocked to see his former wife on his doorstep asking that he allow her to return.

Maurice of course took her in, and was unaware of her planned deceit until he found his bank account empty – and his wife again missing. This was too much for Maurice, and he vowed to end it all. He turned on the gas and stuck his head in the oven, but was fortunately discovered by a neighbour visiting by chance. The after-effects of this on poor Maurice were to leave him with a severe speech impediment. Still bitterly unhappy with his lot, he put on his finest naval dress uniform (complete with medals) and planned to throw himself out of the top floor window of the house. This he did, but fortunately his downward trajectory was halted when he bounced off the roof of a passing lorry. In another terrible twist of irony, the lorry was the one which belonged to (and being driven by) the local coal merchant, with whom his wife was having a liaison...

Once out of hospital, Maurice seemed to come to terms with the terrible hand that fate had dealt him. Deaf in one ear, with a restrictive speech problem, and now with one leg shorter than the other due to the injury sustained in his fall, he decided to write his memoirs. Having completed thirty-six pages of patiently-written script, he needed the lavatory. At the top of the attic stairs, he tripped over the pet cat, and fell down the remainder of the stairs from top to bottom – sadly breaking his neck...

'I might just write that Maurice was a navy hero during the war...' said Nicky.

'I think that might be best...' added Auntie.

Uncle Joe changed the subject by stating, 'Do you know, ever since I took the rear view mirror out of the car – I've never looked back...'

'More tea, Joe?' queried Mum.

Without any prompting or warning, Joe then launched into a verbal assault on the owner of the village television rental and repair shop. This establishment was run by a somewhat withdrawn individual by the name of Mr Dudley Primm. The owner was proud to advertise the fact that this was the only vegetarian television repair and rental shop in the whole county. He had cunningly come up with the title of "Radio Lentils". Joe had marched into Dudley's establishment and ordered the very finest satellite television system from him. The hapless fitter had unfortunately broken the receiver dish when fitting the system. Frog-marched from the premises by an irate Uncle, the fitter was told never to darken Joe's doorstep again, and that he himself would make a new dish for the purpose. He would not pay Primm's exorbitant prices, and he surely had everything which he would need in his famous shed. Joe set to work and made a brand new dish out of an old pudding tin. His argument with Dudley was centred around the fact that try as he might, Joe was only able to pick up Yorkshire...

With the family tree drawn up as far as possible (and the more dubious members pruned out) Nicky's homework was all done, and so he prepared for bed and a few minutes with a good book. He said goodnight to the adults, who were now all chattering animatedly around the kitchen table. He went upstairs to the sound of Uncle Joe recounting the tale of how he called Gamblers Anonymous and Alcoholics Anonymous, and bet them £50 that he was pissed.

Nicky must have been really tired, because he had fallen asleep with his book still open. The new day had already broken, but since no-one had kept the receipt, it was unlikely that he could claim a refund. There was hardly any colour in the grey morning, and the rain was falling heavily as if the clouds could not be bothered to carry it any longer, and had decided to just drop the lot, and go off and have a cup of coffee somewhere.

As he waited for the bus to arrive, the insistent raindrops bounced off the pavement and the road, throwing up a strange mist to knee height. Water found its way through the gaps in the badly-maintained bus shelter roof, and directly down Nicky's neck. The bus came around the church corner slowly and fountained water out from either side, causing the pavement puddles to swell in size, and attempting to dissolve the local postman who was going about his lawful business. In this afternoon's Divinity lesson, Nicky was certainly going to put in a written complaint about that bugger Noah.

It was a very soggy, squelchy puddle-hopping walk to school this morning. The boys seemed to be clustered together as they walked like King Penguins on the march away from the biblical deluge which hammered down upon them. Nicky would not have been surprised to have arrived at the Academy gates with his coat pockets full of fresh salmon. What may have raised an eyebrow is if it had been in a tin...

So the gutters of St Onan's leaked like gossip stories in a cheap tabloid newspaper. Even the inscrutable ravens huddled together under the buttresses like damp undertakers. There were no groups of boys gathered in the quad; all had fled indoors to the relative security of their form rooms, where they could remove their sodden coats, drip onto the parquet flooring in peace, and complain about the sodden weather. Such a gathering was in evidence in Room Nine, where Nicky, Merry, Calderman, Davis and Trevill had removed their raincoats, and stood around admiring the wet from the knee down style of their trousers. The friends all knew that technically, it was not permitted to be in the form room before assembly, and so were keeping the volume of their conversation low. Just as Davis was stretching prior to a major yawn, a tremendous thunderclap tore the air outside the window – and the boys all instinctively dived for cover under the nearest desk.

'Bloody hell, Davis – don't do that again!' laughed Calderman.

As the boom of thunder died away, the boys could plainly hear footsteps coming slowly up the corridor. 'Oh hell – we'll be for it now, here comes Matthews,' said Merry.

'That's not Matthews – listen...' said a nervous Trevill.

The sound of the footfalls was quite plain, but was augmented by a third tap or click just after the second step. The first contact upon the wood floor sounded louder than the others. Merry looked shocked, and stuttered, 'You don't think it's Old Man Bailey do you?'

'Don't be soft, Merry, that's just a story they tell you as a first year to frighten you,' said a rather unconvincing Calderman.

Winston Alfred Bailey had been a master at the Academy for forty-five years. When he was alive, he had a wooden leg and walked with a silver-tipped cane, and the rumour that his ghost still walked the corridors of the Academy was told to every new entrant in the hope of instilling fear. He was reputed to stalk the corridors on the lookout for any boy attempting to skip lessons; and his old class room had been Room Nine. The boys slowly edged to the side of the door, as the sound of the footsteps came nearer. They heard the "click" of metal on wood as whoever it was came up the three steps to the main corridor. All of them were mentally preparing their excuses for being in the room before assembly, when the steps came to an abrupt halt just outside their door. Without warning, the door handle began to turn slowly and precisely. The friends were now frozen behind the door in fear.

Some ridiculous urge seemed to force Nicky to move forward and grasp the door handle. As he opened the door, he began to make his excuse, 'Sorry, sir, we are just putting our wet thi...'He never finished his sentence. In every direction, both left and right, the corridor was empty...

'They must have run off and hidden,' said Nicky.

'Old Man Bailey couldn't have run off that fast, he had a wooden leg!' gasped Merry.

'It was probably just the heating pipes,' said Calderman, himself now scanning the corridor.

'There's usually a perfectly sensible explanation for these things at the end of the day,' said Davis calmly. 'No need to panic over a little noise from an old building.'

As he said this, there was another concussive crash of thunder which made everything in the room vibrate. As one, the gang took off at a sprint down the corridor and headed for the assembly hall, not stopping for breath until they were safely hidden within the mass of fellow students. Once the terror had left them a little, the five friends dissolved into adrenalin-fuelled laughter.

Back in the old block, the door to Room Nine slowly closed by itself, and clicked shut.

The morning assembly took the usual form, with Goodwill preaching to the masses from his position centre stage. Today's 'surprise offering' was a pair of white Y-fronts taped to the front of the lectern. The Academy anthem received the customary mauling by the raised voices of the boys, and Mr Newhouse at the organ was consumed by a fit of barely-contained silent laughter.

Goodwill began, 'Good morning, gentlemen.'

'Good morning, sir.'

'I just have a couple of things to make mention of today. I have been informed that the price of a copy of the recently taken Academy photograph will be ten pounds each. Please place your orders today via your form masters, and Mr Heath will require payment in full by Friday at the latest. I have one name on the Walking List – and that is Mr Richard Weatherill of Form 1A. Please report to my study immediately after this assembly. Thank you...'

With that, the head swept out of the rear doors as usual. The staff followed on, led by Madame Dreadfell and her weapons of Mass Distraction. The boys clustered around Weatherill and tried to ask him why he was bound for the headmaster's study.

'I haven't the faintest idea, chums... ' said the boy. 'But I hope that it's nothing negative...'

Worried about their friend having to pay a visit to the head's study, the boys prepared for their first lesson. Latin was boring today, with just the usual grammar to be dissected and tortured by inexperienced tongues. English was slightly more interesting. Mr Hyde-Jones had come up with the idea that the class should write their own Shakespearian poetry with a goose-feather quill pen. The boys were to make these themselves using a traditional pen knife. The entire class considered this to be a good idea, and were happy to take up the challenge. One person was not at all pleased at the master's scheme (in fact, extremely pissed off at the whole idea)- and that was Baldy the Goose who was now sulking and shivering under cover of the bike sheds.

Presently standing to attention in front of the headmaster's desk, and smiling a faint knowing smile, is one Richard Weatherill Esquire.

Goodwill sat at his desk staring rather angrily at the copy of the long Academy photograph which had been supplied to him by Mr Heath. He regarded Weatherill over the top of his glasses and sighed.

'Mr Weatherill, do you take pride in being a member of this Academy?'

'Yes, indeed I do, sir.'

'Could you explain why?'

'Yes, sir – I appreciate the high standard of education available, and the honour of studying in such historic surroundings, sir...'

'Could you explain why we take a photographic record of the Academy on an annual basis?'

'Yes, sir – to record the whole of the Academy student body for posterity, sir...'

At this point, Goodwill beckoned Weatherill over to his desk and handed him a heavy antique magnifying glass.

'Do you recognise the boy just here?' (He pointed at the photograph)

'Yes, sir, that's me...' said Weatherill.

'And how about just here?' asked the head (Pointing again.)

'I think that may be me also, sir...' said the boy.

'Does this face look familiar at all?' asked Goodwill, indicating a little further across the row.

'That may possibly be myself, sir...' Weatherill answered.

'Do you feel concerned that your time with us at St Onan's will pass unnoticed?'

'Oh no, sir...'

'Then why, may I ask, do you appear on this photograph a total of five times...?'

'Are you sure, sir...?'

'Indeed I am most certain Weatherill – and wearing, I cannot fail to observe, a dizzying variety of headgear...'

'You have told us, sir, that throughout our academic career, we will find ourselves wearing many hats, sir...'

'NOT ALL AT THE SAME TIME – AND NOT IN MY PHOTOGRAPH...' shouted Goodwill.

'Gosh, sorry, sir- it was just a bit of high spirits, a sort of 'spur-of-the-moment' thing, sir...'

'Five different hats in five differing locations is not a "spur-of-the-moment" thing Weatherill, it would have required considerable planning...'

'I shall endeavour to put this planning to a more academic use in the future, sir...' said Weatherill.

'See that you do exactly that, boy... I shall have to try and edit your appearances to a unit of one on the photograph, but I sense that there was no malicious intent. You may go, Mr Weatherill, and ponder upon your future. Should you repeat your ad-lib performance, then that future will be considerably shorter.'

Weatherill said, 'Thank you, sir...' and marched smartly out of his study. Goodwill suddenly called him back. He stood again in front of the head's desk.

'One more thing, Mr Weatherill – before you go, be so good as to put back my mortarboard, which I just saw you take off my hat stand – there's a good chap...'

Due to Everyman's Law of Divergent Opposition and Discovery (Under which calm will reign supreme, until someone discovers that the good advice which they were given by a well-meaning friend has turned out to have a detrimental and irrevocable effect, forcing the recipient to grip the friend lightly by the throat.), there was a suitably heated confrontation taking place in the smoky atmosphere of the staff room.

Professor Strangler had waited in a highly agitated state, never taking his gimlet eyes away from the door. Matthews arrived unsteadily, and trod his normal meandering path toward the coffee table – where he was intercepted by the irate Professor, who greeted his colleague by gripping his lapels and shouting...

'Matthews, you drunken old pillock, I took your advice about legal representation over my divorce – and I want to know just what the bloody hell you thought you were playing at...'

Matthews smiled at him with a look of serene benevolence upon his face.

'I merely tried to assist you in your hour of need, dear boy...' he said.

'You told me to get in touch with this man, who was a friend of yours, and whom you declared to be a "first class barrister" with years of experience,' growled Strangler.

'And you did contact him?' enquired Matthews.

'Eventually, yes – every time I tried to telephone the idiot, he always gave some pathetic excuse about being busy – and seemed to be engaged in making coffee for some other client,' said Strangler. 'I gave him the divorce to handle despite his protestations, and I must say that he made an absolutely piss-poor foul up of the whole damn thing. I have lost my house, my new car, my designer furniture, the kids now hate me, and what is worse is that this idiot, whom you recommended, has saddled me with an exorbitant level of maintenance which I have to pay to the wretched woman in order to be thrown out of my own bloody house!'

Strangler was now foaming at the mouth, and the rest of the staff present were settling in for the rest of the entertainment...

'Just how long did that clown train for?' asked Strangler.

'Nine months, I believe...' answered Matthews.

'NINE BLOODY MONTHS?...' screamed the professor. 'Are you seriously telling me that you referred me to a barrister who has only trained for nine months?'

'To be fair, old chap, I never said that he was an expert lawyer,' said Matthews.

'Oh yes you bloody well did- you told me that he was, and I quote, "a brilliant and fully trained barrister, who is very popular with his customers," you said.'

'Ahh...' said Matthews, 'I think I can see the problem here.'

'So can I – you told me to speak to this man who would be only too happy to listen, and who could advise me' said Strangler.

'I never told you that he was legally qualified...' declared Matthews.

'Highly-skilled barrister, was what you told me,' growled the Professor.

Matthews again smiled at his angry friend.

'I think that there may be a little confusion here. I told you that he was highly-trained barista...'

In the corner of the staff lounge, Messrs Hyde-Jones and Newhouse high-fived each other...

Entering the room with all the inherent stealth of a would-be assassin, the Reverend Gerald Felchingham quietly helped himself to a cup of very strong tea, and slipped into his chair without a word or a glance at his fellow teachers. He had spent the previous evening carrying out another "ritual cleansing" of his house, due to events which had recently transpired in his absence. He had researched ancient Native American rites for ridding the property of unwanted spirits. This had demanded that he burn sage in bundles, and blow the smoke into each and every corner of the rooms, waving the smoke away with an eagle feather. He had been unable to locate or obtain any wild sage from any of his local supermarkets, and the attendant at the late-night garage where he had made enquiries had been quite rude and unhelpful to him. He had been forced to improvise by setting light to a packet of sage and onion stuffing which he had found lurking at the back of a cupboard, and urging the resultant smoke into the corners of the room by means of a feather duster which his cleaner had discarded when she had fled the property in fright after witnessing yet another manifestation of dear old Stan's handiwork.

Felchingham was teaching himself to type, by means of an old manual typewriter which he had picked up for the princely sum of a fiver in the local charity shop. In an attempt to divert himself from his now almost daily supernatural stalking, he had decided to begin work on the book which he had been planning to write for the past few years. This work would outline his struggle with all of the various forms of religions, and would in particular deal with his battle against his conscience; and what may be termed the "Darker side" of belief. He had already come up with what he thought was a snappy title for his book- which was to be called "101 Damnations". The typewriter sat freshly polished and ready for action on his living-room table, surrounded by a city of reference books which seemed to provide a Manhattan skyline of ecclesiastical education. Paper sat across the ribbon of the machine in readiness, but so far he was merely performing exercises to speed up his use of the keys. To build up pace and agility, he had begun typing out the age-old training routine which has been performed by would-be typists for years. He had hesitantly begun to type out the phrase "The Quick Brown Fox Jumps over the Lazy Dog", and had been quite pleased with his progress so far. He had left his task to engage in his late night sage hunt, and upon his return had found that several typed sheets now lay on the floor. Terrified, he stared at the sheets in disbelief. They had all been typed with the same phrase which he was using for practice, over and over again. Well, not quite the same phrase, as a closer look soon confirmed.

His shaking hand pulled the sheet of paper from the typewriter, and when he read the sentence written on it, his worst fears were realised. There, on each of the sheets, with the last one in glorious capital letters, was the phrase which struck terror into his heart.

"The Quick Brown Fox jumps over the Lazy KNOB..."

He then discovered a scribbled note from his cleaner, which stated in no uncertain terms exactly what she was not prepared to put up with, where to send the wages which were due to her, and specific instructions as to where he could stick his job. This had presumably been in response to his previous idea for thwarting the spirit of Stan. The rev. had written out banishment curses and cleansing prayers in a wide variety of ancient runic scripts including Norse, Futhorc and Ogam. These had been placed at strategic points all around the house, and had presumably frightened the living daylights out of his dear cleaning lady. What may have just tipped her over the edge was the manner in which Stan had chosen to respond. She would have been the first person to witness the dozens of post-it notes stuck all around the living room, which were written in a rather shaky, but clearly readable spectral hand. The notes were a direct response from Stan after the rev's latest attempts to banish him. They all read:

"You can Rune... but you can't hide.'

Chapter Sixteen

It was the first lesson after the morning break, which was a double period of biology in the charming care of Professor Darwin. The boys jostled their way into the lab and sat at the benches in their now accustomed positions. Enter the professor, stage right. Note gown trapped securely and efficiently in laboratory door. Please make note of the sound of tearing cloth as the master is almost pulled off his feet when his progress is suddenly halted. Now wearing the surviving half of the gown, the master turned to face the class.

'Hello, boys. Today we will continue to look at living cells and cell structure. I thought that we would enjoy a little look at some of our own blood cells, and the contents thereof. We will prepare microscope slides and have a good old butchers at what is coursing around our body, keeping us alive and healthy.'

'Can we choose who is going to donate the blood for us to look at, sir?' asked Merry.

'Alas no, young Merry – you each will produce a tiny sample of your own, which you will place on the microscope slide for examination,' answered Darwin.

'Will it be much blood, sir?' asked a nervous Davis.

'Indeed no – a little prick is all that will be required,' said the Professor.

'So it's all down to you then Lordsley...' said Calderman, causing much laughter.

The huge shape of Bernie the lab assistant appeared from out of the back room, and began to open the cupboards at floor level and take out the microscopes, which he placed delicately on the benches in front of each boy. They noted that for a man of such immense size, he moved almost silently as he distributed the equipment. He returned the smile from Kendy with a huge grin of his own, and returned to whatever task he had been engaged in within the mysterious confines of the laboratory ante-room. Some unspoken understanding seemed to have passed between them.

'Now then, chaps...' began the master. 'Take the small sharp, and just prick the end of your finger, remembering to clean off with the antiseptic wipe provided. One small drop of blood should be applied to the middle of one of the glass slides in front of you. The other slide should be drawn over the top of the first one, to spread a thin film across the glass. Keep the slides together, and place them under the clips on the microscope shelf. If you wipe off any excess onto the card which I have provided, we can also test your blood grouping as an extra bonus.'

The boys set about the given task. Fingers were jabbed all around the room, with Weatherill now attired in a surgeon's mask and hospital cap. Slides were under construction by all of the class, and some unscheduled direct hits were scored upon the backside of the unsuspecting Lordsley.

'Now we use the smallest magnification first, boys, and we can gradually increase the view until we get a good look at our prey in the eyepiece,' said Darwin.

There were a number of variations on the theme of 'Oooh... Wow... Crikey... and Eurrgh!' from the assembled trainee scientists. 'Now we will attempt to make a simple diagram of what we are seeing' said the master 'and if you have all made your mark on the testing cards, then I will collect them and let you know what blood grouping you have.'

The teacher began to walk slowly around the rows of boys, checking their progress with their drawings of blood cells, whilst also collecting in the testing cards, onto which each scholar had been instructed to write his name. Calderman raised his hand.

'Yes, Calderman, can I help you?' asked the prof.

'I was just wondering, sir. Do you think that if someone were to change their name to "Acula" by deed poll, and then qualify as a doctor, would it really freak people out?'

'Quite possibly, Mr Calderman, quite possibly,' answered Darwin, grinning.

Professor Darwin had laid all of the test cards out on the desk in front of him. He noted that upon counting the cards, there would appear to be one boy who had not handed in a test. Nicky noticed that Kendy was looking nervous, and guessed that it was he that had not volunteered a blood sample for testing. The master put on his reading glasses, and scrutinised the cards in front of him. 'Mr Kendy...' he said. 'You haven't handed in a testing card. Did I hand out enough of them?'

'Oh yes, sir...' came the nervy reply. 'But I'm afraid that I am not allowed to give away any of my blood, sir...' Kendy ventured.

'Ah, religious grounds, I expect...' said the master.

'Well, something like that,' whispered Kendy.

Nicky decided to dive in with an explanation to help his friend. 'Kendy is a member of a particularly observant sect, sir, and he can't use blood for any frivolous purpose...'

This seemed to satisfy the curiosity of the master for the time being, and so he went on to analyse each card which the boys had supplied, and inform them of their respective blood groups. He noted the reaction on the small squares of the testing cards, and called out the grouping to each boy in turn. Merry was tensed like a coiled spring, and seemed to be waiting for something. What he was in fact anticipating became clear when the master called out, 'Now, let me see... ah yes – Lordsley...'

'Dickhead positive' called out Merry, who sat back grinning – mission accomplished.

Lordsley was understandably furious with his classmates at the explosion of laughter which ensued. Even Darwin had to stifle a chuckle at the interjection. What was then clearly audible to all of the boys was the deep-throated laughter which was coming from the laboratory back room, where Bernie had obviously heard Merry's ad-lib. Kendy was pleased that the attention of the class had been taken away from him, and he leaned over and spoke to Nicky.

'Thanks for that, Shep – I just can't do any of that sort of thing,' he said.

'No worries, mate,' said Nicky. 'Is your religion really that strict?'

Kendy stared intently at Nicky, and seemed to come to some sort of decision. 'Look Shep...' he said, 'I may have to tell you a strange secret which will explain a few things – but I need to know that you can be absolutely trusted if I decide to tell you. If you tell anyone else, I will deny it anyway, and you would not get anyone here to believe you – if that is, you believe it yourself...'

This sounded brilliantly mysterious to Nicky. Was this normal yet anxious boy some sort of secret agent working undercover for an evil foreign power? He certainly wouldn't ask Kendy to reveal the "Big Secret" here in front of any of the class, however much he might trust them as friends. Kendy's almost pleading expression made Nicky determined to keep any shared confidence under wraps whatever the facts might be.

'Tell you what Kendy. Why don't you come over to my house at the weekend? Mum would love to meet you, and we can get out my telescope and do some star-gazing if the weather is all right... What do you say?'

For some reason, Kendy found Nicky's remark very funny indeed, but thanked him for the offer, and agreed to come over and stay for the weekend. Nicky asked him if his parents would be happy with him being away from them for a couple of days – at which point Kendy again folded up in laughter, and answered, 'I think that my folks are probably used to me being away from the family...'

Trevill had been told by the professor that he was the proud possessor of a quite rare blood group of AB rhesus negative. The Dorset native was expressing his displeasure at this fact to Darwin in depressed tones: 'Well, that be just moi luck an' no mistake, surr... I could be endin' up loike moi cousin Denzil...'he said.

'It really is not a problem, young Trevill...' said the master

'Well you'm moight think that, surr, but Denzil was a rare blood group too, and he was also findin' 'im self-afflicted by that there Hee-mo-phil-yer. He was a real unpredictable little bleeder, surr...'

'I'm sorry to hear that Trevill,' replied Darwin, somewhat concerned.

'Well... 'tis alroight now o'course – as 'eem had it cured, surr...'

'How on earth did he become cured of haemophilia, Trevill?' asked the fascinated master.

'Well 'ee 'ad it all cured by 'avin' that there acupuncture, surr...'

'We surely live and learn, Trevill...' was the professor's measured response.

The bell called an end to the microscopic analysis and the scratching of pencils on paper. The master was still shaking his head in disbelief at the information which Trevill had imparted to him, and had begun to wonder if it were not time to dash off again on some mission of discovery to parts foreign...He asked the boys to read up on blood cells and their functions for homework, as he could not think of anything else at the moment. He would have to ensure that he did not ask the boy Kendy to perform any experiments that might offend his declared religious sensibilities, and which were utterly alien to him. He was quite unaware that the boy was capable of performing feats which would make him wish that he had never left the dark rainforests of the Amazon. He might have to speak with his colleague the Reverend Felchingham for a little sensible advice.

In the culinary fortress of the kitchens, there had been a meeting of the greatest minds in serving-hatch history. Doris, Agnes and Winnie had held an informal meeting, and decided once and for all to get the problem of the missing food and supplies sorted out. They had decided to put their agreed theory to the test. A batch of particularly splendid muffins had been lovingly prepared. Young Alice had been nominated as the agent who should place the "bait" in the kitchen trap. Three of the wonderful cakes had been placed on the steel work surface above the large floor cupboards which housed pots and pans. Winnie had set up her new video camera to cover the entire area of the worktop, and it would record exactly when (and if) the previously unseen hands lifted the muffins.

All four of the kitchen staff had sat all night in comfy chairs in Betty's office, awaiting any cake-based movement from the main kitchen area. Having plied themselves with cocoa during the twilight watch, the milky beverage must have lulled each of them off to sleep. They awoke in the gentle dawn light, and Alice dashed into the main kitchen to see if the trap had indeed been sprung. What she found was quite touching. The steel worktop had been sprinkled with flour by the team of ladies – to collect any fingerprints from cake thieves. Alice saw three empty circles where the muffins had been previously placed. Sitting on the worktop was a delicate and beautifully-made daisy chain necklace. Written in the flour underneath, were the words "Thank you xxx"' in immaculate copperplate script...

No further photographic evidence was forthcoming, with which the ladies could prove the existence of the remover of muffins. Winnie's preparations had been precise and thorough, with batteries checked, and area of picture coverage carefully set. The tripod had been set and locked correctly, and the motion sensor switched on as per the complicated and specific instructions in the camera manual. Winnie would not be nominated in this year's BAFTA listings however, as she had forgotten to remove the lens cap...

Brigadier Betty was preparing for another dinner service. Her new tablets, which the doctor had hurriedly prescribed and thrust at her without charge, just to remove this raving woman from his immediate vicinity, were having the desired effect. Now strangely calm, she had selected and armed herself with her stoutest kitchen ladle, which she twirled in her fingers as she strode around the kitchen peering into every corner. She had become so calm that when she saw a small, large-eyed child wave to her from the open door of the large pot cupboard, she smiled and waved back...

The boys meanwhile, were amusing themselves over lunch, by calling 'Yoo-Hoo' in the direction of Piper the prefect, and stating loudly that the book which they were currently reading was so good that, 'I was glued to it...'and, 'I've decided to stick with it.' Calderman in particular, made Merry choke on his food when he told him loudly to 'Get a grip'. They all knew that there was not a great deal that the prefect could do to any of them with a bandaged hand. If their collective opinion of the boy was true, then this would also severely curtail at least one of his more disreputable hobbies.

The highlight of the mealtime was the point at which Weatherill was instructed to remove the RAF flying helmet (which none of the boys had seen him put on), and the master who was convulsed with laughter as he instructed him to remove it...

Masters chuckled, boys laughed, Betty prowled, Piper fumed, and lunch ended with the strange "clonk" of the previously sonorous bell. Upon investigation by Dr Chambers, it would appear that some blighter had indeed blighted the bell by placing over it a very generous pair of Y-fronts. The doer of the deed was a complete mystery, as surely no-one capable of wearing pants of that size would be in any way able to climb up the bell tower.

The physics lesson had been a bit of a joke today, and few of the boys actually got it.

Yesterday's thunderstorm and torrential rain had caused one or two worrying problems for Professor Strangler and his beloved Physics Department. Due to the advanced age and decrepit state of the Academy roof, there could be any number of fluid threats visited on the classrooms due to rain. What was presently occupying the pinball mind of the physics guru had little to do with the odd pool of water found on the floor. During the storm, the lightning had decided to send its finger down the old copper conductor which was stapled to the side of the Physics lab. Some student had left a small window open, and the charge had leapt inside and earthed itself via the metal framework which surrounded the "project" currently being worked upon by the

Physics Club boys. There had obviously been some strange change enabled by the lightning strike, which had seemingly created something much more terrifying than that which it had destroyed.

Local plumbers had been called in to deal with what was presumed to be a leak from some of the ancient pipework or guttering, but the two trades people who came to look for the source of the leak (Walter DeViner and Hazel Rodd) were baffled. Strangler pulled down the venetian blind to the workroom, to prevent prying eyes seeing what was taking place inside the room. He could research the reason for what was visible in the centre of the room, with the help of his more accomplished students, and the reference library. Secretly ecstatic over what he had seen created; he couldn't wait to see exactly what it could do. The other matter was one that he had no answer for. Try as he might, he could not figure out any explanation as to why it should be raining – indoors.

He more or less blustered his way through the class, giving the boys work to do on the subject of generating and storing static electricity. As in schools everywhere, there was the usual demonstration of "how to make your hair stand on end" using a Van De Graaff generator. The boys were also technically entertained by the use of the Wimshurst Machine. Whilst one boy was instructed to turn the handles of the machine, the other classmates were told to join hands in a line. Strangler directed the boy at the end of the line to direct the static spark toward the electrical measurement meter. Unfortunately, Merry completely misjudged the distance, and accidentally "zapped" Lordsley. 'Isn't Science wonderful,' said Calderman.

The lesson was interrupted several times, as the professor kept going over to the lab workroom door and peering into the room – as if checking that whatever should (or should perhaps not) be there was still in place. Whatever was going on in there, at least the rain had stopped. He was suddenly blinded by an intense bright blue-white flash from the centre of the room, and he recoiled from the doorway, rubbing his eyes which showed a bright after-image.

'Sorry about that, you fellows...' he declared. 'Just had to check on... Oh... That's strange.'

He more or less blustered his way through the class, giving the boys work to do on the subject of generating and storing static electricity. As in schools everywhere, there was the usual demonstration of 'how to make your hair stand on end' using a Van Der Graaf generator. The boys were also technically entertained by the use of the Wimshurst Machine. Whilst one boy was instructed to turn the handles of the machine, the other classmates were told to join hands in a line. Strangler directed the boy at the end of the line to direct the static spark toward the electrical measurement meter. Unfortunately, Merry completely misjudged the distance, and accidentally 'zapped' Lordsley. 'Isn't Science wonderful' said Calderman.

The lesson was interrupted several times, as the Professor kept going over to the lab work room door and peering into the room – as if checking that whatever should (or should perhaps not) be there was still in place. Whatever was going on in there, at least the rain had stopped. He was suddenly blinded by an intense bright blue-white flash from the centre of the room, and he recoiled from the doorway, rubbing his eyes which showed a bright after-image.

'Sorry about that, you fellows...' he declared. 'Just had to check on... Oh... That's strange.'

'Keep perfectly still for a moment, sir,' Kendy instructed the Professor.

'What the hell is going on Kendy?' asked the confused master

'I think that whatever you have going on in that room has created a Temporal Inversion' said Kendy, matter-of-factly. 'I doubt that the Inversion Field will hold up for very long, but it's best to wait until the surge has passed, sir...'

Strangler opened his eyes fully, and stared at the boy. 'How the devil do you come to know so much about such things, Kendy?' he asked.

'My father has told me about something similar which used to happen to him and the people he worked with in the power plant, sir, and I can help – if you will let me go into the room and try to calm it down,' said the boy.

'You could be killed, boy!' stammered the master. 'You can't go in there...'

'I will be safe, sir, just pull that dimmer switch off the wall and hand it to me please,' said Kendy.

Not daring to resist, yet not knowing why he was doing what the boy had instructed him to do, the master levered the lab dimmer switch off the wall and placed it in the young man's hand.

'And the long steel rule too, if you please, sir...' asked Kendy.

With that, the boy stripped off the plastic coating from the wires of the dimmer using his teeth, and stepped forward toward the door.

'But it's incredibly dangerous..!' said Strangler.

'No, I should be okay, sir; I always use a good quality fluoride toothpaste,' answered Kendy.

Strangler noticed to his horror that the rest of the class seemed frozen. Just as the thought faded, there was the metallic clatter of a steel rule hitting the tiled floor, and another bright flash from the room. He was suddenly aware of a strong smell of burned electrical wiring, and then it seemed that normality had returned, with the boys in the class moving and chatting as if nothing had happened. Kendy emerged from the room smiling, and brushing some burned remains of wire from his sleeve.

'My God, Kendy... it looks like you have saved the day!' said the Professor. 'Are you all right?'

'Absolutely fine, thank you, sir. I have turned down the Inversion by connecting a switch to your circuit. The problem will settle down in about an hour – but I should keep everyone out of that room until it closes down to a safe level.'

'Should I nail up the door?' asked Strangler, nervously.

'Not unless you are certain exactly where the points of the nails are likely to emerge, sir...' said Kendy, 'Best just to lock it up – and I will tell you more about it later if you would like me to?'

'How long will you need?' asked the fascinated master.

'Probably only fifteen minutes – or about a week if you open that door again...' laughed the boy.

As the pants-smitten bell did its very best to signal the end of the lesson, Nicky went over to speak to his friend. 'What were you doing with the professor? Is everything all right?' he asked.

'Yeah, no problem. He just wanted me to help him to save a little time...' said Kendy.

On the way to their Divinity lesson, the boys passed the music master, Mr Newhouse. He was wearing his black gown over his biker's jacket, and had his earphones in – playing a very realistic air guitar as he strode up the corridor. What was clearly visible under his leather jacket (and impressed the boys no end) was his tee-shirt bearing the legend "GO FORTH AND AMPLIFY". As he saw the boys approaching, he beckoned Merry over and passed him one earpiece. 'How's it hangin', gang?' he asked the boys, before saying to the transfixed Merry, 'Eddie Van Halen – I swear the bugger's got another secret arm!'. Catch you later, dudes'. He swept off up the corridor, still soloing for all he was worth. All of the boys thought that the guy was so cool – that you could probably keep milk fresh in his pockets for about a year.

The tormented soul that was the Reverend Felchingham looked like one of the combat troops that had only just returned from Vietnam. He was acutely nervous, and flinched at each and every unexpected noise. Today was not a day on which he would share his personal window of enlightenment on the matter of spiritual discipline. Today was very likely to be the day that he would run screaming from the classroom, and in all possibility not stop running until his feet touched Southern Europe. He decided to play it safe, and give the class instruction on the religion of Buddhism. In a calm and instructive manner, he began by explaining the origin of Buddhism in the sixth century, and how it deals with the pathways to spiritual enlightenment. He had just written on the blackboard the "Four Noble Truths" when he suddenly became fixated by the first three letters in the word "Noble", which seemed to stand out in a neon red glow. He shook his head in order to dispel the vision, and was pleased to note that all was again, normal. He and the boys then discussed the topic amongst all of them (no-Buddhists do not march about singing 'Hare Krishna') and (no, there isn't always a fat one at the back chanting 'Hare Ramsdens').

The Reverend was well on his way to explaining all about the "Noble Eightfold Path" when he chanced to look down at the floor behind his desk. Drawn in chalk on the wooden parquet was a large arrow, which pointed to his chair. Curiosity began to get the better of him, and excusing himself to the class, he began to trace the line of chalk back from the arrow. The line went to the edge of the raised dais, then dropped vertically and unbroken to the floor. Once on floor level, the line ran at an oblique angle out of the classroom door.

The rev. opened the door, not taking his eyes off the white line of chalk. Down the corridor he followed it, as it descended the stairs without any break. Down the stone corridor of the ground floor ran the line, and verily did the rev. follow its path in great curiosity. Without a bend or stutter, the line led him right down the long corridor and past the Honours Wall. Now speeding up slightly, Felchingham continued to track the line like a bloodhound – until it abruptly disappeared under the door of the cleaners' store cupboard just before the main doors to the quad. He knew that the line could not go any further, and he felt compelled to find out exactly what lay at the other end of the line. Twisting the stained brass door handle, he opened the door and let himself into the cleaners' store. The line ended in a chalk rectangle about a foot across and ten inches high. Inside the rectangle was one word – KNOB.

After waiting for quite a while back in the classroom, the boys were beginning to get rather worried about what may have happened to their AWOL teacher. Calderman and Nicky took a group consensus that they should organise a searching party immediately. The group of would-be rescuers set off and followed the chalk line which seemed to have led their tutor into lands as yet unknown. Down the stone stairs they marched, in complete silence. Having followed the chalk all the way up to the door of the cleaners' store, the party came to a halt. There were faint noises emanating from within, and also a weird clanking sound.

'Someone should knock on the door,' said Davis.

'And how do we know that this is where he is?' asked Merry. 'I mean, he may come screaming out at us like a loony...'

'Well we must take some sort of action,' said Lordsley (from the rear of the group). 'I mean to say, you fellows are showing no concern for the poor man – who might be in some sort of trouble. You must do something to help him...'

'I intend to,' said Calderman, 'just as soon as I have qualified as a psychiatrist'.

'I will talk him out of there,' said Ashman.

'Don't be stupid Ashman,' said Lordsley. 'You are not trained as a negotiator, and one idiotic slip could cause a great deal of harm and suffering.'

'So – rather like your Parents then?' answered Ashman.

Nicky attempted to take charge. 'Look, we can't leave him in there, and he might need our help, so let's at least have a try. Speak to him Ashman – but do it politely, and don't say anything which may cause him to panic...' Ashman nodded, and approached the door. Knocking gently on the wood, he leaned down and spoke through the keyhole...

'Sir, you'd better come out – the school is on fire...'

There was commotion from within. The handle turned slowly, and the door creaked open just a fraction, just enough to enable the rev to see out, and the boys to see in.

'Tell him to leave me alone...' said Felchingham in a quivering voice, which was rather echoing and a bit muffled.

Through the gap in the door, the boys could make out the medieval-looking figure within. The rev was poised as if ready for hand-to-hand combat. In his left hand he held a bottle of industrial strength toilet cleaner, and under his right arm was a mop grasped in the style of a lance. Upon his head he wore a steel mop bucket as a helmet, with the handle hanging down under his chin in a casual manner. To the boys assembled outside, he appeared like Sir Galahad of the Round Table, who was about to embark upon a quest to unblock one of King Arthur's more problematic drains.

'Once more into the bleach, dear friends...' said Calderman at the sight of their teacher.

'Come on mate – we can't leave him in there, can we,' said Nicky. 'Sir, whatever the problem is, I am sure that there are enough of us here to be able to help you with it...' he offered.

'He's there... I know he's there... and I'm not coming out,' said the rev, with feeling.

The door was slammed shut with considerable force, and it seemed that for the moment negotiations had come to a grinding halt.

'Should we smoke him out?' asked Jackson.

'No, I don't think that would be a very constructive idea,' said Nicky. 'I suppose we will just have to leave him in there until he feels that it is safe to come out.'

So the boys returned to the classroom, scuffing out the chalk line on the floor as they went in order to prevent their teacher having another attack of the heebie-jeebies if he in fact did emerge from his janitorial sanctuary. As they ascended the stone staircase, Merry was convinced that he heard a dry, throaty chuckle coming from somewhere back down the corridor. Collecting their things back in the Divinity room, the friends were wondering just what could be done to assist their agitated tutor.

'Should we report this, do you think?' asked Merry.

'No, I don't think so, because then the poor bloke might lose his job,' said Nicky.

'As well as his marbles, you mean?' laughed Calderman.

'Perhaps he needs Divine intervention?' said Davis.

'Or maybe just a quick ride in the rubber bus,' answered Ashman (who was still smarting at the mockery of his hostage technique).

Trevill looked very thoughtful for a moment, and then stated, 'Well, Oim no expert as well you know – but Oim thinkin' that our man just moight 'ave some of them there multi-pull personalities see... Should we'em not inform the police?'

'I hardly feel that this is a suitable matter for the police...' said Lordsley, in a haughty tone.

Ignoring the expert on Law Enforcement and Mental Health issues, Trevill continued, 'Only see... Oi was thinkin'... if our fella 'as them multi-pull personalities, and 'Ee threatens to kill 'imself, would the police consider it to be a hostage situation...?'

'Good point, Doctor Trevill,' said Calderman, 'but I think we will be better off leaving the poor man on his own for a bit, and going to our maths class – at least there, things will be a bit more nor – Oh God...what am I saying!'.

So that is what they did. They all set off to the Mathematics lesson. No, they have not arrived yet, give them time for goodness sake, it's a long way across the quad and up all those stairs; and even so, Davis will have to go all of the way back, when he discovers that he has left his pen on the desk. Really, I do wish you might have a little patience, Dear People...

Having failed completely and utterly to achieve any measure of enlightenment from their previous class, the boys made their way up the vertiginous staircase to the maths room in a long line, chanting 'Hare Bannister, Hare Geometry'... like you do. Well, like they did.

Bannister's classes had turned out to be like any other roll of the dice, in other words, there was an even chance of getting something odd. The master welcomed them all to the room, and stated that they would continue to explore the world of Pythagoras and his amazing world of lines and angles. Bannister began to give them a brief "refresher" on the work that they had previously covered, and introduced a whole bunch of new stuff which ended in the term "Hedron". He had not even reacted when Trevill had earnestly asked him when the DoDodecahedron had actually become extinct. The master seemed like a new man, altogether a calmer, more even-tempered version of the amateur ventriloquist which they had seen previously. He had also spent what they assumed was a lot of his salary on smiling lessons, which was a nice change. Something had obviously cheered up the man immeasurably, and Weatherill felt that he just had to comment: 'Wow, sir!...You seem to be in a really great mood today!' he said.

'I am indeed, Mr Weatherill... and in celebration of that fact, I shall permit you to wear that bowler hat for the entire lesson,' Bannister replied, still smiling broadly. 'I believe that an acquaintance of mine has gone on holiday for a few days, and thus I find fewer intrusions upon my time – it really is quite liberating, I can assure y...'

Without any warning, Bannister began to sing 'Midnight' from the stage show *Cats*, in a rather shaky, but nevertheless enthusiastic female contralto voice. His face took on a look of abject horror, and he clamped his hand over his mouth in order to prevent any further unwanted "Lloyd-Webbering" (oh, don't you just wish...). His groping hand found the edge of his desk as he struggled to maintain his balance, and he quickly sat down, changing hands as he did so in case any more feline warbling should escape. Good grief, this was all that he needed, when things had been going so well too. His eyes snapped wide open, as he felt the larger-than-passed-over presence of Mrs Elsie Noakes about to make one of her dramatic appearances:

'Oooh, hello, Miles,' she gushed. 'I have had a really lovely time with my new friends, Mr and Mrs Caldicott. We've been out to the theatre and seen all sorts of lovely productions, and it was so nice. As you know I haven't been into the West End for years since my Horace passed over – and so I've dragged him along to see some lovely musicals...'

'Madam- do you have any idea of the trouble that your constant interruptions are causing?' said the exasperated Bannister, seemingly to himself.

'Oh I know, dear, but I couldn't wait to tell you what we've been up to, and Monsieur Fermat said that you would love it if I got in touch straightaway and told you all about it...'

'Did he now?'

'That's what he said, in fact he insisted. We have been to all sorts of theatres, and we all sat up in the "gods", and we didn't have to pay to get in-although Mr Caldicott did try, but the ticket girl just screamed and ran off...'

'Fascinating, I'm sure...'

'And then I ran into Beatrice from my old Women's Institute group, who was telling me all about her poor son, Gordon, and his trouble...'

'Which you are going to tell me about, no doubt...'

'Well Miles, it seems that poor Gordon had developed some sort of obsession which made him run into newsagents or sweetshops and purchase packets of those little round mints. When he couldn't get them, the poor lad was so depressed. He ended up having to go to the doctor – and the doctor has given him all manner of tests, and finally diagnosed him as "Buy-Polo"...'

'Well I never...'

(Bannister knew a losing battle when he saw one, and even attempting to thwart Mrs Noakes in full flight was like turning up at the battle of Dunkirk armed with a blunt pin...)

The unfortunate Miles realised that resistance was useless, and so he rested his elbows on his desk, cupped his chin in one hand, and prayed for ghostly laryngitis to slow Elsie down.

'Oooh, just listen to me chattering on!' said Elsie.

'Yes, who would have thought it...' said the despondent Bannister.

'I can't stop and natter to you, Miles. I've got a young man coming over to see me later. He's ever so nice – his name is Jimi, and he has promised to give me some guitar lessons – you know that I've always wanted to learn to play the banjo...'

'Why not get Keith Moon to teach you to play the drums while you are at it,' said Bannister.

'Don't be daft love... he's not coming over until Friday,' said Elsie. 'Do you think I should get a small bottle of sherry in, just in case he fancies a little drink?'

'I wouldn't bother, my dear. I've heard that he hardly ever touches a drop...' sighed Bannister.

I'll talk to you later with the rest of my news... Now you be good, and say hello to all of your lovely boys for me. Byeee!'.

With that, Elsie took her leave, smelling just ever so slightly of Teen Spirit.

Chapter Seventeen

Upon his return from school today, Nicky was very surprised to find that the corner of the family living room was now occupied by a huge and imposing writing desk. 'What do you think?' asked Mum. 'It used to belong to your grandmother, and I thought that it would be rather nice to have it back with us here. You will be able to do all of your homework in comfort now, and there is lots of space for all of your books and things.'

He regarded the rather sombre item of furniture from a variety of angles. 'It will be great Mum, thanks very much,' he said, whilst actually thinking 'I could end up like one of the dead pharaohs if that thing falls on me...'

The desk itself was of solid oak construction, with a heavy writing shelf which was pulled down for use – once the ornate and complicated-looking lock had been successfully bypassed, that is. He opened the front carefully, noting the green leather covering. There were tall shelves and compartments for pens and scribing items various, as well as a host of drawers in a range of sizes which were designed to hold goodness knows what. Nicky imagined that these drawers may still contain remnants of a bygone age, such as weird letter openers or sealing wax. He was most perplexed to find that one of the smallest drawers did in fact contain a fresh egg. After dinner, he planned to have a good search around the desk, in order to see if the oaken structure contained any secret compartments. Knowing that one of his Ancestors had been a Pirate, anything was possible. Mum had already augmented the top of the desk with a pristine rectangular cloth, upon which stood two polished wooden candlesticks, and a large fruit bowl placed centrally. He had to admit that the desk did actually look embarrassed at being so swiftly adorned in this fashion.

Mum, Auntie and Nicky had only just sat down at the table to eat, when the telephone jangled into life. Mum drew the short straw, and went over to answer the insistent ringing. From the look on her face as she listened to the words of the caller, she was not too impressed, and said, 'Well thanks for letting us know. I will call you back when I have a little more time...' She paced back to the table with a "complete waste of my time" look upon her face.

Auntie asked her, 'Who was that then?'

Mum answered that although the line had been really atrocious she had just managed to make out what she thought were the relevant points in the very one-sided conversation. It would appear that Cousin Sheila had decided to break with her vegetarian ways which she had religiously followed for the past twenty-five years, and was now intending to return to a diet of pheasant, partridge, venison and grouse.

Auntie was sceptical, stating, 'Are you sure that's what Sheila said?'

Mum gave a non-committal shrug and said 'Well that's what I think she said. She said that Colin had left her for a twenty-year-old from Bristol, with a spray-tan and a Mazda. She told me that he had emptied their joint account, leaving her without a penny. Her exact words were "Well bugger that for a lark, I'm going back on the game..."'

Nicky finished his cottage pie; although who the cottage in question had previously belonged to was never made clear, and neither was the fate of the former occupant. He surmised that both the cottage and the pie crust must surely both have been condemned. Having suffered no lasting damage from the evening feast, he returned cautiously to the brooding desk, and set out some Latin homework. He began to entertain dark thoughts that there might just be a secret compartment somewhere within the structure, in which were located the mortal remains of his granny- a sort of "Bates Motel" for collectors of antique furniture. His mind created the scene where the desk was starring as an object for appraisal by the experts of the *Antiques Roadshow*. As the crucial valuation was about to be disclosed ('Oh no- we'd never ever sell it, it belonged to my late grandfather's milkman, and it's been in the family for nearly two months...Yeah, right), Granny's hand would appear out of the secret drawer and treat the shocked "Expert" to a one-fingered appraisal of her own.

Nicky shook his head to dispel the image, but nothing fell out. He began to struggle with declining verbs again, and however much he tried to get the methods to stick in his brain, they seemed to lift the wire fence of logic, and make a break for the open fields. Incidentally, this was exactly what he wished that he could do right now. The papers would be full of the mysterious tale of the schoolboy who "just vanished into thin air." His Mother would be quoted in the papers, and interviewed tearfully explaining on the six o'clock news that 'I am just beside myself in shame – he made absolutely no attempt to conjugate the Subjunctive Active verbs which he had been given, in the Imperfect Tense – how could he bring such disgrace upon his own family and friends...?' Or maybe the headline of the local rag would proclaim "Shock for Local Youth and family as his head explodes attempting Latin translation".

It was no good wasting time with fanciful imaginings, he couldn't get to grips with the stupid thing, and that was the end of it. He decided to have one last try early in the morning, and so closed up his Latin books and folded up the desk writing shelf. Just before he closed up the desk for the night, he caught a glimpse of two ivory drawer knobs with ebony centres, underneath which was the small ornate brass drop handle for the larger pull-out drawer. Seen together for an instant, he could have sworn that the desk was grinning at him – with an expression that radiated more intelligence than he himself had been able to muster.

Nicky knew that he could write "Fecit" at the end of the homework – and truly mean it...

'I'm going up to bed early,' Nicky told Mum and Auntie.

'Well you can have a nice mug of cocoa before you go,' said Mum. 'Any news on the school photo yet?' she asked. 'Oh yeah, Mum, they told us what the price was today,' answered Nicky. 'But I don't think that I will be getting a copy, cos' they're a tenner each,' he said. The boy knew that his mother was about to say that his 'was bound to be something that we can cut back on' in order to be able to afford the copy of the Academy photograph. He didn't like to be the cause of any unnecessary expenditure in the household, because he knew what a financial struggle it was just to keep him at St Onan's as it was. Mum and Auntie were very proud of him for getting to the prestigious Academy in the first place, but he was acutely aware that pride in this case came with a very hefty price tag attached. Although the family were not exactly on the breadline, there were the odd occasions when they had impersonated Lord Lucan as the rent man had appeared over the horizon. Auntie told him not to worry, as she had 'a little scheme on the go which should help out'. It was a certainty that the 'little scheme' had four legs and a jockey. Nicky kissed them both goodnight, and got a reassuring hug from Auntie before he made his way upstairs to bed.

He lay in bed with his hands behind his head, wondering if there would ever come a point at which any of the stuff which was being hurled at him would ever make sense, and if he would ever feel anything other than terrified and isolated in the strange world of the Academy. His days seemed to be a never-ending film of D-Day landings on the beaches, where unexploded Latin, French and Chemistry books lay hidden just under the sand, ready at any moment to unleash their horrors upon an unsuspecting and ill-prepared boy.

He awoke very early again, and noted the cold mug of cocoa which he had left on his bedside table. He got out of bed, drew back the curtains to reveal tendrils of morning mist still drifting over the fields. Picking up the mug, he opened his bedroom window and carefully tipped the cold cocoa out onto the lawn below, inconveniencing a visiting hedgehog in the process. After he had yawned, stretched, and disappointingly stayed the same size, he dressed and went downstairs. He had suspicions that Mum must be existing on half an hour's sleep per night, because she was always up hours before anyone else in the house. When he had asked her why she seemed to have so little sleep, Mum had replied that "I suppose that I've been the same since the War". He had pointed out that the war had been over for years, but should there be another invasion of foreign forces, then they would never catch Mum by surprise – and in all likelihood she would be on her second cup of tea – and lying in wait for them with the poker.

Mum handed Nicky a cup of tea, and he approached the desk in stealth mode. He noted that the dreaded satchel was lying on the floor under the desk – no doubt busily passing on tips concerning the best and most painful way to trap fingers. Opening the desk writing shelf carefully, he noted that his books lay open on the green leather surface. The Latin text book lay with its pages tucked inside the exercise book as if it had been placed like a bookmark. Nicky opened the slim volume in order to pick up where he had left off from last night. Something extremely odd appeared to have taken place during the hours of darkness. He was mystified to see that all of his Latin homework had been carefully written out and completed in detail. The verbs had all been conjugated correctly, and whoever or whatever had finished his work for him had done so in beautiful rounded italic script. He was both fascinated and horrified at the same time. Just what had happened here? Could it be that Mum or Auntie were secret Latin scholars? What was baffling was the fact that whoever had completed the work had known exactly which section of the Latin text to go to and translate, let alone the effort of putting all of the verbs into their correct tenses. There was one factor however, which caused him the most concern. Whilst he was truly grateful for the assistance of whoever had provided the help which he needed, there was one thing that troubled him.

He could not figure out why the whole of his Latin homework had been comprehensively and accurately written out – in French...

Still pondering the gift of assistance which the desk had provided, Nicky got himself ready for another day of instructive isolation at the Academy. He had also begun to wonder what the big secret that Kendy was about to impart to him might be. As he heard the consumptive coughing of the village bus approaching, Nicky waved to his mother and prepared to once again place his life in the hands of the bus company. The driver was his usual ebullient self, with a face like a Skegness donkey during a national carrot shortage.

'Good Morning to you, sir...' said Nicky as he boarded the bus. 'Isn't it a lovely morning?'

The driver scowled at him as only a man who has seen too many double-shifts, and breathed too much diesel fumes could possibly do. 'It says "Goodyear" on me bleedin' tyres, son, but I ain't havin' one...' was his witty riposte.

Nicky paid his fare, and hastily found a vacant seat. As the bus jerked and shuddered off down the hill, he noticed Uncle Joe speed past with the top down on his car. This was a little unexpected as Joe didn't drive a soft-top.

There were two of the village ladies sitting behind Nicky, who were loudly discussing a horror film which they had apparently just seen on television. 'What I want to know is this...' said one, 'Is it true that Count Dracula doesn't show up in mirrors?'

Her friend said, 'Yes, I think so...'

'Right then...' insisted the first speaker. 'If that's the case, then how come the centre parting in his hair is always so perfectly even... ?'

No better start to the day than blow-to-the-head philosophy, thought Nicky.

As he got off the bus, Nicky could hear raised voices from some way off. It sounded like quite a few voices, all chanting some sort of political mantra as they made their way up the street and past St Onan's. As Nicky got nearer to the marching throng, he saw that it was some sort of local protest march, led by some odd-looking bearded types who were holding aloft a large badly-written banner. As he neared the school gates, Nicky paused to listen to what the crowd were shouting as they passed. The mob was being harangued by one of the bearded types who was shouting into a screeching megaphone. It was difficult to determine exactly where his chin ended, and the megaphone began.

'What do we want?'

'MORE ACRONYMS!'

'When do we want them?'

'ASAP!'

Nicky let the militant throng pass by, then crossed the road, avoiding Gretel the lollipop lady on the pedestrian crossing.(She was not a recognised traffic safety duty holder, she was known as the "Lollipop Lady" because of her large, round and sticky head.)

He met up with Calderman, Merry, Davis and Weatherill just inside the school gates, and the "Musketeers" made their way up to their form room to drop off their bags prior to assembly. The boys were discussing the cost of the Academy photograph, and how they hoped that they had come out looking at least vaguely human, when a familiar voice raised itself in order to ensure that it was overheard by all of the boys. 'Well, I told Papa that it will cost us a fortune to send a photograph to all of my relatives who have requested a copy...' said Lordsley. 'But I know that he can well afford it,' he added, smugly.

Merry tapped the boy on his shoulder. 'Did you say that all of your relatives will want a copy?' he asked innocently.

'Oh indeed they will,' said Lordsley. 'Each and every family member will want one.'

Merry paused, and then said, 'Well it might be expensive for your poor parents if they were to lose it.'

'And why would they lose it?' asked Lordsley.

'Well it can't be easy to try and hold onto a photograph – when you need both hands to be able to swing through the trees...' said the smiling Merry.

Exit Lordsley stage left, with much grinding of the dental equipment.

As the boys made their way into the assembly hall, they were treated to an impromptu rendition of "Honky-Tonk Train Blues" on the organ by the now legendary Mr Newhouse. The master hastily dropped the volume of the organ, and finished the piece before the senior staff came into the hall. Nevertheless, there was enthusiastic applause from the boys, which the master acknowledged with a royal wave. As the staff gathered up on the stage, the boys noticed that amongst their number was an Oriental stranger, who was wearing a black leather trench coat (despite the heat in the hall), and a pair of sunglasses. With his jet black hair swept back into a ponytail, and a white silk shirt, this visitor looked like "Set Meal for One Mafia Hitman" at the local Chinese restaurant.

After the excruciatingly lacklustre performance of the Academy song, Dr Goodwill strode up to the lectern and straightened it to face the crowd of boys as usual. Today's unseen (by Goodwill, that is) offering was an inflated pink rubber glove, the type worn by lovers of pink rubber everywhere, and the occasional washer-up of dishes. It was taped to the lectern front, and swung gently in defiance and a certain squashy subversion. Oblivious to the addition, Goodwill began his address:

'Good morning, gentlemen...'

'Good morning, sir...' (One boy distinctly spelled it "Cur")

'Before I move on to welcome our guest, I would remind you all that the House Music Contest will shortly be taking place. Entries are invited from all boys, and in all classes. The winners of each category will be invited to perform at a special concert which will be attended by the parents. Please collect your entry forms from our esteemed music master Mr Newhouse- who will be happy to assist you with any queries.'

Goodwill then turned to regard the mysterious stranger who was sitting with the staff on the left hand side of the stage. With an expansive gesture of his arm, he introduced the man to the assembled throng of boys.

'Gentlemen... may I introduce to you a very special visitor to the Academy. Our guest is the highly respected artist and sculptor Mr Usimi Japsai, who has most kindly agreed to display some of his new and recently-exhibited work in the quadrangle. I am as excited as I am sure that you all are, to view and appreciate the work of one of the country's most respected new artists. Since his work is frequently sold across the world for very substantial sums, we are fortunate to have him here today to inspire us all with his stunning sculptures. I am sure that you will all make him most welcome, and treat him as a "Fellow Onanist". I am assured that Mr Japsai will be happy to answer any questions which you boys may have about his work and his career in the Art world in general'.

The mysterious visitor stood dramatically, and gave a slight yet formal bow in the direction of the audience. He suddenly caught a glimpse of the rubber glove taped to the front of the lectern, and raised his designer sunglasses for a better inspection. This ad-lib art installation caused the visitor to explode into paroxysms of unsuppressed laughter, and the unfortunate artist had to be helped from the stage by two members of the staff. Goodwill was still unaware of what had amused the man, and assumed that he had been pointing at himself. He made a mental note to only allow this rude fellow to have use of the Academy's second-best cutlery at dinner time. He would also now be cancelling the order for that brand new Toyota that he had been deliberating over – that would teach this upstart a lesson, and no mistake...

Still mentally planning retribution, the headmaster continued, 'I have been asked by Mrs Bradley, our Catering Supervisor, to remind all boys using the hall after school for the rehearsals of the forthcoming play *Oliver*, that they should leave the hall tidy after their rehearsal – as for some reason she feels that she is unwilling or unable to enter the hall during the evenings... That is all, gentlemen, so thank you all for your attention.'

Goodwill turned and began to walk off the stage as the boys stood to attention. He paused just before he reached the rear doors, and came part of the way back into the middle of the stage. Following what he had perceived as a great insult from an invited guest, he had suddenly changed his attitude toward Modern Art – certainly that which had found its way onto his school premises. 'And if you have the time, you may wish to have a quick look at whatever pretentious self-publicising rubbish is lurking under covers in the quad – before it is quite rightly consigned to the recycling skip...'

Having made his pronouncement on the current state of the Modern School of Sculpture, Goodwill left the hall with a fierce scowl firmly displayed upon his face. If Mrs Bradley had unwisely decided to serve Sushi today – it would not go well with her.

There were various incidents, arguments and conversations taking place within and around the staff lounge. Mr Hyde-Jones was convulsed with laughter, and awaiting the entry of his partner-in-crime Mr Newhouse, so that he could recount the unbelievable story which he had just heard.

'Grab a coffee and sit down, Loopy...' laughed Hyde-Jones 'I've got an absolute cracker of a story to tell you; it's one of Matthews' best yet,' he said. Mr Newhouse flopped into the chair beside the English Master, and awaited details of their colleague's escapades.

'Well, it would appear that just before the start of the term, old Matthewselah's missus had been nagging him about his drinking. She had got to the point of threatening him with divorce unless he agreed to attend a residential course for people with alcohol problems. He went all the way down to the Kent coast to an old hotel, where he and a few other poor souls spent a week being counselled and threatened off the demon drink.'

'How did the old bugger get on with that then?' asked Mr Newhouse, grinning.

'Actually, I hear that he did surprisingly well,' said his colleague. 'He was up early every morning, went for long bracing walks on the coast, attended each and every group session with a very positive attitude. He said that he had never felt so well in his life.'

'Good for him...' said Newhouse. 'So I take it that something went wrong?'

'Matthews and the entire group had remained sober and positive for the whole week. At the end of the course they were all presented with official certificates commending their efforts and success. They all agreed to keep in touch, and to stay positive...'

'I sense a "but" approaching over the horizon,' said Newhouse, in anticipation.

'Oh, yes indeed – Matthews thought that they had all done so very well over the course of the week, that it would be a really good idea if he took all of the group out for a drink to celebrate their success...'

'Bingo! The Phantom of the Off Licence strikes again...' laughed Newhouse.

Meanwhile... In the biology laboratory, Dr Darwin was showing his friend the ever-nervous Reverend Felchingham the results of his latest experiment involving goldfish. Having heard that the fish had a notoriously short memory, Darwin was determined to disprove the theory and attempt to teach the little fish to perform small problem-solving tasks. He had dropped the occasional Lego brick into the tank, to see exactly what the fish would make of them. At first, the squad of goldfish ignored the bricks, but gradually, Darwin began to notice that they were taking an increasing interest in the objects which he was placing into their surroundings. He was now showing the rev exactly what the fish had achieved so far...

'See, I don't know how they have managed it, but they seem to have built a small wall with the bricks...' said the enthusiastic Darwin. 'It is almost as if they have been acting under the direction of some outside influence, because they never really showed any interest when I first introduced the bricks into their tank. Look at the face of the wall, and tell me if you can make out anything strange...'

The Rev leaned closer to the tank, and peered with interest in at the inhabitants within the glass, who regarded him with their usual bored indifference. Leaning closer still, he put on his reading glasses, and scanned the small plastic wall in the tank as instructed. Suddenly, he did see what his excited colleague had been referring to...

'My goodness...' he exclaimed. 'Have they actually made marks on the wall?'

'It's better than that, Gerald...' said Darwin. He opened the door to one of the large floor cupboards, and retrieved a very large magnifying glass, which he handed to his friend with unbridled glee.

'Here... if you take a really good look at the wall, you will see that they have actually written letters on it!'

'Don't be ridiculous man – how on earth could fish actually manage to perfect the art of writing in any shape or form?' asked Felchingham.

'Well that's exactly what I thought when I first noticed it,' answered Darwin, 'but the evidence is all there – before your very eyes, there's no getting away from it. Remarkable as it may seem, the fish have somehow managed to form the word on the wall...'

'Honestly? Goldfish graffiti?' queried the fascinated Rev.

'I can't explain it, but they have somehow developed the capability to inscribe something on the bricks...' said Darwin.

Felchingham continued to peer in at the fishes' handiwork. 'I can just about read the word – but I have no idea why they have written "bnok". Do you think it's some strange fish language message which they are trying to communicate to us?' he asked.

'I have no idea – but I'm contacting the *New Scientist* magazine, and the British Society right away; I can see a Nobel Prize in this for me, once they have seen my results for themselves. Nothing like this has ever been seen by human eye, and it is certainly proof that my little gold friends have considerably more intelligence than they are given credit for...'

Felchingham could see that his friend's eyes had glazed over, and he was probably envisioning in his mind's eye the moment when he stepped up to accept the prestigious award in front of other envious colleagues from the Scientific Community at the lavish and famous event. Something about the faint word written on the wall of plastic bricks was causing subconscious panic to rise within the mind of the reverend, something which he couldn't quite pin down for the moment...

As he lifted the lid on the goldfish tank, and sprinkled in a pinch of fish food with his enormous hand, Bernie chuckled to himself.

The boys had convened in their now regular conspiratorial huddle. Nicky had attempted to get more information out of Kendy in order to find out what his "big secret" might be, but for the moment, his friend was remaining tight-lipped. Calderman and Merry listened fascinated as Nicky explained to them the weird happenings concerning the desk at home. His friends decided that the best course of action was to try an experiment with tonight's French homework. The plan was to leave the work in the desk overnight and see what the outcome was – leaving just enough time to complete it in the following morning, just in case the magic which the desk performed failed to materialise. DeVere was missing from the group, and no-one seemed to recollect having seen him since first thing. The boys could not keep a watchful eye on the ground floor doors in case their friend came out as their view was currently blocked by a van which was apparently collecting some musical instruments which were in need of repair. They were all looking at the collection of strange shapes which took up most of the centre of the quad, these being the sculptures brought in by their "visitor", and currently hidden from view under various sizes of dark blue cloth sheets. The covers were to be taken off at lunchtime, when the strangely angular strippers who lay beneath would be exposed to the gaze of the boys, in all their artistic glory.

The first lessons of the day had sort of drifted past without causing any need to get personally involved. Ashman had raised a question concerning the causes and benefits of the French Revolution, and Madame had taken the bait and gone into a long and detailed speech which had lasted some thirty-five minutes. There had just been enough time left in the lesson for her to calm down, sing the "Marseillaise", and hand out the homework. English had been a period of Drama held in the assembly hall. Nicky and some of his friends had performed another short play about homelessness, but had been distracted several times when they were convinced that they had heard voices coming from under the stage. Moving closer to the front of the stage itself, they quite plainly heard whispering, which had abruptly ceased when Ashman had tapped on the wooden panel.

Chemistry too, had proven to be more of a lecture than any attempt at experimental science. A member of staff had attempted to move his car during the lesson. This had proved to be difficult, as so much spare reversing space had been taken up by the covered sculptures in the quad. With the constant revving of the master's car engine, Captain Brayfield had been driven to stride over to the windows which faced the quad, wrench open the frame, and remonstrate with the hapless teacher about the damage which his exhaust fumes were inflicting upon the environment and general air quality. Under such a forceful barrage, the shame-faced master had abandoned his attempts to extricate his vehicle, and had switched off the engine, leaving the car at an odd angle in the quad. When he had closed the window with enough force to almost shatter the glass, Captain Brayfield too went into a long speech about the damage which the internal combustion engine had done, is doing, and would do to the environment. As he strode angrily around the room venting his anger on Henry Ford and fellow car manufacturers, the boys were left in no doubt whatsoever that the captain preferred horses to human beings – and that they should be the only sensible mode of transportation for all. Trevill was tempted to ask the captain how we should deal with the problem of soon being up to our knees in the stuff left on the roads by horses – but he thought that this may well have resulted in the master reaching into the desk drawer for the service revolver, which the boys were all convinced he kept loaded in readiness...

Having been instructed frostily to research the effects of carbon on the gases of the atmosphere, and today being on second sitting for lunch, the boys all gathered with their fellows in the quad to await the unveiling of the art works. It was Doctor Chambers who accompanied the sculptor out in front of the assembled throng of boys, in place of the headmaster, who was still barricaded in his study in a foul temper, and being placated by the ineffectual ministerings of Miss Piggott.

Taking a position right at the front of the group of sculptures, the deputy head announced, 'I shall now hand you over to the artist himself, Mr Japsai, who will briefly explain a little about each of the works which he has created.' Chambers stepped back, and the black-clad artist stepped up and grasped the corner of the cloth which was covering the first of the sculptures.

'I have produced this piece after my experience of being stranded on the Tokyo subway, having lost my wallet and carrying nothing but a copy of the daily newspaper. It speaks of the alienation of Man amongst his own kind. It is entitled *Loss in Colour*'.

The cloth was swept aside, revealing a bright wire shopping trolley, inside which were a small watermelon and a pair of tartan carpet slippers, with the price tag still attached. The front wheel was missing from the trolley, and the slippers were of different sizes.

'How long were you stranded on the subway for, exactly?' enquired Calderman.

'Loss of grip on reality...' said an exasperated voice at the back.

'Exactly...' said the artist.

At this point, several members of staff moved gradually to the front of the crowd, to see exactly what all the fuss was about. Dr Matthews made his way unsteadily to centre stage, whilst clutching a large glass containing a generous sample of Leningrad's finest. He studied the "art" on display with all of the fascination of a one-eyed man in a shop that exclusively sells binoculars. The artist trotted over in a rather camp fashion to the next hidden work, a vertical structure which was taller than a man. He announced:

'My next piece is a single structure which I recently exhibited at the Tate Gallery. It is a work which asks us as males to challenge and question everything about our true masculinity, and where we really fit into a mixed and increasingly female-dominated society. It asks us questions about how we perceive our role in both society and the family. It takes us on a journey to explore our male attitude toward equality, and our right to assert dominance and ownership over our own ego, forcing us to confront who we really are and how we relate to ourselves and our species... It is titled *Morning – And the boy is smiling...*'

He pulled away the covering cloth to reveal the structure underneath.

It would be a fair assumption that none of the assembled audience had been prepared for what their eyes saw as the cloth fell away. There were no sniggers. There were no sharp gasps of breath being drawn. An all-encompassing silence fell over the watchers. Dr Matthews took a massive gulp of Moscow medicine, and with a trembling, pointing finger outstretched, declared... ' Ye gods – It's a seven-foot cock!'

Matthews was hurriedly ushered away from the phallic intruder. As he was pulled out of range by other staff members, he was continually turning around, and could be heard shouting over his shoulder, 'But for God's sake... it's a fibreglass John Thomas!' The helpers managed to get him as far as the doors to the New Block, when he temporarily slipped their clutches, and turned again to say in utter disbelief, 'I mean to say... a great Wooden Wanger!' The last thing that the boys heard from Matthews was just as the double doors closed, and he spluttered out, 'A bloody great Plastic Pr...' before a hand was judiciously clamped over his mouth.

With a contemptuous look back at the vertical pink structure, the boys dispersed, having had their fill of Contemporary Art. They had decided to spurn *Autumn and Electric Thighs*, as well as *Neon Lady who is nearly not...*. The highlight of the afternoon was just after lunch, when a truck driven by some itinerant scrap-metal collectors screeched into the quad, having seen the piles of what they assumed was scrap from the road opposite. A furious fight had ensued, during which Japsai had been assaulted with pieces of his own artwork, and had in turn applied his own expensively-veneered teeth onto the ankle of one of the scrap collectors. In a bid to escape the thrashing being meted out to them by the staff, and to avoid the further cannibalistic dental attentions of the artist upon their persons, the scrap dealers piled back into their truck and fled. In their haste, they inadvertently put the truck into reverse gear, and jerked backwards, knocking down the oversized male member which had formerly stood so proud in the quad. It fell in a graceful arc until it came into contact with the ground floor windows of the Boarding House. There was a tremendous crash of breaking glass as the tip of the sculpture thrust into the ground floor room.

An unidentified voice from within was heard to exclaim 'Thank You Jesus...'

Later analysis would lead investigators to conclude that the grateful voice had most likely belonged to none other than the Matron, the occasional "Public Servant" and self-confessed player of the pink oboe, Miss Lucretia Dipper...

Having been somewhat subdued by having been offered another large glass of Chateau Damage de Cranium, Matthews was being berated by the French mistress.

'You cannot continue to drink so much without doing great damage to your 'ealth,' she proclaimed.

'That's a bit rich, coming from the nation that tests positive for Beaujolais...' answered the affronted Matthews. 'Anyway, I am looking after my health, Madam, as a matter of fact.'

'And how on earth can you possibly justify that statement?' asked Madame

Matthews took a health-giving gulp of his drink, and explained his reasoning.

'Dear Lady: I would draw your attention to the fact that vodka is in fact made from the humble potato. If you look up "potato" in the dictionary, you will quite clearly see that it is indeed a vegetable. So you will see that there is no reason at all why what I am drinking can not accurately be classed as "Salad". The defence rests, m'Lud...'

A heartfelt round of applause erupted from the other staff members.

Chapter Eighteen

As the last of the ambulances left the quad, and the scattered remnants of the "art display" had been swept up and hurriedly disposed of, the boys made their way up to the games field. As they passed the houses which lined the road to the sports field, they were discussing what could have happened to their friend DeVere, or rather, how they thought he may have made his latest bid for freedom. They had heard a rumour that his discarded uniform had been found on the floor of the Music room by a cleaner, but of DeVere himself, there was no trace.

A strong wind had sprung up in complete defiance of the nice man who had given the weather forecast, which was on the whole, rather rude. The gang got changed into their rugby kit, and lined up outside the changing rooms ready to be split up into teams for the afternoon's punishment. Mr Carter was resplendent in his battered track suit again, still resembling the fitness instructor from the local council tip. All of the boys noted that he was wearing a woollen hat over the animated feature known as the toupee, which normally led an independent existence from the vantage point of Carter's skull. He appeared to have secured both the hat and toupee with a medium-sized elastic band (he had obviously heard about the gusting winds – and was taking no chances with either tape or glue).

'RIGHT LADS...' he bellowed. 'LINE UP, WARM UP, AND TEAM UP.

'And throw up...' added a voice from the wings.

The homicidal maniac that was Mr Burke led them all off to the centre of the nearest pitch. Here, they were instructed to windmill their arms and run on the spot, and there were ten press-ups thrown in for good measure. When the sadistic master gauged that the boys were sufficiently near the point of passing out due to lack of oxygen, he ordered Ashman to collect the bag of balls.

'Today we are going to learn how to get this ball over those goals, and between those posts,' declared Burke. Carter stood some distance away, leaning into the wind and adjusting his home-made wig restraining unit. Each boy in turn was made to place a ball on its point end, and kick it over the rugby posts in order to achieve a "conversion". The wind was playing merry hell with every boy's attempts, and more time was seemingly spent in fetching back balls that had escaped, aided by wind power. Kendy was the surprise star of the show. With every successful kick that he achieved, Carter moved the ball further and further back. The ball was placed well over the half-way line, and a smirking Carter invited Kendy to 'Try your luck from here then, Mr Professional...'

Without hesitation, Kendy repositioned the ball, and studied the gusting wind. Pacing out a short run-up, he again paused for a moment. He then took four swift paces forward before making contact with the ball, which arced into the air and headed for the right of the posts. Carter watched the ball veer to the right, and sneered, 'Oh hard luck, lad, still, you can't be perfect all of the time...' At that point, all of the boys watched as another strong gust caught the ball in the air, and steered it straight between the posts with absolute precision. Carter stood open-mouthed, with hat and wig listing badly over his left ear. He may have found a new star for the First Eleven rugby team, and if he could get a few impressive wins under his belt as team manager, he might just be able to lever a pay rise out of old Goodwill.

It was Nicky's turn next. He placed the ball as the other boys had done, and performed the same exaggerated backward stepping away from the ball. He waited for a moment as he studied the wind, then ran forward and kicked the ball as hard as he could. He saw it take off skyward on the required trajectory, and turned to accept the congratulations of his friends. As he did so, he heard them shout something, and at the instant that he turned around, he felt a terrific bang right in the middle of his face – and everything went black.

He came to lying on one of the wooden slatted benches in the changing rooms. The first thing that he saw was Calderman on all fours, crying with laughter and gasping for breath.

'What happened?...' asked the groggy boy.

'Oh Mate – that was absolutely brilliant!' said Calderman, through the laughter. 'You really gave the ball a good clog, and it took off like a rocket. Just as you turned round though, the wind caught it and it hit the left hand post, and came back, spinning. When it hit you between the eyes we all thought that you were dead!' he spluttered.

Just then, Merry poked his head around the corner of the changing room 'Are you all right, Shep?' he asked. (He too laughing at Nicky's misfortune.) 'Carter sent me over to see if you were okay – and he said to stay here until you feel a bit better. No-one has been able to play for the last fifteen minutes, because we can't stop laughing – sorry mate...'

'Tell him I'll sit it out until I feel better,' said Nicky.

Calderman decided to stay with his friend just in case there was any delayed concussion, and helped him wipe off nearly all of the blood from his shirt. When he felt a bit more conscious, Nicky suggested that they get some fresh air, so they walked slowly out of the changing room and up along the tall hedge which followed the edge of the sports field. The two boys paused a little way along the hedge, and were both frightened out of their wits as the foliage suddenly erupted to reveal a humanoid figure...

The vision which now stood in front of them was terrifying to say the least. It looked like some alien life form made entirely of the same leaves which made up the hedges. The hellish being gave a cough, spat out several leaves, and said in its deep alien tongue, 'Bloody hell – Sorry Lads, I very near fell on me arse then...'

'Who are you?' asked a frightened Calderman

'It's me, Albert Brooks, you silly sod...' answered the creature.

Lifting his balaclava, Mr Brooks the Groundskeeper revealed his friendly, smiling face. He had camouflaged himself from head to toe using the identical foliage to the hedges, and so had been able to 'disappear' amongst the leaves completely. 'Sorry to give you a scare, boys,' he said, 'but I've been lying in wait for the bugger who walks his bloody great dog up the side of the playing fields. The damn thing seems to think that it is a good idea to crap in the middle of my cricket pitch, so me and the shotgun were hoping to convince them that it is a bad idea...' He chuckled. 'Actually, I'm just on my way over to the Small Range, so you can come and help me if you like.' With the appearance of Clint Eastwood at the Chelsea Flower Show, how could the boys possibly resist his offer?

Shedding leaves as he walked, like a marching sample of autumn, Mr Brooks led the two boys to the smaller of the concrete barn-like structures right at the end of the playing field. From somewhere about his camouflaged person, he produced a massive bunch of keys on a brass ring. Selecting a key with a red tag, he approached a small door set into the side of the building, and beckoned the boys to follow him inside. Both of the boys were apprehensive as they stared ineffectually into the gloomy void beyond the door opening. There was a dry rustling as Brooks walked a little distance away from them, and then there was a click. The boys quickly shielded their eyes from the sudden glare of the lights which burst into life. Looking down the length of the building, the lads saw what appeared to be lanes, set out as one might expect to see in a bowling alley. There were four of these long lanes marked out at varying distances, and at the far end of the strips were twelve school desks arranged in four rows of three. Both of the boys were wondering if this building was part of some secret installation specifically constructed for the purposes of extreme detention (Just how wrong would you have to get your homework in order to be incarcerated here?). At the top of the lanes adjacent to where they were standing, were two large brass levers of the type seen in old-fashioned railway signal boxes.

Brooks reappeared, now only leaf-bound from the waist down, but still wearing two belts of shotgun cartridges which he wore crossed over his chest. This "Garden Centre Rambo" now addressed the boys in a happy voice. 'Righto then, me boyos! Who fancies a decent cup of tea eh?' Still rather disorientated, the boys both nodded in agreement. Brooks reached back over his shoulder, and produced what looked like a large shell for an artillery gun. Both boys instinctively dived to the floor for cover, and Brooks gave a loud laugh which echoed around the vast empty room. 'Stand easy lads... It's only me flask!' he chuckled. He elbowed the small wooden door behind him without looking, and it swung open. From the cupboard, he produced two enamel mugs and a packet of ginger biscuits.

As he poured out the strong tea for the boys, and urged them to take a biscuit, Brooks began to explain. 'I don't suppose you lads 'ave 'eard about this little place 'ave ye?' he enquired. The boys shook their heads, and Nicky spilled hot tea down his leg.

'What is this place, sir?' asked Calderman 'It looks like a bowling alley with desks.'

'Don't call me "Sir", Lad, save all that cap-doffing shite for them as thinks they need it,' said Brooks. 'Seein' as you are now good friends of mine, you can call me Albert.' The boys now began to relax, as the smiling groundskeeper really looked as if he meant what he said. 'There's not but a few who knows about this place – and ye'll 'ave to keep our secret between us. This is the Small Range where I am obliged to try and instruct yon masters in the art of ballistic accuracy with classroom equipment. You know when them buggers in the gowns hears you talkin' to yer mate and launches a piece of chalk at Ye? Well I teaches 'em to be accurate on this range, as ye can't 'ave untrained pillocks lobbin' chalk all over the show – cos' someone could easy lose an eye. I'll show ye if ye like...'

Brooks walked over and grasped one of the large brass-topped handles which rose from floor level. He depressed a lever and pulled the lever back – and from behind the rows of desks at the bottom of the lanes, cardboard targets in the shape of schoolboys popped up in the seats. Brooks took a small cardboard box out of the cupboard, selected a new piece of number three chalk, and took up a position behind the first marking on the middle lane. He spoke as if repeating a well-used mantra 'Four yards... full stick... no breeze... target chatting... FIRE.' The chalk missile flew down the range at incredible speed, and decapitated one of the targets in the middle row. The boys stood open-mouthed.

'Ah...a bit hard there maybe, new chalk is always a problem,' said Brooks. 'I normally teaches 'em to just ping the chalk off the boys head as a warning...' He laughed and turned back to face the boys. 'Unless it's a prefect or some other Rich Nobby Gobshite...'

He walked back to the levers, and pulled the other handle a short way back. At this action, the desk lids rose slightly, presenting slightly less of a target area for the prospective sharp-shooter to aim at. 'This is the "Boardrubber Deflector" setting,' he informed the boys. Brooks again reached into the cupboard, this time selecting one of the fearsome wooden-backed erasers with which the blackboards were cleaned. He measured the distance for a few seconds, and then turned back to the two boys who were happily crunching their biscuits. 'You were right about the range looking like a Bowling Alley, son...' he said. 'I got the idea from when I had a job in just such an Alley near the town centre. It wasn't a permanent job though – It was only tempin'...' Without warning, he spun around and launched the board eraser down the lane at a target. The projectile hit the slightly raised desk lid just in front of the target, making a loud bang and causing a shower of chalk dust to erupt into the air and showering the cardboard "schoolboy". 'That's how it should be done, mates!...'Brooks stated with some considerable satisfaction. 'Maximum shock and surprise – but no casualties...'

Brooks then adopted a serious tone to his voice. 'Trouble is – most of them so-called "masters" is power-crazed old nutters, who don't care if they injure someone. One of these days I shall be only too happy to show them the error of their ways, you mark my words...'

'Don't you get on with the teachers?' Nicky asked.

'Bunch of toffee-nosed inbred morons who couldn't find their arse with an atlas...' said Brooks.

'We'll take that as a possible "no" then, shall we?' asked Calderman.

'The day will come when ordinary working people come to realise that they have had enough of being downtrodden by the so-called "Ruling Classes", and I will be more than ready to help strike a blow for equality and a Fair and Just Society...' Brooks growled.

'What do you have planned for the "Toffs" then, Mr Brooks?' Nicky asked.

Brooks dived back into the cupboard and reappeared holding a short dark green tube. He knocked the cap off the end, and pointed it down the range. There was a terrific bang as some sort of rocket projectile flashed down the centre lane, and almost instantly there was an explosion which hurt the ears and left a red after-image on tightly shut eyes. When the monstrous noise had ceased, the boys felt brave enough to get up off the floor of the range and look down the target alley. Desks four to seven had ceased to exist, and only some twisted metal framing still stood upright. Dust, chalk, and wood splinters were still raining down.

'I shall insist that they "See Me"...' said Brooks, without any expression.

Brooks blew the smoke away from the end of the bazooka tube, and stood it upright on the floor. 'Come on then... I'll show you my equipment for settling cultural and sociological disputes,' said Albert the Revolutionary. He led the two boys down to the very far end of the building, through the still acrid cloud of smoke which was gently drifting across the firing range. He paused in front of a small metal plate in the floor, and undid four squared pins with another key from the collection on the ring.

Lifting the metal trapdoor, the boys could see down a short set of metal steps which obviously led down into some sort of cellar or basement beneath the building. At the foot of the stairs was another metal door, which would be quite capable of excluding any intruder not armed with either a tank or nuclear warheads. Brooks punched in a sequence of numbers on the keypad at the side of the door, and the door swung open noiselessly. The light inside was akin to natural daylight, and showed up the items stacked upright in glass-fronted cabinets all along both walls. The cellar looked like the garden shed of an international arms trader. Stored in all of the cabinets were an alarming variety of rifles, pistols, grenades, and things designed to inconvenience an enemy – mostly permanently and very finally.

Brooks turned to the two stunned boys and said, 'And not all of these are replicas...'

'Why do you need all of these guns – what have you got planned?' asked Calderman

'Something to deal with any eventuality...' answered Brooks.

'Wouldn't a Swiss Army Knife take up less room?' asked Nicky.

'Knives are dangerous, in my opinion...' answered Brooks. 'You will be well aware that ten per cent of the people of this country own ninety per cent of the wealth – so you tell me exactly what is wrong with that sentence...What you see here is a few small articles which I have collected to help me gain the attention of the people to whom I am attempting to make my point clearly.'

Nicky was eyeing the point on the bolt of a hunting crossbow behind the glass, and wondering just how much the person would have to be missing the point before they metaphorically got the point, so to speak...

'In the meantime...' Brooks continued, 'I suggest that we reinstate the rather noble tactical group formally known as the ODD – or Onan's Disruption Department.

'What is that?' queried Nicky.

'It is a covert tactical unit designed to confound and frustrate the ruling classes of the teaching fraternity, or maternity, whichever may be applicable,' said Brooks.

'Exactly what is involved here?' asked Calderman.

Brooks grinned an evil grin. 'We take each and every opportunity to disrupt, frustrate and confuse the enemy by means of practical operations and effective action,' he said.

'Which means...?' asked Calderman.

'We set up as many booby traps as we can on a daily basis, our prime objective being to take the piss with maximum effect at every possible opportunity...' answered Brooks.

'Sounds like a plan...' said Nicky.

'Good lads, now, do either of you know Morse Code?' asked Brooks.

'Will we need to know the code in order to pass messages?' asked Calderman.

'No – I just wondered if you knew it. I can't stand the bloody thing – it always reminds me of a woodpecker with Tourette's syndrome. If you have any plans for disruptive action, you can put a note under my door, or let me know via Mrs Finucane the cleaner – she is one of my other undercover toff-botherers. She is known as Agent J-Cloth.'

Brooks then led the boys out of the cellar warfare supermarket, and back up into the main range building. 'Remember, lads...' he said. 'Not a word to any of 'em – and certainly not to anyone who you can't trust. Secrecy is our currency, and hot cross buns are our currants, see?' The boys both grinned conspiratorially, like the black-cloaked villain who has just tied the heroine to the railway tracks. As they were just about to exit the shooting range, Brooks turned to them and casually asked, 'Oh by the way, have they told you yet where this term's school outing will be going to?' The boys both confessed that they knew nothing about any such trip as yet.

'Is this a regular thing then, Albert?' asked Nicky.

'I'm sorry to say that yes, it is...' said Brooks with a sad expression.

He explained to the boys that the school outing was far from being a jolly trip away to some place of historic interest. The St Onan's quarterly school outing involved a coach load of boys and Staff setting off to some pre-determined location, where they would expose hitherto closet homosexuals...

With the profound words of their own personal revolutionary still ringing in their ears, the boys made their way back to the sports changing rooms, where the other pupils were now emerging from the icy showers after their forced exertions on the rugby field. The boys were still laughing at the incident which had taken place earlier, and nearly all of them took the opportunity to examine Nicky's face for signs of the impact. Carter showed no concern at all for Nicky's injury, and merely shouted at the boys to hurry up and vacate the changing rooms, whilst struggling with his wig-containment system which had migrated northward with the rubber band now tightly under the man's nose, and which was distorting his already odd features into an even more strange shape.

Nicky crunched up the long gravel path and out of the sports field. Gently examining his nose, he crossed the road and headed for the bus stop. As he sat down on the bus in a seat behind the driver, he glanced out of the window, and could just make out the shape of Mr Brooks crawling over the roof of the small range- no doubt lying in wait for the dog owner and his canine accomplice.

Mum was very concerned at her son's sporting injury, and listened to the story of how it came about with great concern. Auntie added that it was a well-known fact that wind could be unpredictable, and then disappeared out into the garden laughing. With no real or lasting damage seemingly done to his face, Nicky was more interested in setting up the "experiment" with the new desk, to see if the miraculous results of the previous evening could be replicated. He would place his French homework in the desk as before; leave it overnight (again allowing a "safety net" of time in the morning) and see if the task would be completed by unseen hands. This was not due to laziness on his part, but if he could get any help at all with a subject that he was struggling to understand, then he would gladly take it.

As usual, there was a discussion which involved the latest antics of the legendary Uncle Joe. He had telephoned Mother and informed her that when he had been shopping in the village, he had found a twenty pound note in the street. As he was a man with great social conscience and responsibility, Joe had pondered over what his next course of action should be. Finally, he had asked himself, 'What would Jesus do?' The answer had come to him in a flash – so he turned the £20 into wine. Joe was also somewhat disgruntled as he had explained that some interfering member of the public had reported him to the police again. It would appear that the story that had been relayed to the authorities was that Joe was a secret Arms dealer. Joe had a visit from a couple of the local police squads finest, and was forced to explain that the confusion had arisen when he had sold some prosthetic limbs to the local hospital. The officers had warned him about wasting police time, and Joe had made a mental note to do something unpleasant in the informant's garden, should the opportunity present itself.

Auntie had returned from outside, having calmed down a little, and was scanning a copy of the local paper in order to see if anyone she knew had done anything unspeakable or even more weird than normal. She read out one particular article of interest. 'It says here that local archaeologists have been called in after the council had dug up a part the Lincoln road for widening, and have found an ancient burial site. The historians have been working on the area, and have unearthed twenty Roman skeletons,' she announced.

'Remains to be seen' answered Mum, at which point tea came down Nicky's nose.

Auntie had found another interesting advert in the paper. 'It says here...' she began, 'that some bloke has recently demolished an old barn on his land, and is offering to give all of the bricks away for nothing if anyone wants to collect them. I wonder if Joe might be interested?'

Mum thought for a moment, and then answered, 'No, I wouldn't even ask him if I were you – you know that he has always been violently opposed to Freemasonry.'

It looked like it was going to turn out to be one of those evenings again.

With no other homework looming over his head like a hawk of doom, and the "experiment" all set up within the confines of the desk, Nicky decided to have an early night. Actually, whatever he had decided, the night would have happened at exactly the same time, as having it earlier in the day would have been inconvenient and confusing for the public at large- even the smaller ones. He fell into a fitful sleep, and dreamed of row after row of shotguns, which were all marked "for use on detention boys only". He awoke early, and made his way downstairs to the bathroom. He regarded his reflection in the bathroom mirror, and noticed that his right eye was reddened and swollen. 'Oh great...' he thought. 'Something else that the other boys will be able to mock me for.' He washed, and then dressed, returning to the kitchen table where Mum was already on her third cup of tea. She took him over to the kitchen window, and examined his face in better daylight.

'You are going to have a really nice black eye there...' she stated. Mum gave him a cold flannel to hold onto his eye in order to bring down the swelling, which he clutched to his face as he drank his tea. It was strange how a cup of the hot beverage had the amazing ability to make you feel so much better, and he thought that if only the National Health would invest in a few million decently-sized tea urns, Mum could affect miracle cures throughout the Nation for a fraction of the current budget. Patients who had elected to "go private" could also have a biscuit with it, should they so wish.

He was putting on his blazer, and attempting to tie his tie (which was writhing around in an attempt to defy being knotted) when he suddenly remembered the French homework which was sitting inside the desk. With his tie hanging loosely around his neck, he hurried over to the desk and carefully pulled down the front shelf. There, sitting neatly was the homework. Slowly and nervously, Nicky opened the work book and checked the contents. He could scarcely believe what he saw in front of him. Every single section of the French homework which he had been dreading had been meticulously completed. He spent several moments staring in disbelief at the pages, trying to fathom just how this miracle had come about. He packed the rest of his work into the fearsome satchel, which had somehow managed to wrap its strap around the leg of the desk. Mum was calling to him from the kitchen. 'Hurry up Nicky – you will miss the bus.' But as he fought with his tie, his mind was completely preoccupied. He caught the morning bus in the same state of absent-mindedness, almost missing his stop due to his distraction. The walk to the Academy was completed in silence as he continued to ponder the mysteries of the desk. He would like to have handed in the French homework with the confident air of one who has spent time in deep concentration, and has striven to complete the task to the very best of their abilities. Just for once, he would like to experience the same smug feeling that the other boys seemed to radiate when they handed in their own work, knowing that it was correct, and anticipating a good mark from the teacher for their efforts.

He knew the work was done. He was certain that nothing had been missed or omitted, and that simple matters like grammar and punctuation had been correctly addressed. What was worrying him right down to the very pit of his soul was the fact that whatever forces were at work within the desk had brilliantly completed his French homework – in Norwegian...

Chapter Nineteen

As Nicky and his schoolmates were once again swallowed by the great stone throat of the Academy gates, they were all completely unaware that there were various scenes of chaos and confusion being enacted all over the school.

A somewhat "relaxed" Dr Matthews was being berated by Rundell the Latin master, who was declaring in his clipped, upper-class tones 'One of the drawing pins with which you had put up your details of the Historical Society on the notice board, has come out and stuck through my rather expensive shoe, piercing my foot.'

Matthews regarded the irate man through blurry eyes and responded, 'I'm dreadfully sorry, old man – it would have appeared to have completely escaped my notice...'

Bell-Enderby, the Art master, was arguing with Dr Chambers, the deputy headmaster, and pressed him for an answer as to why 'He had not even bothered to take a look at the Japsai'. Chambers responded by stating forcefully that not only did he have no interest whatsoever in the collection of Modern Artworks, but that should the so-called artist ever present himself on Academy premises again, he would have no option but to take down the two swords which were mounted above the fireplace in the head's study, and put them to the purpose for which they were originally intended.

Mr Newhouse and Hyde-Jones were in the corner of the staff common room, both giggling away like a couple of their pupils. The Music master was recounting the story of a recent christening which he had attended, and the bizarre events therein. Newhouse had attended at the express wish of two of his close friends, but had done so under protest having clearly stated that 'Rock is my Religion...' The ceremony was being held in an out-of-the-way Baptist church somewhere out in the sticks. It had the unfortunate added ingredient of being held during one of the frequent and eagerly-awaited hosepipe bans which are imposed upon our parched island. There were several other unfortunate and highly amusing circumstances, which would ensure that the event stuck in the memory of all concerned, if not the innocent around whom the farce was centred.

Newhouse almost choked with laughter as he described the so-called "Musical accompaniment" that had preceded the Main Event. Set up at the front of the church was an eclectic and diverse set of would-be musicians behind very expensive instruments. Their skill however, had obviously come from a Pound Shop. Without any warning, there had begun an 18- minute version of that Rock Classic "Amazing Grace". (Of Grace, there was no sign, but trust me – amazed she definitely would not have been.). Stepping forward to treat the congregation to a guitar solo sounding like a ring-tailed lemur being water boarded, was a serious and dangerously thin man with a hockey-team beard (seven per side). His bald pate, yet flowing locks at the rear, reminded Newhouse of some sort of comet featuring a hard-boiled egg as the nucleus. To make matters worse, when he broke a string (surely proving the existence of God) it had wrapped itself around his left hand, presumably in an attempt to prevent further offence to the ears. Flailing desperately to free himself from his single "handcuff", he had struck his boom stand microphone, which swung and hit the bass player straight in the eye. Reeling backwards from the blow, the bass player head-butted the enthusiastic lady standing directly behind him, and her tambourine rolled offstage like the surviving car tyre at the end of a Hollywood car crash. The keyboard player made a lunge for the falling woman, but had unfortunately only succeeded in thrusting an arm down her loosely fitting tee-shirt. All had gone deathly quiet after the melee, except for Mr Newhouse, who could not resist calling out, 'I'm afraid it's a no from me...' Ignoring the scowls directed at him, he quickly loaned a handkerchief with which to wipe his eyes, and help to muffle his laughter. The walking wounded left the stage without attempting an encore, and their place was taken by the new-age vicar, who took up station at the side of the font.

The vicar then began a rather confused litany about taking in the Holy Spirit, and Newhouse was convinced that he had heard a voice sounding very much like Dr Matthews heartily agreeing with the principle. A rather large woman had risen like a swollen tide at this point, and stood in the aisle with a baby under her arm, looming large like an untethered airship. As the vicar proceeded to deliver his speech. The woman became more and more enthusiastic, and each time the vicar said the name "God", she would punch the air and shout "Amen". This carried on for a long while, until the vicar mentioned "Satan", at which point the woman punched the baby.

With the sermon finished, and the over-enthusiastic woman led out of the church to calm down, attention was turned to the first family who had chosen today to name their offspring. Due to the water shortage, and due to the fact that the family were as pretentious a set of chinless inbred cretins as you could possibly hope to meet, they had filled the font almost to the brim with Perrier Water to add a certain nobility to the occasion. The first family in the queue were baptising twins. Being very sensible and safety conscious, the father had insisted that each baby wear a tiny life jacket, and that a Church of England Life Guard was standing in attendance at the side of the font in case of any emergency.

After yet another lecture delivered in earnest by the vicar, the standard question was asked, 'What name have you chosen for this child?'

The father stepped forward and declared, 'Marmaduke Johann Bethelridge...'

The vicar was horrified, and with a barely-audible, 'I'm not having that for a start,' immediately placed his right arm on the edge of the font, and offered to take on the father at arm-wrestling, best of three, in order to give the poor infant a more bully-proof nomenclature. Having won the test of strength, the vicar repeated the question, and was told simply, 'Colin...'

The man's wife however, had decided that her daughter deserved a name which conveyed all of the high-ranking status to which she desperately aspired. After hours spent poring over names in a baby book, she had finally agreed on a suitable name – and hence, the baby was christened Chlamydia... With the ceremony now concluded for the first family, the proud parents stepped away from the font, with a grin from Hyar to Hyar.

Hyde-Jones had now choked on his tea, most of which had come out of his nose and distributed itself across his clean shirt. Trying to calm down his hysterical laughter, he was gasping for air, and thumping the arm of the chair.

'Sorry Roy,' said Newhouse 'but it got worse after that...'

It was now the turn of the party which included Mr Newhouse to approach the font and the still-hyperventilating vicar. As the vicar briefly turned away from the group, Newhouse had noticed that the man had very obviously cycled to the church whilst wearing his immaculate white surplice. This was obvious for two reasons: one was the fact that he was still wearing his bright orange cycle clips, and the other reason was the two-foot long skid mark which extended right up to the man's shoulders. At the sight of this, Newhouse had apparently had to dash outside and laugh in private, aided by a quick cigarette. When he returned, he noted that the font had been emptied of the effervescent fluid by the previous family. There was now the pressing problem of how to baptise a child with an empty font.

It came to a distant and rather vacant Cousin Roger to step up and save the day. He was a travelling salesman for a well-known chocolate firm, and had some fresh new samples in the boot of his car which he was certain would get the job done to the satisfaction of all. He sped out of the church, and after a whispered conversation with the vicar, assumed his position within the group.

It was thus that little Grant Williams was christened by cracking two crème eggs on the side of the font. The happy, smiling and extremely sticky baby was handed back to his proud parents, who did not look as if they would ever be able to put him down (well, not for some hours and without judicious use of moist wipes). Apart from the problem of unwelcome attention from wasps for the rest of the afternoon, there would be, in later years, a far more terrifying problem with which to deal. Poor Grant would have to include several supplementary sheets with his future passport application – upon which to include his full name of "Grant Sugar Glucose Syrup

Skimmed Milk Powder Cocoa Butter Lactose Hydrolysed Milk Protein Barley Malt Extract Whey Powder Suitable for Vegetarians Williams..."

All had concluded well, if you ignore the crying, screaming and general wriggling about during the first family's christening. Eventually, the vicar had insisted that the mother either shut up, or leave the church...

Hyde-Jones would take many hours to recover from this anecdote, and would certainly not risk another cup of tea until his hysterics had completely subsided.

Rundell was now explaining to Dr Matthews in a highly-animated manner that *Howards End* was definitely not a work of Gay Fiction, a point that the somewhat lubricated master failed to concede. Bannister, the Mathematics tutor, had not at all helped to calm the fraught situation by suggesting that Matthews should have his own personal entry in the *Record Book of Guinness*. Matthews had retorted by pointing out the dangers in what Bannister was himself drinking – iced mineral water. He declared in a serious tone, 'I had a good friend who always drank Vodka on the Rocks – he died of liver failure. My own father passed on after continuously sipping Scotch on the rocks – due to kidney damage – so you must be able to see that ice is bloody dangerous stuff...'

'Miles is perfectly correct about that...' said Mrs Elsie Noakes, out of Bannister's mouth, 'I have met some of the poor Souls from the *Titanic*'. At that point, Dr Chambers made a dramatic entry into the room, and swept up the various staff members ready for the morning assembly. As the boys and staff all stood to attention awaiting the entry of the head, the boys could clearly see this morning's addition to the front of the lectern. The object of interest today was a rather impressive black leather brassiere, with a fierce array of studs dotted around its edges. Clearly, somewhere within the environs of the Academy, Boudicca was already catching a cold, or perhaps Miss Dipper, the Matron would discover her underwear drawer to be slightly lighter today. The head grasped the sides of the lectern and swung it to a central position, causing the threatening undergarment to swing alarmingly, and also cause similar alarming swings within the libidos of the older boys (one boy actually realised that he preferred the rubber chicken – but I can assure you that he will receive the very best help and care available).

After the daily massacre of the Academy Anthem had taken place, Nicky was certain that he had heard whispering coming from the space under the stage. Against the background murmuring of the other boys he could not be certain of the exact location, but made up his mind to enlist the help of his friends to investigate just as soon as the opportunity presented itself.

In their form room prior to the register being called, the boys were discussing the most recent disappearance of their friend DeVere, when the mocking tones of Lordsley rose above the general chatter. He was prodding the amply-upholstered

Davis in the stomach and announcing, 'I don't see why they sent you here at all, because let's face it, you will never be able to add to St Onan's sporting records you fat oaf...'

Calderman, Merry, Trevill and Nicky all rounded on him in defence of their friend. 'Leave him alone you inbred little prat, or you will be having your lunch through a drip-feed,' snarled Calderman. Lordsley saw the error of his ways, and turned away from his victim to face the front of the class.

'Thanks Ian,' said Davis, 'but I don't pay any attention to him – I am used to him insulting me'.

Nicky asked him how he could possibly get used to insults from such an unpleasant character such as Lordsley.

Davis explained, 'I was at prep' school with Lordsley, and he used to torment me there too. He found out that I have an allergy to peanuts, so he spread the word around the school.'

'And that was helpful, surely?' asked Merry. 'No it wasn't...' replied Davis. 'At break times they used to grab me and force me to play blindfold Russian Roulette with a bag of Revels...'

It turned out to be a weird morning (for a change). The Geography master had apparently had to go on an emergency call to a local supermarket – and had become hopelessly lost in the maze of aisles within. It was rumoured that there had been a sighting of him somewhere in the area of the tinned fruit and vegetable section, but this was as yet unconfirmed. Mr Baker had done his best to fill in for the absent Thwaite, but had easily been side-tracked into telling the class all about his recent camping holiday to Wales. He had shown the boys several photographs showing his wife and himself atop various rain-soaked hills, climbing Mount Snowdon (in the rain), and shots of the two of them surrounded by sheep, (very wet and rain-soaked sheep). The water was all-pervading, even causing the room of their lodgings to develop a leak through the ceiling. Returning still dripping from their excursions, Baker had put out a mouse trap outside their bedroom door to catch any local vermin – and in the morning found that he had caught an angry otter. Even on a Sunday, when all other shops were closed, the purveyor of rain remained open, and was happy to distribute free samples to all and sundry.

Chemistry had turned out to be even more bizarre. Goggled and white-coated, the boys were once again investigating the reactive properties of various metals when exposed to water, and were expected to make detailed notes on the results. Captain Brayfield took exception to the fact that Kendy was a second or two too slow to respond, when the master called for silence. He bellowed at the boy, and made him stand in front of the class and explain why his conversation was so much more important than the experiments in front of them. An embarrassed Kendy stood stock still, and locked eyes with the captain. His hands were clenched and his knuckles were showing white. When the master had finished berating the boy, it was almost thirty seconds before he noticed that every single dish on the benches containing water had frozen solid...

Physics had started to go quite well, with the professor managing to keep his pinball mind under relative control, and actually teaching the boys some interesting things about circuits and electricity in general. They all had a great deal of fun constructing and then testing their own circuits with the object of getting a small lamp to light up. Merry discovered that even more fun was to be had by connecting up batteries in series, and discharging the current via the backside of the unsuspecting Lordsley whose shouts of alarm were mistaken for whoops of delight by the professor and amazement of the brigade of boys who had chosen Lordsley to receive retribution, Strangler strode around the benches and inspected their individual circuits, correcting and re-connecting the wiring.

'Should work fine now Merry, just connect this resistor, yes, that's got the blighter, now try again,' he said. Merry connected the bare end of the wire to the posterior of Lordsley, who leapt a few inches into the air to prove that the circuit was correctly connected – but rather disappointingly, failed to light up.

The professor was strangely silent when he approached the bench at which Kendy was working, and saw the bulb glowing dimly and extremely brightly with alternating pulses. Kendy stood upright and smiling in front of the work bench, seemingly pleased that he had achieved what had been asked of him. What amazed the master even more to the point of disbelief was the fact that the battery was not connected to the circuit...

Just then, the tension was broken by the sound of cheers and applause coming from other classrooms. All of the boys ran over to the windows which faced the quad, to see what the source of the clamour was all about. Across the quad, again flanked by two severe-looking masters, was the escapee, DeVere, who was struggling to shrug off the grip of his captors. At the end of the path to the headmaster's study, DeVere defiantly threw off the hands that held him, and marched proudly up the path on his own, to shouts of 'Bad luck Mate' and 'Tell them nothing Davey'. DeVere gave a one-handed clenched-fist salute back towards the quad, as he opened the door to face the wrath of the headmaster.

The boys were summoned away from the windows, and the lesson was gradually wound down. The same could not be said for Lordsley, who was still twitching like a wild creature about to spring, or at least one who looked to be ever-ready.

Just before the start of the lunch break, Dr Darwin had sped through the corridors in a frantic search for his friend Felchingham. The Reverend was the only other staff member who ever showed any interest in the extra-curricular experiments which

Darwin was so enthusiastic about. His recent fish tank experiment had taken a dramatic turn, and he was desperate to share the results with his fellow tutor. Breathless and dishevelled, he flapped across the quad and flung open several of the classroom doors in his hunt, leaving a trail of bemused masters and startled pupils in his wake. By the time that he caught up with Felchingham in the corridor, he was quite out of breath, and could hardly gasp and splutter out the reason for his urgent searching. 'Quick Gerald,' he panted, 'something wonderful is happening in the fish tank – you simply must come and see.'

Although the Rev failed to share the immediacy of whatever the fish tank residents had managed to achieve, he was curious as to what had produced such a level of hysteria in his colleague, and so he allowed himself to be herded across the quad and over to the Biology laboratory where the magical event was taking place. Darwin almost pushed his friend through the door to the preparation room, and pointed to the large fish tank with an outstretched and trembling finger. 'Look, look, Gerald, see what they are doing – I told you that they are far more intelligent than we thought...' stammered Darwin. Felchingham peered into the tank, and noted that the four goldfish were working in pairs to move two of the lego blocks with which they had previously constructed the small wall in the midst of the gravel. Darwin was now quite frantic...' See Gerald, they are swapping the two end blocks over...' he stammered. The Rev saw that the fish were in the act of replacing the two end bricks. Previously, he had seen that some hitherto unrecorded skill on the part of the fish had enabled them to write the word "BNOK" on the plastic wall which they had constructed. The fish were now earnestly engaged in the act of swapping the two end bricks over. It was the matter of a second or so before Felchingham worked out just exactly what the new word on the "wall" would spell. 'See now Gerald – the graffiti now says...'

'I am well aware of what it says, Jonathan... and I will thank you not to bother me again with such trivia,' said Felchingham, through firmly gritted teeth. Daily attacks from Stan were one thing, but now it would appear that he had coerced a group of innocent goldfish into taking the piss...

Lunchtime was spent quizzing the recaptured DeVere, who was fast becoming a hero to the other boys. Everyone wanted to know just how he had managed to escape this time, and what unfortunate set of circumstances had led to his unwilling return to the fold. Young Master David explained to his fascinated audience that he had seen a piece of paper in the music room. The sheet had been the bill for the repair of the double bass, which was to be collected by a firm from Nottingham. He had noted the date of collection – and had (with some considerably skill and difficulty) secreted himself inside the large instrument just before it was taken away for repair. The restorer who had intended to begin work on the bass had been completely taken by surprise when he found a small boy inside it. DeVere had made a bid for freedom, but this had been somewhat doomed to failure from the outset – because a boy wearing only his pants was not going to get far before being noticed, and so he had little choice but to surrender to the inevitable. The headmaster had not been too harsh on him, and had seemed much more concerned as to why any boy should not want to stay at his Academy, and was at a loss to comprehend why an individual would not wish to stay and take full advantage of the facilities on offer: i.e. cold and draughty dormitories, poor food, constant bullying, and the unpredictable nocturnal visits to the dorm from Dr Matlock, who for reasons of health, stalked the corridors dressed only in helmet, cricket pads, and a Gentleman's Protector. Throw in the regular early morning five-mile runs in all weather, the cold showers, and a plague of mice in dormitory five – and what more could a boy want.

The head had asked the boy, 'Look, DeVere – just what is the problem?'

DeVere had answered him honestly, 'Home sickness, sir...'

The head looked puzzled. 'But during term time, boy, the Academy IS your home...'

DeVere paused. 'Yes, sir – and I'm sick of it...' Actually, what DeVere wanted was for his father to take notice of the constant letters which he sent pleading for help, and for his parents to get a refund of the fees which they had paid in order that the Academy had the chance to inflict mental and physical torture upon their son. His letters fell upon a deaf desk – and so DeVere was determined to put as much distance between himself and St Onan's as he could, whenever the opportunity might arise. Even as the head had been lecturing him in his study, DeVere had been glancing sideways out of the window, and noting exactly at what time the kitchen catering lorry turned up and left. His next attempt may well involve Royalty- as he estimated that he could easily fit into one of the sacks which contained King Edward potatoes...

Throughout lunch, Mrs Bradley had paced up and down the aisles of the dining hall, whilst peering into every corner of the ancient enclosure. Although still deeply troubled by the constant removal of items from her kitchen, it was obvious that the medication which her doctor had prescribed in order to calm her was beginning to have an effect. Her mind was on her investigations, but seemingly also on 1970s music. She could clearly be heard gently singing the odd Hendrix ditty to herself when scanning the hall's nooks and crannies, 'Scuse me, while I kiss the Pie...' At one point, her fellow workers had become most concerned, as she had leapt up onto the long kitchen table and executed a very creditable air-guitar solo on a large ladle. The headmaster was now monitoring her behaviour closely. This had become necessary after Betty had picked up a large leg of roast lamb, and had proceeded to give it the identical treatment that Mr Pete Townshend regularly gave to his Les Paul guitar. The head demanded that she come immediately to his study, and in severe tones, explained that the kitchens were to confine themselves to matters of beef stock – and not Woodstock.

If Nicky had any hopes of being able to get through his first days at St Onan's without being put into the spotlight of embarrassment, then this hope was about to evaporate as rapidly as Dr Matthews' grip on sobriety. Since first finding himself in the horrible position of having to study Latin, Nicky had continued to find the whole subject utterly baffling, and filled with intermittent terror at the prospect of being asked any question. Rundell the Latin Supremo summoned the class into the room with his customary barked instruction. As the boys sat in their now accustomed rows, it was obvious that the man was in a foul humour.

Rundell shot up out of his seat and addressed the class. 'There are, I am sorry to have to point out, gentlemen, certain elements within the class who do not seem to share the thirst for a skill in the Latin tongue. Indeed, there are boys here that show little or no aptitude for my subject, and all that it has to offer. I have recently corrected preparatory work which quite frankly, I would have been embarrassed to have handed in, were I a student. There is one such boy among us, who thought my subject of such little importance that he could submit his work in another language. I was certainly not impressed or amused by this little stunt. Let me make the position abundantly clear, gentlemen: I intend to impart into your young brains such Latin as may complement your education and enrich your vocabularies and social skills in the years to come. Not to dwell on the point, I fear I may be wasting my time with certain boys in this class – but be assured boys, I am here to teach you, and learn you most certainly will. This may well prove to be a painful process for some of you, but I will never let it be said that a dull or uncultured boy has ever left my classroom without a firm grounding in the subject of Latin. Am I wasting my time with you Mr Shepherd?'

To Nicky's utter horror, the entire class swung around to view his embarrassment and shame at being singled out by the master. 'N-n-no, sir...' he stammered.

'Then why do you display such a competent incompetence at the subject, boy?'

'I just find it hard, sir, and I've never had to learn languages before.'

'I doubt, Shepherd, that if I sat and made you decline Latin verbs for the next twenty-five years, that you would grasp it,' said Rundell. 'It is probably just as well, because I cannot imagine for one moment that your future employment will cry out for a complete understanding of the Latin parlance.'

There was a collective snigger from the more able section of the class, and Nicky could not help but notice that the loudest laughs came from the wealthiest students. Unwilling to bite back with any response to the master, the boy simply sat in silence, although the fires of resentment and anger were beginning to heat up the boiler of revenge in his soul. He paid little or no attention during the rest of the lesson, and was caught out when Rundell asked him a question out of the blue. 'I don't suppose that you were paying attention, were you, boy?' sneered Rundell.

'Not in the slightest, sir – not that you would think that it would do me any good,' Nicky answered.

'Leave my class, Shepherd...' demanded Rundell. 'A spell in the corridor may allow you to consider your future conduct.' Nicky left the room shame-faced, and stood with his back against the ancient plaster wall outside the classroom. Just as he was pondering the prospects of joining DeVere in an escape attempt, Miss Piggott the Academy secretary and would-be personal assistant to the headmaster appeared around the corner.

'What are you doing in the corridor out of lessons?' she demanded. 'Church of Scotland – I am excused Latin during the feast of St Ludicrus,' explained Nicky.

The woman gave him a blue-rinsed look of confused scorn, and scuttled away down the corridor on whatever urgent errand she was engaged upon. All of the boys were aware of her fanatical devotion to the head, and rumours about her private sherry mornings abounded. She was the owner of a small and quite bizarre dog. The pooch was a cross-breed, with half of its parentage being Pit Bull Terrier, and the other half Poodle. The resultant offspring was absolutely no use as a guard dog – but it turned out to be a vicious gossip...

Suddenly, Nicky caught the smallest of motions out of the corner of his eye. Doing his best to look right, whilst trying to observe to his left, he saw one of the long corridor cupboard doors come slightly open. Trying not to look as if he had seen the door move, he heard whispering from within the cupboard, and then what sounded like two young voices giggling just before the door closed with an almost imperceptible click of the latch. He held his breath and waited to see if another door should come open somewhere along the corridor, but there was no further movement or sound – until he was forced to remember to breathe again. Eventually, the bell for the next lesson sounded, and his classmates spilled out of the Latin class and made their way down the corridor for the next session. Calderman, Merry, Trevill and Weatherill (resplendent in an oak-leaf crown) all tried to lift the spirits of their friend. 'Don't Ee bother about yon teacher – the man's an arse!' declared Trevill. Calderman told Nicky to ignore the comments which Rundell had made, and insisted that all the master had achieved was to make himself look like a bully and a misguided snob. Merry came up with the best suggestion of all – and that was that they should report the master's conduct and attitude to their newest and most secret friend, namely Albert Brooks. With Mr Brooks' hatred of the so-called "Upper Classes", he would certainly have something to say about the way in which Rundell had chosen to belittle one of his pupils. The boys had a vague idea of exactly what Albert's response might be. No doubt he would suggest that this could well be a job for the ODD.

Chapter Twenty

Still smarting from the haughty reprimand which he had suffered from the Latin master, Nicky was somewhat relieved to attend the next lesson, which was English with Mr Hyde-Jones. This temporary relief was shattered when soon after the class had all sat at their desks, the door to the classroom had swung open to reveal Miss Piggott in all her sycophantic glory. She ignored the assembled boys, and strode purposefully up to the master's desk. She declared in a voice designed to be heard in the next county that 'The head has instructed that Shepherd be punished due to the fact that he was excluded from a Latin lesson earlier, so I will leave it up to you Mr Hyde-Jones to arrange a suitable detention and task for him.'

To his credit, Hyde-Jones gave the woman a look of suspicious contempt, and merely answered, 'I shall arrange something appropriate- do please inform the head that it has been taken care of.' At this response, the woman turned around quickly and stomped toward the classroom door. She pulled at the handle with considerable force, which had absolutely no effect. She then seemed to lose her iron self-control, and gripped the door handle with both of her pink podgy hands and began to frantically tug at the door for all she was worth. Her glasses fell from her head, and swung about her person on the purple string to which they were attached.

Hyde-Jones managed to stifle his laughter at her predicament, and enquired in a silken voice, 'May I perhaps be of assistance, Miss Piggott?' (The boys noted that he placed distinct emphasis on the "Pig" syllable of her name.)

She rounded angrily on the master, foaming ever so slightly at the corner of her mouth, as she declared, 'My name should be pronounced PIE-Gott if you don't mind...'

The master stood up and gave a slight bow, as he answered, 'My profound apologies, madam – I will endeavour to remember that. Just to keep a sense of equity and balance, I should point out that my own name ought to be pronounced 'Hy-de-Jo-ness' if you would be so kind.'

'And I am Miss – not Madam' declared the now furious secretary.

'I have absolutely no doubt that you are indeed...' said Hyde-Jones, leaving the response hanging in the air. He calmly walked over to the door, gently removed both of her hands from the door handle, and with a sweeping fluid movement, pushed open the door which she had been tugging at in maniac fashion. The master stared after her for a few seconds, and then pulled the door closed, shaking his head and declaring 'What a terrible thing it is when you mistake HRT for HRH.'

Hyde-Jones cast over a sympathetic glance at Nicky, and said, 'I'll have a word with you after the lesson about all of that nonsense.' He then began giving the class an enthusiastic introduction to the wonderful world of that virtuoso of the printed word, Mr Charles Dickens. With the very mention of the name, Nicky's heart sank. Atop the tall standing book case in his living room were several thick volumes which comprised the complete works of Mr Dickens. Nicky had taken one of the books from the shelf, blown off the dust from the cover, and made a futile attempt to read it. He found that the prose and style were almost impossible to read, and he could not identify with any one of the characters in the story. Although his mind had taken precautionary steps to delete any memory of the actual content of the book, Nicky had more or less worked out how this, and every other Dickens story would develop.

Abel Pecksniff and Dolly Crotchpin had got married and settled in a grimy back street in old London town, where they toiled as shoe lace engravers to the public from their homely hovel-cum-shop. One day, their evening's gin-gathering was interrupted by a sound outside their tiny front door, which had rickets. In a wicker basket on their doorstep was the foundling young Rupert Twistcock, with a note placed in the basket indicating that the baby had upper-class roots, but could not be kept by the family for tax reasons, and the risk of dandruff.

Local merchants Mordecai Greyspube and Daniel Bitchgrinder would of course call at the house and notice a significant birthmark upon the little mite. The Reverend Grimley Cleftclinch will have received a mysterious letter which tells of a secret benefactor who has pledged a great sum of money to assist with the upbringing of the infant Twistcock (now Pecksniff by deed poll).

Crispin Slyme the lawyer will seek to relieve the family of the secret bequest, for his own nefarious ends (as he can only afford one end at present). He is saving up to take all of his thirty-four children and his wife to "PauperWorld" on the Dorset coast, where the consumption can be caught much more cheaply than is the case in the City of London. Twistcock will reach the age of sixteen, when the discovery of yet another letter will reveal that he is in fact the illegitimate son of Sir Rustyc-Burpe, and the rightful heir to the lonely yet majestic Gusset Hall on the edge of Dartmoor. He will have made friends with a humorous cook by the name of Mrs Dumpling, who will declare that, 'Oooo-This is a fine carrying-on Master Twistcock, and no mistaking.'

By this time, he will also have formed an intimate but tragic bond with Matilda Futtock. She is working as a maid for a firm of horse polishers in the City, but is in fact Twistcock's twin sister, who has been searching for her missing sibling for the past ten years. She will be forced into a marriage to the tyrant and mole-beater Clement DeCluster, but will leave him fuming at the altar of the quaint village church, and speed back to the arms of her long-lost brother (after receiving yet another mysterious letter by means of consumptive pigeon post, and then eating the pigeon).

All will end well, except for the boy Lumpy Little Leonard, who will sadly die after getting his string vest caught in a passing military parade...

Nicky begun to think that Dickens was exactly the same as Latin – in that neither were for people from the lower social orders, and certainly it was only rich people that he had heard declaring a love for Mr Dickens (sometimes in Latin). He began to think that the reason that he did not "get it" was that deep down, he was not supposed to. Maybe the very words themselves contained some hidden repellent which was put there to ward off the less financially established reader. It was the same with mathematics – so he reasoned that if he was obviously so bad at maths, then he would be prevented from working out just how poor he and his family actually were. Was this some massive social conspiracy on behalf of the upper classes? Was it some hideous scheme to prevent the lower classes from getting ideas above their station? (Certainly, his father had ideas above his station, but this actual idea was to pinch all of the lead from the station roof.) Or was Dickens just some overblown Victorian turd, who should not even have been allowed to write a note for the milkman..?.

Despite Nicky's natural aversion to the author, the lesson actually passed off in a reasonably fine fashion, with the natural acting talent of Hyde-Jones showing through, as he portrayed all of the characters (and the author), with enthusiasm and skill. At the end of the lesson, the master indicated for Nicky to remain behind as the rest of the boys filed out of the room. Hyde-Jones smiled at him, and invited him to 'park it on the end of the desk for a moment, while we sort out this crap'. Nicky had certainly never expected such a relaxed attitude from a teacher.

'Look mate...' the master began, 'It's like this – I can't go against the head, because I have got used to too many luxuries, like food, and living indoors, but I don't agree with all of this "crime and punishment" rubbish. We will have to agree on some small task after school that we are both happy with – so that their "justice" is seen to be done. I hear that you are a good artist, so how's about helping us to paint the back scenery for the school play, that shouldn't be too much of a terrible punishment will it?'

Nicky agreed that this proposal didn't actually sound too bad, but said that he would have to let his mother know that he would be late back from school. Hyde-Jones was pleased that they had reached a suitable solution, and told Nicky to go down to the school office and call his mother from the telephone in the room next to the head's study. Nicky was a bit nervous in case he came face-to-face with the Gorgon-like Miss Piggott, but he thanked the master, and set off to make his call. As he was just going out of the door, Hyde-Jones called out to him, 'Don't worry – it really will get better!' Nicky prayed that the master was correct.

He took the steps down to the quad two at a time, and raced across the concreted area trying not to attract the attention of any passing prefects. At the end of the path to the offices and the head's study, he paused and took a deep breath, before walking as confidently as he felt able up the high-walled strip and up to the oaken door. He suddenly realised that he was not entirely sure exactly where the school office was located, and dreaded the thought of having to try every door along the corridor, in case the horrors which no doubt lurked within should be released. The corridor itself was eerily silent as Nicky tried the third door handle, and found it to be locked. At that point, he noticed, a little way down the corridor, that one of the doors was slightly ajar. The door had a square name-plate fixed to the top of the timber, which simply said "Baxter", picked out in the usual gold italic script. There was no handle at all on this door (which Nicky thought was a little unusual), but there was a large and highly-polished brass push plate fixed on the door about three feet or so from the floor.

With cold sweat gently running down his back, Nicky slowly eased open the door and looked into the room. The contents of the office were similar to any of the classrooms throughout the entire Academy, with a parquet floor, ancient and tatty rug, and the standard dark oak desk upon which stood the telephone. Nicky pushed the door a little further open, and called out 'Hello – is there anyone here?' His call was greeted with silence, so he raised his voice slightly. 'Hello, is it okay if I just use the 'phone?' Nothing. He noticed that in the far corner of the room was a large wicker basket, in which sat an equally large chocolate-brown Labrador dog who was busy doing his afternoon ablutions, so to speak. As he knew that he would only be a few seconds when using the telephone, Nicky decided to risk it. He carefully lifted the receiver, and was relieved to hear a dialling tone. He quickly dialled the number, and was surprised at the speed with which the call was answered.

'Oh hello, Auntie,' he said. 'Can you please tell Mum that I will be late home from school tonight, because I am going to help to paint the scenery for the school play' (he chose to gloss over the real reason as to why he was kept behind).

'Yes, Dear,' answered Auntie.

He was just about to ask if everything was all right at home, when a smooth, cultured and aristocratic voice enquired, 'I do hope that you intend to make adequate remuneration for your telephonic communication...?'

Nicky froze, but turning around slowly, he could see no-one else in the room, apart from the dog which was still engaged in the act of gnawing at a back leg. 'Sorry Auntie, I can't talk at the moment, but I will see you later tonight,' he said nervously.

Again, he heard the upper-class voice say, 'I do hate to rush you, young man, but I am expecting a rather important call myself...'

Nicky replaced the receiver quickly and scanned the room. The only occupants of the office were still himself and the brown Labrador. He carefully paced around the room seeking the owner of the voice which he had heard, watched by the dog who was wagging his tail in a friendly manner. When no other person could be found, Nicky leaned over to the dog in the basket, and gently stroked his noble head saying, 'You are a good boy aren't you...?'

'So are you – it would appear,' said the dog.

Nicky leapt back in stunned amazement, with his eyes wide open in shock. 'You can talk!' he stammered.

'No,' said the dog. 'Everyone who knows anything about animal physiology will tell you that canines do not in fact possess the ability for intelligible speech.'

'But you are talking...' was all that the stunned boy could utter.

'My word – you know, you may actually be correct about that,' replied the dog.

'But how?'

'Although your sentence construction does lack a certain finesse...'

'But I don't understand.'

'But me no buts young sir – I shall explain, if you have time?' said the dog. 'You will note that my door is the only door without the addition of a handle. This is because paws and door handles are not a mutually beneficial combination. My name is Baxter. In addition to being the much-loved pet and companion of Dr Goodwill, I have my own office here because I am also employed as a Stock Market and Investment advisor to the MidShires Banking Group. I am also the consultant on etiquette for several local newspapers, and an expert on wines of all vintage. I am also kindly afforded the status of expert in several other areas..'

'Which areas are those?'

'Well, trees mostly, to be quite frank.'

'Are you qualified as an expert on trees?'

'What do you think...?'

'I think that it is an honour and a privilege to meet you, Mr Baxter,' said Nicky.

'What a polite young man you are, and I thank you for that. Please accept the use of my telephone for free, as a gift from one new friend to another. However, if you do feel that I should be awarded some recompense, then I would point out that a large marrowbone is always acceptable...' said Baxter.

'How many other people know that you can talk?' asked Nicky.

'Not another living soul, dear boy, and if ever you should feel the need to recount the story of our chance meeting, then I will be happy to revert to the canine vernacular' answered Baxter.

'Sorry?' asked Nicky, not quite understanding the statement

'Woof, bark et cetera...' said the dog. 'Now I will let you go about your business, and I do have several important matters to attend to before I take my business calls, if you do not mind.'

'And are these important things anything which I can help you with?' enquired the boy

'I think that I will need no assistance with washing my arse, thank you...' said Baxter.

Nicky went a little red, and left the office, having given his new friend another stroke of his well-bred head. He closed the door behind him and hurried off to his lesson feeling as if he had somehow been given a walk-on part in an episode of *The Twilight Zone*. When he finally arrived in his art class, he was more than a little gutted to find that he had not even been missed. He thought it appropriate to produce a painting in the art class which was undertaken in the Impressionist style. The picture was of a large chocolate-brown dog sitting behind a desk, whilst on the telephone, and smoking a large Cuban cigar. The Master told him that he admired his technique, and asked where the inspiration for the subject of the painting had come from. Nicky merely told him that the idea had come from a meeting with a friend (he failed to mention the fact that instead of a mobile phone constantly by his side, his friend had a squeaky bone).

With the end of what for the majority of the boys had been a normal day at the Academy, Nicky slouched his way up to the assembly hall, where the cast of the play were beginning rehearsals, and the stage crew were busying themselves with the painting of backdrops and various scenery. He reported to Mr Hyde-Jones, who welcomed him and directed him to join Merry, Davis and Jackson (all volunteers as opposed to detainees) in the painting of a large street backdrop which was in the early stages of preparation. Each of the boys had been given a massive tee-shirt to wear over their white uniform shirts. The state of these "overalls" seemed to suggest that they had been evacuated from some recent armed conflict, and the shirt that Nicky was given looked as if someone had merely evacuated over it. The Art master and his chosen apprentices had drawn out the lines of the "street" in perspective, and it was the task of the rest of the crew to fill in the colour and shaded detail to give the illusion of a London street. Jackson suggested that they paint in a couple of muggers and a mime artist, in order to give the scene authenticity, but Merry had threatened to do something biologically interesting with one of the smaller brushes if he tried it. With an old black and white photograph and a colour illustration pinned onto the backdrop for reference, the boys set about recreating a snapshot of Victorian London. Even after Merry's threats, Jackson could simply not resist adding in one of his own "personal touches" to the scene. It would be only on the final night of the actual performance, that one of the cast would notice the naked lady looking out of her bedroom window some way down the street.

As with some onerous tasks which miraculously turn out to be quite good fun after all, none of the boys noticed that a whole hour had simply flown by. Their work was coming along very nicely, and had received positive comments from Hyde-Jones, between calling out direction to the cast who were completely failing to dance, sing, and not collide with the props at the same time. Davis suggested that they take a quick five-minute break, and so the boys sidled off to stage left where cola and crisps magically appeared from the pockets of Davis.

It was whilst in mid-crunch that Merry raised his hand in alarm, and called out, 'Shhh, I heard something.'

Nicky said 'What was it then, Gerry?' but his friend urgently waved him into silence.

Merry put down his crisp packet, and bent forward, straining to hear the sound which he had noticed, and walking like a Ninja along the back wall.

Davis and Nicky followed him as silently as they could, pausing when Merry again raised his hand commando-style to call for silence. For a few moments, all three boys stood statue-like, hardly daring to breathe. It was Davis who broke the silence, well, actually the silence was broken by Davis breaking wind. He looked shamefaced, and silently mouthed the word 'Sorry' to his friends. Then suddenly, they all heard it...

From behind the wall, where the fire hose cupboard doors were located, came the sound of two children's voices giggling. The boys looked at each other in apprehension. Now they knew that the sounds which they heard were not a figment of schoolboy imagination. Someone was definitely behind those cupboard doors, presumably in the wall cavity which the fire hoses were set into. Gingerly (okay – strawberry blonde then), they edged back away from the fire hose doors, and re-grouped stage left.

'Right, chaps...' said Merry, 'we are going to get to the bottom of this.' What I propose is that we try to lure out whoever is behind the wall, with some sort of bait.'

'I don't have anything that we could use,' answered Nicky.

'Well, I might be able to come up with something,' said Davis 'I may have a little piece of chocolate which we could use.'

From pockets various, and with much rummaging, Davis began to pull out a startling array of chocolate bars from who knows where. Like a Cocoa Cornucopia, he began to pile up an astonishing selection of clandestine confectionary. There were two Mars bars, a Twix, a larger bar of Dairy Milk, two Snickers bars, a Twirl, three Milky Ways, two packets of smoky bacon flavour crisps, and a lone Crunchie. 'Sorry Lads, that's all that I can find,' said Davis.

'So do we use these as bait – or open our own sweet shop?' asked Merry.

'My God, Davis,' declared Nicky. 'You want to be careful that you don't put on any weight eating all that lot'.

'It's okay,' said Davis, 'I make sure that I only drink Diet Cola...'

So rather reluctantly, Davis helped the boys lay a trail of the confectionary away from the wooden doors from which they had heard the sounds. Nicky and Davis took up position at the far end of the right hand side of the stage- but with a clear view across to the doors. Merry being the smallest of the group, hid himself beneath a heavy stage curtain right at the side of the doors. Before covering himself with the heavy cloth, he signalled to the other two boys to begin talking (they got the message, but for a while it looked like the world's worst ventriloquist act). Nicky and Davis began chatting idly between themselves, all the time with a casual eye on the fire hose cupboards. The lighting back stage was almost non-existent, and so they could not clearly see Merry under his camouflage curtain. Just as they thought that their plan had been a complete waste of time and effort, the right hand door began to open slowly. Nicky saw Davis's eyes widen, and in a whisper he asked what he could see. Davis said nothing for a few seconds, because he was transfixed as he saw a small girl peer around the door, then slowly reach out and pick up the first of the chocolate bars. Her hand darted back inside, but after another agonising few moments, she reached out even further and claimed two more of the free sweeties.

'Don't turn around...' said Davis very softly, 'but I think that the plan is working.'

The girl had obviously reached the conclusion that there was no danger present, as she now edged out of the cupboard completely. Davis was shocked to see that she was followed out of the door by a small boy. They began to pick up all of the chocolate which had been placed at intervals of a foot or so in a trail which led away from the door. The girl passed back bars to the boy every so often, and paused when the crisp packet gave a warning rustle. As the two children neared the end of the trail, Merry's hand shot out from under the stage curtain and shut the cupboard door with a click. The two children looked around in abject horror – seeing that their escape route was now closed behind them. The girl looked as if she were about to flee, but the small boy just stood in terror, with large tears rolling down his cheeks and leaving salty trails through the dust and grime which covered his little face.

Merry was the first to speak. 'It's all right... don't be frightened, we will not hurt you... we just wanted to share our chocolate with you.'

'That's right...' said Nicky, in as pleasant and calming a voice as he could manage 'We were just worried that you were shut in behind the wall – we just wanted to be your friends.'

The girl and boy looked at each other, and then rapidly at the three boys in quick succession. They seemed to come to the conclusion that they could not escape right at this second, and seemed to slightly relax in front of the boys.

Davis spoke next... 'Look, we don't mean you any harm, and we promise not to tell anyone that we have seen you. You can have more chocolate if you want some?' Davis sat down on the floor, and defied the laws of Physics by producing yet more confectionary from hitherto undiscovered pockets. The other two boys took this as their cue to also sit down, and to their amazement, the two children did exactly the same.

Nicky decided on Choccy diplomacy, and tore open a bar of Dairy Milk – offering it to the little boy, who took it very carefully. 'My name is Nicky,' he began. 'What are your names?' There was silence for a few seconds, as the boy was chewing happily on the chocolate, and then the girl suddenly spoke up 'We are Ursula and We are Thomas. We are sorry that we have done thee a wrong deed.'

'You haven't done anything wrong, and you are not in trouble' said Davis.

'Thee have given us a share of thy food – and yet we have done ye wrong by taking that which does not belong to us – we bring shame to ourselves,' she declared in a small voice.

'You are welcome to share the sweets – and we will bring you more if you like,' said Merry.

'Thou are good to share with us, but HoBi has told us that it is wrong to steal,' said the boy Thomas, his words made difficult to understand as he munched hard on his chocolate.

'Where have you come from?' asked Nicky, but the girl cut him off before he could ask any more questions.

'We thank thee, and we make a promise to return. We must go back now, as the Elders will be angry with us. We make this promise, and HoBi tells us that it is wrong not to keep a promise which thou has made...'

The children edged back toward the fire cupboard doors, which Merry had opened for them. The boys remained seated so as not to frighten the smaller children, and watched them as they disappeared through the doors and presumably back into the wall somewhere. Nicky noted that their clothing had looked very old-fashioned (from what he could see in the poor light behind the stage), and that both children did look rather thin. Not knowing quite what to make of the experience, the three boys began to laugh amongst themselves. Just then, the cupboard door opened slightly, and a small and grubby hand gave them a wave – before quickly closing the door again.

'Okay, chaps- we say nothing to anyone... right?' said Merry.

The three friends shook hands to seal the deal. They returned to their painting, and accepted with good grace the slight "ticking off" which they received for disappearing from their job. The conversation now changed back to the normal light-hearted ribbing of school friends everywhere.

'Did you see that they are asking for volunteers to go on a mission to Mars?' said Nicky

'You should put your name down for that, Davis,' said Merry.

'Why would I do that...?' Davis asked.

'Well, if you get to Mars and you don't like it, you could always eat it...'

Chapter Twenty-One

There was still something deeply disturbing and generally "wrong" about having to attend school on a Saturday morning. Apart from having driven a totally unwanted and unwarranted educational wedge into his weekend, Nicky hated the fact that being forced to attend St Onan's on a Saturday morning prevented him from meeting up with any of his village friends – who were not subject to the torture of extended education. He wondered if the ritual of Saturday School had been put in place to give the masters some measure of enforced continuity, without which they might suffer from a dilution of their knowledge, and not be fully able to remember whatever it was that they were supposed to be teaching. Friday was the day on which you were allowed to eject the CD of learning, and not press "play" again until Monday morning. Still, there it is, and here we are, and although there are no bears in the local woods, if there were, then I am sure that they would...

The morning had begun with an excited and highly animated Uncle Joe calling on the telephone. He had asked Mum and Auntie if they had anywhere that he might store some "merchandise" if he decided to go ahead with a little venture which he was thinking of getting involved in. It would appear that he had been having discussions with one of his many "contacts", who assured Joe that he had an absolutely "can-not-fail" business opportunity for him. Joe told Mum that he was intending to purchase a large quantity of "pre-market samples" of a best-selling substance with hundreds of uses around the house and workshop. He was sure that he was going to make an absolute fortune from selling the stuff, but needed somewhere to keep boxes of the product. On further questioning, it turned out that Joe intended to buy test samples of a product that was later re-named and marketed across the world – how could he possibly lose?... It also soon became clear that what his mysterious seller was trying to offload was a small warehouse full of WD39.

After getting ready (grudgingly) for school, Nicky waited near the bus stop for the lift which had been arranged for him. Eventually, Merry's mother's car came lurching around the church corner, driven by Merry's grandmother. The car shuddered to a halt some way past the point at which Nicky was standing, and he had to run several yards to get to it. It was during this short sprint, that the satchel saw its chance, and dropped its strap down and under the running boy's foot. Nicky suddenly found himself airborne, and created a very detailed imprint of his face on the passenger side window as he made contact head-first with the vehicle. A dishevelled and semi-concussed schoolboy reappeared at the passenger side window, and carefully opened the door. He dropped himself into the seat, and said 'Good morning,' to the driver.

Granny peered back at him through extremely thick spectacle lenses, which would undoubtedly be banned in the National Park districts due to the very real danger of causing fires. Grinning like a maniac, she let out the clutch and shot out into the traffic. Nicky was convinced that she had been given driving lessons by Uncle Joe. The car seemed to have only two speeds – that is off, and seventy-five miles per hour. Their progress down the hill was slowed a little, as they found themselves behind a refuse wagon, piled quite high with a variety of household detritus. After several minutes spent behind the lorry, Granny was about to pull out and around the leviathan, when without warning a large, very pink sex toy flew off the back of the dust cart, and bounced off the bonnet of the car.

Merry's little sister was shocked, and instantly said to her grandmother, 'Granny! What was that which just bounced off the car?'

There was a short embarrassed silence, until Granny recovered her composure and replied, 'Oh it was nothing, dear, it was only a fly...' The journey continued in silence for the rest of the way, until Granny screeched to a halt outside the Academy.

Just as Nicky and the boys were getting out of the car, they heard little Millicent ask her grandmother, 'Granny – did you see the size of the willy on that fly...?'

Meeting up with their comrades, Nicky and Merry made their way up to their form room for registration. Even before the boys entered the room, they could hear the rich tenor voice of Dr Matthews raised in song, and extolling the virtues (or rather lack of) pertaining to some young maiden of France. Matthews greeted the boys at the door holding what should correctly be described as a 'flagon'. 'Aaarrh! Greetin's Me Hearties...' quoth the master in pirate tones, and waved the boys into the room. No-one was quite sure exactly what Matthews was drinking out of his large vessel, but it had obviously put him in a very good mood. Most of the class were pleased to see their form master in such high spirits, but Trevill in particular thought that it, 'was a bit of a rum do...'

With the register called, or rather intermittently slurred, the boys made their way down to the Geography room, urged on by the call of, 'Sail on to be a-learnin' of the ways of maps, charts and the lands of buried treasures, me boys...' from Matthews. It was a fair bet that Matthews would be some time out sailing in the notable company of Captain Morgan.

Entering Mr Thwaite's room, the boys were fascinated to see their master engaged in a life or death struggle with the long wooden pole with which the top classroom windows were opened. They were also fascinated to note that Mr Thwaite had seemingly decided to 'go blond' overnight. In addition to his painted fingernails, false eyelashes and higher-than-usual heels, he now spoke in a voice which was quite a few tones higher than his normal speaking manner. This would seem to be another of Thwaite's 'quirks', and none of the boys paid much attention to their teacher's new look.

'Today, fellows...' he began, 'I thought that we might take a look at glaciers and how they affect the surrounding geography by their weight and slow passage.' (Nicky hoped that he was not referring to Cousin Sheila, who had much the same effect upon her surroundings.) This topic seemed to go down very well with the class, and Weatherill was spotted having donned a downhill skier's cap for the occasion. He was urged by Thwaite to remove the goggles, but was allowed to remain fully hatted throughout the lesson. There followed a great discussion focussing on the great glaciers of the world, and quite a bit of information concerning Drumlins, Kames and Eskers (many other brands of glacial feature are available at an eroded valley near you). In his haste to capture the information, our man Trevill produced detailed notes on the various attributes of Goblins, Canes and Buskers. The class were then asked to draw a detailed diagram of a typical valley created by the passage of a large body of ice over the centuries. Mr Thwaite appeared to be applying some fine powder to his cheeks, and hurriedly hid whatever equipment he was using when he noticed that some of the boys were regarding him with a certain degree of confusion. He asked the class to produce a list of associated glacial features for the next lesson (with illustrations, please), and ushered the boys out of the room just as the bell sounded.

On their way to English class, Nicky, Merry, Davis and Jackson were quietly discussing their recent encounter with the mystery children from behind the wall. Jackson was insistent that they should inform a member of the staff. Merry was dead set against that idea – telling Jackson firmly that no-one should be told anything, until it had been established exactly who could (or could not) be trusted. Nicky stated his personal concerns that the children may be ill or under-nourished, judging from the way in which the boy had demolished the chocolate bars, but general agreement was reached that they should get more evidence and at least explore a little more, before committing themselves to any further course of action. They agreed at least that Calderman, Trevill, and DeVere could be told of the incident without any security risk. They did wonder however, if any other boys from the Academy had seen or met the visitors, or had they just become the most recent recipients of common knowledge?

With Mr Hyde-Jones in mischievous mood today, the English lesson was really good fun. They had begun discussing William Shakespeare, and what it would have been like to have attended the theatre of his time. The master had informed them that in Shakespeare's time, a visit to the theatre to see a play would have been quite a riotous affair, with much audience participation encouraged by the actors. Hyde-Jones told them that the audience would have behaved like a modern day football crowd, and the odd cabbage was very likely to have been flung at the villain onstage (possibly caught by one of the other cast members, as a good cabbage was hard to come by in those times). The boys were then split into groups – one group would be the actors, and the other section the crowd. The 'actors' were given a short piece of drama to recite, and the 'audience' were instructed to act accordingly. This led to much hilarity – with some singular exchanges between the two groups taking place.

During a scene from 'The Scottish Play' (as Hyde-Jones referred to it), three Black and Midnight Hags were heckled by the crowd with chants of 'Sing when you're Witchin' – you only sing when you're Witchin' and that old Stratford favourite – 'Can yoo 'ear the Witches sing? Noo, Noo'. The King had fared little better, himself being drowned out by the chants of 'One Thane of Cawdor – there's only One Thane of Cawdor, One Thane of Caawwdorr...'

Although it is generally accepted that Iago may well be the most evil character which the Bard ever created, Hyde-Jones was forced to step in and calm the crowd who had gotten far too deep into their character, and were pointing and lunging at the boy who was playing the role, whilst singing 'Who's the Bastard in the Black...?' Hyde-Jones was well pleased with the boys' efforts, and suggested that he try to organise a trip out to see a performance of Shakespeare in its authentic form as soon as possible- although he would insist that the boys let the actors perform their craft without interference.

And so, with the sound of Dear William of Avon gently spinning in his grave complete with revolving quill pen in hand, the boys set off for their Music period. All of the pupils really looked forward to their weekly music lessons, which was due in no small measure to the popular and stylised teachings of Mr Newhouse. As the boys piled into the music room, he took out his headphones and greeted them with a friendly, 'Hiya, dudes!' The lads sat down eagerly, and awaited whatever treat for their ears was in store from their favourite teacher. 'Okay, Rock and Rollers,' he began. 'Let me just tell you about the upcoming House Music Contest. The idea is that all of the houses enter contestants in all of the categories, such as choirs, treble solo, and instrumental classes. There will be plenty of chance to show off your musical talents lads, so if you fancy entering on behalf of your House, just let me know, and I will provide you with an entry form. If you have managed to get a group together, I'll be happy to help you with rehearsals'.

Nicky eyed the drum kit in the corner of the room, and wondered if he might just be able to recruit any of his friends into forming a band who could perform at the contest. It was rather short notice, but this was a chance far too good to miss.

'Anyway...' Newhouse continued, 'I have received a complaint from the parents of a certain individual, concerning the music featured in our appraisal of last week. It would appear that the said parents feel that musical education and appraisal should be confined to the classical form – and that modern music is far too frivolous to be studied by the serious student.'

The boys looked around the room at each other, in order to try and work out exactly who had complained about their Hero, and reached the conclusion that there was only one candidate who ticked all of the boxes when it came to suspects.

'I humbly and profoundly apologise for any offence which I may inadvertently have caused to any boy, concerning my musical choices. Furthermore, I intend to deal with the complaint in two ways: the first will be a hearty recommendation that at the earliest opportunity, the complainants should be so kind as to kiss my arse.

The second part will involve a fresh selection of an album for us to review- in accordance with the wishes of Lo – of the parents of one boy. I intend to invite you to listen and write a short review on what I consider to be a supreme musical opus – and definitely a "Classic" by any standard'. Newhouse crossed the room, and taking an album from the shelf above the record deck, proceeded to take it out of its sleeve with much reverence and due ceremony, before placing it upon the deck. He turned on the record unit, wound up the volume on the wall-mounted speakers, and paused. Before placing the needle into the groove of the record, he turned to the boys and smiled his knowing smile.

'Gentlemen – may I present for your delectation... that classical meisterwerk known as *Powerslave* by Iron Maiden...'

With their ears still ringing from their musical appraisal of the Classics, the boys dispersed across the quad, eager to reclaim the rest of their Saturday for their own uses. This was the weekend that Nicky had arranged for his friend Kendy to come over to his house and stay. He was really looking forward to showing his chum around his village, and had planned a few "activities" which he hoped that his friend would find interesting. The boys said cheerio to the rest of the group, and then gathered up their belongings in preparation for the trek home. Nicky had done his best to prepare Kendy for the experience of a trip on the village bus, and just hoped and prayed that the never-fragrant Mrs Jenkins would not be on the bus. Even a person with the very strongest of constitutions would soon find that in her presence, their olfactory sense would shut down in an attempt to prevent irreversible sinus damage.

As it happened, the boys were spared the pungent perils of Mrs Jenkins. With a scream of burning rubber, who should pull up at the bus stop, but a Knight in Shining Zodiac – Uncle Joe. 'Fancy a lift, lads?' he asked, and the boys gratefully slid onto the enormous leather bench seats. 'Have I seen your face somewhere else, son?' Joe asked Kendy.

'No, sir- I always keep it on the front of my head...' he replied, without a trace of sarcasm intended.

'I might be having a bit of a run out on Sunday, if you fancy coming along?' asked Joe, but then corrected himself, saying, 'Oh, sorry, lads, I forgot that I've got to give that talk on guided laser weaponry to the Women's Institute on Sunday evening, so we might have to make it another time eh?'

Nicky looked across at his friend for a sign of a reaction, but the boy was too busy clinging onto the upholstery of the car as Joe screeched around the traffic in front of them to react in any way whatsoever. Three near-misses and two shouted threats later, the boys got out of the car. As they closed the doors, Joe sped off at light speed, causing the local vicar and his antique bicycle to take an unplanned diversion through a newly-creosoted fence. What the vicar shouted at the retreating vehicle must have been a quotation from the first book of St Genghis Khan.

Mum was waiting for the boys to arrive back from school, and had prepared a light snack of sandwiches and orange juice. She introduced herself, although Nicky had to point out that he already knew who she was – but would be happy to see any official identification if she had any about her person. Kendy seemed bemused by this exchange, and shook her hand saying, 'Hello, Mrs Shepherd. Thank you very much for inviting me to stay. My name is Jonef, but please call me 'Jon' as it is easier to remember.'

'You are most welcome, Jon' said Mum, 'now you can get changed if you wish.'

At this statement, Kendy looked a little terrified, until Nicky told him 'Mum means, out of our uniform. We'll just stick our jeans on, and I will give you a guided tour of the village.'

Their discarded uniform now heaped up in the corner of Nicky's bedroom, the two boys set off on their trip around the sleepy village and its collection of sagging-roofed relaxed houses. The village was identical to small rural hamlets everywhere, with its random gatherings of brightly-coloured plants in pots and hanging baskets outside the dwellings. Kendy had the look of someone who was completely unfamiliar with architecture – and showed a marked fascination with features which Nicky no longer gave a second glance to. It took them some time to reach the top of the village, as their progress was continually halted by local inhabitants who all wanted to be introduced to Nicky's new friend. On the plus side, the boys were given free ice-creams by the keeper of the village shop, although Kendy had been extremely confused at the shopkeeper's refusal to accept his offer of payment.

Leaving the shop and its friendly proprietor, Nicky led the boy a little further up the main street, and turned left into a much narrower avenue. Wiping off the ice-cream that had dripped down his arm, Nicky paused outside a house on their right and declared, 'And this is where I was born...'

Kendy stared at him in horror. 'You were born on this doorstep, in the street?' he asked.

'No Jon, I meant that this is the house which I was born in. We moved out of here when I was six years old, to where Mum and Auntie live now, but I really miss this house and all of the fun I used to have here.'

'Shall we go in and look around?' asked Kendy.

'No, I don't think the people who live here now would like that very much, especially if we drip ice-cream all over their carpets,' said Nicky.

'But that is your house, isn't it?' asked Kendy.

'Well it used to be, but someone else has bought it, so we can't go marching in and demand to be allowed to climb the big apple trees in the back garden – although I would like to...' Nicky replied.

The two walked on, and Nicky pointed out a small overgrown cottage, which was next to a rather more imposing Georgian-style grey stone house.

Kendy was seemingly baffled by the difference between the two dwellings, and asked, 'Why is that house so much bigger than the other one?'

'Because they have a lot more money than those people,' answered Nicky.

'So the people had to buy a bigger house to keep all of their money in?'

'No Jon- that house was more expensive to buy.'

'So why didn't they buy a smaller house, and give some money to the people next door so that they could buy a bigger house?'

'Because they probably needed more money to buy another house.'

'But they already live in one house, why would they be able to live in two places at once?'

'Well maybe they wanted to rent the second house out...'

'Why would they do that?'

'To make more money, I suppose.'

'But then they would need to buy another house to put the extra money in?'

'No Jon, they would keep the money in a bank.'

'Wouldn't the money be just as happy in a smaller house?'

'No – they have to keep it in the bank.'

'But why?'

'Because in addition to being a greedy bastard, the man who owns this house is the local bank manager.'

'So then! – (Kendy looked triumphant...) they could give the bigger house which they have just bought to the people who only have the small house, and they could give their house to someone who doesn't have a house at all.'

'Kendy...'

'Yes, Nicky?'

'I don't seriously think that I can see any future for you as an estate agent...'

The boys walked and talked all the way along the narrow and winding path that followed a recently-ploughed field, until they came to one of Nicky's favourite spots in the entire village. It was his "drawing spot", where he would often come armed with blue paper and chalk, and lay for hours sketching the ever-changing clouds. Beneath a weathered tree was the equally weathered bench seat, where weathered villagers would sit and gaze out across the Vale of Belvoir, taking in the serene view of the rolling fields of wheat and the gentle curves of the hills. Nicky was bursting to ask Kendy the question which had been at the front of his mind all day – perhaps now was the time?

'What was this big secret that you were going to tell me?' he asked, casually.

His friend was silent for quite a time, seemingly taking in every detail of the countryside which surrounded the two watchers. In utter fascination, Nicky suddenly noticed that several birds had landed on the arm of the bench at the side of Kendy, showing absolutely no fear of the boy. As he extended an arm and allowed one of the birds to perch on his outstretched finger, Kendy turned and smiled at Nicky. 'Do you ever wonder if there might be other worlds out there in the Universe just like this one?' he said.

'Oh gosh yes – all the time...' Nicky answered, still fascinated at the close encounter of the sparrow kind, which had now proceeded to perch on Kendy's shoulder. 'When I am out with my telescope at night, I sometimes think that there might be other people who are watching me through a telescope of their own...'

'Oh yes – we do..' said Kendy.

'Yeah, and I have even thought of trying to – hang on a minute... what do you mean "we do"?'

'You are right about there being millions of other worlds like this out there in your galaxy and beyond,' said Kendy.

'You sound very sure when you say that, have you studied the stars, or seen something on the telly?' Nicky asked.

'I just know,' said Kendy.

'How come you know that – are you an expert?'

'No, I don't need to be.'

'Then why are you so certain about life on other planets?' asked Nicky.

Kendy let the little bird walk down his arm and back onto the bench. He sat perfectly still and crossed his hands in his lap, staring straight ahead out at the rolling fields.

'If you look up at the Constellation of Cygnus, you can easily spot the star Deneb. Draw a line from that star down into Pegasus, and you will come to (seen from Earth) a very faint star of twentieth magnitude. This star has a 'sister star' at the same distance from its companion as the sun is from Earth. Around these two binary stars are fifteen planets, seven of which are very much like the Earth...'

'Wow – how do you know? Is your dad an astronomer?' asked Nicky.

'No, not as such...' said Kendy with a chuckle. 'That's where I live...'

Chapter Twenty-Two

Once Nicky realised that he was staring at his friend, with his mouth hanging open in shock, he shook himself mentally and let the torrent of questions come pouring out...

'But you're – I mean you are an – Are you the – how did you – Oh blimey, Kendy!... are you sure?'

Kendy gave Nicky a look, and both boys collapsed into fits of laughter. 'Yes, I think I am pretty certain, now you mention it...' said Kendy.

Nicky was pleased to have been nominated in the "Silly Arse Question of the Year" category, and hoped that Mum would be able to find shelf space for the trophy.

'I know what you want to ask...' said Kendy, 'so I will be brief. Two eyes, two arms and two legs is pretty much the standard as regards evolved species throughout the galaxy, at least in the higher end of the animal kingdoms. Some beings on other planets are taller or shorter – depending on their planet's individual gravity, but we are all very much the same to look at- if you ignore the odd huge fang or claw...'

'Oh very funny...!' said Nicky.

'I wasn't actually making a joke there,' said Kendy. 'Some of the races which we have encountered are not quite as cute as the one which I believe you call ET.'

'Is your planet like this?' asked Nicky.

'Very nearly identical in most respects, except that we don't allow pollution such as you have, and we don't dig dirty great holes in it or burn down the vegetation which helps to provide our oxygen,' Kendy replied.

'Are there any dangerous species?' asked Nicky.

'Oh yes – but you are all down here on your own planet...' laughed the boy.

'I meant, anything like lions or tigers or sharks?' asked Nicky, the Interplanetary Biologist.

'Well yes, we have some dangerous species, but we know how to deal with them,' said Kendy.

Nicky just had to know. 'How do you deal with something like a lion, if it pops up in front of you without warning?'

Kendy stood back and studied Nicky with a critical eye for about ten seconds. 'Right – stand up and close your eyes,' demanded the boy. Nicky did so.

'Okay – you can open them now,' said Kendy.

The warm breeze blew softly across the small hill upon which stood the bench and the aged tree. The golden stalks of wheat danced in the breeze like a rippling yellow sea. Woodpigeons called from the distant tree line, and a skylark sang its joyful melody as it rose vertically from the amber field.

Standing in front of the bench seat, face to face, were two Nicholas Shepherds...

When the initial shock and terror had dissipated, Nicky was captivated by what his eyes told him was before him – yet his brain would not quite accept to be true.

'Wow!' was all that he could utter. Kendy asked him to close his eyes again, and when he was told that it was safe to look, his friend had resumed his usual and familiar shape.

'How on Earth can you do that?' Nicky stammered.

'Well, on earth, I probably wouldn't need to do it,' answered Kendy. 'Let's just say that my people have retained the ability to mimic the physical characteristics of any species that is posing a threat. It's a sort of defence mechanism, and trust me, it works. No predator will attack if it can see that its intended prey is exactly the same size and shape as itself, and so will think better of it and go away.'

'Would a creature not notice the difference in smell?' asked Nicky.

'It depends on how sudden the surprise of seeing the predator is...' answered Kendy, with honesty.

'So tell me about your planet, is it like ours?' Nicky said.

'Oh yes – very similar. A bit bigger, more islands, hotter deserts, but nearly identical in every respect' Kendy answered.

'But... but – how did you get here?' Nicky asked his friend. At this point, a passing wood pigeon decided to vacate onto Kendy's shoulder. 'That's supposed to be lucky' said Nicky.

'How is that considered to be good luck'? asked the bemused friend, wiping off the offending gift with a handkerchief.

'Well, it's lucky that it didn't land on me for a start... ' said Nicky.

'I came here because we picked up requests for exchange students which were sent out by St Onan's Academy. My Elders thought that it would be a great opportunity for me to 'get out into the world and broaden my horizons' (so they told me). I was prepared for the journey by learning the languages of Earth, and your customs and habits – so that I would not "stick out like a sore Bum".

'The actual phrase is "Sore Thumb", Jon,' Nicky hastily corrected.

'Well, sorry, yes – I was brought to Earth in my relative's transporter, although we had some trouble when we initially ended up landing in completely the wrong destination due to a rubbish navigation aid which my father had obtained from a man here on Earth. The man who sold it to my father claimed that its voice-recognition system was foolproof. This was not the case. We travelled here using what you might refer to as a "wormhole", and set the co-ordinates for the village of Little Pendleham on twenty-sixth of December 1980. We ended up landing in your county of Suffolk, and got completely lost in a forest in a place called Rendlesham. Father says that he will do damage to the idiot who sold him the faulty navigator, if he lays hands on him again. If I remember, his name was "JaPrentiz" or something similar – but that's all I could read on the receipt which he gave Father.'

Nicky froze, because at the back of his brain, some tiny hand was hammering on the door of recognition. It would be a coincidence too ridiculous to contemplate – but what if, or just supposing, that the actual name on the worthless receipt was in fact, J Prentiss... This would mean that somehow, Uncle Joe may have flogged a dodgy sat-nav to visitors from another world. This was worse than the time that Uncle had to "lie low" after being sought out by the unlucky customers who had chosen to invest in his Underwater Gardening kits.

Nicky was determined to plough on with the array of vital questions which his brain was seeking clarification upon (not necessarily all concerning alien agriculture). 'So are there other kids who have been sent here?' he asked.

'Oh yes, of course; and also we have sent other children off to other planets throughout the galaxy in order to enrich their knowledge and experience, so that they can make our own world a better place when they return,' replied Kendy.

'But what is your society like at home?' Nicky said, looking serious.

'We live exactly as you do – in great cities and smaller towns. Some even choose to live on the outskirts of civilisation in close proximity to the jungles and deserts. The ones that don't get eaten or fried tell us that it is good to "commune with Nature", mostly wearing their liquid-proof body suits and overboots. Some even take time away from the cities to erect temporary shelters in which to stay for a short time, but Father always complains that they clog up the intercity travelways with their auxiliary habitation pods'.

'Ah...so you have caravanners too then eh?' laughed Nicky.

As the two boys walked and talked about the similarities and differences between their respective home planets, Nicky was enthusiastically pointing out all of the interesting things which he assumed that Kendy would be unaware of. He paused at a thick bush, and bending down close to the ground, parted the thick foliage to reveal a tightly-woven nest – inside which could just be seen a very comfortable-looking dormouse. Kendy was fascinated by the various items of rural interest which his friend was pointing out, and Nicky was proud to act as temporary authority on the flora and fauna of Planet Earth. The lads walked down narrow seldom-trodden pathways which were known to only the more adventurous and curious village children. They climbed through a gap in a wire fence, and climbed to the top of another small hill, which was in fact the top of the local branch-line railway tunnel.

Kendy was very interested in the train and the railway lines, asking why seemingly so much effort and fuel were required to transport people from place to place in a straight line. 'Do people not think that this system wastes such a lot of energy and resources?' Kendy asked.

'Don't worry,' said Nicky, 'the trains are usually cancelled if they spot a stray leaf on the line'.

Nicky was becoming increasingly concerned at the number of "followers" which the boys seemed to have magically acquired. Something about Kendy had lured a variety of woodland creatures out of the safety of the undergrowth, and they were currently being accompanied by three rabbits, two weasels, several pheasants, countless field mice and an elderly badger who was doing his best to keep up with the Tour Group. When Kendy and Nicky paused to admire a lightning-damaged oak tree, several of the group collided in a heap, with rather embarrassed looks all round. A small argument had broken out at the rear of the group, as the badger (who had by now caught up with the main body of creatures) had accidentally relieved himself over one of the slower field mice.

Kendy laughed, and bent down to place his hands on either side of the moist mouse, with his palms open. In a couple of seconds, the water flew off the coat of the unfortunate little animal, leaving him fluffed out like a dandelion clock. The mouse gave the badger a smug nod, and moved back to the rear of the group. Kendy thought that he should explain: 'Yeah, we can also manipulate fluids if we concentrate, it helps to dry off in an emergency,' he explained. Nicky made no comment, and had made up his mind that as far as his friend Kendy was concerned, then the impossible was likely to be perfectly ordinary behaviour. He was also secretly thinking of just how he could persuade him to perhaps unleash some of his extraterrestrial skills upon the inhabitants of St Onan's.

They climbed carefully down the slope of the tunnel top. Pacing slowly up the hill once again, the boys came to the large wooden farm gate which had marked their starting point on the ramble. Kendy turned and faced the animals which had followed them, and said something which sounded friendly, in a language which Nicky took to be his native tongue. The creatures dispersed back into the hedges and fields, but Nicky was convinced that before shuffling off through the undergrowth, the badger head given them a cheery wave...

Back at the house, Mum had already prepared dinner. Nicky had already informed his mother that his new friend was a strict vegetarian, so they all tucked into a pasta casserole. Mum seemed rather nervous and a little fidgety at the table, and Nicky knew that she was bursting to ask all of the "Mum Questions" which parents are legally obliged to subject visiting school friends to. He didn't have to wait very much longer for the barrage to commence:

'So, Jon – tell me about your parents,' said Mum.

'Not much to tell really, Mrs Shepherd,' said Kendy. 'They are just normal people just like anyone else I suppose.' (Nicky thought to himself – yes, normal in every way if you ignore the fact that they live about two point five light years away.) The conversation and questions mirrored those asked by parents all over the world, and were just as intrusive in any language...

'So Jon, what does your father do for a living?'

'He's a scientist.'

'That must be a really interesting job.'

'It is – but Mother hates it if he brings his work home with him.'

'What sort of science is he involved in?'

'Bio-mechanics and advanced stasis enhancement technology.'

'That sounds very complicated.'

'It was when he had to explain to Mother why the robotic stasis subject which he brought home to work on ran amok and re-painted our living quarters bright pink.'

'What is your house like?'

'Oh, it's just a small average living space, like many of the others in our Community'

'Do you have any brothers or sisters?'

'Yes I do – I have an elder brother called Karis, and a sister named Pleiia,' he replied.

'How old are they?' asked Mum (here it comes...)

'Pleiia is sixteen, and Karis a hundred and three,' said Kendy.

Nicky leapt into the conversation swiftly, and said, 'Pay no attention, Mum – he's always joking around, Karis is thirteen.'

Mum went from mild shock to happy normality – but he would have to have a quiet word with his friend about being too candid in the future when answering any other questions. Mum settled back into her script. 'How do you like your new school, Jon?'

'Oh it's fine, Mrs Shepherd, thank you, I have made really great new friends, and the lessons are really interesting,' he replied.

'Nicky is having trouble settling in – but I hope that you and his friends will help him to enjoy his time at St Onan's' said Mum, going for maximum embarrassment to her son, and qualifying for the finals with ease. 'Right then,' she declared brightly. 'Who would like a nice cup of tea?'

Both of the boys nodded their agreement to this, and as she left the table, Nicky hissed to his friend, 'Careful with the questions, Jon – if you are not sure, then just tell Mum that you didn't understand, and that where you come from is very different – you won't be telling any lies!'

Mum came back to the room bearing the tea tray, on which were arranged the tea things which only saw the light of day on special occasions. She daintily poured the tea into their cups, and reached back for the blue-and-white hooped milk jug which bore the phrase "Make hay while the Sun shines" on its side. She poured milk into Nicky's cup first, but slightly miscalculated the angle of attack as she came to Kendy's vessel. 'Oh dear... never mind, I'll just go and get a cloth,' she said.

Without warning, Kendy held his open hand over the spilled milk, which rose in a small column and leapt back into the jug. Jon smiled, but Nicky was making frantic "don't let on for goodness sake" type hand signals. Mum returned, and was confused when she could find no trace of spilled milk, or a dampened table cloth.

'I managed to catch most of it in the saucer, Mum – no problem,' he lied. He just hoped that his friend (who had-ironically also arrived via a saucer of a different kind) would not expose any more of his extraordinary abilities for the time being. Mum shrugged, and returned the cloth to the kitchen, but did deliver a quizzical glance or two back at the table.

Nicky informed his mum that the two boys were going up to his bedroom to listen to some music. Later, they would do a little observation of the heavens with the telescope.

'Very well,' said Mum, 'but not too loud if you don't mind – because you might upset Dave.'

'Who is Dave?' asked Kendy.

'Dave is our pet chicken who seems to have adopted us,' said Nicky, as Dave pecked happily at Kendy's foot.

'He says he likes Rock music, Mrs Shepherd...' said Jon.

'He said what – who said he – what say – pardon...?' said Mum, back in Confusionville.

'Only joking, Mum,' said Nicky, glancing sideways at his friend.

'Well, you two are a double act, if ever I saw one,' said Mum. 'Go on then- I'll see you later.'

The lads went upstairs, and Nicky played a selection of his favourite Rock tracks, beginning with Queen, Iron Maiden, Rush, and Van Halen. Kendy sat on the bed staring at the CD cases, seemingly taking in every printed note and detail. After he had played his friend a good list of tracks, at what might be termed "intimate volume", Nicky asked Kendy. 'Do you have the same sort of music on your planet, mate?'

'Well yes, we do have music, but it is considered one of the highest honours to be allowed to study music as a career, and a privilege to be able to play it for the People. I must say that our music is much more like your Classical type of composition – and we certainly don't have anything as uplifting as your Rock and Roll. Are all people allowed to play music for a career without any training?' asked Kendy.

'Oh yes...' said Nicky, 'but sometimes the two types are played together. We also have some comedy stuff which you might like...' He played his friend, "Ernie- The fastest Milkman in the West", some Goons stuff, as well as David Bowie singing, "The Laughing Gnome".

Kendy sat back, looking very impressed. 'Your civilisation has certainly produced such wonderful music...' he said.

'You have obviously never heard of Eurovision or Jedward...' said Nicky, sadly.

Having gone some way in providing Kendy with the beginnings of a musical education, Nicky hoped fervently that when it came time to return to his Home World, that Jonef Kendy would be easily distinguishable by nature of the fact that he was the only alien wearing ripped jeans...

Now it was dark, and thus time to sneak a peek at the stars with a mate who had absolutely, "been there, seen it, and bought the tee-shirt" for real.

The boys set up the equipment on the side lawn, complete with star charts. What Nicky really wanted to do was see if it was possible to get a look at the region of the stars from which his friend had come. While he fiddled with lenses and filters, Nicky chatted to Kendy about what life was like on another planet.

'So does everyone on your planet have enough to eat?' he asked.

'Oh certainly' Kendy answered, sounding somewhat surprised at the question. 'Long ago, the Elders eliminated hunger by using bio-engineering and equality of distribution all over the planet. We care too much as a race to allow any member of our species to be without nourishment,' he stated, in a very matter-of-fact way.

'What do you do about the problem of crime up there?' Nicky enquired.

'We don't tolerate any criminal or deviant behaviour,' said Kendy. 'Any person electing to display behaviours likely to cause harm to others is brought before the Governors. They will offer a choice of correction or treatment, which if it is refused or not adhered to, will lead to instant exclusion.'

'Do you mean that they are locked up?' asked Nicky.

'No – I mean that they are excluded permanently by means of off-world relocation to a suitable site where they will pose no possible threat,' said Kendy.

Nicky thought about this for a moment, and then said 'So you don't have any criminals at all on your planet?'

'No,' answered his friend. 'We could not possibly tolerate behaviour likely to cause harm – relocation is the only answer. I will tell you a little of our long past history. But please do not be angry when I give you all of the facts,' said Kendy.

'Well, okay then, tell me all about it...' said Nicky, rather hesitantly.

'Millions of years ago, the problem of violent and criminal activity was becoming more and more of an issue for us. Property was not safe, and apparently women could not freely walk the streets without fear. The senior governors made a decision to ensure the safety and security of our world by re-locating all offenders to a separate planet. Because of our strict moral code, this world would have to be chosen as a site which could supply all of the needs of those who were relocated there, but of course, they were only given basic weapons necessary for survival. A site was selected that would provide adequate food resources for the excluded persons, and which did not already contain deadly predators which might pose an immediate threat to them.'

'But you removed them from your planet – why would you bother what happened to them?' asked Nicky.

'The governors insisted that they should not be placed in a situation of immediate harm, as killing is a violation of our global code. After a detailed search which lasted for quite a few years, a suitable location was eventually found. The site that was eventually chosen was very similar to our own planet. The one major problem was that the indigenous animal life on the planet had already evolved a large and highly dangerous group of predators, who were top of the food chain.

'In order to allow the excluded a chance of survival, these major carnivores had to be eliminated, and this was done by means of programmed machines. The plan did in fact work very well, except for the slight problem that occurred some months after the initial culling had begun. Soon after, a large asteroid smashed into the chosen planet and killed off most of the large animals anyway. The governors were apparently furious, as they could have saved a fortune if they had only waited. Many of those excluded also perished, but Father told me that the survivors eventually interbred with the evolving species of ape-creature, and repopulated the planet.'

There was a "clunk" in Nicky's brain as the penny dropped...

'You sent all of your criminals here, then killed off the dinosaurs, didn't you...?'

'I was never told about the exact location of the planet which they were sent to,' said Kendy.

'But it is a tiny bit of a coincidence, don't you think?' Nicky answered.

'I really can't be sure, and as I have said, there are thousands of very similar planets to yours out there- it could have been anywhere.'

'But it is highly likely that cavemen with criminal tendencies were stealing each other's antelope legs, hitting their neighbour over the head with Brontosaurus thigh bones, and painting graffiti on cave walls (not to mention groping the bear-skin clad cave ladies) because your ancestors decided to dump them here. I wonder if any passing T-Rex bothered to read the sign which said, "Cretaceous Extinction Sale – everything must Go!".'

Kendy looked very apologetic, and tried to calm the situation by saying, 'But everything has turned out all right, hasn't it?'

'Well it would mean that we might just be able to explain Great Uncle Mortimer's slight criminal tendencies, and put it down to genetics...' laughed Nicky. 'Come to think of it, the inbreeding with Neanderthals might also explain Cousin Sheila!'

Still reeling from his friend's ancient historical revelations, Nicky set the telescope to view the constellation of Pegasus. After setting the target in his sights, he switched to his highest-powered lens and focussed down the tube. 'Have a look Kendy...' he said, 'I can see your house from here!'

Kendy peered into the eyepiece, 'No, not quite,' he said, 'but you have got a great view of the place that we usually go on holiday...'

Nicky jumped back to the telescope, and was squinting to take in the detail when he heard his friend giggling. 'It's a pity that I haven't got a great big telescope,' Nicky said. 'Then we might actually be able to see your home star.'

Kendy rummaged around in the pocket of his jeans, and produced what looked like a large iridescent marble. 'Okay...' he said. 'Just please don't let on that I have shown you this, because my father said that I should only use it if I really have to.' He placed the ball in his upturned palm, and then gave the top section a half twist. Using his finger and thumb, he opened up a quarter section of the sphere with a soft click. He then adjusted the telescope slightly, and put the ball onto the end of the eyepiece. 'Okay, now look at the fence,' he said. Suddenly, there was a muted flicker as a wide view of the stars appeared as if projected onto the dark fence panel. The image was the size of a large television screen, and the picture was crystal clear. Nicky could see two bright stars in the centre of the view, and three much dimmer objects in a line to the left of the brightest star. 'The third planet on the left is home...' said Kendy. 'We call our planet Alta Media, as it is the middle planet of the three home worlds.' Nicky was speechless.

Kendy then told him, 'I will turn the device off now, to save power, and I wouldn't want the amplified light to melt your telescope.'

'Wow...' said Nicky, 'I have got to get one of those things!'

'I will try and get you one for Christmas, if you promise to be good,' laughed Kendy.

Nicky then thought for a moment and said, 'Sorry, Jon, you must get very homesick seeing your planet so far away, and you stuck here with us...'

'Thank you, but I'm fine about it,' said Kendy, smiling. 'I know that they will be coming back for me quite soon anyway. This is just a thing that lets me send the odd "postcard" back to my parents.'

They then spent hours sweeping the skies for more interesting objects. Mum popped out to check on the boys, saying 'You were both so quiet; I thought that you might have been abducted by aliens!' Both boys laughed heartily at Mum's observation, and wondered what she would have thought if she only knew the truth.

Because it was the weekend, and also because she was pleased that her son had made a firm friend at his new school, Mum let them stay out much later than would normally have been the case. Auntie had now returned from her evening out at a Country and Western night at one of the local village halls. Although she liked the music that was played, she had suspicions about some of the dancers who seemed just a little bit too animated, and who would disappear off into the toilets – and reappear in an altogether more animated state. She told Mum that she was certain that a bit of 'Bolivian Marching Powder' had been involved, and that she now knew why it was called "Line Dancing"...

Sunday was normally a day for church. Nicky was an occasional member of the occasional choir who sang in the church – assuming that they all turned up (which only happened occasionally). Nicky had woken up still laughing at an incident which had occurred the previous evening. The boys had just gone upstairs to get changed, and Nicky had shown his friend into his bedroom. Kendy had come flying out of the door in a state of panic, and flattened Nicky against the wall, saying, 'Don't go in there – there's something dangerous...'

Nicky had pushed past his worried schoolfriend, and looked into the room. Nothing was out of place, and there was certainly no present danger contained in the bedroom. 'What is the problem, Jon?' he had asked.

With a trembling finger pointing to the wardrobe in the corner, Kendy had stammered, 'There... don't move, it might not have seen us'. Nicky was completely nonplussed as to what could have caused his friend to panic, so he instructed him to point out exactly what the problem was. 'It's resting on top of the tall cupboard,' Kendy whispered.

The only prominent feature on top of the old wardrobe was Watkins, Nicky's old and much-loved teddy bear. 'You don't mean Watkins do you?' laughed Nicky, and took the bear down from its lofty perch. Kendy slightly backed away from the toy, until he was sure that it was not alive, and could pose no threat to the boys. 'I've had him ever since I was a baby – he's my oldest friend,' said Nicky.

Kendy drew in a relieved breath and explained. 'Sorry Nicky, I panicked for a couple of seconds there. You see, we have a creature which looks identical to your bear on our planet, except you would not want to play with it. We call it a 'Yagga', and they are extremely vicious carnivores which hunt in packs. Three of them can strip a man clean in minutes, and they often "play dead" so that they can lure prey closer. If they get into your house, they will eat everything in sight; drink anything which they can find, leave their dung everywhere, as well as creating a disgusting mess.'

'We call them "Family",' said Nicky.

Kendy had been particularly impressed with the early morning "mushroom hunt". He had wolfed down a couple of the larger fungi, like the Lycanthropic vegetarian that he was. He had asked Nicky 'How is it that your auntie seems to be so good with plants?'

Nicky answered that, 'She just has green fingers.'

Kendy wasn't satisfied with this, and said, 'No, I mean how does she know to be good to them?'

Nicky told him that Auntie could get a lollipop stick to grow if she planted it, and that she always talks to her plants.

'I know,' said Kendy, 'and they appreciate that, they really like her...'

Nicky was not about to ask him exactly how he could possibly know that, but decided to add it to the list of amazing skills which his friend possessed.

He asked Kendy if the people on his planet were religious.

'Certainly,' was the answer. 'We believe in everything and everyone as part of a single consciousness.' Kendy was a bit confused over one particular issue, and that was the matter of churches. 'If there is only one God...' he had queried, 'then how come he owns so many houses – and which one does he actually live in?'

Here was a boy that failed to see how a God which he could not see had so much property, and yet the homeless people which he could see only too clearly had nowhere to live. Rather than risk an ecumenical argument of biblical proportions breaking out involving the vicar, Nicky decided that it might be a wise decision to give church a miss. There would be no escaping Kendy's logic, or that calm smile which made you want to explain yourself, and why you weren't a better person all round, now you come to think of it. If Kendy had managed to meet Jesus, the two would have chatted very amiably. The boy from Alta Media would have listened politely to everything which was told to him, all the while smiling that disarming, patient smile. He would then have no doubt expounded his own philosophy as to how the world could be a better place.

Jesus would have then said to the boy, 'Wow Dude, you really have got it all together – now can I have another look at that "marble" of yours?' The Bible would then have contained detailed descriptions of how Jesus had ditched the sandals, and was frequently seen in torn jeans and trainers, searching the streets of old Jerusalem for indie record shops, and clutching a batch of Heavy Metal albums... "The Sermon in the Mosh Pit" would become legendary.

As it was, the boys spent most of the day flying model aircraft in the big field, and climbing the tall trees which were still in full leaf. Kendy met Nicky's village gang at the bomb crater, and as expected, got on well with all of them immediately. One hairy moment occurred when Kendy slipped from an overhanging branch and landed in the local pond. Nicky was able to distract the others just in time to prevent them witnessing Kendy's "Look Ma-no hands instant dry-as-a-bone" technique, but it was a very close call. Being witness to such an incident would have set off a mass panic that would rival that created by Orson Welles when he broadcast his *War of the Worlds* adaptation – especially in a small village which went into mass hysteria if the cost of a pint went up by 5p in the local pub.

The local public house was another cornerstone of village life. It had stood at the top of the village since medieval monks had decided to build themselves an out-of-the-way sanctuary where they could enjoy the fruits (fermented) of their brewing labours without the constant nagging of the overbearing Abbot. The original structure was a small stone-built room with a disco at the rear (Gregorian Chant-Rock being very popular at the time), and ample cart parking (atheist coach parties by arrangement only). Over the centuries, the hostelry had grown considerably, although some of the original pickled eggs were still available. The pub had been given various names over the passage of time. It had featured in the legend of Dick Turpin, who had apparently said of it, "I wudde note be seen dedde in that dyve..." Locals at the time had taken quite a shine to the outlaw despite this critique, and so the pub had been christened "The Dick's Head". Sometime after, there had been a campaign to re-name the pub in order to put a stop to ridicule. It was decided that two sets of paper slips would be put into a hat. One set bore the name of various occupations, and the other the name of a variety of everyday objects and tools. A slip would be drawn out with a profession on it, and the second slip would be added as an "and", so to speak. During the draw process, the label in the hat must have come adrift, and thus the pub became known as the "Nun and three eighths".

Since then, it had been known as The Merry Monk, The Poacher's Sack, The Crammet Inn, and The Proud Cock. It had recently been taken over by a group of local Real Ale enthusiasts, who had instantly re-named it as The Five-Legged Horse. It boasted of a real old English Pub Atmosphere. This was perfectly true: it was a theme pub- and the theme was manic depression. It had new carpets that smelled of old Jack Russell terriers, baffling toilet signs for the Gents and Ladies, and a resident ghost named Bernard, whose hobby was the breaking of spectral wind during lunch servings. The pub had once been the victim of a terrible thunderstorm. A bolt of lightning had hit the roof of the building, and the resulting explosion had caused almost five hundred thousand pounds worth of improvements.

At any time of night or day, there were the two village drunks (both curiously named Lesley) sitting opposite each other on high stools – but both far too inebriated to see the other.

Auntie was the reigning darts champion at the pub. Her deadly accuracy was known and feared county-wide. She would place bets on herself to win, playing deliberately poorly until the odds on her winning went up in her favour. She was temporarily under a ban from the pub Bowls Team. They played on a bowling green which faced the main road through the village. The match had been a tight one, and an opponent had left a wood resting on the jack. Auntie stepped forward for her shot, and was instructed by the captain of the team to 'tap it out of the way'. Dear Auntie let fly with the bowling equivalent of the Dambusters Raid, with her bowl bouncing Barnes Wallis style down the green. It struck the jack with considerable force, and leapt salmon-like into the air, over the edge of the bowling green, and through the windscreen of a passing car. An act of God had decreed that the vehicle was being driven by none other than her arch-enemy Mr Seaton...

And thus it came to pass that Auntie didst win the bowls match, and didst amaze the locals with her ballistic skills, and verily, she did render the Seaton unconscious. So, on the whole, not a bad day's work at all.

Chapter Twenty-Three

As a special treat for Sunday tea, Auntie had purchased a very sugary cake which had come all the way from Austria. Mum was delighted, but Nicky was not comfortable with the thought of handling Stollen goods. After tea, the boys both lent a hand with the washing up. Kendy was given the task of drying the plates, and Mum was amazed at how quickly he did it.

Auntie suggested that they have a good old family "Film Night", and this suggestion was well received. Mum suggested that the boys should finish any outstanding homework before they settle down, which cast a slight shadow over the proceedings. Nicky knew that he still had some outstanding Latin to complete – but no idea how he was going to do it. He dare not risk the unpredictability of "the desk" again, as he was not sure that answers in Swahili would be very well received.

Kendy of course, breezed through his verbs and translations, and had finished his work long before Nicky had begun to panic over his task. The boy sat at the side of his friend, observing the anguish and terror which alternated in the expressions upon his face. Finally Nicky cracked under the pressure, stating, 'Well, bugger it then – I'll just have to be "Mr Thick" again, in front of that stuck-up Rundell.'

'What's the problem?' asked Kendy.

'I just can't do it, and Rundell knows I can't do it – he's just waiting for me to make a fool out of myself,' Nicky said. 'I can't get languages – it just won't sink in. I stare at the book for hours, but it might as well be written in Martian – no offence.'

Kendy came over and stood behind him. He reached out and placed each of his middle fingers on both of Nicky's temples. 'You just need to let your eyes see the sounds,' he said. As the boy was speaking, Nicky began to feel distinctly lighter, and a distant noise which was on the threshold of hearing suddenly became much louder. Nicky then heard a sound like a firework being let off backwards...' Now try reading the text again,' said Kendy. The page in front of Nicky's eyes was blurred, but began to swim into perfect clarity. He was shocked to see that the Latin text seemed to have translated itself into English before his eyes. 'See,' said Kendy. 'All you need to do is concentrate, and it will become clearer. This is a trick someone taught me at my previous school.'

Still not quite sure what had just happened, Nicky not only completed the translation, but understood every word of it. He flicked further through the textbook to see what would happen, and the result was the same. '*Non Me Stultus Est,*' he declared – and meant it.

Kendy had patiently listened whilst Nicky had explained everything which he had been able to deduce concerning the random activity of the desk. In the drawer today, he had found the latest offering from whatever dimension the desk had an account with, comprising of a freshly laundered pair of khaki socks, a small penknife, and a pin badge from Butlin's holiday camp in the 1950s. Nicky felt a little uneasy at keeping the items which the desk provided, and elected to keep each and every one of the objects safely in a box under his bed should the desk request their return at any point in the future. Kendy however, was fascinated by the mysterious drawer of delights. He hurriedly wrote a letter to his parents, in strange handwriting (that Nicky thought more closely resembled footwriting), and asked him to put the paper into the secret drawer. 'Well, I have a feeling that it might just get there,' he said. Nicky asked his friend if they had a postal system on his planet which was anything like the one here on earth.

Kendy answered, 'Oh yes we do, but we mostly use teleportation for written messages, if our computer link system is not available.'

'Gosh – that's really neat!' said Nicky. 'Is it really fast?'

'You bet,' said Kendy. 'Sometimes it can take a whole two minutes for a message to be lost...'

'Yep,' said Nicky. 'Identical.'

There was a selection of films on the television later on that night. As per usual, the various channels had elected to show a collection of cinematographic delights that would be completely new to the viewer. Hence, the choices on offer were *Bridge over the River Kwai*, *The Great Escape*, *The Dam Busters*, *Rocky VII*, *Star Wars* and *The Sound of Music*. The war films were the cause of bewilderment to their guest, who could not grasp the concept of one section of humanity wishing to inflict damage upon another.

'Why is that man so happy at the thought of killing people?'

'Because they belong to the opposing army, and because they are at war.'

'But why are they at war with them?'

'Because they want to take over the world.'

'But they already own the world.'

'Yes, but they want to run it their way.'

'Do they want to change it for the better?'

'No – they want to dominate it and impose their own rules.'

'And that's why the man wants to bomb them?'

'Yes.'

'Isn't that a bit of a childish point of view?'

'Well – they started it.'

(Things were no better when Mum turned over to the boxing film.)

'Why is he hitting that man?'

'It's not real – he's an actor.'

'Why does an actor have to hit another actor?'

'Because it's all part of the script, dear, they are friends really...'

'So if they are friends – then why is he punching him?'

'Because it is part of the story.'

'Is he angry because the other actor is paid more?'

'No, he's just pretending to be angry because he is trying to win.'

'What is it that he is trying to win?'

'He's trying to win the World Title.'

'What – "Best Actor who hits people for less money"?'

'No, the title of World Champion.'

'Do all actors go around punching people?'

'Only in the *Daily Mail*, dear...'

Mum changed channel again, and was forced to hope that Rocky would find his way onto the picturesque mountains of Austria, and belt the living daylights out of that Singing Nanny. In a moment of panic, she tried another station, and found herself seeing conflicts fought out in the far reaches of another galaxy. Mum and Auntie thought that *Star Wars* was futuristic nonsense; Nicky thought that it was a load of special effects just pasted together without any real plot or purpose. Kendy thought that it was documentary.

It was by sheer good fortune that Auntie took command of the remote control, and managed to find an altogether more wholesome choice of film. *It's a Wonderful Life* enthralled them all, and Kendy sat in rapt wonderment as the story unfolded itself before their eyes.

When the film had finished, the boy excitedly told them, 'I must get a copy of that film – the people back home will love it.'

Nicky wondered just what format his friend would require in order to play the film back at home, and could only imagine the look on the face of the poor unfortunate shop assistant who was asked to supply a copy, suitable for use with alien technology...

Film night now having come to a satisfactory end, with Clarence the Angel flapping off happily into the sunset; it was time for bed for the lads. Nicky climbed into bed, and was soon asleep. Kendy was on the camping bed – placed suitably far enough away from the bear Watkins (on top of the wardrobe) that further panic would not occur.

Both boys woke up early, to the sound of the rain hammering on the bedroom windows. It was impossible to see even a few yards across the garden, as the rain sheeted down the glass, giving a clue that persons with webbed feet were the only people who were likely to have a good day. Nicky decided to check the secret drawer of the desk, just in case, and discovered that not only had his friend's note disappeared, but the desk had decided to take liberties by donating a small bottle of high-factor sun cream.

Kendy spent quite a long time profusely thanking Nicky's Mum and Auntie for having him stay for the weekend.

Mum told him that 'He was welcome any time,' and 'what a pleasure it was to have such a well-mannered young man in the house'.

Auntie agreed, stating that 'You would think that most of the kids you meet these days have come from another planet...'

Waving hastily to Mum and Auntie, the boys sprinted up the front garden path, and sought sanctuary from the deluge within the wooden bus shelter. Kendy looked around. 'What is it that Wendy does, exactly?' he asked his friend.

'What do you mean, Jon?, and who is this Wendy, exactly?'

'Well, someone has written a message on the wall here, to let us know that "Wendy does it", but they do not say exactly what it is that she does.'

'I don't really know, Mate,' said Nicky, 'but she obviously does it up in the village phone box too.'

'Have they got the words wrong?' asked Kendy.

'What do you mean?'

'Well, confusing "Wendy" with "Easy".'

'I don't think there's any confusion, Jon,' said Nicky.

Before the subject began to get completely out of hand, neither boy being suitable knowledgeable to give an opinion on Wendy's apparent expertise at whatever, the village bus crawled around the church corner (or perhaps it may have been breast stroke, it was difficult to see through the rain). It was the usual driver, with his usual doomy look welded to his face. The boys paid their fare, and edged down the bus aisle to the last two remaining vacant seats, dripping all the way. Kendy offered his seat to a lady who got onto the bus at the next stop. She thanked him as she sat down, and Kendy told her, 'You are most welcome – my name is Jon.'

'What a well-mannered young man you are – my name is Wendy,' she answered.

'Oh really,' said Kendy, looking pleased. 'In that case, can I ask you, exactl- whnnf ghnn fnuggh...?' Nicky shot out of his seat and clamped a hand over Kendy's mouth, and pulled him away from the woman before he could do any irreparable damage. He really would have to speak to his friend.

The bus was now full to capacity, and the passengers were suddenly surprised at the loud guffaws which came from the front of the bus. It would seem that the driver was brightening his morning by seeking out the deepest and widest puddles at the road side, and ploughing through them in order to drown the would-be passengers who emerged from the bus shelters in eager anticipation of a dry ride. Before they knew it, the bus had reached their stop, and the boys made their way forward to get off. Nicky had stowed the killer satchel away in the front luggage space to prevent any unpleasantness. As he made a grab for the school bag, the satchel saw its chance and looped its strap around the handles of a passenger's baby buggy. When Nicky attempted to lift the satchel out, it brought with it the buggy, and a large golf umbrella, which flicked open and showered adjacent passengers with water. Kendy attempted to assist his friend, but only succeeded in looping the strap tightly around his neck. The buggy and the umbrella fell to the floor of the bus in an untidy heap, and the two boys dived off the coach still tied together – and back into the deluge.

After a few moments of careful pushing and pulling, the satchel was persuaded to release its death grip on Kendy's neck. Nicky apologised to his friend, and made sure that he dragged the satchel through several puddles as a punishment for its homicidal actions. The walk to school turned into an Olympic sprint, in order to escape the rain which hammered down onto the head. Just inside the Academy arches were gathered a group of bedraggled boys who were attempting to shake off the water from their outer layers. If anything, the rain seemed to be coming down even heavier now, and once inside the buildings, the boys could hear the thunderous roar of the rain on the roof.

Sodden coats were hung up in the form room, and the lads made their way to the assembly hall, pausing at the doorway to pull up their blazer collars over their heads before dashing across the quad. There was much pushing and shoving of damp students at the hall doors, before a master appeared and restored some semblance of order.

'Order – order I say!' called the master.

'Mine's a pint then,' called Weatherill, at the back of the jostling crowd of boys.

'Weatherill – I know that's you... Get up those stairs right now..' shouted the master.

'Yes, dear, if you say so...' called Weatherill.

Cunningly concealed within the group of soggy youths who made their way up the stairs, Weatherill was able to avoid any comeback from the member of staff for his cheek. The lads huddled together at the front of the hall, as the masters came in through the rear doors of the stage. Because the scenery backdrops were now in place for the forthcoming dramatic production, this gave the somewhat bizarre spectacle of a group of berobed men walking into a snapshot of Victorian London.

Affixed to the front of the lectern was a red warning triangle sign bearing the legend "Wide Load". Goodwill the headmaster paced out his normal route to the front of the stage, and pulled the lectern straight. He regarded the boys with a piercing stare, and then looked over to where Mr Newhouse was sitting at the organ, and gave a quick clap of his raised hands. Some unseen boy called out 'Ole'.

There was a general chuckle, before Newhouse crashed out the opening chords of the Anthem. The song was sung with all the enthusiasm of a condemned prisoner, and little panache, (Actually, "panache" is exactly the sound made when a pair of hi-hat cymbals slips to the floor – sorry, just thought that I would mention that fact. It is also reputed to be all that remained of Peter, after Captain Hook had set light to him.)

After boring the boys with a list of forthcoming events, Goodwill instructed the assembled masses, 'And due to the somewhat intemperate weather which we seem to be experiencing this morning, I would require all boys to report the location of any leaks.'

'Wales...' said an unknown voice.

Goodwill ignored the comment, and continued. 'Please report any pools of water which you may encounter in the classrooms or corridors, because, may I remind you...'

'You should have gone before...' the voice interjected.

'CEASE THESE INTERRUPTIONS.' thundered Goodwill. 'This assembly is turning into a pantomime.'

'Oh no it isn't...' the voice replied.

His anger overriding the need to locate the phantom ad-libber, Goodwill turned and flapped out of the doors, leaving the staff looking embarrassed and unsure what they should do next. Hyde-Jones was doubled up with laughter, and even Mrs Dreadfell was wearing a broad grin. Mr Newhouse sat at the organ, with his back toward the audience, but all of the boys could see his shoulders shaking in silent mirth. Dr Chambers stepped forward and dismissed the boys, and the masters filed out of the hall.

Back in the form room, Dr Matthews was doing his best to call the form register. His concentration was suddenly disturbed when he discovered that there was no boy in his form called "B.Rakes-Faulty". He discovered that he was in fact reading from the form which the local garage had supplied to him when he had submitted his car for its MOT test. As he scrabbled amongst the various sheets of paper which seemed to litter his desk, he came upon another mysterious page. His bleary eyes attempted to focus on the name of the person to whom this letter was addressed, but he had to admit defeat, and called to Nicky to assist him. 'I say Shepherd, old chap – could you be so kind as to help me here? This letter has the correct address of the Academy, but they seem to have put the wrong name on it – do you know some chap by the name of "Reminder" by any chance?'

Nicky whispered to the master that it was a bill.

'Bill Reminder? Never heard of the blighter...' growled Matthews. 'Probably hidin' out from the authorities in one of me cupboards, I'll be bound. Right then, we'll flush this Johnny Hideaway out, and tan his hide for him. But before we start, would you please nip down to the kitchens and get the Bradley woman to send me up some ice. Make sure that it's fresh though – I don't want any more of that frozen muck...'

Nicky hurried off on his errand. When he got to the kitchens, he knocked at the small side door, and went in. He was surprised to see a small procession taking place. Walking slowly around the perimeter of the hall were Betty, Doris, Alice and the other kitchen staff. At the head of the slowly marching column was a strangely-dressed gentleman with very long black hair, tied back into a pony-tail. A beaded headband crossed his forehead, and garish feathers were stuck into the back of it. He wore an extremely well-worn leather jacket with fringes on the sleeves, and hand-made moccasins. As he led the column of worried-looking staff around the room, he was making sweeping motions into each corner with what looked like a bundle of dried herbs, which were alight, and smoking furiously. He was also performing some sort of low chant or song as he walked around like some trainee ethnic arsonist...

Betty had in fact unleashed the latest weapon in her war against the unseen removers of food. The man was in fact acting out the role of a native American shaman, delivering a blessing in order to banish evil spirits from Betty's kingdom. She had found him via the Yellow Pages, and he lived not far away, in a mystic bungalow on the outskirts of the village of Lower Grayford. His tribal name was "One Grey Wolf". His real name was Arthur Hebblewhite, and his spiritual or ancestral connection to the noble tribes of America was tenuous at best. He had spent his gap year in Arizona as a student (many years ago), and had worked in a native American restaurant as a Sioux chef.

With "One Grey Arthur" temporarily preoccupied, Nicky sidled up to Betty and made the request for ice. She indicated the large refrigerator in the corner, and left him to work it out himself. Nicky found a glass measuring jug, and after a few floor-covering attempts, managed to fill the jug with ice cubes from the dispenser. As he turned, he was surprised to see Ursula, the small girl from "behind the walls" waving at him from an open cupboard door. She was grinning from ear to ear, as if extremely pleased to see him again. Almost without thinking, Nicky snatched up one of the many jam tarts that were on the kitchen worktop, cooling down. Walking nonchalantly past the cupboard, he passed the jammy treat to the eager hand of the little girl – and heard her say, 'Thank you, our friend.' Before closing the cupboard door. Ignoring whatever ritual was still being concluded by "Tonto Pronto" in the hall, he left hurriedly by the same door through which he came in.

Dr Matthews was plainly delighted at Nicky's return. 'Damned good show that man – top marks for ingenuity, well played,' he declared. He opened the bottom drawer of his desk, and the boys heard the rhythmic "glug-glugging" of a large glass being filled. Matthews raised the jug full of ice level with his glass of Glaswegian Jollity, and attempted to tip some ice into his drink. He managed to fill the ink well, the top of his desk, and his top pocket with ice cubes. The boys left him to his task, and went to their lesson, to the sounds of Dr Matthews chasing ice around the floor and calling, 'Come hither, you slippy little buggers!' and, 'Better get m'skates on. Heh! Heh! – just like that pair who did the *Bolero* – Pearl and Dean...' to no-one in particular.

English with Mr Hyde-Jones was the first lesson of the day, and the boys were looking forward to easing their way into the new week courtesy of the more relaxed teaching style of the master. As the class made their way into his room, Hyde-Jones was sitting with his feet up on his desk, dipping a biscuit into a very large cup of tea.

'Morning, guys- how's it hanging?' he asked. 'I've looked at your prep work, and I think we will take a look at the use of "irony" in language and poetry. Irony is a device which we find in language which can carry a sarcastic or sardonic hint within the actual speech. Can anyone give me an example of irony?'

'The school railings?' said Trevill.

'The fact that the film is called *The Day of the Jackal,* but it only takes an hour and a half to watch it?' said Jackson.

'The situation where the country is threatened by escaped venomous snakes – and so the Government convenes the COBRA Committee?' asked Nicky.

'The fact that there is only one Monopolies Commission?' said Merry.

'Overlook and Oversee meaning totally different things?' asked Calderman.

'The stuff that they serve in the kitchens actually being referred to as "food"?' said Davis.

'The fact that many Americans take their dog to a pet psychiatrist- when they know that they won't be allowed on the couch?' asked Nicky.

'A seal that decides to go out clubbing?' ventured Trevill.

'Yep – I think that we've all got the message now' said Hyde-Jones. 'Now I want you to go through the scenes of *Macbeth* that we looked at, and highlight the use of irony in the text. Give me a bit of a critical appraisal, you might say.'

'Well, Oi think that Oi'm speakin' for us all, when Oi say that we'em thinkin' that you're a pretty good bloke...' said Trevill.

'No, not an appraisal of myself – although I thank you for your kind remarks, I meant a short illustration of how Shakespeare uses the devices which we have mentioned.'

The boys set about their allotted task, with many a tongue poked out in concentration. The exercise took up nearly the entire lesson, which was suddenly interrupted by a persistent drip of water coming through the ceiling above Hyde-Jones' desk.

'Sir- there's a drip in here,' pointed out the ever-observant Lordsley.

'Ironic...' said Calderman, and the class dissolved into laughter. Hyde-Jones himself was laughing at the comment as he grabbed the waste paper bin, and placed it on his desk to catch the water.

'I think we'll call it a day chaps – and please remember to bring your umbrellas with you next time,' said the master. The boys handed in their work, and left the classroom, carefully navigating their way around the front desk and its new shower fitting.

Now this was the lesson that Nicky dreaded. For some reason, Rundell the Latin master seemed to have taken an instant dislike to him. Whenever he entered the classroom, the boy felt dread in the pit of his stomach. The only question in his mind was just how long it would be before the master managed to make him feel inadequate and stupid. Having been summoned into the room, the boys saw that Rundell was standing behind his desk with a look of utter distaste (even more than usual). He pointed at Trevill:

'You , boy- fetch me a char...'

'Pardon, sir?'

'I said, fetch me a char.'

'You want a tea lady?'

'No, you imbecile, I cannot sit on a tea lady, now can I...'

'Well Sur –You can at the place which moi dad goes to of a Wednesday, in fact...'

'I will go and get you a chair, sir,' volunteered Nicky. (Anything to get out of the room.)

'Well, yes, thank you, Shepherd,' said the master, grudgingly.

Nicky walked down the corridor and listened at each classroom door which he came to. Hearing no sounds of teaching in progress from one room, he opened the door and took the chair from behind the front desk. No doubt his choice of seat would attract criticism, and he was certain that Rundell would find some fault with it. When he returned to the Latin class, he stepped onto the raised dais at the front of the class, and placed the chair at the desk. Rundell gave the object a look of contempt, and flicked a silk handkerchief out of his top pocket, with which he began to dust off the seat and arms of the chair. When he seemed satisfied that he had brushed away all debris likely to pass on some awful disease (like becoming Working Class, heaven forbid), he carefully sat down.

'Now, gentlemen, today we will discuss and translate one of the most famous legends in mythology, which appears on page twenty-seven of your texts. You will note that it is a Latin rendition of the Ancient Greek, but we will study this as I consider it vital to your education in the Classics – at least for some of you. (Nicky saw the glance in his direction, and the fear began to rise.) We will just find out what, if anything, you may know about the voyage and trials of Jason and the Argonauts. Would anyone care to start us off on the subject?'

Now there were immediately several hands raised in the classroom, each eager to share their knowledge on the subject in hand. With a combination of looks and gestures, the eager participants began to lower their hands in response to received signals from their fellow pupils. This was a major task. This was a challenge. There was only one man for the job – and little by little, he remained the only boy with his hand held proudly aloft... After staring hard around the room for a couple of minutes, Rundell was forced to admit defeat.

'Very well, Mr Trevill... please share your knowledge with the class.'

Trevill stood up at his desk, cleared his throat, and began...

'Firstly, Oi will quote a famous saying – and that is that ooever the gods wish to destroy – they'm first make 'em listen to Madonna...' (He assumed a dramatic pose in readiness.)

'Roight then: 'ere's 'ow I sees it all goin' down...

This is a story what's come out of the Thistly region of Greece. Here's yer man Jason, he'm bein' brought up by some bloke callin' 'imself Sharon. Ee'm a centre-forward or suchloike for some Greek team. This 'ere Jason is set a task by some king called Perilous, whereby 'eem as to go all the way to the island of Colchester (or Duodenum as the Romans called it) and collect a sheep what is a-sufferin' from golden fleas. Well, obvious loike, ee'm not about to set orf on 'is own, so ee 'as a word with one or two with his drinkin' pals to come along with 'im.

They'm settin' off and buyin' themselves a ship from Argos – which is why they'm callin' 'emelves "Argonauts" for a laugh, see... They'm 'avin' it fitted with a talkin' figurehead, seein' as how sat-navs were a long way off yet, and yer man Jason dedicates it to the Goddess, and sings "We don't need another Hera".

'Roighto- so they'm a-comin' to an island where they finds a blind prophet bloke livin' there, whose name was Phineas Fogg Oi think, and 'ee is 'avin' 'is life made misery because he is plagued by herpes. He can't see any way out of it – but Jason and his Agronaut lads are after buildin' a cage and trappin' the buggers so they'm stop pinchin' all of his grub. Well now, yer man is well happy, and gives the lads directions to the island – but tells 'em to look out for these 'ere rocks, what tend to clash all of the time, and do no good to sailors.

Jason 'as a word in the wooden ear of 'is figurehead sat-nav lady, and she tells 'em to sail through the rocks, and she'm give 'em a hand. Well Oi never! Just as the rocks come crashing in to give 'em a squashin', up pops her mate from the bottom of the sea, and 'olds the rocks apart so that Jason and his Aqualungs can pass safely loike. If Oi remember correct – Jason 'as to fit a Triton shower or somethin' before they leave. Anyhow, they'm endin' up on another island where there is a great big tall 'efty bloke what uses far too much bronzer and fake tan – called Talos, or possibly Tardis. Ee'm not 'appy when one of the lads pinches a big pin off him, and 'ee didn't 'alf kick off. Jason 'as to pull the plug on 'im, and they all leg it a bit sharpish.

Then it's on to the island of Colchester, where Jason makes a dash to grab the sheep with the golden fleas, what 'eem seein' hangin' in a tree, casual loike. But before he can get the fleas, Jason 'as to get rid of the dreaded Hydrant what is in the way. The name of the Hydrant is "Gordon" apparently, and Jason cuts the top off it. He finds a set of false teeth, which he buries in case anyone asks any questions – but the teeth grow up loike, and turn into supermodels with swords, and chase 'im all over the place. Well now, our man Jason 'as 'ad about enough of all this, and dives off a cliff and swims back to the Amphinauts on their boat. Now 'eem got the golden fleas, its plain sailin' all the way back to Greece.

When he gets 'ome, some girl asks 'im if 'ee will marry 'er – and he tells 'er 'Yes, Me Dea'. I don't know what 'appened to the rest of the lads, I think some stayed on some island and made a pig of themselves, and Hercules went on to become a professional wrestler. Years later, I hear that 'eem got crushed by the bow of the ship *Tesco* – which just goes to show that you should always keep the receipt...'

Trevill gave a polite bow to his audience, and resumed his seat.

His appreciative audience gave him the kind of applause which would normally be reserved for a cup-winning football team; another thunderous standing ovation. Trevill took the praise very humbly, and thanked his fellows for their accolades. Rundell sat at his desk with his head in his hands and waited until the clamour had died down.

'Thank you, Mr Trevill...' was all that he could manage. Some people in life aspire to greatness, some will read about greatness- and some are fortunate enough to have Trevill thrust upon them.

Rundell recovered his composure, and strode down off the dais, collecting the Latin homework from the boys. When he got to Nicky, he stood at the side of his desk and opened his Latin book. The master studied the boy's homework intently, and as he did so, his eyes widened in shock. 'You have, Mr Shepherd, completed all of this work by yourself?' he said.

'Yes, sir,' answered Nicky. 'With no outside assistance or influence of any description?'

Nicky looked honestly up at the man. 'No, sir...' he answered.

'Well, well, Mr Shepherd, it seems that we may finally have shone a tiny light into the darkest corners of your mind at last,' he said.

'I didn't cheat , sir, if that's what you were thinking,' Nicky heard himself say.

'Perish the very thought, Mr Shepherd, my concern is merely the surprise at a very average pupil achieving a very high standard of work for once...' sneered Rundell.

Kendy signalled to Nicky from an adjacent seat, and mimed the action of applying his middle fingers to his temples, as he had done at Nicky's house. The "hint" was received, and Nicky applied his two fingers to the side of his head, just briefly and casually enough so as to not attract the attention of the master.

'I can see that I shall have to keep an eye on you in the future, Mr Shepherd...' said Rundell.

Out of nowhere, Nicky got the feeling of stepping off a moving roundabout. Not knowing exactly how or why, he turned his face up to the master and proudly declared, '*Ut ego non possum stolidus, Magister...*'

Rundell was dumbfounded, and stuttered out his reply. 'No, Mr Shepherd, I am sure that you certainly are not as stupid as you may look.'

Nicky now took control of the exchange, and resting both elbows on his desk, raised his voice and declared, 'And do forgive me, sir, but I really must point out that '*Callidus aperuisti os tuum donec ego credebam te esse.*' Rundell opened and closed his mouth like a stranded fish. For once, the eloquent and florid speaker's oratory power seemed to have deserted him. He turned away from the boy, not bothering to collect the rest of the books, and flopped down into his chair. The chair exploded underneath him – showering the various parts, screws and fixings across the room. Rundell was invisible, now himself collapsed behind the desk. As he fought to regain his balance and dignity, he discovered a small white business card which had been taped to the underside of the chair. Written on the card was the simple phrase which declared "This has been an ODD job".

''Ooo the bloody 'ell knows owt about this then?' screeched Rundell, his flowery tones having temporarily fled. 'I mean to say, what is the meaning of this outrage...?' The boys all stared at their teacher with genuine innocence.

'Right, forget it – out, the lot of you...we will carry on next time,' said the man.

The boys hastily left the room, carefully stepping over the pieces of disassembled chair.

'Blimey, what on earth was all that about, Shep?' asked Calderman.

'I have no idea, I suppose that the chair just broke...' said Nicky.

'Not the chair, you silly bugger – I meant what on earth did you say to Rundell that freaked him out? asked Calderman.

'Oh that,' said Nicky, in a matter-of-fact way. 'I just told him that until he opened his mouth, I thought that he was clever...'

'That thur explodin' seat were a maasterstroke...' declared Trevill.

'Yes, I suppose it was – but I had nothing to do with it!' protested Nicky.

'Well, we'em all see'd you go and get it for old Stuckup,' said Trevill.

'Yeah, but I had no idea that it was booby-trapped,' Nicky answered the boy genius.

Calderman looked thoughtful. 'Do you chaps recall one person in particular, who declared to us that it was his mission to strike a blow against "The Knobs"?'

'Yes, I remember, but Brooks has never heard me say that I was having a problem with Rundell. Even when we have talked about it between ourselves, there's been no teachers around who could have heard what I said. The only Academy staff member that was around at the time was the cleaner – that nice Mrs Finucane, and I hardly think that she...'

'AGENT J-CLOTH...' all of the boys said together.

'Wow! Imagine that,' said Nicky. 'A pre-emptive strike by the ODD...'

'Us One... Dickheads nil,' said Merry.

'What about Rundell, do you think that he'll have it in for us all now?' asked Davis.

'*Copulatus Ipse...*' said Nicky – with considerable feeling.

Chapter Twenty-Four

The Reverend Felchingham sat forlornly in his gloomy poorly-lit classroom. The man was beside himself with despair, and neither of them would make very good company on a long-haul flight. The cause of his deep melancholy was the brand new car which had just had delivered. Whilst most drivers who had spent hours poring over the pictures in a car brochure would have been eagerly planning their first excursions in their new vehicle, the Rev was an abject picture of misery.

It had all begun when he had unexpectedly won £666 pounds on the Premium Bonds (surely an omen). Fed up with the aged two-tone (maroon and rust) car that he had owned for years, he vowed to completely change his four-wheeled image and purchase a brand new car. He thought, 'Maybe something a little racy, a little sporty, and something that will really get me noticed.' He searched the catalogues, and found the ideal vehicle for him- appropriately named the "Diablo". Obviously, he chose a hellish fiery red for the colour scheme. With deposit paid, and delivery dates agreed, all he had to do was to sit back and await the arrival of his life-changing transport. But Lo! He didst espy an advert in the Sunday paper. This was just what he needed to complete his transition from ordinary sedate motorist, to Black Arts Playboy. Why not treat himself to a private number plate? He could afford it, and it would complete the look that he wished to achieve. He had called the number in the newspaper with a trembling hand. Yes, the registration GNO666 was still available, and, yes, he could reserve it. He paid by credit card there and then, now feeling that his boring life was about to take a turn for the better. Now people would notice him, now people would take him seriously. No more "sad Gerald" would there be, as he sped past at 100mph with the top down. It was Life in the Fast Lane for this boy now – he would put the "Rev" into "Reverend".

All was rosy in the land of Rev. Nearly.

The shiny new car was delivered. The smart delivery driver showed the Rev over the car, handed him his log book and paperwork, removed his red trade plates and wished him safe and happy motoring. Felchingham walked around his new pride and joy, stroking a hand over the immaculate shiny paintwork. He bent down and peeled off the paper which was stuck over the number plate and stood back.

Oh dear...

The personal number plate was slightly different from the one which he had ordered. There had been a hideous mistake – and he knew exactly who was responsible for said mistake. His new cherished number was there for all to see.

KNO 8

From behind the hydrangea bushes came a distant throaty chuckle...

There was much discussion amongst the group of boys who comprised Nicky's gang. He had tried to convince Kendy that his 'talents' were far too good to be permanently hidden, and that he should share his secret with the rest of the group. The boy was understandably nervous about revealing his true nature to the Academy in general, and had been sternly spoken to by his father not to show off. Merry did not believe a word of what was told to him, and was dismissive (right up until the point that Davis actually wet himself, when Kendy suddenly appeared in front of him as a mirror image).The boys agreed to protect Kendy's secret from the world in general – but should the opportunity arise where they could make use of his skills, then they would take full advantage. The poor boy was subject to the same barrage of questions about his home and family, with the most pressing of these being "But do you own a death ray gun?". Kendy did his best to reassure his friends that he was just a young boy like themselves, except for one or two special talents. From now on, the lads would regard him with a mixture of pride, awe, and just a hint of trepidation.

Someone else currently experiencing a level of anxiety was Dr Strangler the Physics tutor. He had encouraged his after school Physics group to construct an experiment in Temporal Dynamics. (No, me neither, but he seemed to know what he was doing.) This experiment had all come from an idea which Strangler had whilst in the bath. It should have stayed there. He had contemplated the "Mobius Strip", and how when the edges were joined to form the infinity symbol, one edge and one side were lost. The boys had constructed two such strips from the plastic racing track for Hot Wheels toy cars. The two tracks crossed at a central point. The idea was to electrically charge one car positively, and one negative, and to send them around the interlinked tracks in order to see the reaction where they would cross paths in the centre. The results had been poor to begin with (but great fun for car racing). He had decided to let the lads ramp up the charges on the small vehicles, and increase the speed. Boy, did this work...The combination of the Mobius tracks and the opposing charges on the cars produced a small neon-blue point of light in the centre of the experimental structure. Strangler of course did the sensible thing at this point, namely: shutting down the whole experiment, writing down the facts obtained, and taking time to study the results in depth. (No – of course he didn't, he went out and bought two more powerful generator units, an industrial-sized transformer, and hooked them all up to the tracks.)

Not only had the experiment opened up a large vortex in its centre, which looked like a waste-disposal unit designed by a special effects team, it had an alarming habit of producing random actinic flashes in an attempt to earth the temporal flux build up which was being generated. Strangler had come up with the bright idea of earthing the random discharges by running a conductor wire to the largest metal object in the room; an old empty metal filing cabinet. The temporal flux peaks were now localised, so much so that within the confines of the old cabinet, they created a transfer interface for Dimensional Osmosis. Say hello to St Onan's very own time machine...

(This is not an uncommon phenomenon. When humans feel thirsty, the personal electromotive field gives off vibrations at very specific frequencies. These are picked up by drinks vending machines, whose suppliers know a good deal more than they are letting on. This can also manifest itself as a small flux overload – causing the unexplained appearance in drawers of foreign coins which come from countries which you have never visited. Next time you are searching for a bottle-opener and find a Ten-Zloty piece, earth yourself quickly...)

The effects were soon witnessed throughout the Academy. Biologist and egomaniac Darwin was gazing out of the laboratory windows one bright morning, whilst chatting to his friend Strangler over a cup of coffee. 'You know, Dick,' he said. 'I love mornings like this, where we can just look out and watch the blue tits on the bird table. It's so nice to see tho- GOD ALMIGHTY- IS THAT A DODO?' 'Don't worry about them,' said Strangler, casually dunking a Hob-Nob biscuit 'they are really friendly, and they're no trouble to feed – they're quite fond of Custard Creams actually.'

Darwin had fainted...

In addition to the birdlife which had hopped into the Academy grounds via the Wormhole (actually a bit bigger than your run-of-the-mill wormholes, and so was christened the "Viper Vortex" or "Anaconda Gap"), a splendid example of Homo Erectus had found himself standing a little too close to the wormhole when it discharged. This much-bearded and animal skin wearing chap could be glimpsed sneaking stealthily around the campus, and was often mistaken for a member of the Faculty. He was from a time where the area was part rainforest, and part swamp, and so was permanently afflicted by excess moisture. Because of this fact, Strangler and his boys had named him "Stig of the Damp".

Chemistry today had been livened up to the delight of the entire class. Captain Brayfield had been illustrating distillation effects involving chlorophyll by means of a complicated set of equipment on the front bench. The boys were to then test the resulting liquids produced with litmus paper, and write up their conclusions. As per usual, the man was in a foul mood, and had adopted a "Shout-one-scowl-one-free" attitude from the very start of the lesson. His mood was not helped when he noted

Kendy talking to Davis at the end of the workbench. 'GET TO THE FRONT NOW, BOY...' he bellowed at the poor lad. Kendy duly slunk to the front of Brayfield's desk, where he stood without expression.

'Do you find this lesson boring, Mr Kendy?' demanded the master.

'Certainly not, sir...' answered Kendy.

'Then why in the name of God's trousers do you feel it appropriate to chat to your friends when you should be concentrating upon the lesson?'

'I had already written down what I expected to see, sir' answered the boy.

'And what did your psychic powers tell you would be the result – eh? Mr Kendy?'

'That the chlorophyll would react with the litmus paper indicating an alkaline solution,' said Kendy.

'Are you trying to be smart, boy...?' said Brayfield, now edging toward a purple tint to his face.

'I shall only consider myself to be smart, sir, when I have acquired as much knowledge of the subject of chemistry as you have...' said Kendy, honestly.

'Don't try and be clever with me, Kendy,' said Brayfield.

'But I thought that was the general idea, sir?' the boy replied.

The rest of the boys could see the vast pit opening up before their friend, and knew that he was far too literal and genuinely honest not to plunge headfirst into it. They all had their fingers crossed that some "earth sense" had been absorbed by Kendy, and that he would not continue to play verbal tennis with the angry master.

'I have little time for boys of your ilk, Kendy,' said the teacher. 'You assume that I am a stupid old duffer who has nothing interesting to teach you. Oh yes – I have met plenty of your sort of boy, who think that because they have been at this Academy for a whole five minutes they can unlock the secrets of the Universe without effort. I can assure you Kendy, the work which we do here is the result of hundreds of years of painstaking study by clever thinkers, who could actually be bothered to listen to the advice and teachings of their tutors...'

Brayfield continued his rant without taking his eyes off his prey. What he could not see was that out of the adjacent sink, a column of water was slowly rising. The water spiralled up about two feet, and was about as thick as a man's arm. As the master continued to berate the smiling Kendy, the top of the column began to thicken, until it resembled a fist. The rest of the boys remained transfixed as one by one, fingers unfurled from the top of what was now clearly a watery hand. The hand slowly turned toward Brayfield, and the class were gripped with horror as to what might happen next. The fingers flexed, and then folded up, leaving the middle finger standing alone – and displaying a completely unmistakable gesture...

Brayfield finished his attack, and the water column collapsed back into the sink. The master turned to look as water splashed onto the bench, but assumed nothing out of the ordinary.

'Have you anything else to say for yourself, boy?' asked Brayfield.

'Only to offer my unreserved apologies, sir' said Kendy.

'Do we understand each other?' demanded the master.

'You have made your point, sir, and I hope that I have made mine...' Kendy answered.

Master Jonef Kendy was now the toast of Form 1A. He had to endure much back-slapping (done quite respectfully, might I add) and yet further questioning from the rest of the class who had been previously unaware of his "little abilities". A Form meeting was hurriedly convened, and the whole group sworn to secrecy under pain of – well, lots of further pain. Kendy in return had to promise not to reduce any of his fellow students to a pile of smoking ash with his death-ray gun...

Across the quad in the staffroom, there was a tense and foreboding atmosphere as Hyde-Jones and Newhouse faced each other across the table. The battle had been going on for some time, yet neither of the two men was willing to yield. Newhouse leaned back in his chair and took a pull on his cigarette, his eyes never leaving those of the man opposite. Hyde-Jones edged forward and rested his elbows on the stained table. A bead of perspiration ran down the back of his neck, the only movement visible as the two vied for supremacy.

The English master narrowed his eyes at his opponent, and spoke with a harsh rasp. 'Okay, Newhouse... let's do this thing.'

Newhouse showed no emotion, his face a blank sheet which Hyde-Jones could not read. 'You wanted it – You got it...' he croaked.

The air between them was charged with electricity...

'Was it Miss Scarlet, in the Library, with the Cucumber?'.

'No – Ha Ha!! It was our friend the vicar, in the drawing room, with the egg whisk...' said Hyde-Jones. 'That's six quid you owe me, my Rock God friend...'

'I deeply regret the day that we altered these cards,' said Newhouse. 'I find myself temporarily embarrassed in the pecuniary department – will you accept payment in kind?'

'I will consider it kind if you pay me at all...' said Hyde-Jones, in his best Groucho Marx voice. The two waggled eyebrows and imaginary cigars.

'Hey Loopy,' said Hyde-Jones, 'Penny Dreadful was asking where you were earlier – did you go up and see her?'

'I went up to her room, but I couldn't get past her bouncers...' laughed Newhouse.

The two raised their coffee cups and clinked them together, in recognition of a gag well executed. Hyde-Jones arose and assumed the pose of a vicar about to deliver a sermon.

'And yea verily I say to you my flock; her double D cup runneth over.'

'It's all a colossal front, you know.'

'The plan went completely tits-up...'

Both masters were now laughing and struggling to breathe, until Newhouse caught sight of the familiar Gallic silhouette standing right behind them, hands on her hips.

'When you gentlemen can take a break from being juvenile, perhaps you can help me with a problem,' said Madame.

'Made a bit of a boob have we?' asked Newhouse, still chuckling. His colleague waved him into silence, as she looked in a dangerous mood.

'How many boys are in the cast as '"urchin extras" for the play?' she demanded.

Hyde-Jones answered, 'Twelve, for the group scenes – why?'

'Because at last evening's rehearsal we had twenty-one boys, and I only have costumes for fifteen of them at a push' she stated.

'Sounds a bit weird..' said the English master, 'I'll try to find out what's going on.'

Madame turned on her designer heels and flounced out of the room.

'Is there a problem, Roy?' asked Mr Newhouse, noting the concern on the face of his friend.

'I have no idea, mate, unless that bugger Darwin in the Biology department has tried his hand at cloning again...'

The answer was a lot simpler than either of them could imagine.

As the rain paused for a sandwich and a cup of tea before resuming its monsoon deluge, the boys were growing restless as they waited for Dr Matthews to turn up for their History class. 'I expect that the old soak is still across the road, at the bar of the 'Five Crowns' – or possibly under it...' said Calderman.

Nicky had an idea – 'Hey Kendy, can you "do" old Matthews for us?'

'No, I don't think that would be very nice,' Jon replied.

'Oh go on, we'd all like to see if you can be him for a few minutes,' said Davis.

'Please Jon – see if you can do it,' asked Weatherill, now sporting a rather fetching Trilby hat.

Rather embarrassed at being the centre of attention, but not wishing to disappoint his friends, Kendy shrugged his shoulders, and walked across the classroom and into the stationery cupboard. From within, there came the sound of an empty bottle landing on the floor and rolling a short distance. Suddenly, the door opened, and, walking the walk of the pleasantly inebriated out came Dr Matthews. He tripped and staggered his way to the front of the desk, and folded his arms in Churchillian manner.

'Do (Hic) pardon me you fellows…' he said 'but some (burp) absoloute bounder seems to have been helping themselves to my twelve-year old bottle of Glen Hoddle. I was saving that for a special occasion – such as if I ever found myself sober...' The boys applauded the perfect performance.

'We will study (hic) the rise and fall (burp) of one of the most notable (fart) figures in English History-ry. Open your p-pages at book thirty-six, and we will (hic) get ourselves acquainted with Mr Oliver Crim-Crumb-Cromwell...'

The real Matthews had just meandered his way up the corridor, and managed with effort to locate his teaching room. He opened the door, and stared glassy-eyed at the scene before him. He then gave a small bow to the room and said, 'I am most sorry to have interrupted you – please accept my apologies...'before turning and closing the door again behind him. Out in the corridor, Captain Brayfield was passing, and saw Matthews emerge from the classroom looking puzzled and bewildered. He approached Matthews, who seemed to be trying to work something out.

'I say Matthews, is everything all right, old chap?' he asked.

Matthews looked up into the tall man's face and brightened. 'Oh yes, everything is under control – I'm already in there teaching them about the Civil War...'

Chapter Twenty-Five

It was that time in the academic year when certain unavoidable extra-curricular activities would come to the fore within the day-to-day routines of Academy life. Most of the boys had elected to become members of various clubs and societies, whose dubious practices were "enjoyed" after school hours. In addition to the more literary-based groups, which regularly met in the library in order to give the impression that they had a thirst for the Classics, there were a number of activities which took place far beyond the school walls. Orienteering and abseiling were very popular – and nearly all of the boys came back unscathed from their expeditions. One pupil had reputedly slipped the bonds of Authority whilst out in the countryside, and now lived a nomadic existence in and around the caves of the Peak District in Derbyshire. His parents had of course received a hefty bill for the cost of his missing tent, equipment, and the packed lunch with which he had been supplied, I mean – fair's fair.

The Archaeology Club had been a keen choice for many of the boys, and Nicky and his friends had signed up straightaway. For some bizarre reason, Mr Thwaite the Geography master had taken charge of the club, although his attendance was often marred by the wearing of completely inappropriate stiletto-heeled footwear. The supervision of the lads was undertaken by three "helpers", who seemed to have some vague connection to Mr Duggan the Metalwork tutor. So it was, that the Academy gained the services of Messrs Norman Figg, Adrian Swall, and Bert 'Bendy' Fletcher. The boys were regularly taken out of school in the minibus to an increasingly weird set of locations. The routine was always the same – Figg would produce a map, Swall would hand out tools for digging, and Fletcher would stand around smoking surreptitious cigarettes, and speaking in low tones to the other men out of the corner of his mouth. Their digs had taken place in such diverse locations as the side of busy roads. Yes, officer- we're investigating the site of a Roman massage parlour, pub car parks, yes, landlord – we're looking for the burial place of Caesar's cat, we'll put it all back – I promise, and the gardens of several of the larger local houses, yes, madam – we're looking for the lost Golden Pants of the Vikings, we'll put yer azaleas back where we found 'em.

The boys were happy to unearth examples of Roman pottery and the odd clay pipe, but if any coins were located, there would be a mad rush to examine the find by the three men. Should any of the boys hit anything which sounded like a metal box, then they were hastily bundled out of the way until the find had been inspected. Nicky noted that strangely, very few notes were taken, and the only reference material used seemed to be the increasingly grubby map which Figg kept about his equally grubby person. The boys were confused as to why some of the more well-known Roman sites in the area were not regularly visited, and why the three insisted on referring to possible finds as 'loot', and not 'artefacts' – hmmm… strange that.

The other "non-study related" event was the House Music Contest. This was one of the more eagerly-awaited events in the school calendar, with the chance for the students to show off their musical skill and prowess, or in many cases, the complete lack of it. Mr Newhouse in particular, dreaded the approach of the contest, as he would have to provide pieces of music for the entrants in each class to perform. He and Hyde-Jones would place bets between them on how long it took before the Music master became sick of the sounds of a violin being tortured, or solo singing from boys who could clearly not hold a note in a bucket. At this time of year, it came as no surprise to find that the second tympani drum in the music room was actually full of ice, in case Newhouse felt the urgent need for liquid sedative to calm his frayed nerves.

One highlight that the boys were eagerly awaiting was the appearance in the contest of the Academy Rock Band. These comprised a motley crew (!) of fifth-formers, who had convinced themselves that they were going to be "The Next Big Thing" on the music scene. They had started out on borrowed equipment, thrashing away at various rock numbers in the Academy rehearsal room. Newhouse would often go across to the music room, open the door, and listen to the would-be band in rehearsal. He would then nod, close the door as he left, and wish that there was some way that he could weld it shut.

The name of a band is a very important thing, as any up-and-coming musician will tell you. It can convey what you need to know about the music, and the people who play it. The choice of a name can be a very strong selling point when it comes to live gigs – and it absolutely must look good on a cheap A4 hand-produced poster. The band name will also be the major cause of arguments and spontaneous violence amongst the band members. This band were definitely a Rock outfit (No Keith – we're either Metal, or I'm leaving again...). They had been "Zip Fastener and The Studs", "Sex Thieves" (until Brian's mum put her foot down), "Steel Bender", "Gender Criminals", "Whipsuckin' Mamas", "Tofu Dildu" (during a brief electro-pop experiment), and "TazerPants". It was decided that the band needed a much stronger image, and a much more Heavy Metal name, and so the arguments had begun. After the damage had been cleared up, and most of the injuries treated, the name of "Death Member Warrior" had been chosen. It was pointed out by the band's "manager" (Brian's mum) that this would cost a fortune to print on the tee-shirts which they wanted. A new title was swiftly selected, and after some hasty editing by the censor (Brian's mum), they were all agreed on the name which would propel them to fame, fortune, and a possible date with Colin's sister.

Ladies and Gentlemen... Will you please welcome –

FUNDERTHUCK.

Their set consisted of a variety of Rock standards, which they would murder with little or no conscience, and their own self-penned songs. These tracks were based on their favourite classics, but with their own particular twist, spin, and dislocation. So at any local gig, the audience could be treated to:

Run Through the Bills

Stoke on the Water

Where the Sweets have no Name

Bohemian Raspberry

Layby

FreeBurger

Paraglide

Ain't Talkin' 'bout Gloves

And of course, who could possibly forget their show-stopping finale – "Stairway to Helen".

There was already a general buzz of excitement about the fact that the Academy would actually have a band appearing in the contest. The masters however, were not so thrilled by the intrusion of what they termed "Heathen Music" (surely a great title for the first album) being perpetrated on St Onan's premises. Well now Mr Newhouse had done his very best with the contestants, and so now it was up to them to prove their worth in front of their fellow students. Dr Chambers in particular, had been horrified at the thought of what he termed, "Heavy and Mental Music" being allowed at his Academy. His belief was that proper music should be played by a String Quartet, preferably under weeping willow trees and dreaming spires – by young gels wearing very short...(here his reverie was abruptly terminated, before the authorities were called).

DeVere was very satisfied with his progress as a participant in the Archaeology Club. He cared not a jot for Roman pottery or coinage. He gave scant regard to Norman architecture, or the chance discovery of Anglo-Saxon jewellery. While they were at it – the Vikings could kiss his bum. What pleased him the most was the acquisition of a handy stainless-steel trowel, and a small wooden-handled pick, with which he would facilitate his latest escape attempt. He had concealed these looted items about his person, and discretely hidden them in his boarding-house mattress. There had been an unfortunate incident in the night, when he had turned restlessly in his sleep, and accidentally picked his nose, but his plan was coming together nicely.

The plans for rehearsals in the music room were not going nicely at all for the band. For some reason, they were having great trouble starting their songs, and things looked like coming to blows – 'Look, Brian, why did you come in early?' said the drummer.

'I wasn't early, Spider, you stupid turd (there's always a drummer called 'spider') 'cos I heard you count me in,' snapped the guitarist.

Spider stood up and pointed at Brian. 'Look, I heard you count me in just then, so stop messin' about.'

Spider did as he was told, but he would have to make Brian pay for showing him up in front of Liam, Dave and Crusty.

This time, he shouted "One-Two-Three-FOUR" to make sure that they got the message loud and clear.

In an adjacent storeroom, a dust-covered DeVere paused with pick in hand. He waited until the band were in full flow before he started his chiselling again. It was his ill-timed blows at the stone which the band members next door had heard, and had taken as their cue. Just a little bit more to hack out of the mortar, and he could lift out the stones which barred his path to freedom. The loud music was the perfect cover for his demolition work, and he knew that as soon as he burst through to the cavity behind the storeroom, he could edge his way along the wide gap – and out of the Academy. When he had removed the blocks, he could place them in front of the door to severely delay the progress of any would-be pursuers...

Lessons for the rest of the day were suspended, as the entire Academy would be crammed into the assembly hall in order to witness the music contest. Those who were not quick enough to claim chairs were forced to sit on the floor at the front of the hall. The overall effect was that of a very respectful and well-dressed Free Festival. Weatherill was sitting at the front wearing a long ginger wig and hippy headband, plus a pair of round blue-tinted glasses.

'Are you all right there, Mr Weatherill?' a master had enquired on seeing the boy.

'Cool, man...' came the response, complete with "Peace" sign.

The first class to be heard by the panel of judges (Newhouse, Bell-Enderby, the Town Mayor, and Dr David Hickley – Professor of Music at Kings College) was the Treble Solo class. A parade of younger boys walked hesitantly onto the stage, and one by one sang the same piece of music until they had all been individually heard. The piano accompaniment was provided by Forster, one of the sixth-form students. His lively rendition of the chosen tune was regularly punctuated by a ferocious sneezing, during which he was forced to play one-handed.

The next class was for Duo, Trio, Quartet, and anyone who had managed to talk four mates into competing. There were a variety of melodies attempted. The best effort came from four fourth-year boys, who sang as a Barbershop Quartet. Mr Newhouse had high hopes that the barber would be Sweeny Todd...

Tap, Tap, Tap... DeVere wiped the sweat from his eyes – nearly there.

Weatherill turned to Nicky and said, ''Scuse me, mate, I've just got to go to the toilet.' With that said, he took off his long wig and plonked it onto Nicky's head. 'Don't forget the glasses, man,' he added, laughing. 'Be back in a jiffy – keep my place for me.' He disappeared toward the back of the hall, picking his way through the seated throng. It was halfway through the next category when Weatherill returned, saying as he sat down, 'Job done, now let's have me gear back, Sheppo,' as he reclaimed his wig and glasses. This class was the string section, with some very competent entries, but alas, some who did things to a poor defenceless violin and cello that should really be reported to the police.

It was now time to sample the delights of the Brass section. Weatherill rubbed his hands together and said, 'Oh Yes! Where there's Brass there's Muck...'

'Surely that's the wrong way round isn't it?' asked Nicky.

'Nope. You just wait and see,' replied the grinning Weatherill.

There were one or two entries which displayed a very good standard. One was a third-year boy who delighted the crowd with a trombone rendition of a tune normally heard at circuses. He received tumultuous applause, and cries of 'Encore' from all sections of the audience. Eventually, a familiar figure emerged from behind the curtain, and took up his seat on the stage. The masters cast angry glances around the room, trying to identify which boys were responsible for the chorus of hisses which greeted the entrance of the contestant.

The boy with the tuba was the prefect, Piper.

His chosen piece of music was "The Elephant" from *The Carnival of the Animals* by Saint-Soëns. Mr Newhouse gave him the signal to begin, and Piper gave a quick twiddle on the valves of the instrument. He began with a long, low note which slowly rose up the scale. Just as it seemed that he was about to begin the tune in earnest, there came a completely different and gruesome sound from deep within the tuba. This was not the melodic, deep tone of brass, and had absolutely no connection to any pachyderm, unless it was one who had ventured a suspect late-night kebab from a dodgy stall, following a good night out with the lads at the local watering-hole. This sound had very much more to do with something frequently left by elephants upon the plains of Africa, especially after a Vindaloo curry. The boy stopped blowing into the tuba, and regarded the wide horn of the instrument in horror. He peered cautiously into the brass mouth of the device.

Tap, Tap, Tap...DeVere clawed at the loosened blocks – just a little bit more...

Piper rested the tuba on the floor, and thrust his arm into the horn to investigate the blockage. He was angry and embarrassed, and could feel the eyes of the audience boring into him. What he hated most was looking a complete prat in front of the school. His assumed air of superiority evaporated away as he poked around in his instrument hoping to clear whatever obstruction was causing the problem.

He located the source of the blockage.

He tried to grasp it and pull it out.

He withdrew his hand, staring at it in disbelief.

'Is there a problem, Piper?' called Mr Newhouse from the podium of judges. 'If you are unable to continue, we will have to get on with the next classes.' The prefect was still staring at his hand in disbelief, and decided that there was only one course of action open to him.

He threw up.

After an emergency "operation mop" from the ever-vigilant Mrs Finucane, the stage was once again fit for the next contestant. Piper was led away and cleaned up by his fellow prefects, and the contaminated tuba was removed for a thorough deep-clean and disinfecting.

'Well, that was disappointing,' said Dr Hickley to Mr Newhouse.

'Yes, utter crap,' replied the Music master, barely stifling a snigger.

Tap, Tap, Tap, CLUNK. The two heavy blocks fell away. DeVere smiled...

Mr Newhouse then stood up on the podium, and announced that they would now break for lunch, with the "Miscellaneous" category being heard when they reconvened. The boys all rose as the masters and visitor left the hall. Across the quad, DeVere looked at his watch. 'Right, better rejoin the school for lunch. Don't want to arouse any suspicion, so I'd better make sure that I dust myself off properly.' After checking his appearance in a small mirror, DeVere quietly closed the door. All he now needed to do was to collect his "escape kit". This time, there would be no problems.

At this precise moment, problems seemed to have been reserved for Nicky and his friends. Before they had the chance to queue for the dining hall, they were confronted by an extremely furious Piper. He pushed into the group of boys, and selected Davis as his primary target, grabbing him roughly by the lapels, and shouting into the terrified boy's face 'Right, you fat little cretin – I know it was you and your bunch of peasants who did it, and this time you will not get away with it.' Nicky and Calderman squared up to the Prefect, in defence of their frightened friend.

'Take your hands off him now,' said Nicky.

'Or what?' sneered the bigger boy, twisting his grip on Davis. 'What else do you and your little bunch of morons think you can do? I'll get you expelled for this – then maybe the Academy will be fit for decent people.' Weatherill stepped forward at this point and confronted Piper. He had his thumbs tucked into his lapels, and from somewhere had acquired a barrister's wig. He cleared his throat.

'Ahem... My client will be making no statement at this time until the exact nature of the spurious charges which you have levelled against him is garnished with some measure of proof. To wit – any accusations against said Client should be set out in full, and only when these allegations have been fully considered will a response be forthcoming – which, might I add, will neither confirm nor deny that my Client was in any way involved with the incident or incidents which may, or may not have occurred at the time in question. In the meantime – it will prejudice any future claim which you may make, should you fail to observe the legal principle of "Habeas Corpus".

'What the bloody hell are you talking about, you little oik?' said Piper.

'I am merely suggesting that unless you let go of our friend, then I shall kick you in the scrotum so hard that you end up with three Adam's apples...' said Counsel for the Defence.

Piper looked into the face of the smiling Weatherill. A small crowd was beginning to gather around the group, and Piper was getting a little uncomfortable, having been the focus of much attention earlier. He released Davis, flinging him toward Nicky and his friends. 'Here, take your Piggy friend – but you haven't heard the last of this. I will get rid of you bunch of bastards, you mark my words.' He stormed off, bumping into Mrs Finucane as he did so. He mumbled an apology, and hurried into the dining hall.

'What was all that about?' asked Nicky. 'Are you allright, Davis?'

'Yeah, I'm okay,' said the boy, still shaken, 'but why pick on me?'

'Something's upset him,' said Weatherill.

'But why would he go berserk at us like that?' asked Merry.

Weatherill gave the group a knowing grin, and said, 'I think that even I might be rather upset if someone shat in my tuba...'

Mrs Finucane had seen and heard the whole incident.

It was agent J-Cloth, however, that would put a plan into action...

Chapter Twenty-Six

DeVere had decided to skip lunch. He was unlikely to be missed, as those masters on the first sitting would assume that he was on the second, and vice-versa. He walked confidently along the echoing corridors of the Boarding House, and into his dormitory. Leaning under his bed, he opened the cardboard box and retrieved the pack of items which he had assembled in preparation for his trip. He rolled his "day clothes" into a tight pack, and left the room without glancing back. At the main house door, he checked left and right for any casual observers before ducking into the doorway of the adjacent storeroom. He made one last check of his "kit", then tested his torch. Satisfied that all was in order, he stepped through the hole in the wall like a diminutive Howard Carter in the Valley of the Kings. Slowly but with determination, he walked along the narrow space between the thick walls, casting a protective circle of light before him.

The boys had wolfed down their lunch, and hurried back to the assembly hall to resume the programme of afternoon entertainment. It was the turn of the pianists to show their mettle first, and the grand piano stood proud and imposing, centre stage. There had been a brief flurry of activity as Mr Newhouse dashed onto the stage in order to remove a hastily-remembered bottle of Jack Daniels from beneath the piano lid. Returning to his seat amongst the judges, he nodded to Hyde-Jones on the stage, and the first boy scampered on to sit behind the noble Steinway. The boy flexed his fingers, settled himself, and played a low chord. He then amazed the audience and the judges by belting into a storming version of "Honky-Tonk Train Blues" by Meade Lux Lewis. As the piece slowed to a halt, and the final chords rang out, the boys were already on their feet and applauding.

''Ave some of that, Doc!' said Newhouse, punching his fellow judge on the shoulder. The visitor's gold fountain pen leapt from his hand, and created a spontaneous Rorschach Test on the white shirt of a boy sitting innocently on the left of the podium.

That would be a hard act for anyone to follow. Newhouse called for quiet, and the next boy walked timidly across to the piano. It was the walk of one who has entered the contest under protest, and is desperately trying to become invisible. Rigid with fear, the boy attempted to copy the routine which the previous pianist had shown. Unfortunately, there was slight difference in his preparations. He played a low chord, flexed his fingers, and soiled himself...

With the standard of musicianship displayed by the rest of the participants in the piano class, Mr Steinway would have insisted that he refund the cost of the piano to the Academy, no questions asked. Nicky and his friends were huddled with the rest of the latecomers from lunch, in the back corner of the hall near the large windows. They found themselves sandwiched between the fire hose and a rather glazed-looking Miles Bannister, the Maths tutor. He was looking toward the stage with a definite waxwork quality to his face, like an animatronic puppet whose batteries had been removed. Calderman said, 'Good afternoon, sir. What do you think of it so far?' but got no response.

Merry was brave enough to wave a hand in front of Bannister's face, at which point, the soothing yet concerned voice of Mrs Elsie Noakes told him, 'Oooh, be careful, Gerald, you nearly had his eye out there!'

Nicky moved back in shock at the female voice which issued from the tall man – without any change to his glassy visage. 'Please excuse me,' he said, 'but who is it exactly that I am talking to?'

There was a friendly auntie-like chuckle, and Elsie answered, 'It's Mrs Noakes Lovey – but you can call me Elsie, now that we're friends.' The boys looked at each other, and Merry asked, 'Sorry to ask, Mrs N, but how come you are here?'

'Oh blimey, I never miss the Music Contest,' she said. 'I make sure that I'm here every year – I love all of the singing and tunes, although I'm a bit disappointed that no-one has done "Nissan Dormant" yet.' There was slight pause, until the penny (or Lira) dropped.

There was particular look that came over the face of young Master Trevill, whenever he was about to say what everyone else was thinking, but daren't articulate. Such a determined aspect was very evident now, as he said, 'May Oi arsk you summin,' Mrs Noakes?'

'Yes of course you can, deary,' she answered.

'Well, Oi bin' wondrin' see, what is that death actually loike? – I mean, Do it 'urt?'

Elsie began to chuckle, and it sounded as if the question had really hit her funny bone. 'Ooh no, deary, it didn't hurt a bit. Death is nothing that you need to be worried about, it was a breeze – mind you, I was a bit stiff the next morning...'

Mr Newhouse was now calling the first of the contestants for the Miscellaneous category. This would include the band – whose appearance was eagerly awaited by the entire crowd. There was a sigh from Elsie... 'You know,' she said, 'I always fancied myself as a singer...' Just as Nicky was about to ask Elsie another question, Bannister (or Elsie and Bannister, or both – oh you get the picture) suddenly set off toward the panel of judges. The boys noted a whispered conversation between

Bannister and a rather bemused Mr Newhouse, and then saw Bannister walk to the stage and take up a position in the centre.

The Music Master stood up and turned around to address the crowd. 'Before our next acts come on, there is a surprise entry from one of our very own members of staff – who would like to entertain you all with a song.' He beckoned over Forster, and whispered something in his ear. The boy shot up to the stage and took up position at the piano.

Bannister turned and politely nodded at his accompanist, who began the opening chords of the song. Instead of the rich baritone which the boys may have been expecting, there was the sound of a pleasant (if a little reedy) contralto voice from the master- who went into the theme from *The Sound of Music*. Surprisingly, when he/she had finished, there was a standing ovation from the boys. Elsie took the applause politely, making a gracious bow to the crowd. Bannister suddenly shuddered, and glanced around himself in complete horror as he found himself centre stage, in front of a cheering crowd, with absolutely no recollection of how he came to be there. In confusion, he managed to squeak, 'Hello,' before fleeing the stage at top speed.

Mr Newhouse let the audience settle down, and then announced, 'And now to introduce the entry that you have all been waiting for, I will hand you over to our esteemed guest judge, Dr Hickley, who will introduce them...'

The announcement caught Hickley completely by surprise, and he rose from his seat looking nervous. 'Well, err, I would like to introduce the next contestant in this category, which, err, is indeed, erm, a group of contestants, who, erm, I believe are called, (Newhouse handed him a piece of paper with the name of the band on it) sorry, I can't read that... oh, is it? Okay then.' Brian's mum would be furious, as he mispronounced the name of the band – as Newhouse had hoped...

A roar went up from the crowd as Brian, Liam, Dave and Crusty took up their places. Spider sat behind his kit and attempted to twirl a drumstick, but only succeeded in poking himself in the eye. Liam stepped up to the microphone...

'Hello, Granchester!' he managed to shout, before accidentally pulling out the lead. After being hastily re-connected by Dave (who would speak to him afterwards), he announced, 'We're going to play you a song that we wrote last week – this is "Flat Bosomed Girls..."'

The song was quite possibly the worst attempt at Rock music that Nicky and his friends had ever heard. True, the guitars were good and loud, but there was not enough Spider, and altogether far too much Liam. Nicky turned to Weatherill, who now resembled Slash from Guns N' Roses, resplendent in top hat and dark shades. The lead guitar solo had been a revelation, especially the bit where Dave caught his hair in the strings. Even above the amplification, most of the boys heard him use a word which would earn him a stiff telling-off from Brian's mum.

All too soon, the song came to a crashing end. The last chord rang out as Crusty raised his guitar in salute (the effect was slightly spoiled by the glancing blow to Dave's chin on the way up). 'Thank Yew Granchesterrr... and goodnight!' screamed Liam. The band left the stage waving to the crowd, and Spider got caught in the heavy stage curtains.

Mr Newhouse tapped Dr Hickley on the shoulder, to let him know that it was safe to remove his fingers from his ears. He then stood up again, and announced the woodwind class. Now that the bit of the "show" that they had waited for had finished, the majority of the boys beat a hasty retreat out of the double doors at the back of the hall.

DeVere was busy beating his own leisurely retreat, down the dank and spider-haunted narrow corridor between the walls. He had progressed about forty yards along the passage, constantly brushing the clinging webs from his face. He calculated that he was just about at the point where the dining hall ended, and the even older wall of the so-called "Dark Tower" began. From his numerous reconnaissance missions, he knew that just around the corner would be one of the many half-sized doors which were an easily overlooked feature of the outer structure. The doors were old, and the wood should not provide much resistance to the determined hands of an escapee. All he had to do was lever the door open; clear the Tower grounds, and hello world!

Squeezing past some strange fungi which clung to the wall, DeVere at last found the corner and turned left. A little way down the passage he saw his target. The wood of the tiny door was set in a stone arch, but seemed to have a decent gap all the way round – into which his borrowed pick could be inserted. He brushed the dust and accumulated debris from the wall behind him, and angled the torch upwards from the floor to illuminate the doorway. Inserting the metal edge of the pick into the gap in the door, he took a breath of the dank corridor air and heaved. The door moved back about an inch and a half. Although the wood of the door was ancient, time had set it like steel. He paused for a moment, and tried another position on the door which looked as if it might give way. It didn't. He picked up the torch and carefully examined the frame all the way around. There were two places which looked promising – one of which he had already tried. Spitting on his hands, he thrust the pick back into the gap and redoubled his effort. This time, the door came open about four inches, and he quickly jammed the handle of the trowel into it to prevent it slipping back. Looking again with the torch, he could clearly see the problem. The hinge side of the door had been nailed through, and over the years, rusting must have acted like adhesive, cementing them into the frame. He could certainly get the door to move if he could only get a bit more power and leverage. There was perhaps one way to get the job done, but it would be risky.

He asked himself, 'How badly do I need to escape?'

He made up his mind. Some risks were worth taking...

He would get help from his friends.

The lads were gathered in the corner of the quad, some way apart from the other groups of boys who were larking around and laughing, some imitating the mannerisms of the band which they had just seen on stage. The band themselves had sought out their musical mentor, Mr Newhouse, for some constructive criticism on their performance (absolute crap – Liam in particular just wanted to hear how great they were, and when the American Tour should be booked by Brian's mum).

'There are no adequate words which would describe your performance...' Newhouse had said. Actually, he had thought of quite a few, but wouldn't use them for fear of reprisals from Brian's mum.

The conversation had strayed onto a matter that had been playing on Merry's mind for ages. 'We really need to do something about those kids,' he said.

'How do you mean?' asked Nicky.

'Well they don't half look thin for one thing, and how do we know that they are not sick or anything?' said Doctor Merry.

Nicky replied that they had seemed cheerful enough, and told the boys about handing over the jam tart the other day. Davis was very concerned that he might be required to provide chocolate with which to tempt the children out on a more regular basis, but Nicky calmed his nerves by telling him that he had a plan.

'I intend to feed the kids behind the wall...' stated Nicky, with feeling.

'How do you know that they want to be fed?' asked Davis.

'Well, we did all see how thin and scrawny they looked,' Nicky answered.

'Can I just ask a quick question here?' said Calderman. 'Do we know just how many kids we are talking about? I mean, there could be loads of them in there...'

'Okay – then it is our duty to feed them all,' said Nicky.

'Corrr – listen at yourself, you'm soundin' loike that Bob Gelding feller...' said Trevill.

'I have an urgent request,' said a serious-looking Merry.

'The floor is yours, Geraldo...' said Calderman.

'If you are going to organise a big benefit gig – then for god's sake don't have that band we just heard playing anywhere near it – they were shite!'

When the laughter had died down, and Nicky had released Merry from the playful headlock which he had him in, they got down to detail on the "plan".

'I think it should work something like this...' explained Nicky. 'We know that normally on a Thursday they serve up those individual pies for lunch. The pies are all cooked and set out on the worktops about the time of the morning break. This is where timing will be crucial. We have to get into the dinner hall and grab as many pies as we can carry, when Mrs Bradley and her staff are having their morning coffee. The masters will be in the staffroom at the same time, so we should be able to get in and out without any interference. We take the pies up to the assembly hall, and hand them over to Ursula and Thomas for distribution to all of the other kids. We know that they have a "secret hatch" behind the stage, so it's just a case of getting some sort of message to them, to let them know that Thursday will be "National Pie Giveaway Day".

Trevill had his hand raised...

'Can Oi just arsk...' he said slowly, 'Just 'ow it is that you propose we carry the gravy?'

'Any chips to be supplied with the pies?' said Davis.

'Look- we'll cover the detail later, once we've settled on the main plan,' said Nicky.

'Is there to be a vegetarian option?' asked Calderman.

'Will they supply their own cutlery and napkins?' asked Merry.

'Oh of course – and we'll make sure that we send 'em the wine list well in advance... Look, there are some parts of the scheme where we are just going to have to wing it – but does everyone agree with the basic idea?' said Nicky.

'Yes I certainly do – I can't stand the thought of being hungry...' said Davis.

'That's true...' said Weatherill, 'I once saw him put mayonnaise on an aspirin...'

The boys all laughed, and Weatherill added, 'And Davis, my hungry little mate – we will be counting those pies...'

The rest of the afternoon had been designated as "Free Study" period, to enable those with a more Classical interest to listen to the last classes of the Music Contest. The gang were just about to go up to the library for the last forty-five minutes, when they were suddenly confronted by a slightly out-of-breath DeVere.

'Hiya Davey, what are you up to?' asked Calderman.

'Actually, chaps, I have come to ask for your help – it's really urgent,' said DeVere.

'Happy to help Davey – fire away,' Calderman said.

DeVere explained. He looked nervous, yet resigned to his task. There was no question at all that any of the boys would not assist their friend – who they knew was suffering at the Academy. He told them how far he had got, what he needed to do, and what help he needed from them. Without realising it, the whole group had begun to drift over toward the storeroom next to the Boarding House. One by one, they checked for observers, then darted inside and into the room where DeVere had breached the wall. Davis had to be left outside as lookout, due to his acute claustrophobia. It would be unwise (as willing as he was) to risk a boy of his size having any sort of panic attack in a narrow gap. The remaining boys climbed through the hole and inched their way down the tunnel. Suddenly, the group were startled by a light which appeared on the roof some way ahead of them. They stopped dead, and Merry turned around, and a blinding light shone straight into his eyes. There was a brief moment of panic, until it was discovered that the source of the extra light was Weatherill, who was wearing a miner's helmet, complete with lamp on the front... Shortly, they came to the small door which was all that stood between imprisonment and happy release for their friend.

Trevill borrowed the torch, looked around the door and said, 'No problem, boys, we 'em just got to get 'old of that thur frame and give a bloody good pull'.

Easing back the door edge with the pick, the boys managed to all get a grip on the handle side of the timber.

'Right...' whispered Trevill. 'When Oi says Three... One, Two, Thr...' The door broke off, leaving the splintered hinges hanging, and a pile of pupils sprawled on the damp tunnel floor.

'-ee...' said Trevill, 'Oh bugger, Oi've dropped the torch.'

Light flooded in to the tunnel, revealing much more detail of the floor and walls than the boys were comfortable in seeing, but more importantly, revealing DeVere's route to freedom. The boy began to babble his thanks to the group, but Calderman just said, 'Don't waste any time, Davey – just leg it. Send us a postcard if you get the chance – now bugger off, and good luck, mate...' DeVere grabbed his escape kit and his rolled clothing, and vanished through the splintered remains of the door.

Nicky and Merry began hunting for the shattered remains of the torch. Having located the object, the team turned to go back up the passageway, but were halted by Calderman.

'Hang on a minute, chaps...' he said. 'I just want to have a quick look inside the Dark Tower.'

'Are you mad?' said Merry. 'I'm not going near that place – I've heard rumours...'

Calderman stared at his friend. 'What sort of rumours would those be, then?'

Merry shivered, and answered, 'I've heard that all manner of dark and evil practices have taken place in the Dark Tower, and it doesn't do to mess or meddle with forces which we know nothing about...'

'What sort of forces are you referring to?' asked Calderman.

'I don't know what forces it is that I don't know anything about...' said Merry, 'but I do know that I'm not about to start meddlin' with them.'

''Ow is a mortal man supposed to combat the forces of Doom, Destruction and Despair...' said Trevill, in hushed tones.

'Well, the lamp on my hat is pretty good...' said Weatherill, brightly.

'Fair enough then,' said Merry. 'We'll have a quick look, but if there's any forces about- I'm legging it.'

A small courtyard lawn led them to the side door of what had become famed as the Dark Tower. This was the second oldest building on the whole Academy campus. It loomed over the quad with an air of melancholic foreboding. Its gothic arched windows had acquired a thick patina of dust, which made them blend in with the gloomy stonework. As with any old building left unused and empty for any length of time, it soon gained the reputation of being the site of haunting and demonic ritual. In keeping with the various signs affixed to the outside of the structure which declared 'Building unsafe – keep out', the tower was given a wide berth by even the bravest students. Pieces of the internal structure and ceilings would occasionally surrender to dry rot and gravity, and plunge to the ground with loud thumping sounds, which were often mistaken (especially during the hours of darkness) to be the movements of some beast that dwelt within. During a particularly violent thunderstorm, one of the ancient gargoyles had fallen from the corner of the tower. Rumours were that it had flown away to chase some intruder who had dared to venture inside. Another legend was that an angel had smote it with a mighty smite when it came alive during said storm. It had actually fallen off and landed upside-down in an adjacent drain, where it still blew bubbles when the drains could not cope with the heavy rains. Trust me, it will not be long before we start hearing stories about haunted gutters.

There was however, a very real and valid reason as to why the building was given the title of the Dark Tower. This was the fact that there had been no lighting in the building since 1947.

The boys had their quick look into the gloom of the tower via a ground floor window. From what they could make out (or at least, what the grime-encrusted window would allow them to see) the room space only contained a large table, four chairs, and what might be an old oak settle, or perhaps a rescued church pew. In the centre of the far wall was a very old stone fireplace, but little else could be seen.

Nicky peered in through the filthy glass, then turned his head toward his friends saying 'We'd better get back now, team – it's mission accomplished...'

He fell backwards in terror when he saw the face looking out at him.

They ran, they stumbled, and they skidded along the passage in a frantic attempt to get as far away from the tower as possible, as fast as possible. They tumbled out of the hole in the storeroom wall that DeVere had carved, and without speaking, quickly piled up the blocks back into the hole to seal it. Running outside and into the quad, the boys stood against the wall, trying to regain their breath. Davis was involved in a life-or-death struggle with a packet of crisps, and asked them, 'Well, chaps – how did you get on?' The lads burst out laughing, more out of nerves than humour. They told him about the passage. They told him about the door. They told him that they had helped to liberate their fellow inmate DeVere. For some reason, no-one mentioned the face at the window...

Chapter Twenty-Seven

Following the cavalcade of carnage which had comprised the House Music Competition, after which the mortal remains of several legendary composers could quite plainly be heard revolving in their graves at an alarming rate of rotation, there came the ceremonial and ritualistic event which comprised Founders' Day. This solemn occasion celebrated the founding of the Academy, and its inception as a seat of learning. To mark the occasion, the staff would bedeck themselves in their ermine and robes, to celebrate the untimely passing of furry animals and silk worms. The complexities of the rituals were a mystery to the newer boys at present, who knew absolutely nothing of "Beating out the Wolds" or "Chasing up Charlie's passage", not to mention "Binding of the Nethers" of the Third Year Boys.

The main points that the new intake had managed to absorb were that: best uniform was to be worn (without stains, however obtained), statues of the Founders were to be bowed to and honoured (notwithstanding the plasticene appendage added to the image of Bishop Foxe), and an extremely long church service, during which some of the congregation would pass away, the vicar would in all likelihood pass out, and the choirboys would pass through puberty. At the evening service, the parents lucky enough to have received an invitation, or have purchased a specially vetted ticket, would assess each other's dress sense upon entry, and anyone deemed to have not spent the required amount on clothing would be shunned and sent to sit behind the largest pillars, with no clear view of the priest, or his threatening nasal hair...

Founders' Day was thus perhaps the most venerated date on the entire Academy calendar, and there was much personal preening and "gentrification" attempted by the staff, or at least those who could spell it. As with every previous year, there would be pockets of resistance to the overblown peacock-pride of the occasion, led by Messrs Newhouse and Hyde-Jones. Even Betty in her kitchen enclave would choose and put on her very finest ceremonial corsetry for the look of the thing (most certainly a thing never to be looked at, if it could be avoided). To all intents and purposes, the Academy of St Onan's would be thrown open to the parents of its students, who would be given a guided tour of the school by boys especially chosen for their image and charm (i.e. those scant few who could be nearly relied upon not to slur, spit, fart, or scratch themselves in front of the visitors). The other reason for carefully 'vetting' the so-called guides, was that if they could do a convincing enough job of selling the Academy to the visitors – then there was every chance that they would send their younger offspring to St Onan's, and once again, the headmaster would dance the dance of one who is soon to be the recipient of grossly inflated school fees a-plenty.

Nicky in particular was dreading the occasion, as he just knew that he would somehow be instantly spotted and then targeted by the rich boys, who would no doubt have a "How to spot your Peasant" chart lovingly fixed to their wall by their butlers. He had visited Uncle Joe's rambling domain in the village, in an attempt to seek solace. Uncle had been there, seen it, and done it (and better still – there had been no witnesses, so no-one could prove a single thing). As the boy walked up to the open back door of Uncle's house, he could hear the pleasant tenor voice of Joe singing an old cowboy melody...

'Ooooh – give me a home–
Where the Buffalo roam–
And I'll show you a carpet
Covered in cowshi... 'Oh, hello, lad! To what do I owe this pleasure?' said Joe.

There was no point in trying to hide anything from Uncle, so Nicky told it like it is...

'It's Founders Day tomorrow, Uncle, and I know that the posh kids are going to humiliate me,' he told him.

'Pay the buggers no attention, son,' said Joe. 'You have got there because you had enough brains to pass the exam, and so did I, but them bastards have only got there because daddy has a nice fat cheque book, or because they are the spawn of Lord Nobbsey-Nobb of the Shire of Toffington. When you get a bit older, then you will understand how it all works my lad. When it comes to dealing with the Silver Spoon Brigade it's all about tolerance, and of course, don't forget about your arse...' Joe told him.

'What do you mean, Uncle?' asked Nicky.

'I told you – tolerance' said Joe.

'I still don't quite understand what you're getting at,' said Nicky.

'I mean use tolerance the same way that you would use your arse,' said Joe.

'What – just sit on it?' asked Nicky.

'No , son – you grin... and bare it,' said Uncle with a cunning smile.

'Anyway – while you're here, I shall disclose to you my very latest invention, which will make me a millionaire without a shred of doubt. Picture the scenario. You are setting off with your family on a long car journey from here all the way down to Cornwall. You have packed all of the usual holiday paraphernalia in the car, but my oh my... have you forgotten something? Yes you have indeed – you have forgotten the woeful lack of toilet facilities available to the long-distance traveller as he navigates the highways and byways down to the coast. Crossed eyes and legs are no friend to the long-distance driver, and so with this in mind, I have invented a reasonably-priced emergency kit for the holidaymaker in dire need...'

Joe reached under the table, and swiftly dropped a small shoe-box sized package onto the table top. He lifted the box lid with great ceremony, and proudly placed a stout greaseproof-paper packet in the centre of the table. 'There she is,' Joe beamed. 'Contains everything necessary for those stops along the way which you would rather not make. There is the packet itself, with full instruction booklet for use, the required amount of paper for a family of six, and moist wipes. All in a handy-to-dispose of packet which is hygienically sealed and eco-friendly. Trust me – I'm gonna clean up with this little beauty...'

As per usual, Joe's research was sound. His product was practical. His sales pitch was perfect. The name that he had chosen for his product was not quite as well thought out. It was extremely unlikely that "Bog in a Bag" was destined to become a best seller...

Dread the prospect or not, there was nothing that could be done to prevent the spectre of Founders' Day from stalking the land. In a ritual no doubt played out in the homes of most of the boys of the Academy, the students were condemned to a "special wash", as they were to be on view to the rest of the visiting parents. The Boarding House boys were subjected to a good hosing-down by a rather over-enthusiastic Matron, who had "seen it all before" and so rumour would suggest, possibly in the same quantities...

Putting the thoughts of Founders' Day to the back of his mind for the time being, Nicky remembered all about his plans to distribute food to the poor thin kids from wherever. Arriving at the Academy decked out in their finest attire as occasion demanded, the group of friends assembled like a committee of Victorian philanthropists about to achieve great things. The plan was gone over in some considerable detail, to ensure that the removal of the pies would take place as smoothly and covertly as possible. As the morning break approached, and the time for action arrived, the boys huddled in the far corner of the quad – where Weatherill was politely but firmly instructed to remove the black balaclava which he had donned for the occasion.

At Calderman's signal, the boys divided up into two groups, comprising of Trevill and Nicky, Merry and Calderman, and the lone unmasked raider known as Weatherill. Davis was again asked to act as lookout, because as Merry had stated, 'We can't give 'em any half-eaten pies – it wouldn't be right'. Davis had grudgingly agreed to his given role as trouble-spotter. Also spotting the boys' actions from a discreet downstairs window, was the ever-vigilant Mrs Finucane. Weatherill casually sauntered into the dining hall through the main door, and finding Betty Bradley already on patrol, asked her if he could possibly have a glass of water. Betty told him to help himself – an unfortunate if accurate choice of words on this occasion. Before moving over to the serving area sink, Weatherill slunk back to the dining hall door, and gave the thumbs-up signal to the other boys, indicating that it was safe to proceed. The other members of the gang edged into the kitchen, taking up station behind the serving area door. Only one hatch was raised at this time of the morning, and so it would be easy to duck under the steel serving units and grab the pies which were laid out in rows. Weatherill had already opened the rear door to the kitchen, in order to facilitate a speedy escape if plans went awry. One by one, the boys approached the resting flock of pies, and quickly wrapped each one in a serviette before filling each of their pockets with the tasty stolen booty. As the last pie was lifted and secreted, Weatherill calmly walked over to the sink and filled a glass tumbler with water. If he was now seen by Betty, it should raise no suspicions on her part. The boys walked nonchalantly out of the dining hall, waddling slightly under the weight of knocked-off steak and kidney delights.

Re-grouping in the far side of the quad, the gang were well pleased with their achievements.

'Well done, team!' said Nicky. 'Now we need to get over to the assembly hall and get rid of the evidence before we get caught with pastry on us.'

Calderman agreed, 'Nice one, mates, well played. We'll try and make contact with the kids via the fire hose cupboard at the back of the stage again.'

Still looking over their shoulders just in case they were being followed, the group made their way into the echoing assembly hall and up behind the stage, with every footfall ringing out like a challenge to intercept them all. Merry went over to the cupboard door which was set into the wall next to the fire hose, and tapped loudly on the wood. When there was no response after a few minutes, he turned to his friends and declared, 'I don't think anyone is at home.' He got a sharp shock when as he turned back to the wall, the door was ajar, and the bright and hopeful face of Ursula was staring back at him. 'Bloody hell!' gasped Merry. 'You didn't half give me a fright there...'

The girl frowned at him, then said, 'HoBi says that thou must not use profane language, it is a bad thing.'

'Yes, you're right err – sorry, Ursula' said a chastened Merry.

'We brought you pies!' said Davis, spraying out pastry crumbs over innocent bystanders.

'One less than we thought... so it would appear,' said Calderman, doing his best to scowl at his munching friend.

The boys began to unload their stolen cargo from their pockets, and soon there was an impressive stack of pies on the floor in front of the door. Trevill produced a supermarket carrier bag, and having filled it to the brim, handed it over to the girl. 'Take these 'ere poise, Hurdler... and please share 'em with your friends.' Despite the unprompted change of name, the girl took the carrier bag and its contents, and looked genuinely moved. Merry handed over a mysterious small package and said, 'Tell Thomas that I sent him this...' Nicky had the distinct feeling that Thomas would be the only child "behind the wall" who would be wearing a Ramones tee-shirt.

'We will bring you some more food if you let us know what you would like...' offered Nicky. The girl was staring past the group of boys to a point up above their shoulders.

'Pray do not tempt the child...' said a man's voice behind them.

The boys spun around, and found themselves staring up at a tall, thin man with a rather severe look on his face. 'We live, we thrive, and we ask no contact with the Upper World,' he said.

'Who the hell are you?' asked Calderman.

'I am Gideon of the Third Family,' he answered. 'I am elder and teacher. Thee should not tempt the young ones with stolen food. To steal is wrong, to steal is immoral, it is against the teaching of HoBi – who will be displeased...'

'Sorry Mr Gideon, but we just thought that the kids did look a bit thin, and we were worried about them,' said Merry. The man studied Merry's earnest expression, and all of the boys noticed that the man had very large eyes, which gave him the impression of an authoritative Bush Baby.

'Where'm you from then, Mr Giddyup?' asked Trevill, ''An 'ow comes you'm lettin' kiddies roam all about the place behind walls and suchloike?'

'I shall tell Thee when it is time for Thee to know...' said Gideon.

Ursula must have seized the moment, and the pies, as the door closed with a loud click. The group of boys spun around to see what the noise was, and when they turned back, there was no sign of their mysterious friend. The confused silence was broken by Trevill, who announced in a loud panicky voice, 'Oh Buggerr!... Oi've forgot that Oim supposed to be helpin' with the Parents' Tour, and showin' 'em one of our classes...'

'Which class are you helping in?' asked Calderman.

'English – an' Oim supposed to be givin' 'em some Shakespeare too,' answered Trevill.

The boys looked at each other.

'God help us...' said Merry.

It was testament to the somewhat malicious wit of the staff, that some of the boys chosen to show parents and guests around the Academy were the least competent at the designated tasks. In the eyes of Mr Hyde-Jones, there was only one boy who could raise the bar of the English Language to its highest level, whilst providing perhaps the finest ad-lib comedy guaranteed to enliven a boring event such as Founders' Day. The lads had all planned to sneak into the class in order to witness the Bard being pinned down by Dorset sniper fire.

Weatherill had already been summoned to the Deputy Head's office, and was told in no uncertain terms by Dr Chambers, 'Now look here, Weatherill... With parentals and visitors being admitted to the Academy today, you will cease and desist in your persistent and wholly bizarre practice of adopting inappropriate headgear...'

'Sorry, sir? I'm not too clear...perhaps just a small Trilby?'

'NO WEATHERILL – PERHAPS NOT A SMALL TRILBY UNDER ANY CIRCUMSTANCE...' shouted Chambers 'And another point of order, Mr Weatherill...'

'Why yes, sir?...'

'YOU WILL WEAR A TIE – DO I MAKE MYSELF CLEAR?'

'Absolutely clear, sir, happy to oblige,' answered the boy.

As Weatherill crossed the quad, he saw high above him the ravens, with their "Been there – seen it – done it – crapped on the tee shirt" attitude of superiority, who were riding on the thermals above St Onan's (apart from one rather elderly raven called Keith, who for some weird reason was riding a tiny red moped). Just then, he noticed Chambers and the dreaded Piper rushing over to the assembly hall, on some urgent mission. To make matters worse, when the vindictive prefect noticed Weatherill across the tarmac, he halted mid-stride and pointed him out to Dr Chambers. From an upstairs window, Mrs Finucane waved at him.

Before the tour of the Academy began in earnest, or possibly in harness (if Matron was in any way involved), there was an intimate soiree being held in the headmaster's chambers. Nicky noted that the procession of parents making their way to the chosen venue were only the ones who had arrived by Bentley. He could not see his mother, or the parents of any of his friends being ushered up the leafy path to Pale Sherry City. Prefects were standing guard outside the entrance to the head's study, and were looking like rather camp bouncers in their heavily-embroidered waistcoats and high collars. At this precise moment, the jealous and utterly smitten Miss Piggott was no doubt dropping sedatives into the glass of the head's wife- who had quite spoiled her day by attending the event. With Mrs Goodwill temporarily incapacitated, she could assume her rightful place as the head's consort and companion for the duration of the day. Mrs G was fully aware of the situation, and of her rival's motives – and had launched a pre-emptive strike on the Piggott with a chocolate éclair laced with a powerful dose of laxative...

The parents not lucky or rich enough to have been given a golden ticket to sip cocktails with the head, were welcomed into the staff lounge, where a table buffet had been laid out. There was a space on the table which should have been occupied by several specially-prepared meat pies, but Betty had temporarily "mislaid" them, and had set about filling the gap with a delicacy of her own creation. All was well again, her staff were happy, the parents looked happy, and she was happy that her new medication was having wonderful effects. She couldn't wait to see the look on the faces of the visitors when they sampled her chocolate and Marmite dipped fish fingers...

Whilst the parents braved the various exotic concoctions which Betty's prescriptions had led her to create, no-one particularly noticed Stig of the Damp queuing up with his plate in order to partake of the fare on offer. The parents assumed that he was part of the entertainment provided, and agreed that the smell which emanated from his vicinity was jolly authentic.

No-one had noticed that Davis had been separated from the gang, and was at this moment standing in the corner of the prefect's common room, staring at his shoes, and trying not to cry. He had been lured up to the room by a haughty prefect named Winstanleigh, on the pretext of having been given a special task. He now stood red faced and fighting back tears, as he was berated by the prefects.

Piper stood with his hands on his hips, leaning over the terrified Davis, and shouting into his face, 'So what have you got to say for yourself, you useless fat little pig?'

Davis remained silent.

'You are a fat peasant. I have no doubt that your parents are morbidly obese, and that your sister is a flabby, lonely, friendless object like you are. You probably have a Labrador dog who has been so overfilled with leftovers that it looks like a drooling fur-covered barrel.'

Davis stood impassively, but his shoulders shook as he sobbed.

'What use are you to this Academy?' asked the prefect Morris.

'You don't have a waist measurement – you have a postcode,' sneered another, called Greggs.

'Oh Yah... the last time that I saw an arse as big as yours – it had a plough behind it...' laughed Hope-Stanleigh, prodding the boy.

'Why don't you leave me alone?' pleaded Davis.

'Because fatty, scum like you have no place at this Academy,' said Piper. 'You lower the tone and embarrass us all waddling around in the uniform which you have no right to wear, so why don't you clear off and leave the Academy for those who deserve it?'

'I passed my exams, I have every right to be here,' mumbled Davis.

'Don't answer me back, you little oik,' shouted Piper.

'Why not – it's better looking than your front,' said Davis.

The first blow came out of nowhere, and Davis fell sideways, hitting the door frame as he spun to the floor. There was a flurry of punches and kicks, which rained down on the poor boy as he tried in vain to protect himself. A hard kick to the stomach knocked the wind out of him, and as he tried to get up, another prefect hit him in the mouth. He was now only semi-conscious, and was sure that he had lost a tooth. He felt himself being dragged upright, then along the corridor. The prefects carried the bleeding boy down to the foot of the stone staircase, where they dropped him roughly to the floor.

'Now you breathe a word of this to your peasant friends or any of the masters, and next time it will be worse. You tell everyone that you fell down the stairs – understand?' warned Piper, and with that, the prefects departed laughing.

Seconds after they had disappeared, Nicky and the gang came around the corner of the corridor, and spotted their friend slumped against the wall. Dabbing at his mouth with a handkerchief, Calderman asked Davis, 'What the hell happened, Mark? We found half a Twix in the quad – and sent out a search party. Who did this, mate?'

Davis regarded his friends through eyes which were already beginning to swell up. 'Fell down th'stairs...' was all he could manage to mutter.

'Don't bother, Mark...' said Calderman. 'I can see the shoe prints on your uniform, and they look like expensive leather soles – worn by expensive arseholes. Okay lads- we'll clean up Mark here, then we will see how we want to deal with this.'

As the boys helped their friend to stagger away, Mrs Finucane was already busy mopping up traces of blood from the bottom of the stairs. She reached into her tabard overall, and after checking that she was quite alone in the corridor, spoke into a two-way radio...

Things had gone swimmingly at the headmaster's little gathering of the Gin-and-Thank-you-for-your-generous-donation set. Goodwill was holding court with the lady mayoress, Matron had disappeared off into her "private rooms" with Stig of the Damp, having much admired his superbly developed musculature, and Miss Piggott was still sitting on the lavatory, trying to hold the door closed whilst on her second can of air freshener. Grinning like a Cheshire cat, the head began to usher the tipsy guests out of his study and back to the throng of parents engaged in the tour of the Academy – trying to stuff various cheques on which the ink was not yet dry, deeply into the pockets in his ceremonial gown.

The crowd pressed into the English classroom, and parents and boys huddled together in anticipation as Mr Hyde-Jones introduced his protégé, one William Trevill Esquire. The boy was wearing a wig with a bald top and hair at the sides only, in the manner of the Bard of Avon (of course, loaned to him by Weatherill).

'Shakespeare is what Oi calls a Man for All Seasonings...' he began. "Oi arose, and by some other name, smelled of sheep". Who can ever forget some of Ee's most classic lines – such as (he struck a dramatic thespian pose) "Now is the winter – in a discount tent, made nauseous summer boi this 'ere ton of pork..." and who hasn't 'eard of the famous line "Is this 'ere a digger wot Oi sees afore me? A Norse, an horse, me kingdom is an arse – roll Meo, oh roll Meo, wherefore art the rodeo?"' Trevill, now completely in the swing of it all, clambered up onto a handy desk and proclaimed '"Two Bees are not Tubby! That's the question Oi tell Ee... Whether 'tis knobblyer in this 'ole to suffer the slingin' of marrows, for a contagious fortune – or take up in yer arms the disease of truffles – and by supposing, bend 'em..."'

The boy took in the sea of astonished faces which surrounded him. Trevill in full flow was an unstoppable force, against which Nature had no defence. Hyde-Jones was crying with laughter at the back.

'"To sleep – per chance with cream, and there's the rubber..."' declared Trevill, bowing low to his adoring and amazed audience. 'And his girlfriend, Anne, was in fact an Avon lady.'

'I thank 'Ee one and all...' said Trevill. 'Ladies an' gentlemen – all the wheels are sage, and we are merely potaters, an' if Ee cut us – it don't arf bleedin' 'urt, Oi tell Ee...'

The room was shaken by the applause which erupted. Hyde-Jones walked through the crowd and ruffled the boy's hair whilst still wiping his eyes. 'Trevill...' he declared. 'You're a bloody genius.'

By now all of the boys in Nicky's form had been told about the attack on their friend Davis, and it had taken some severe negotiation led by Calderman, Jackson and Merry to prevent Mob Rule taking over in order to exact revenge.

Piper was in fact engaged in another act of vengeance against the boys– which he hoped would bring about their expulsion from the school. He and a couple of his sycophantic hangers-on were outside the form room of Nicky and the gang. They had just discharged three of the fire extinguishers along the corridor, all the way to the stairs, and were standing outside the doors to the chemistry laboratory watching as the water rippled its way along the parquet wooden floor.

'Right fellows...' laughed Piper, 'now let's get over to the Dark Tower and seal the fate of our little peasants, shall we?'

Piper had already grabbed the attention of Dr Chambers, and had led him into the assembly hall in order to show him the trail of flaky pastry crumbs that led from the rear of the stage. The fact that Mrs Bradley had reported the disappearance of several pies just as Piper was talking to the deputy head was too good a coincidence to waste, and rather than merely report the boys for having been in the hall without good reason, he had been able to creep in ahead of Dr Chambers and liberally distribute fragments of piecrust about the stage. He now took the bemused deputy head over to the Tower and around to the side garden. He pointed out the small door which appeared to have been forced from the inside. Chambers inspected the door with a forensic eye.

Piper declared in mock horror, 'I mean, sir, my only concern is the fact that the boys could have been seriously injured, sir, and the notices to keep out are quite clear. It really is irresponsible and dangerous to have come in here, sir, but I suppose that we must expect village boys not to have respect for instructions, sir..'

Chambers regarded the prefect suspiciously, but grunted in agreement.

'And sir, I was wondering who might have been responsible for the damage, when I came across this...' He produced a crumpled and rather stained white handkerchief. Chambers took the item carefully, and unfolded it. There in the corner was the sewn-in name tag of the owner. The handkerchief would appear to belong to G MERRY.

'We appear to have our culprit named and shamed Mr Piper,' said Chambers.

'Indeed, sir, but I am certain that he and his band of anti-establishment rebels had a hand in the liberation of DeVere from the Boarding House, sir,' said Piper, grinning behind Chambers' back. 'I wasn't going to bother you with this, sir, but earlier on I chased one of their group out of the corridor where he was not supposed to be, sir, and he fell on the stairs. When I went back to check if he was injured, I found, sir, that he and his accomplices had flooded the top corridor out of spite, sir...'

Without comment, Chambers turned and walked briskly across the quad, waving away Mrs Finucane as she attempted to get his attention. He strode up the stone steps two at a time, pausing at the top, when he was greeted by a very small waterfall making its way down the steps in a leisurely fashion. 'Do you have any idea who is responsible for all this calamity?' he asked the prefect. 'This is the last thing we need on a day like today. I want names, Piper, and I want them now.'

There was virtually no pause between the last syllable of Chamber's words and Piper's instant reply – 'Merry, Calderman, Davis, Jackson, Trevill and Shepherd, sir- and don't forget DeVere, sir, who has absconded again , sir...'

'Mr DeVere has been captured and is being brought back to the fold,' said Chambers. 'I want the other boys sent to the headmaster's Office as soon as the mayoress has given out the prizes at the awards ceremony. I feel that I shall have to recommend severe action be taken over the conduct of these pupils. I commend your diligence, Mr Piper, it shall not go unrewarded,' he added.

The master sped off to organise a clean-up on the corridor, and Piper strode off with his hands in his pockets, enjoying the satisfaction of a job well done.

Darwin was revelling in the attention of the crowd of visitors who had thronged into the biology laboratory. He had instructed Bernie to lay out microscopes on all of the benches, and prepare the scene as if it were part of a forensic police unit as seen on television. There was the all-pervading smell of formaldehyde within the room. The lady mayoress walked between the benches, glancing with some barely-concealed revulsion at the poor laboratory rats, which had been laid out on boards as if awaiting dissection. Kendy and Merry had managed to insinuate themselves into the party, and Merry had prompted Kendy to utilise his "special talents" in order to liven up the proceedings. Whilst Darwin urged the mayoress to look at a particularly interesting microscope slide, Kendy sidled up to the last bench, where another unfortunate rodent lay supine upon its board. Concentrating hard, the boy gently stroked its cheek, then melted back into the crowd of observers. The mayoress had now moved to the last work station. She leapt back from the bench in fright, Mayoral chain of office swinging wildly, when the rat suddenly stood up, looked around at the crowd – then threatened the horrified Dr Darwin with a scalpel – before making an obscene gesture to the onlookers, and fleeing out of the door.

Having been revived with soothing words and smelling-salts, the confused mayoress was led out of the room by a contrite and apologetic Darwin, and taken over to the physics laboratory. As the audience of visitors left the lab, Bernie's deep, coarse laughter could be heard right the way up the narrow corridor.

It was destined to be a day which the poor lady was unlikely to ever forget. Professor Strangler had taken the unprecedented step of showing off his "Wormhole". (Oh please – do let's try and be adult about this, if you don't mind...). He had ranted on about Temporal and Magnetic Flux vortices, and attempted to give a practical demonstration of the phenomena by dropping a ball of waste paper into the vortex. Whoever the recipient of the paper ball was, and whatever epoch of time the vortex led into, the person at the receiving end took great exception to his cross-dimensional littering. Strangler stood back and addressed his attentive group: 'And that, Lady Mayoress and gentlemen, is the effect whi- OW! BASTARD!' Back through the vortex had come quite a large rock, which struck the professor squarely on the side of the head...

'Fifteen Love...' called an unseen voice.

Chapter Twenty-Eight

With a glazed expression, and a very nervous twitch, the mayoress was ushered by kind and caring hands into the assembly hall for the prize-giving ceremony. The hall had been set up with a long highly-polished table on the left hand side of the stage. The plan was that boys receiving prizes would ascend the steps stage left, collect their award from the lady mayoress at the table, and after a brief chat with the visiting dignitary, exit stage right down the other steps and back into the audience. Having completed their duties as "tour guides", the boys had returned to the hall where they stood to attention in well-groomed rows.

Doctor Gerald Goodwill led in the staff and esteemed visitors. He whispered to the mayoress, who seemed to have recovered some of her composure, and walked over to the lectern. In time-honoured fashion, he pulled the lectern into its required central position. Nailed to the front, was a large black wellington boot.

Goodwill gave a slight nod in the direction of Mr Newhouse at the organ, who immediately began to crash out the tune "Oh I Do Like To Be Beside The Seaside" until a very audible cough from the head halted the melody. Once the laughter had subsided, Goodwill called for the singing of the Academy anthem. When this was finished, all were agreed that it had been totally uncalled for.

'Welcome gentlemen, Lady Mayoress, parents and Onanists past and present,' began Goodwill. 'Today we have the very great honour of having the mayoress – well, not actually having – I mean I've not actually had – I mean she is doing us the great honour of attending our Academy. She will be handing out the Founders' Day prizes for academic achievement, and musical prowess, and of course the Sporting Victor Ludorum...'

Nicky wondered who the hell "Victor Ludorum" was. Jackson wondered why he had obviously not shown up. Trevill wondered why they were awarding prizes for Ludo...

The boys were all smartly attired in their best dress uniform. The lads had done their best to get Davis presentable following his beating, and he stood nervously between Calderman and Merry. Even the recalcitrant Weatherill had followed the instruction of the deputy head as far as dress standards were concerned. The boy stood surrounded by his friends with an angelic smile on his face. He had done as he was instructed, and was wearing his tie–

Just the tie...

Scarcely daring to look over at the cherubic smile which beamed back at her, the mayoress leaned over to the headmaster and whispered, 'Why is that boy naked..?'

The panicked head took a second to scan the ranks of his pupils, until he located the source of the problem near the rear of the hall. 'Ahh... Sorry ma'am, that boy is a strict Episcopal Penitent, and it would appear to be the Festival Day of St Ephraim of the Divine Peasecod – it has fallen early this year as I am sure you are aware... We at St Onan's are proud to respect religious diversity in all its many forms.'

The Lady Mayoress fell silent. Goodwill glared at Weatherill. The boy smiled back.

So began the handing out of the prizes for all manner of excellence. There were sashes for sporting prowess, books, badges and tokens for literary success, and a host of strangely-shaped cups and trophies for everything from Mathematics to Art and Drama. Goodwill was praying to any god which he thought might possibly be listening, that the boy Weatherill had not won any manner of award. He began to make a mental list of the more remote islands within the South Seas, to which a chap might retire, just in case his worst fears were realised.

Some boys strode up the steps in a proud and manly fashion to collect their award. Others seemed rather embarrassed to be singled out in front of their fellow pupils. One or two crept up the steps like escaped prisoners, desperate not to be recognised by the public at large. At that very moment, one of St Onan's own escaped prisoners was being returned to the confines of the Academy. DeVere had made it home, only to find that his father had been called away to France on a business trip. The rest of the family had decided to go with him for a short break, and after several nights spent sleeping in haystacks along the way, poor David had returned with his heart bursting with joy, only to find an empty house... A concerned neighbour had taken him in and fed the starving boy, and had disclosed the destination of the family holiday. DeVere had immediately raided his piggy bank, and set off in hot pursuit – only to be apprehended at the port of Calais by an eagle-eyed gendarme with the worst case of anti-English prejudice and halitosis that he had ever come across.

He now sat cowed and gloomy in the back seat of the large car which belonged to one of the Academy porters. Dr Chambers had been sent out to supervise the collection of DeVere, and he was busy delivering an eye-watering dressing-down to the boy.

DeVere asked, 'Excuse me, sir... but are you by any chance related to any French policemen?'

'Why the hell are you asking me that?' demanded Chambers in furious tones.

'Just wondered, sir...' answered DeVere.

With the prospect of taking part in some ritual humiliation of one of the younger boys, Piper and some of his lackeys had made their way outside "to assist the deputy head". As the boy was roughly manhandled out of the car by two burly porters, Piper leaned toward the boy and demanded, 'Why must you insist on absconding all of the time, DeVere?- what is wrong with you boy?' DeVere looked him defiantly in the eye and replied.

'Because this place is the opposite of a hedgehog, that's why.'

Piper and Chambers looked puzzled. 'Be so kind as to explain that remark,' said the deputy head.

DeVere pulled out of the grip of the porter who was holding him, squared up to Piper, and without showing any trace of fear informed him, 'Because with a hedgehog – all the pricks are on the outside...' The two porters had to turn away and have a hearty private giggle.

Back in the hall, there was a whispered conversation going on between Kendy, Calderman, Nicky, Merry and the boys. 'Go on – please do it Jon, you know that he deserves it, and look what he has done to our friend Davis. You can help us get our own back...'

'Well, I really don't think that I ought to,' said Kendy, looking doubtful. 'I mean, won't I get into terrible trouble if I do it?'

'No, mate – but that pompous prat certainly will. Look – you owe it to the gang to help us get even with Piper, and this is the best way to do it. Please, Kendy, give it a go for the lads eh?' Nicky pleaded.

Kendy looked from one friend to the other, then at the battle-scarred Davis. He made up his mind. 'Right...' he declared. 'I will just need to study him for a few seconds, to get it right.'

'He's outside, shouting something at Dave DeVere – have a quick look out of the window,' said Merry.

Kendy made his way to the large glass pane which looked out over the quad. He stared intently at Piper for almost a minute, only stepping back when the prefect glanced up at the window. 'Got it, chaps...' he said 'Now I need to hold it until I am ready.' At that point, the headmaster announced that a special "Mentor Award" was to be presented to the pupil who had shown the most caring and skilled leadership for the term. The award had apparently been voted upon by the prefects, and there would be no extra prizes given out for guessing just who the likely recipient of the award would be... Money talks, and the boys could already hear it calling for a servant to throw another polo pony onto the fire.

'And so it is with great pleasure, that I award the Mentor prize to one of our hard-working prefects, Mr Bertrand Aloysius Piper II of School House.' The head attempted to start the applause, with which only the prefects and a couple of staff members joined in. From the mass of the assembled pupils, there came the sound of muted hissing.

'Now Kendy – Go for it!' urged Nicky. Kendy began to walk forward through the throng of boys, but it was Piper who ascended the steps to the stage in his usual arrogant manner, and extended a hand for the mayoress to have the privilege of shaking. The whole audience fell silent as Piper collected the small trophy, and the envelope containing the cheque. He smiled as he walked calmly to the centre of the stage, and then stopped and turned his back to the crowd. There was a dramatic pause of several seconds as he did nothing. Suddenly, and without warning, Piper dropped his immaculately-pressed trousers to floor level, and bent over to expose his backside to the entire hall. There were gasps of astonishment and disbelief from the boys, and a resounding crash from the left hand side of the stage as the lady mayoress fainted and fell to the floor. Pandemonium erupted, and in the confusion that followed, Piper made a dash out of the rear stage doors. No-one could hear the frantic banging on the hall window, or the cries of despair uttered by the real Mr Bertrand Aloysius Piper II, who had to his horror just seen himself flash his arse to the whole Academy and staff...

As the stunned mayoress was stretchered out to the ambulance which had been called, the Head Master (now bordering on a state of complete hysteria) was being comforted by his wife (whose own borderings were almost complete wistaria). Dr Chambers reappeared in the hall, and whispered into the ear of the man, passing him a handwritten list of some description. Goodwill studied the list. He cleared his throat, gripped the sides of the table for support, and barked out 'THE FOLLOWING BOYS WILL REPORT TO MY STUDY IMMEDIATELY – CALDERMAN, MERRY, SHEPHERD, JACKSON, DAVIS, TREVILL...'

'Why all the fuss, eh Shep?' said Calderman.

'Dunno, mate,' said Nicky. 'It must be a full moon...'

Chapter Twenty-Nine

The little group of boys made their way up the path to the headmaster's study, slowly and in complete silence. None of them wanted to the first to reach the door, and be the first casualty in the war of words which they were sure was about to follow. The path seemed to stretch far into the distance as they walked, and Nicky was sure that he saw the ravens gathering in the tree on the lawn, no doubt to pick over the remains when the head had finished with them. They halted before the main door, looking at each other in trepidation. It was too late to get a plan together – or to build a convincing alibi. Anyway, there was no telling what they were about to be accused of.

Miss Piggott was already waiting at the study door, with a barely-concealed look of contempt on her face. Without speaking to the boys, she flung wide the door, and permitted them entry to the dragon's lair. Nicky heard the door close behind them with the sound of the door closing on a condemned cell.

Already seated behind the head's tidy desk were Dr Chambers and the head himself. Whatever conversation had passed between the two men prior to the arrival of the boys, had hardened their attitudes to steel. Dr Goodwill's normal manner was one of gentle eccentricity, like a favoured grandfather who had recently taken to wearing his underpants on his head. Now he sat before them with his face set, completely devoid of any emotion. This was not just anger; this was the expressionless fury that chills the soul, drawing out energy from the air and leaving a fearsome vacuum. Miss Piggott scampered around to the side of the desk and sat down. She picked up a new notepad, and attempted to release the pen which had attached itself to the string which her glasses dangled on.

The boys stood in a nervous line at the edge of the carpet. It was Dr Chambers who spoke first, in words chosen carefully for their forensic precision.

'You have been called here in respect of certain incidents and behaviours which the head and I consider to be in direct conflict with the standards of conduct and behaviour expected at this Academy. Several occurrences have been brought to our attention, all of which it would appear, involve you boys in some capacity. I refer to the theft of comestibles from the Academy kitchens, damage to the fabric of the Academy building, trespass into areas clearly marked as "out of bounds" to boys, wilful and flagrant violation of Academy uniform codes, and vandalism in the old block corridor – which may as yet cost the Academy a significant sum to repair...'

He paused, and continued. 'Gentlemen... the founders of this noble enclave established this school and its curriculum because they had a vision...' (This was true – and if they had studied it in any sort of depth, then they would have told the founders to shove their vision right up their collective arse – but that's hindsight for you...)

'The founders hoped to raise and maintain the very highest standards of morals and behaviour amongst their charges – standards which it would appear that you boys wish to pay no heed to whatsoever,' he stated.

'Should such charges be proven, and likewise your actions proven to be complicit in same, then we must consider very severe penalties against all of you. I am particularly appalled that these actions have occurred in your first few days at the Academy, and, gentlemen... this does not bode well for either your reputations, or your future at this establishment – which may well prove to be considerably shorter than any of you may have envisaged...'

Right – so they were all well and truly in the deep end. There didn't seem to be any grey areas in Chamber's narrative – but all of the lads could see a very deep brown one.

'We will begin with the theft of foodstuffs from the kitchen. Have any of you any valid explanation as to why you thought it appropriate to misappropriate pies from Mrs Bradley?'

'Dr Chambers... it doesn't look very good to use "appropriate" and "misappropriate" together in one sentence...' said Miss Piggott, who was furiously taking notes.

She was silenced, as both men turned to face her slowly, and subjected her to twin stares of disapproval. She hurriedly hunched back over her notepad, and an awkward silence settled on the room. Finally, Chambers could stand no more, and shouted 'PIES – FOR GOD'S SAKE... WHO TOOK ALL THE PIES?'

Nicky was just about to attempt some vague explanation, when Calderman came to his rescue. 'Sir, I will be the first to admit on behalf of my friends and I that we did in fact take pies out of the kitchen. We accompanied our friend Weatherill to the kitchens, sir, as he urgently needed a glass of water, because he was feeling ill. The pies were on the side worktop, sir, not in the serving area, and we thought that they were a batch of products which Mrs Bradley had discarded as unfit to serve, sir.'

'Why did you think it acceptable to steal them?' asked Chambers.

'Sir, we merely thought that we could save Mrs Bradley and her staff the trouble of disposing of them- and perform a charitable service at the same time...'

'How so, Mr Calderman...?'

'Well, sir, we boys have become increasingly aware of the increasing proportion of the population of the town who do not have the advantages that we have been given. It cannot have escaped your notice that there are rising numbers of people either sleeping on the streets, or begging. We decided that along with the need to educate ourselves at this venerable Academy in order that we can make the world a better place, should, and surely must, come the social responsibility to extend care and support outside these walls to those who we can see are in desperate need of it. We were merely attempting – albeit on a small scale, sir, to provide food for those who it would appear were in urgent need of it. We thought that this would be an action with which the Founders would have been happy, bearing in mind their own attempts to stave off hunger and poverty by means of philanthropic intervention...'

'You gave away food to the hungry?' asked Chambers.

'Indeed, sir- what other motive could we possibly have?'

'Without asking permission?' Chambers queried...

'We do not seek any recognition, sir... just the knowledge of a good deed done for its own sake,' said Calderman.

'I see... And the damage to the storeroom wall?'

Merry seized the moment, 'We did not damage the storeroom wall, sir. We did investigate when our friend DeVere brought the damage to our attention, but we did not cause the damage. We were told that part of the wall had somehow collapsed, but could not discuss the matter further, sir, as DeVere did not seem to be on the premises...'

'There is also the matter of trespass into the area of the Dark Tower. The area is very clearly marked "out of bounds", and yet you chose to gain entry.'

'We were lookin' for our, mate, DeVere, Surr... ' began Trevill, 'with 'im not bein' settled at the Academy an' all, it were a bit of a worry to everyone, Surr... We didn't loike the thought of 'im bein' stuck or injured in there Surr... so we'em goin' to 'ave a quick butchers to make sure Ee 'adn't come to any misfortune, Surr – out of brotherly concern, you might say...'

'Might you then be able to say something concerning the flooding of the upper corridor then, gentlemen?' asked the disbelieving Chambers.

Jackson pulled himself up to his full height. 'Sir, you will have noted that the level of standing water in the corridor upon your initial inspection was quite significant. The water had only just begun to flow down the steps to the lower floor. We were not in the corridor at the time, as we were all in the assembly hall; moreover, it is not permitted for boys to be in the corridors or classrooms outside lesson times,' he said. 'Had the alleged offence been perpetrated earlier, sir, then the water would have soaked into the parquet flooring to a much more severe degree, and the steps to the lower floor would have all been wet with the cascade of water coming down them from the corridor above...'

'So...?' said the deputy head.

'So we weren't there, and didn't do it, sir – that is my point...' answered Jackson.

Chambers stared at the boy for a moment, and then opened the headmaster's desk drawer, and pulled out a crumpled handkerchief, 'Mr Merry – can you explain to us why this item was found in the annexe garden passage near a damaged door to the Dark Tower? I believe that the name tag sewn onto the item would seem to clearly indicate you as the owner of the item?'

'I have no idea why my handkerchief could have been found near the Tower, sir...' said Merry. 'Seeing as I gave it to my friend Davis, when we found that he had been beaten up and left bleeding in the lower corridor, sir...'

The two masters looked aghast at each other. Goodwill removed his glasses, and said, 'Step forward, Davis, let's have a look at you, boy.' He studied the boy's facial injuries and swollen eye, before declaring, 'Looks like you just played a game with the First XV, son – better get Matron to see to that eye...'

'Who did this, Davis?' asked Chambers. The boy did not answer.

'Oh do come along Davis... we cannot tolerate this sort of thing at all – we can't have chaps physically assaulted unless it's during games period,' said Goodwill.

To hell with not 'snitching' on your fellows. It was about time that Piper and his cronies were exposed for the bullying scum which they were. Nicky answered...

'It was Piper and some prefects, sir' he said. The masters looked shocked. 'We have all been picked on and bullied from day one, Sir, and Piper and his gang are always pushing us around and telling us that we have no right to be here at the Academy. That's why Davis was beaten up, that's why DeVere keeps on trying to escape, and that's why the prefects have planted evidence to make it look as if we have done all of these things...' He felt anger rising from within him, and seeing as how they were in trouble anyway, he thought, 'What the hell...' and continued, 'and to be honest, sir, if all that this place can teach you is how to behave in an evil way to anyone who you don't think is up to your social standing – then you can stuff it! I will be happy to remain a village peasant thank you so very much.'

'I feel you have said quite enough, Mr Shepherd,' said Chambers.

'I shall speak to the headmaster about what course of action we feel is appropriate. This will include an interview with Mr Piper, who I am led to believe did the image of the Academy an uncharacteristic disservice this afternoon, and I shall inform you of what you may expect in respect of punishment. I feel that I must point out that at this moment, we are very much given to considering your immediate expulsion. The head will write to inform your parents. You, gentlemen, will await our further deliberations – now get out...'

The friends filed out of the head's study with heads hung low. Each of them was playing out the scene in his head when the letter arrived informing the parents of how and why their son had been expelled. Although the visions contained differing degrees of shouting and thrown items of household cutlery, the essential script would be the same in every household.

Just then, the smirking spectre of Miss Piggott appeared behind them. 'Ger– that is… the headmaster has instructed that you are all banned from this evening's music concert for parents..' she stated.

'Thank you, Miss Piggy...' said Calderman, graciously.

'Oi wonder 'ow old she is in human years?' said Trevill.

Merry addressed the gang. 'Well, lads, it looks like we are really in for it now. We will probably be marched out of the Academy in disgrace. By the look on Chambers' face it might be the firing squad...'

'The situation is indeed grave. We need help, chaps, specialist help from a very specialised team,' said Calderman. 'Who we gonna call?'

'Toff-Busters!' chorused the gang.

'You better believe it – right, Kendy and Merry, you try and find Mrs Finucane – Trevill and Davis, you go and see Albert up at the Games Field. Shep, didn't you say that your Uncle Joe was a solicitor?' asked Calderman.

'No – he was once accused of soliciting, I think...'

'Well best double-check; because we will need all the assistance we can get on this one.'

The boys split up and went about their covert errands. The cheerful and ever-friendly Mrs Finucane was found enjoying a crafty cigarette behind the gymnasium bin area – and was given a full account of proceedings so far. She listened patiently as the facts were explained to her. She then nodded sagely, and said, 'Don't be worryin' about it, me boyos, I'll contact ODD headquarters immediately, and sort out something suitable for himself as thinks he's Top Dog...'

Albert Brooks had already been contacted by Agent J-Cloth by the time that the boys met him on the games fields. He had startled the boys by appearing as if from nowhere by abseiling down from the changing-room roof in full combat gear. He promised swift and immediate action, and to be truthful, neither boy cared just how violent or unpleasant that action might be.

Nicky had a flash of inspiration. There was indeed some extremely learned authority that would be able to advise him on what to do about the threat of expulsion. If anyone had the answer, then this chap was the one to see. He could not risk being seen calling on him, but he knew the telephone number on which his potential saviour could be reached...

Sneaking over the road, Nicky counted out what loose change he had, and began dropping coins into the slot of the telephone box. He looked up at the wall opposite, and discovered that the Publicity Department for Wendy had been very thorough indeed in their coverage of the area. The writing above his head declared in capital letters that she "did it" in this telephone box too. He also noted a small card tucked behind the steel frame of the instruction panel, and was immediately struck by the resemblance of the lady offering "Specialist Services" to the Academy's own Matron. The telephone was answered after five rings, and the deep, cultured voice which he had been expecting introduced itself. Nicky explained in some detail the circumstances in which he and the gang now found themselves, and the voice answered with brief comments of, 'I see...' 'Please continue...' and, 'Indeed...' At the end of the call, Nicky asked, or rather pleaded for help. The voice instructed him that he was well aware of the ill-treatment meted out to some of the poorer boys. He also informed Nicky that it was very likely that he and his friends would be called back to the headmaster's office tomorrow morning. He told him that he was fully aware of the head's daily routines, and that he would personally telephone the head at 10.34 a.m., as he knew that he regularly walked his dog shortly prior to that time. He reassured the boy that he would render him whatever assistance might be necessary in order to resolve the matter swiftly, and with the minimum of fuss. He assured Nicky that his bite and his bark were of equal degree of severity when required.

Nicky thanked him profusely, just before his money ran out. He crept back into the Academy and sought out his friends. 'Okay, gang,' he told them. 'I've managed to get some pressure of a legal nature brought to bear on Goodwill – I'm sure that my contact will do his best for us.'

'What do you think the Old Geezer and Chamberpot will do about Piper and his performing jacksie show?' asked Merry.

'He'll have to do something,' said Jackson. 'I heard that the mayoress has refused to attend the evening concert – and has vowed never to set foot in the Academy again.'

'Wot will Ee do to 'im do you think?' asked Trevill.

'He'll most likely be charged with arson – sorry!' laughed Nicky.

The boys disbanded and set off for their respective bus stops. Nicky was suddenly a bundle of nervous tension, as the gravity of the potential consequences began to sink in. He sat on the bus and stared out at the passing scenery without paying any attention whatsoever. How on earth was he going to explain to his mother and Auntie... He was dreading the conversation.

'Hello, dear, how did you get on at school today?'

'Great thanks, Mum. I met up with the lads, showed parents around, went to the prize-giving, and er... got slightly expelled.'

What he was dreading most of all was the anticipated look of disappointment which he knew would come from Mum. Auntie would most likely call him a silly prat and give him a clip round the ear, but it was letting them both down that made his heart sink. There would probably not even be a long lecture; he might be left to mull over his mistake on his own, in complete silence. To make matters worse, he could only imagine the humiliation which Mrs Hislop would bestow upon his mother when she found out that he had not even completed a full first term at St Onan's. Her false and over-dramatic sympathy would be too much to take, and the speed of her gossiping would mean that most of the planets of the Solar System would know all about it well before lunchtime. He would be outcast, and pointed at in the street. Crowds of villagers would drive him out with pitchforks and burning torches, and effigies of him would be burned on ceremonial bonfires on the village playing field. Clergymen and nuns would seek him out, and would shout rude words at him. Small children would be encouraged to throw stones at him in the street. Dave the Chicken would attack him and peck mercilessly at his – 'OI! THIS IS YOUR STOP.'

The call of the bus driver broke the spell, and Nicky more or less fell off the bus in panic. Wait a minute... as long as he got to the post first, he could mislay any letter from the Academy before it could fall into friendly hands. With luck, his legal contact would be able to press the "stop" button on the moving staircase of terror – and stop things escalating...

Yeah... Panic over, he thought, failing utterly to convince himself one iota.

As it turned out, events were overtaken by a small family-sized bargain crisis. There was a telephone call from the police at around seven o'clock. Mum took the call, and was some time talking to the constabulary on the other end of the line. It would appear that Cousin Sheila had visited a zoo with some of her fellow inmates as part of a "Girls Only" night out. After what the officer referred to only as "an incident", it would appear that Cousin Sheila gained possession of a rather lively young male okapi. She thought that it was a capital idea to take it home on their mini-bus, with a view to keeping it as a pet in her third-floor flat – or selling it on E-Bay as an unwanted gift should things not work out as planned. They didn't.

The enraged okapi did a considerable amount of damage in a very meaningful way to the inside of the hired mini-bus. The dry-cleaning bill for the rest of the passengers alone was likely to run into hundreds of pounds, as a frightened okapi tends to have a loud noise at one end – and a complete lack of discretion at the other. How the creature was loaded into a taxi was a mystery. More puzzling still, was how Cousin Sheila had got it up to her flat in the lift. Mother listened very patiently to the concerned policeman, and then suggested that they free the okapi without charge and return Cousin Sheila to the zoo – before hanging up the telephone. Hopefully, the zoo would not have a captive breeding programme...

Nicky had a very restless night. What little sleep he managed to achieve was interrupted by frightening dreams where he was being led in chains to the gallows, on a foggy morning, which was very cold, and wearing trousers of a rough material that he knew were not his own. He awoke with a start, and immediately put on the clothing of dread, which had hung all through the night in the wardrobe of shame. Right then, the plan... He had to act casually, but make sure that he was as near to the front door as possible, ready to snatch the written evidence of his misdemeanours as soon as it fell through the letterbox. He carefully lifted the flap of the letterbox and scanned the road through the slit – no sign of the cheery, whistling postman going about his morning walk, or the miserable grouchy old bastard that delivered their post either. Mum made him toast. He ate the toast sitting on the small seat just inside the front door. The letterbox gave a rattle. He dropped the toast (yes of course, butter side down). Oh my Lord – there was no letter from the Academy. He yanked open the door and called to the postman, 'Is that all?'

Postie answered, 'Oh deary me... now you come to mention it, I've got a cheque here addressed to you for two million quid – yes, that is all you're gettin' – you cheeky little bleeder.' He closed the door quietly.

He handed the letters to Mum with a sense of relief. She took them with a sense of sticky distaste, as he had handed over a well-buttered piece of his toast with the envelopes.

Wiping her hand on a tea towel, Mum asked, 'Is everything all right? You do seem a little jumpy this morning.'

'Sorry Mum, I didn't get much sleep,' he answered, hoping that relief didn't show on his face.

He got ready for the ritual of the daily bus ride to town. The satchel made a spirited attempt to strangle him with its strap, but he was ready for the attack, and knotted the leather with force in order to shorten it. He was already playing out in his mind just how things were likely to go during his meeting with the headmaster later on that morning, and hoped that his friends were doing the same. He was also hoping that Kendy would remember to bring his Death ray Laser gun in case things didn't go too well.

Shortly before Nicky arrived at the Academy, things were about to go not so very well at all for Mr Piper. He had once again located and isolated Davis in a corner of the quad, and was haranguing the boy with a view to preventing any disclosure of his actions on the previous day. Davis as usual, stood in the corner, with his head bowed and a large plaster over his left eye.

'The point is Davis, you loathsome overweight little oaf, that I enjoy a certain standing within this Academy, and so if you have any intention of blackening my character by making false and spurious accusations against me, no-one will believe you. There is no good running to the headmaster and telling tales, because Daddy plays golf with old Goodwill, and got him into the Freemasons. Rest assured, you little tick, it doesn't matter how well you think that you have done to get here, you and your ilk are never going to aspire to anything significant. No matter how hard you may work, and however hard you may turn the pages with your fat fingers, I will always beat you to a better job, a much bigger house, and a much grander salary – because my father is an Earl...'

Davis stood up straight, and looked the surprised prefect directly in the eye. 'Look Piper – my father is a clergyman. Every night I say my prayers, and I can honestly say that those small prayers have been answered.'

'Oh really, Fat Boy?...' said Piper, turning to laugh with his cronies.

'Oh yes indeed. My prayers have been answered – because I have not grown up to be a self-loving, pompous, overbearing, toffee-nosed, pretentious, arrogant, sententious, conceited supercilious little arsehole like you...'

Piper moved to strike the boy, but noticed out of the corner of his eye a sign which had been hung on the wall of the physics block. There was a large white piece of card about three feet square, suspended by string at each top corner. Written upon the card in large capital letters was the legend "PIPER IS A POMPOUS TWAT". The prefect was incandescent with fury, and ran over to the wall, where he began to make frantic leaps up at the sign, which hung tantalisingly just out of reach. By now, boys had begun to arrive in the quad, and a circle had formed around the screeching prefect.

However high the prefect attempted to leap, the sign hung there, just defiantly out of reach of his clawing fingers. There were flecks of foam in the corner of his mouth as he bellowed at his entourage, 'Well don't just stand there you buffoons, give me a hand.' He pulled two of the prefects toward the wall, and forced them to bend over and give him a platform on which to stand. The others followed like sheep, and formed a pyramid, up which the angry Piper began to climb. 'Someone is going to be bloody sorry that they did this...' he growled, as his fingers finally gripped the bottom of the notice. He shakily stood up, and gripped the sign with both hands, and gave it a vicious tug. The sign came away in his hands. Someone was instantly very sorry that they had done this, oh yes indeed. Balanced on the deep cill of the first floor window, was a large plastic garden flower trough. It had been attached to the sign by fishing line at both front corners.

The surrounding farmlands around the Academy were famous for producing the very finest potatoes, beans, peas and brussel sprouts. The local pig farms also produced a great deal of pig manure. It was a mixture of such waste (both liquid and slightly more solid) that cascaded down into the upturned face of, and over, the Piper-topped pyramid of prefects. There was now a writhing heap of foul-smelling humanoid shapes in the quad. Piper sat up, almost in tears, and wiped the effluent from his eyes. As he did so, a small white business card floated down from heaven and stuck to his forehead. He gingerly peeled the card from his head, and read the inscription. It said... "This has been an ODD job".

The fascinated audience of boys behind them applauded wildly, then scattered...

Piper had an early appointment with the headmaster, following yesterday's unexpected revelation, in which he revealed something which no-one expected... Firstly, he had to dash back to the Boarding House and scrub himself clean, and seek out a uniform which did not smell of little piggies.

The head had lectured Piper on the subject of behaviour expected by Academy Prefects, and the laws governing indecent exposure. Having seen himself do the deed in question, even Piper was not arrogant enough to deny the offence. 'It was a skilled make-up job, sir, designed to ruin my reputation and make me look a fool in front of the Academy,' was all he could muster.

'And from where I was standing, they bloody well succeeded!' was the response from Goodwill. 'Anyway, on the telephone, I have someone who wishes to speak with you, it would appear that he is a little upset at your performance...' The head passed the telephone over to Piper.

On the line was his father. The conversation went on for some time, with Piper standing in complete silence, but going red in the face, then white, then ashen grey. After some minutes, the prefect handed back the receiver to the head. 'Thank you, sir. He's gone.'

'Yes, Piper... and I'm afraid that so are you,' said Goodwill.

'Pardon, sir?'

'You will pack your things. You will finish term early. You will not attend the Academy drama production or the church service. You may consider yourself expelled, pending reports. I have heard of your bullying, and witnessed your loutish behaviour – I shall tolerate neither. Get out.'

Piper left the head's study in shock, and slunk across the quad with only a swarm of flies for company. His normal ostentatious strut had been replaced by the slouch of the recently shamed. Ignoring the calls of his fellow prefects, he made his way up the stairs to the prefects' common room. This enclave of the privileged was set out with comfy chairs, a large study table, and lockers which filled one wall. He flung himself onto the tattered sofa. His world had just come crashing down around him (damn those peasants) and he suddenly felt eight years old again, standing in front of his father in the study – as he was told that he was to be torn from the bosom of his family and sent away to Boarding School. He shuddered at the memory, and his conscience jabbed at him with a sharp finger for what he had allowed himself to become. In his locker was a secret gift from an uncle – a bottle of fine brandy, and he felt that his nerves needed a small nip of the forbidden fluid.

Just then, his friend Hugo opened the door. 'I say, Pipes, old chap – is everything okay?'

'I just want a little time on my own Hugo, do me a favour and lock the door on your way out will you?' he replied.

His friend did as he was told, and Piper helped himself to a glass of the brandy from his locker. He sat on the sofa and rolled a cigarette. (Two forbidden acts in one day – but what did it matter now?) Lying full-length on the ragged furniture, he took a long pull on the cigarette, and contemplated his possible options. Another glass of brandy followed, and then another, with another badly-rolled cigarette as a side order. In no time at all, he drifted off into sleep, the cigarette falling from his limp hand, and down between the floorboards. It was a matter of minutes before the accumulated detritus of the years which lay beneath the floorboards began to smoulder...

Chapter Thirty

Nicky, Calderman, Kendy, Trevill, Davis, Merry and Weatherill stood in front of the headmaster's desk, looking as apprehensive as the queue for a cross-eyed dentist, with a nervous twitch. It was 10.29 a.m. by the clock behind the desk. Goodwill began his speech:

'As headmaster of this noble Academy, there are very few things which I absolutely insist upon. I insist on the very finest standards of education, and the highest standards of punctuality and conduct from all pupils. It is this high standard that sets us apart from the "Other Establishments" in the area, who have the temerity to call themselves "Schools". They are nothing more than zoos full of young tearaways. I will not have delinquent behaviour exhibited within these walls. This leads me to ponder what my course of action should be, when faced with young men who show no regard for the standards expected of them.'

The group of boys were startled when the telephone on the desk suddenly shrilled into life. Goodwill fumbled the receiver, and ended up attempting to speak into it upside-down. The boys could clearly hear the clipped tones of Miss Piggott saying, 'Sorry to interrupt, headmaster, but I have a call from a gentleman identifying himself as "Barker", who insists on speaking with you.'

'Very well, Emilia – put him through,' said Goodwill. It was 10.34 a.m. precisely.

A very calm, cultured yet determined voice spoke to the headmaster, causing him to sit up straight in his chair. The caller informed the head that he had been made aware of "certain punitive actions that were currently under consideration against some of the Academy's students". Goodwill attempted to explain about pies, bricks, escaped students, and flooded corridors – but was halted by the calm (but now insistent and full of unspoken menace) voice.

'I fully understand the need to enforce certain standards,' said the caller, 'but with the academy rigidly enforcing its rules and tradition, we must be very sure that when we "Insulate" – we do not "Isolate". Without crushing the Human Spirit, we cannot ignore the values of Friendship, or Curiosity – or we are in danger of suppressing individuality in young minds. It is a group of minds such as these that founded the Academy. Whilst I can fully appreciate your need to protect your charges from the banalities of "the outside", it is unfortunate if you allow the School to become too rigid, and your educational archipelago becomes an institution. Ipso Facto headmaster, your pupils become institutionalised...'

Goodwill had begun to look confused. His brain rummaged around for a response, but all he could muster was 'Yes.. Ahh.. Well.. But You see.. But the damage!'

'High spirits, head – Boys will be boys, after all,' said the voice.

'All well and good, my man…' said Goodwill, 'but the cost alone…'

He was interrupted by the voice, who was clearly going in for the kill.

'Ah yes… Costs. May I just enquire, headmaster, as to when your Academy had its last full audit? I have a note here which would seem to indicate some rather puzzling "irregularities". Anyway, I am certain that any full and frank financial disclosure would not bring any manner of discredit upon you and your splendid Academy?' purred the voice.

'Oh yes indeed – no need to bother… Ha Ha! I will deal with it – just telling off some young rascals for a bit of high jinks, as it happens… thank you for calling – must dash,' stuttered the head. He replaced the receiver, shaking slightly.

'Sir…' said Merry.

'Right, boys – I think that due to the fact that there is no firm…'

'Sir…'

'Don't interrupt boy. I cannot see the point in taking…'

But, sir…'

'For heaven's sake, what is it Merry?'

'Sir – the Boarding House is on fire.'

There was a panic as all of the boys, plus their headmaster, attempted to get through the doorway at the same time. Miss Piggott had come up the corridor to see what the commotion was all about, and was spun backwards down the passage by several running boys and a flapping head (an event unlikely in the extreme ever to be repeated in her leisure time, however hard she might wish). A crowd was beginning to gather in the quad, around the Boarding House door.

'Don't just stand there, you fellows – call the bloody Fire Brigade!' screamed Goodwill. He took off up the stairs, closely followed by Nicky and the boys. They turned the corner, and saw smoke billowing out from under the door of the prefects' common room.

Just then, Hugo pushed his way past the group, and said to Goodwill, 'Piper is in there, sir, and I have lost the key!'

'Right then, boys…' said a determined headmaster. 'We have to get that door open.'

Behind him, Davis was frantically opening the wall cupboards, and stuffing books under his jacket to create large shoulder pads. 'I need a helmet –quick,' he said. From out of nowhere, the ever-reliable Weatherill produced a motorbike crash helmet. The headgear gave Davis the appearance of a rather well-padded American Football

Quarterback. Davis paced back a few steps and said, 'Right. Now you buggers get out of my way – I'm going in!'

With that, the boy set off at a furious pace down the corridor, tilting his head down as he ran. There was a tremendous crash of splintering timber as Davis the Battering Ram hit the door at full tilt. Smoke billowed out of the room, and all of the boys could clearly see flames leaping up in the background. Nicky and Merry tried to see inside the room, but were beaten back by the intense heat and smoke. Anxiously awaiting the siren of the fire engines, the group (now joined by several masters and boys) stood in a huddle some way down the corridor – all fearing the worst as time dragged on. They all heard a loud thump from inside the room, followed by another crash as part of the ceiling came down. Suddenly, a blur shot out of the room through the curtain of choking smoke, as Davis came hurtling out with the limp body of Piper slung over his shoulder...

He hit the crowd square on, and the boys and Staff were sent flying like skittles. Davis did not stop until he hit the wall cupboards at the end of the passage. Weatherill leapt over to his smoke-blackened friend...

'Talk to me Mark – say something...'

'This bleedin' 'elmet is jammed on me 'ead...' said the Hero of the Hour.

Piper was taken off to the local hospital in the ambulance. Davis was carried shoulder-high around the quad by his friends, whilst a local reporter snapped pictures of the heroic pupil. Everyone was far too busy congratulating Davis to notice that one of the ambulance crew was considerably shorter than the others, and was wearing a surgical mask to avoid being recognised. DeVere had seized his chance when he saw it...

The fire had been put out, with no significant structural damage having been caused. A bottle of vintage Cognac had been found near the charred table, and was removed by Dr Matthews, 'In case it should be required as evidence later...' The reporter was busy taking details about the dramatic rescue, and was grilling Davis for juicy detail.

'Well it's a bit ironic really,' said Davis, 'because me and my mates are going to b...'

'... Be greatly and properly rewarded for their heroic efforts – my word yes!' interrupted Goodwill. 'This just goes to show the lengths that an Onanist will go to, in order to safeguard his fellow members..' The reporter raised an eyebrow. 'These boys shall have seats of honour at the forthcoming dramatic production'

'With drinks and popcorn thrown in...' said Davis, hopefully. 'Absolutely!. said Goodwill, 'Nothing is too good for our very own hero and his esteemed friends.'

'Three cheers for Davis!' shouted Weatherill, now resplendent in a fireman's helmet.

And so it came to pass that the lads and their families did get the best seats in the house for the production of *Oliver*. Drinks were slurped, and corn was mightily popped for all. The drama group equitted themselves excellently, putting on a really first-class show. Not noticed by the majority of the audience, but certainly spotted by the boys, was the addition to the cast of urchins which doubled their scripted number. Still, they knew all of the numbers and the dance routines perfectly, so no harm done. Nicky had to laugh when during the 'Food Glorious Food' number; various items of edible fare were danced out of the wings – to be laid out on the long bench table. As it landed, each tray of food was whisked down the table, and made its way offstage by means of a human chain of "extras". Merry and Calderman were doubled up with laughter, as they spotted one of the ragged youngsters was wearing a "Ramones" tee-shirt... Further fun ensued during the scene where the evil Bill Sykes was being pursued by the police. The baddie had climbed up the scenery to evade capture. When the policeman (Ardley Senior in a huge stuck-on moustache) pointed to the man with his truncheon it had flown from his grip and hit "Bill Sykes" in the groin.

'Bullseye!' shouted Davis.

Chapter Thirty-One

The Founders' Day church service historically marked the last official day of the Michaelmas Term. It was the time when each and every member of the staff would don their finest robes and ermine. Mr Newhouse had already laid out his best "Rush" tee-shirt to wear, and Hyde-Jones had chosen a rather fetching black fedora hat. Prior to the ceremony, toasts would be raised to The Founders, and after a few of these, attempts would be made to raise Dr Matthews. Miles Bannister had quite a funny turn, when via the spirited attempts of Mrs Elsie Noakes, he found himself shopping for a "posh frock" to wear for the occasion. The Reverend Felchingham was being very secretive as usual, whereas the French mistress was upfront about the whole thing (ahem).

Dr Goodwill had been surprised by the mystery gift of two pounds of best steak, which some generous benefactor had given to his dog.

Chambers had finally calmed down when he had read the glowing reports of the fire incident in the local press. He even featured prominently in the photograph which was printed, although he was partly obscured by a Stetson hat being worn by Weatherill.

The boys had decided as a group to lay low after what they considered to be a "lucky escape". Davis was enjoying his now legendary status, and Kendy too (for his services to prefect eradication) was much lauded amongst his companions.

Betty Bradley was extremely happy. The effects of her new medication were such that she didn't notice that she had ordered one thousand aubergines, instead of the normal hundred. She was still happy when the huge lorry turned up to deliver the order. She selected the vegetable which she thought most pleasing to her eye, stuck two wobbling eyes into it, and named it Bernard.

Winner of the, "I am not happy at all and my life is one steaming pile of crap" award was the Reverend F. He had all but given up even attempting to play Scrabble with friends. Whatever letters he put down on the board, they mysteriously conspired to score him ten points (thirty on a Triple Score, but that's not the point). Now Children... can you guess which letters are worth five, three, and two at one point each? – Bingo!

He had stormed out into the garden, where an aircraft was flying overhead, towing a banner which read "SunTrips – Book Now – Book Now". When the plane flew back over his house, he noted that the majority of the stick-on letters advertising the holiday firm had fallen away. The banner being flown around his house in circles two hundred feet above his head now read "k N o- B..." Thank you Stan. Thank you so very much.

He resolved to summon help with the banishment of the tormenting old wretch, and made his mind up to do so when the rest of the Academy were at the church service. This time he would bring out the big guns... No messing. Once and for all. Done and dusted. Gloves off. Sorted.

Dear God... what do I do if I can't shift the old sod?

'Well...' said Nicky, 'that turned out a lot better than I expected.'

'True, mate,' said Davis. 'I found the other half of the Twix that I had forgotten about.'

'Don't you ever think about anything but food?' laughed Merry.

'Yeah – of course! There's milkshakes and cola and all sorts of stuff to consider...' he replied.

The lads decided to nip over to the church, where Mr Newhouse was sitting astride the colossal organ (now stop it – I've already warned you). He waved at the boys and launched into "Fanfare for the Common Man", complete with Emerson Lake and Palmer ad-libs. He then entertained them with a superb version of '"Lazy" by Deep Purple. The basso profundo pipes on the organ shook the pews, and made hymn books skitter off shelves like surprised starlings.

'Tell you what,' said Calderman, 'I fancy a quick look at the Piper Barbeque shop – anyone care to join me?' The lads didn't see any harm in visiting the scene of the fire, and with any luck they might persuade Davis to re-enact the daring rescue, subject to the appropriate chocolate bribe, of course. No-one paid them any attention as they made their way across the quad (avoiding Keith the Raven, who was busy changing a tyre on his moped) and up the stairs to the prefects' corridor. The air was still acrid with the stink of smoke, and the judicious use of water by the Brigade had left a smell like the morning after Bonfire Night. They approached the taped-off doorway with caution, and leaned into the room for a better view of the damage.

'Cor! What a mess,' said Merry.

'Let's go in and look,' said Calderman.

'Don't be daft,' said Jackson. 'The floor might be dodgy, and we might fall through into Matron's "Special Rooms". They had all heard stories – some of them written by Matron herself and published under an assumed name in plain covers. Youthful curiosity overcame them, and they edged slowly into the soot-blackened room, where they studied every detail of the charred wood and twisted metal.

Nicky came to the far wall, where he noticed something strange... 'Look at this, chaps,' he said. 'It looks as if there is another door under the plaster here.' The boys stared at the wall, and yes, there did seem to be the outline of a slightly smaller door visible under the charred plaster.

Calderman said to Jackson, 'Johnny – pass me that stool, mate...'

Jackson handed him the heavy-based stool, covering his hands in soot as he did so. Calderman grinned at his friends, and gave the wall a stout blow with the stool. Much of the damaged plaster fell away, revealing the ancient door beneath.

'I hate it when he does this – I know what's coming next,' said Merry.

'Oh Wow! We have ab-so-lutely got to explore this...' said Calderman (Merry was bang on the money).

The door had fallen away, revealing a shaft. On the wall of the shaft was fixed a metal ladder, which judging from the scuffs on the rusted rungs, was in regular use. Calderman darted inside, and began descending. The shaft was lit by curious pools of soft light, and after climbing down just a short way, the boy found that the illumination of the shaft was achieved by strategically placed mirrors – each angling light down from the roof, from one to the next. The boys still in the room listened to the rhythmic clang-clang of his footsteps as he climbed ever downwards. They looked at each other, shrugged, and joined their friend in his decent into the underworld.

The church meanwhile, was beginning to fill up with the masters and invited guests for the Founders' Day service. Captain Brayfield had already commandeered the best front pew, and sat ramrod-straight in his seat, in full Cavalry uniform. Behind him sat Mr Thwaite, who had chosen to present himself (after getting lost twice in the crypt, and once in the vestry), in a rather shocking long auburn wig. He wore deep scarlet fingernails, and earrings that resembled small Renaissance chandeliers. With his kohl-lined eyes and deep eye shadow, he gave the impression of a rather fey Pirate.

Having set up his "get-rid kit" in his classroom, Felchingham was preparing to evict his burden, Stan, from his life forever. He had drawn a large pentagram on the floor (Mrs Finucane would do him bodily harm when she saw it), and had lit a forest of black candles. He had opened his rare copy of the "Black Bible", and sacrificed a portion of fresh chicken nuggets. He placed the ouija board in the middle of the pentagram, placed the cards out in their correct order, and began...

(Now it should be pointed out that the Legions of the Underworld were well aware of the Reverend Gerald Felchingham, and of his surreptitious plans to gently convert boys into the realms of Satanism. They were also exceedingly aware that he had about as much talent at being a servant of the Dark Master as a squashed gnat. He wasn't very good at it, and not to disguise the point – they were all getting pretty pissed off with this black-clad loony calling them up every five minutes and talking out of his bum at them. They appreciated the gesture, but capturing souls this early seemed a waste of everyone's time and effort- because when some of the boys became Members of Parliament in later life- they would get their soul anyway).

They had decided to make an example of this pain in the cassock, and teach him a lesson which should put him off "dabbling" for life.

As the Rev continued with his summoning of the dreaded guardian of the dark portal, the Lords of Hell summoned their secret weapon. Now – in any factory or workplace throughout the land, there is an individual on the payroll who, quite frankly, would not get to work if the trees were all cut down. This will be the person who will always be told to make the tea, sweep the yard, or paint something – anything to get them out of the way of normal employees who genuinely want to work. There is no job which you can give them that they will not walk away from. They will argue for fifteen minutes as to why they cannot do a five-minute job. If Management want to scupper a proposed merger with a rival company- this is the dozy fuckwit that is sent in to negotiate on their behalf.

The Lords of Darkness have summoned the demon Abolochyn...

(If you were determined to mess with forces that you knew nothing about, and use stupid methods over which you had little or no control, then it was inevitable that you would get Abolochyn.)

The boys had reached the foot of the metal ladder, and were congregated around the bottom, trying to dissuade Indiana Calderman from continuing on his quest. Their attempts were doomed to failure.

'Don't bother, Gerry,' Nicky said with conviction. 'We all know that it's futile.'

Trevill immediately asked what it had to do with Japanese beds...

Jackson seemed to take charge at this point. 'Right, we will go a little way into the tunnel, but we can't be long – otherwise we will miss the church service,' he said.

'Are you very religious then, Jimmy?' asked Merry.

'Not really – I am what you might call a "Jehovah's Bystander" I suppose...' answered Jackson.

Nicky just had to ask, 'And what is that exactly?'

'Well, I do believe in a Supreme Being – but I just don't want to get involved,' answered Jackson, earnestly. Trevill had found a thin stick from somewhere, and was using it to tap the wall and floor as the group of boys slowly edged their way up the dark tunnel. Ahead of them, a thin shaft of light beamed down from the roof, but all that managed to do was to ruin their night vision.

'Ooo do you think 'as made all these 'ere tunnels?' asked Trevill.

'Probably left over from when the priests had to do a runner during the Reformation,' said Nicky.

'Might have been the Gas Board?' said Merry.

'A bit big for Cable TV I think,' laughed Jackson – 'It might even have been the Vikings.'

Trevill pondered... 'Yeah – probably that Valerie Halla or whatever 'er name was, runnin' up and down in these 'ere caves in their Long Boots.'

Whoever had made the tunnels was obviously keeping them in a good state of repair. There was no water running down the walls, and not a trace of a single rat (for the sake of balance, there were no married ones either). The tunnel turned to the left, and then curved slightly. The boys walked slowly down the corridor in complete darkness, with Trevill waving the stick in front of them like a Jedi Knight. At the next corner, there was a muted light permeating from a large room ahead. The lads paused at the doorway. At the far side of the chamber, were two stubby candles set into recesses in the wall, and it was these that provided the thin wash of light within the room. Merry assumed the position of a Secret Agent at the side of the door – hands clasped and holding an imaginary pistol.

'Okay...' he said, 'I'll check it out, then we move on my signal.'

There was a bang behind them, which scared them all and sent them tumbling into the room. The source of the 'pop' was Davis, who had opened a packet of crisps by squeezing the bag.

'You silly sod, Davis,' said Calderman. 'What did you do that for?'

'I didn't want to frighten you – sorry,' said Davis, now munching happily.

Nicky pointed out a wooden box-like structure in the middle of the room. The boys slowly approached it, looking over their shoulders as they did so.

'It's like Dungeons and Dragons isn't it!' said Davis. 'You keep expecting a gruesome beast to come drooling around the corner at any second.

'Thanks, mate,' said Merry. 'I feel a lot better now you have told us that.'

Nicky, Calderman and Kendy were busy looking at the plinth in the centre of the cavern. On top of the angled stone top, was a very thick book. The book was old, very old. At some stage it had obviously survived a fire- which had burned away almost all of the gold lettering which had previously adorned its cover. Nicky ran his hand over the scarred leather, and suddenly, the penny dropped. The wording on the front had originally read "Holy Bible", but now only the first two letters of the title had remained intact. 'Well now, Calderman – at least we now know who "HoBi" is, ' he said.

The questions came thick and fast. Whose Bible was it? How did it get there? Why was it still here? Who comes in here to read it? Did anyone have any more crisps? (that was Davis, of course).

'Look!' exclaimed Trevill. 'The buggers 'ave pinched one of our bookmarks!'

There was indeed a St Onan's hand-tooled and gold-embossed bookmark (£12.99 from Simper and Crouch Ltd. of High Street) between the well-thumbed pages. There were more questions, this time a little more worrying. Where was "Gideon"? Who else was down here? What would they do if they found the posse of boys creeping around their tunnels? Kendy suggested that the boys should leave the place immediately and return to the church. Calderman however, was of the opinion that since they had explored so far, a little more investigation was unlikely to hurt anyone. Trevill said that 'It was whatever's in 'ere 'urtin' me that Oim worryin' about.' A vote was taken. There was a vote of 'Yes' to press on with their explorations from the rest of the group- and a "crunch" from Davis.

The church was now almost full to capacity. The congregation sat in their rows, checking out the people on either side of them, and trying to ensure that they noticed the new clothing which they had purchased especially for the occasion. There were some very expensive and exclusive designer outfits on show – the overall effect being spoiled for some, due to the fact that the labels had been left hanging down the back. They had been joined by Stig of the Damp, who had acquired evening dress for the occasion. He sat proudly in a state of Neanderthal elegance with his beard plaited, and feathers woven in. Hyde-Jones was already bored, and had sneaked outside for a crafty cigarette. He was approached by one of the boys who had arrived a little late.

'Excuse me, sir...' stuttered the boy. 'But can I ask you a question?'

'Yeah, of course, Matthew, fire away,' said the master.

'Is punctuation the most important thing in the English Language?' asked the boy.

Hyde-Jones was a little taken aback. 'Well, it's quite important, especially when you are writing a letter or an essay,' he answered. 'Why do you ask?'

'Because I was worried...' said the boy, with a look of anguish on his face. 'You see, sir... My dad told me that he used to go out with an English teacher. He was crazy about her, and he wanted her to marry him. She was obsessed with punctuation, and Dad said that is why she finished with him.' 'What – because of punctuation? How come?' said Hyde-Jones.

'Well – Dad said that she ended their relationship due to my dad's improper use of the colon...'

'I shall have a serious chat with your father at Parents' Evening,' replied Hyde-Jones.

Mr Newhouse was giving the organ some serious exercise, and was playing what the congregation thought was a rather soothing and atmospheric melody. What he was in fact playing was a slowed-down and slightly amended version of "Aces High" by Iron Maiden. He was just considering moving into the "Overture" theme from the Rush album *2112*. Oh Yes – praise the Lord mightily, and hold the Red Star proudly high in hand...

Still seeking to contact an entirely different kind of lord, was the Reverend. He had chanted until he began to feel light-headed. He had burned enough incense to set off the smoke detectors in a Hare Krishna temple. Still nothing.

In his despondent state of mind, he had not noticed the smell of sulphur and brimstone which had begun to permeate the atmosphere within the room. He raised his hands aloft in desperation, and cried, 'Oh Forces of the Darkest Realms, I crave an audience with thee... See how I make sacrifice with Bl...'

A broad column of foul-smelling smoke began to form within the pentagram, and the hideous shape of a figure rose up through the floor.

'...oody Hell...' said the Rev.

The ghastly form was well over nine feet tall. Its long and gangly arms dragged on the floor, and ended in vicious-looking horny claws. It wore a ragged loincloth, and a scowling expression of pure hate. The awful vision turned this way and that, as if trying to work out where it had materialised, and then turned to fix its evil countenance upon the cowering Reverend Felchingham... It opened its drooling maw and growled:

'Is yoo that daft sod Fletching-Ham?'

'I am the Reverend Felchingham, Yes...What do you want, Foul Demon?'

'NO need for that, mate- only doin' me job...' said the demon.

'I am trying to contact the Dark Lords,' said the Rev.

'Yurs... we know. I 'ave brung a massage.'

'A message – yes, what is your message, oh vile one?'

'Don't get lippy, you sarky little dick...' said the demon.

'Sorry... Please give me your message, oh great Demon' asked the Rev.

The demon cleared its throat with a sound like the emptying of septic tanks, produced a parchment scroll from somewhere about its glistening person, and began to read – a clawed finger tracing the words slowly.

'THIMBLE, IN-SIG-NIFF-IC-ANT MENTAL...' growled the demon. 'I BRING A MASSAGE FROM THE DARK SID- FURRY YE MENTALS AND COWL...'

The Rev stepped forward and took the scroll. 'Would you mind awfully if I take a look? I'll read it for you shall I? It says "Tremble, Insignificant Mortal, I bring a message from the Dark Side – Fear Ye Mortals and Cower..." The demon nodded, causing something to fall from behind its left ear, and scuttle off into the corner of the room. It stood still, and looked as if it were about to whistle, out of boredom.

'Is that all?' asked Felchingham.

'No, it ain't...' said the demon. 'I 'ave anuvver message for yer...'

'And what is this other message, please?'

'Message is – (It paused, as if trying to remember the script.) Oh Yurs... (cough) 'PACK IT IN –YOU ANNOYING LITTLE TURD...'

Felchingham folded his arms. 'And that is it, nothing else?'

'Yurs...LEAVE THEM KIDS ALONE – OR THE BOSS SAYS THAT YER ARSE IS TOAST...'

'What about helping me get rid of Stan?' pleaded the Rev.

'Hur Hur! It were Stan wot tipped us orf...' said the demon. 'Can I go now?'

'You might as well...' answered Felchingham.

There was a small thunderclap, and the visitor from the Nether Hells disappeared in a cloud of sulphurous smoke, leaving only a slight smell of unwashed pants behind...The Rev sat dejectedly in the middle of the scuffed pentagram, and idly kicked out at the ouija board, upon which, four letters were glowing brightly. Guess which four letters?

'Oh, bollocks...' said the Reverend.

Back in the church, the Founders' Day service had begun. It had begun with a spirited rendition of the Academy anthem. In the case of Dr Matthews, the spirit of choice today was "Sporran's Revenge" – a peaty single malt, in his largest hip flask. He was to give the Founders' Day address, and so had availed himself of a little "Dutch Courage". Unfortunately, he had already extended the borders way beyond the land of clogs and windmills, and was currently 'courageous' enough to cover most of Europe.

Ironically, most of Northern Europe was in the midst of a UFO flap. An unidentified craft had entered European airspace at a tremendous rate of speed, and had made its way toward central Lincolnshire. Typhoon fighters had been scrambled from RAF Coningsby, but had lost contact with the intruder somewhere above Granchester. The Flight Commander made a frantic call to his control room...

'Red Base One... Red Base One... This is Arrow Leader, repeat, this is Arrow Leader. We have contact with Alien craft – repeat; we have radio contact with Alien craft...'

'Arrow Leader... Arrow Leader, this is Red Base One, what is this contact – repeat; what is this contact – over...'

'I think he's asking for directions, Red Base One...'

By some strange combination of events, the parents of the boy Kendy had in fact received the message that he had placed in the drawer of the desk in Nicky's sitting room. The letter had contained a reminder to try and attend the Founders' Day service. After much argument, Kendy's father had given their larger flying saucer a thorough polish, and set off. There had been far more intense argument at the toll booth near the wormhole- when Kendy's mother discovered that she had left her credit unit on the kitchen table...

With their eyes now a little more accustomed to the dim light of the tunnels, the boys were walking along yet more narrow passageways. Here and there, were thick candles set in wrought-iron holders affixed to the wall. Only one in four was actually lit, and the boys hurried from one welcome pool of light to the next.

'That room must be directly under the church..' said Calderman 'You can hear the organ, and I'm sure that I just heard old Goodwill giving one of his speeches.'

'We had better get back sharpish then,' said Nicky. 'We'll be in more trouble if the service has started and we're not in the church.'

'We're in trouble as it is, mate...' said Merry. 'That's the third time that we've been past that narrow doorway with the carving on top – we've been going round in circles...'

In the great tradition of exploration parties everywhere, a furious row broke out as to whose fault it was that they were lost, and whose job it had been to navigate.

Kendy raised a hand for silence and declared, 'Look, lads – don't panic; I am not at all lost. Just follow me, and we will soon be out again.' He strode purposefully up the passage and turned left. Coming to another narrow door, he turned, smiled at the boys, and disappeared inside. After a short while, he reappeared and said, 'Okay – so it's a toilet...'

Davis suddenly let out a sharp yell. The entire group jumped in fright.

'What's up, Davis?' said Nicky. 'Are you okay, mate?'

'Look at this!' said an excited Davis. The boys scanned the tunnel – but could see nothing unusual. 'No – I mean here...' he said. 'I've just looked inside the wrapper, and I've won a free Mars Bar!' The clip around the ear which he received from Trevill was well deserved...

High above the Academy, the jet fighters were circling... 'Arrow Leader to Red Base One – We have visual, repeat, we have visual...'

Hovering over the quad was a sixty-foot silver flying disc, with a sticker on the bumper which read "Roswell or Bust". Inside the control deck, a furious argument was in progress.

'I told you to set off earlier – now look what's happened; it's always the same every time we go anywhere.'

'It's not my fault that the ruddy school has not allocated ample parking, now is it, dear..I just can't find a space.'

'Look – there's a gap at the side of that long red sports car – put us down there.'

'The gap's not big enough – and I'm not risking another row with the TransUniversal Insurance Company – I didn't get paid out last time you scratched the ship.'

'Oh that's right – blame me, that Zark was right up my exhaust pipe!'

'When you argued with him – it was me that ended up getting punched!'

'It was only one little punch.'

'Yeah, but those bloody Zarks have six arms, dear...'

Dad had now had enough of trying to find a parking space, his wife's nagging, and the unwelcome attention of the RAF. It was decided that they would come back later and collect their son, Kendy. They might even have time to track down the bloody con-artist who sold them the crappy Space-Nav.

Dr Matthews would definitely have been described as a great customer for any seller of navigational aids. Wreathed in alcoholic fumes, he had painstakingly weaved an unsteady path between the church pews on his way to the lectern, in order to deliver his speech. He took out the couple of pages which comprised his notes, fumbled for his reading glasses, and then turned to address the figures in front of him. Smiling benevolently, he was about to launch into his speech, when he realised that he was in fact about to deliver his words to several marble statues of saints who stood unsmiling and impassive against the transept wall. He giggled to himself, and turned through ninety degrees to face the congregation.

'I bid you welcome, Ladies, Gentlemen and Honoured Guests...' he began. 'Bread, Milk, Sugar, half a dozen eggs and...' (His sheet of notes was hurriedly discarded when he realised that he was reading his shopping list.)

'It is my great pleasure – (well, not as often as one might like, to be honest) to welcome you to the Celebration of our Academy Founders. It was indeed on this day, many years ago (can't remember when exactly, should have written it down – bugger.) that our Noble and Venerable Enclave of Academic Excellence (damn good phrase that) was founded. Personally, I didn't even know that it had ever been "Losted"! – sorry, just my little joke. The Founders saw a need to provide a top-class education for every boy in the county, so this Academy was founded, and very well founded indeed. There were those who told them that they were mad – but their fears were unfounded – unlike the Academy.

We celebrate all of the (hic) bishops, knights (don't understand all that moving sideways malarkey, never did) and men of the church who got laid and stoned...sorry – stayed and loaned, no- LAID THE STONES (yes – that's it, sorry) (burp) to form the walls within which we enrich the lives of our pupils. I am gratified to see so many familiar faces here today, who I have had the pleasure of teaching (fart) over the ears – over the years, sorry. Let us all look forward, Ladies and Gentiles, (unless we are reversing of course – damned dangerous thing to do) to moving forward, and showing forward thinking (hic). We shall fight them on the beaches – we will fight them on the landing grounds (sorry, I have no idea what happened there.) He fished out the hip flask from his pocket, unscrewed the top, and took a large series of gulps.

You see, the thing is... the thing is – these bastards have been trying to retire me for years – oh my word yes. They say that (hic) I am past it (don't think I don't hear 'em talking about me) and I should be put out to grass. But I tell you – I am like a fine wine (burp), and you don't waste a classic (fart, burp) vintage, now do you.' He took another large sip from the flask, and leaned on the lectern. 'I've told 'em – I'm part of the very fabric, nay, the very foundations of this Academy, and none of you young upstarts are going to (hic) push me out.'

Goodwill sat with a look of horror on his face, and Dr Chambers made his way up to the lectern, to call a halt to the "speech" before more damage could be done. Matthews peered at the deputy head, before pointing an accusatory finger at him. 'And you are one of the worst, you miserable sod...' he told the stunned Chambers. The deputy head put a compassionate arm around the shoulders of the History master, who looked lovingly up at him, and through a fog of whisky fumes declared, 'I didn't mean it, son (hic)- You're my Best Mate, you are...' as he was led back to his seat...

Chapter Thirty-Two

Unaware of the drama being played out above their heads, the boys now stood in complete darkness, at a bend in yet another narrow tunnel. Curiosity and bravado had now evaporated along with the last remaining traces of illumination, and the group were huddled together in a state of communal fear.

Davis had begun to sniffle, and even the normally tough Calderman was regretting his decision to lead the boys into the labyrinthine passages. Terror had begun to seep down through the roof of the tunnels, when the boys were suddenly provided with their own personal soundtrack for their explorations. Above them, Mr Newhouse had played Bach's "Toccata and Fugue" on the massive church organ. This was an atmospheric piece of music at any time, but in the alternating gloom and total blackout of the tunnels, it chilled the souls of the boys. Now confronted and swallowed up by the clinging dark, the boys' imagination seemed to be sent into overdrive. They had so far seen nothing but empty rooms and clean corridors, but now they were lost – and alone. The only sound which they could hear was the sound of their own breathing, the inky void sucking away all noise. In the blackness, the monsters which their minds created were so much bigger than any that they had seen on television.

'We're going to die, aren't we...' said Merry, quietly.

'No, Merry – we are certainly not going to die. We will carry on up the tunnel, and there will be a vent or something in the roof – and we will shout for help.'

'What if no-one hears us?' said Jackson.

'Then we shout louder, or maybe Kendy can blast us out of here with his ray-gun,' Calderman answered. No-one laughed.

'Look, the longer we wait here, the longer we will be stuck in these tunnels,' said Nicky. 'I will go in front – pass me the stick, Trevill.'

The boy was terrified, but on the basis that escape or rescue could lie around the next corner, Nicky decided to face his fear and take control for the sake of his friends. Tapping the walls with the stick, he led the party onward slowly. The passage curved to the right, and suddenly there was a different sound as wood made contact with wood.

'It's another doorway – follow me in,' said Nicky.

This time, their footsteps echoed back to them from all around. Whatever space they had entered was obviously a very wide one. Nicky felt for the wall at the side of the door, and after edging a few steps into the darkness, felt something hard and cold under his questing fingers. 'I can feel some sort of panel on the wall – spread out and see if you can feel what it is' he said. With fear still doing its best to prevent them from moving, the boys reluctantly began to spread out along the wall.

'There's another panel over here!' called Kendy, as the echo died away.

'And here too,' said Davis.

'Lads, I've found something...' said Calderman. 'It feels like a shelf or something, just under the panel.'

Nicky called out in reply – 'Yes! There's one here too – and I think I've found a candle!'

In the dark, the boys all made their way slowly over to where Nicky stood. Feeling gently along the shelf, he was relieved to recognise the shape of a box of matches. He carefully took a match out of the box, turned the box with the sanded side toward him, and struck the match. The match spluttered, then went out. They were back in total darkness.

'Look – don't panic, I'll try again,' said Nicky.

He withdrew another two matches, and holding them together, struck them against the match box. This time the matches flared into life, and Nicky made a grab for the thick stub of candle which was on the shelf in front of him. The candle wick caught light, and although it protested slightly, a small flower of flame began to grow above the wax.

'Oh Wow!..' shouted Trevill, 'It's a mirror!'

The walls of the cavern were gently illuminated as the candle began to burn properly. Nicky was turning the candle this way and that, trying to make sure that it stayed lit. He had found two more similar candles, and was trying to light one from the other.

'Oh, bloody hell, Shep... ' said Calderman, gripping his friend on the shoulder.

'Hang on Ian – I'll have it going properly in a moment,' Nicky answered.

'No, mate – look in the mirror.'

The boys all leaned forward to look into the mirror. It reflected their worst fear... They saw over a hundred faces, in a circle behind them...

*

Coming Soon!

The riotous sequel to *Michaelmas Term* and next the chapter in the academic year at St Onan's...

Nicholas Barrett brings you: *Advent Term* (or – 'Yes, we've all seen it, now put it away, Boy...')